系列

108課綱、全民英檢中

進階英文字彙力
4501~6000 PLUS⁺ 隨身讀

三民英語編輯小組 彙整

📱 APP　　🎧 音檔

三民書局

序

英語 Make Me High 系列的理想在於超越，在於創新。
這是時代的精神，也是我們出版的動力；
這是教育的目的，也是我們進步的執著。

針對英語的全球化與未來的升學趨勢，
我們設計了一系列適合普高、技高學生的英語學習書籍。

面對英語，不會徬徨不再迷惘，學習的心徹底沸騰，
心情好 High！
實戰模擬，掌握先機知己知彼，百戰不殆決勝未來，
分數更 High！

選擇優質的英語學習書籍，才能激發學習的強烈動機；
興趣盎然便不會畏懼艱難，自信心要自己大聲說出來。
本書如良師指引循循善誘，如益友相互鼓勵攜手成長。
展書輕閱，你將發現……
學習英語原來也可以這麼 High！

使用説明 ▶▶▶

符號表

符號	意義
[同]	同義詞
[反]	反義詞
～	代替整個主單字
-	代替部分主單字
<>	該字義的相關搭配詞
( )	單字的相關補充資訊
▲	符合 108 課綱的情境例句
💡	更多相關補充用法
＿＿/＿＿	不同語意的替換用法
＿＿/＿＿	相同語意的替換用法

略語表

1. adj. 形容詞
2. adv. 副詞
3. art. 冠詞
4. aux. 助動詞
5. conj. 連接詞
6. n. 名詞
   [C] 可數
   [U] 不可數
   [pl.] 複數形
   [sing.] 單數形
7. prep. 介系詞
8. pron. 代名詞
9. v. 動詞
10. usu. pl. 常用複數
11. usu. sing. 常用單數
12. abbr. 縮寫

電子朗讀音檔下載方式

請先輸入網址或掃描 QR code 進入「三民・束大音檔網」。

https://elearning.sanmin.com.tw/Voice/

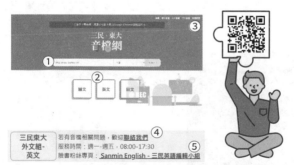

① 輸入本書書名即可找到音檔。請再依提示下載音檔。

② 也可點擊「英文」進入英文專區查找音檔後下載。

③ 若無法順利下載音檔，可至「常見問題」查看相關問題。

④ 若有音檔相關問題，請點擊「聯絡我們」，將盡快為你處理。

⑤ 更多英文新知都在臉書粉絲專頁。

英文三民誌 2.0 APP

掃描下方 QR code，即可下載 APP。

開啟 APP 後，請點擊進入「英文學習叢書」，
尋找《進階英文字彙力 4501~6000PLUS》。

使用祕訣

① 利用「我的最愛」功能，輕鬆複習不熟的單字。
② 開啟 APP 後，請點擊進入「三民 / 東大單字測驗」用「單
　機測驗」功能，讓你自行檢測單字熟練度。

目次

嗨！你今天學習了嗎？
一起使用進度檢核表吧！
學習完一個回次後，你可以在該回次的◎打勾。
一起培養進階英文字彙力吧！

我的進度檢核表，
學習完成就打勾✓！

Level 5-2	① ② ③ ④ ⑤ ⑥ ⑦ ⑧ ⑨ ⑩ ⑪ ⑫ ⑬ ⑭ ⑮ ⑯ ⑰ ⑱ ⑲ ⑳
Level 6	① ② ③ ④ ⑤ ⑥ ⑦ ⑧ ⑨ ⑩ ⑪ ⑫ ⑬ ⑭ ⑮ ⑯ ⑰ ⑱ ⑲ ⑳ ㉑ ㉒ ㉓ ㉔ ㉕ ㉖ ㉗ ㉘ ㉙ ㉚ ㉛ ㉜ ㉝ ㉞ ㉟ ㊱ ㊲ ㊳ ㊴ ㊵

Unit 1

1. **attendance** [ə`tɛndəns] n. [U] 出席 <in, at>
   - ▲ All the executives were in attendance at yesterday's meeting. 所有的主管都出席了昨天的會議。
   - 💡 take attendance 點名 | regular/poor attendance at school 都有 / 不常去上學

2. **briefcase** [`brifkes] n. [C] 公事包
   - ▲ My neighbor usually wears a suit and carries a briefcase to work.
     我的鄰居通常都穿著西裝、提個公事包去上班。

3. **clinical** [`klınıkl] adj. 臨床的
   - ▲ Clinical trials show that the new medicine is quite effective. 臨床試驗證明這個新藥相當有效。

4. **compliment** [`kɑmpləmənt] n. [C] 讚美 <on>
   - ▲ The whole class paid the student great compliments on her speech. 全班都很讚賞那位學生的演講。
   - 💡 take sth as a compliment 把…視為稱讚

   compliment [`kɑmplə‚mɛnt] v. 讚美，稱讚 <on>
   - ▲ The judges all complimented us on our performance.
     評審都稱讚我們的表演。

5. **conversion** [kən`vɝʒən] n. [C][U] 轉變 <to, from, into>
   - ▲ The country is undergoing a conversion from monarchy to democracy.

該國正在從君主政體轉變為民主政體。

6. **defendant** [dɪ`fɛndənt] n. [C] 被告
   ▲ The defendant denied all charges and pleaded not guilty. 被告否認所有指控，不肯認罪。

7. **directory** [də`rɛktərɪ] n. [C] 姓名地址錄，通訊錄，名錄 (pl. directories)
   ▲ Joe found the company's number in the telephone directory. Joe 在電話簿裡找到那家公司的電話號碼。
   ♥ business directory 企業名錄

8. **entitle** [ɪn`taɪtl] v. 為 (書籍等) 命名；使享有…資格或權利 <to>
   ▲ The magazine is entitled *Newsweek*.
   這本雜誌名為《新聞週刊》。
   ♥ entitle sb to do sth 使有權做…

9. **exterior** [ɪk`stɪrɪɚ] n. [C] 外表 [反] interior
   ▲ The teacher hid his anger behind a calm exterior.
   老師平靜的外表下隱藏著怒火。
   ♥ the exterior of a building 建築物的外部
   exterior [ɪk`stɪrɪɚ] adj. 外部的 [反] interior
   ▲ The exterior walls of the building are made of glass.
   這棟建築物的外牆是用玻璃做的。

10. **gloomy** [`glumɪ] adj. 沮喪的；陰暗的 (gloomier | gloomiest)

▲ My aunt was very gloomy after losing her job.
我的阿姨失業後很沮喪。

11. **ideology** [ˌaɪdɪˈɑlədʒɪ] n. [C][U] 意識形態，思想體系
(pl. ideologies)
▲ Some people say that elections are about ideology.
有些人說選舉和意識形態有關。

12. **interval** [ˈɪntɚvl̩] n. [C] (時間或空間的) 間隔
▲ The singer returned to the stage after an interval of
two years. 那位歌手隔了兩年重返舞臺。
💡 at regular intervals 相隔一定的時間或距離

13. **masterpiece** [ˈmæstɚˌpis] n. [C] 傑作 [同] masterwork
▲ Van Gogh's *Sunflowers* is considered a masterpiece
of Impressionist art.
梵谷的〈向日葵〉被視為印象派藝術的傑作。

14. **narrative** [ˈnærətɪv] n. [C] 故事，敘述 [同] story
▲ This novel is a gripping narrative of the explorer's
adventures across the Sahara Desert.
這本小說是引人入勝的橫跨撒哈拉沙漠探險故事。
narrative [ˈnærətɪv] adj. 敘述的
▲ Epics such as *The Iliad* and *The Odyssey* are
narrative poems.
像是〈伊利亞德〉和〈奧德賽〉這樣的史詩是敘事詩。

15. **pastry** [ˈpestrɪ] n. [U] 油酥麵團；[C] (派、塔等) 油酥糕
點 (pl. pastries)

▲ Cut the pastry into small pieces and then roll them into balls. 將油酥麵團切成小塊然後把它們搓成球狀。

---

16. **porch** [pɔrtʃ] n. [C] 門廊

▲ On summer nights, Ted and his family would sit on the porch and gaze up at the stars.
在夏天的夜晚，Ted 和家人會坐在門廊上看星星。

---

17. **quota** [`kwotə] n. [C] 配額，限額 <of, on>

▲ The boxer avoids exceeding her daily quota of calories so as not to gain weight. 那名拳擊手為了不要增加體重而避免攝取超過每日配額的卡路里。

💡 introduce/lift a quota on sth 對…設定 / 解除限額

---

18. **republican** [rɪ`pʌblɪkən] n. [C] 共和主義者

▲ Many republicans want an elected leader instead of a king or queen. 許多共和主義者想要經由選舉產生領導人，而不要國王或女王。

republican [rɪ`pʌblɪkən] adj. 共和的

▲ In a country with a republican government, the ruler with real power is an elected leader, instead of a king or queen. 在有共和政體的國家中，擁有實權的統治者是經由選舉產生的領導人，而不是國王或女王。

---

19. **scope** [skop] n. [U] 範圍 <of, beyond, within>；機會 <for> [同] potential

▲ The task lies beyond the scope of the novice's ability.

這件工作在那位新手的能力範圍之外。

💡 widen/narrow the scope of sth 擴大 / 縮小…的範圍

---

20. **sibling** [ˋsɪblɪŋ] n. [C] 手足，兄弟姊妹

   ▲ Tom has 4 siblings: 2 brothers and 2 sisters.
   Tom 有四個兄弟姊妹：兩個兄弟、兩個姊妹。

   💡 sibling rivalry 手足鬩牆，兄弟姊妹之間的競爭

---

21. **spectrum** [ˋspɛktrəm] n. [C] 光譜；範圍 <of> (pl. spectra, spectrums)

   ▲ When light passes through a prism, you can see the spectrum. 當光線通過三稜鏡時，你可以看見光譜。

---

22. **stink** [stɪŋk] n. [C] 臭味 <of>

   ▲ Do you smell a stink? 你有聞到臭味嗎？

   💡 the stink of smoke/sweat 菸 / 汗臭味 | cause a stink 引起軒然大波 | give sb the stink eye 非常不滿地看著…

   stink [stɪŋk] v. 發出惡臭 <of>；讓人感到糟糕，討厭 (stank, stunk | stunk | stinking)

   ▲ That drunk's breath stank of alcohol and smoke.
   那個酒鬼的呼氣有酒臭味和菸臭味。

---

23. **testify** [ˋtɛstəˌfaɪ] v. (尤指出庭) 作證 <for, against>

   ▲ The victim's neighbor testified that she heard a gunshot. 被害人的鄰居作證說聽到一聲槍響。

   💡 testify for/against sb 作有利 / 不利於…的證詞

---

24. **trim** [trɪm] v. 修剪；削除 <off>；裝飾 <with>

(trimmed | trimmed | trimming)

▲ I got my hair trimmed. 我剪頭髮了。

trim [trɪm] n. [C] 修剪 (usu. sing.)

▲ Kate's hair needs a trim. Kate 該剪頭髮了。

trim [trɪm] adj. 苗條健康的 (trimmer | trimmest)

▲ Ann keeps trim by swimming.
Ann 靠游泳來保持苗條健康。

25. **verdict** [ˋvɝdɪkt] n. [C] 判決，裁決

▲ It took the jury 5 hours to reach a verdict of not
guilty. 陪審團花了五個小時才做出無罪裁決。

Unit 2

1. **attic** [ˋætɪk] n. [C] 閣樓

▲ The kids found boxes of old books and letters in the
attic. 那些孩子們在閣樓發現好幾箱舊書和信件。

2. **bronze** [brɑnz] n. [U] 青銅；[C] 銅牌 [同] bronze medal

▲ The statue is made of bronze. 這座雕像是青銅做的。

🕯 the Bronze Age 青銅器時代

bronze [brɑnz] adj. 古銅色的

▲ The designer wanted the model to be a young man
with bronze skin.

設計師希望模特兒是有古銅色肌膚的年輕男性。

bronze [brɑnz] v. 使成古銅色

▲ The athlete's skin has been bronzed by the sun.

太陽將那位運動員的皮膚曬成古銅色。

---

3. **cluster** [`klʌstɚ] n. [C] 串，團，群
   ▲ Sightseers were standing in a cluster around the famous statue. 觀光客在那座著名的雕像旁圍成一團。
   🍷 a cluster of grapes/stars 一串葡萄 / 一群星星
   cluster [`klʌstɚ] v. 聚集，群集 <around>
   ▲ Tim and his friends clustered around the campfire. Tim 和朋友們聚集在營火周圍。

---

4. **comply** [kəm`plaɪ] v. 遵從，遵守 <with>
   ▲ All of us should comply with the epidemic control regulations. 我們都應該要遵守防疫規定。

---

5. **convict** [kən`vɪkt] v. 宣判…有罪 <of>
   ▲ That man over there was convicted of theft and fraud. 那邊那個男人被判犯了竊盜和詐騙罪。
   convict [`kɑnvɪkt] n. [C] 囚犯
   ▲ The police are chasing the escaped convict. 警方正在追捕逃犯。

---

6. **defy** [dɪ`faɪ] v. 違抗
   ▲ The couple got into trouble because they openly defied the law. 那對情侶因為公然違法而惹上麻煩。

---

7. **disapprove** [ˌdɪsə`pruv] v. 不贊同，不認可，反對 <of>
   [反] approve
   ▲ Eunice strongly disapproves of drunk driving. Eunice 強烈反對酒駕。

disapproval [ˌdɪsəˈpruvl̩] n. [U] 不贊同，不認可，反對 <of> [反] approval

▲ The principal expressed strong disapproval of their plan. 校長對他們的計畫表示強烈反對。

💡 shake sb's head <u>in/with</u> disapproval 搖頭表示反對

---

8. **entity** [ˈɛntətɪ] n. [C] 獨立存在的個體，實體

▲ These countries are all regarded as separate entities.
這些國家都被視為獨立的實體。

---

9. **fabulous** [ˈfæbjələs] adj. 很棒的 [同] wonderful

▲ I am a big fan of the fabulous dancer.
我是這位很棒的舞者的熱烈崇拜者。

---

10. **gorgeous** [ˈgɔrdʒəs] adj. 非常漂亮的，很美的；美好的，
令人愉快的 [同] lovely

▲ Jenny looked gorgeous in her new dress.
Jenny 穿著新洋裝非常漂亮。

---

11. **idiot** [ˈɪdɪət] n. [C] 笨蛋

▲ It's not polite to talk down to people as if they were idiots. 以居高臨下的態度跟人說話、彷彿人家是笨蛋似的，這樣很無禮。

idiotic [ˌɪdɪˈɑtɪk] adj. 愚蠢至極的

▲ What an idiotic question! 這是什麼愚蠢的問題啊！

---

12. **intervention** [ˌɪntəˈvɛnʃən] n. [C][U] 干涉，介入 <in>

▲ People are opposed to military intervention in other countries' affairs.

人們反對軍事干涉他國事務。

---

13. **mattress** [ˋmætrəs] n. [C] 床墊
    ▲ Many people prefer to sleep on soft mattresses.
    很多人比較喜歡睡軟的床墊。

14. **negotiation** [nɪˏgoʃɪˋeʃən] n. [C][U] 商議，協商，談判
    <with, between, under>
    ▲ The treaty is still under negotiation.
    條約還在協商中。
    💡 in negotiation with sb on sth 與⋯針對⋯進行協商

15. **patch** [pætʃ] n. [C] 補丁；(與周圍不同的) 一小片 <of>
    ▲ The frugal farmer often wears jeans with patches on
    the knees.
    那位節儉的農民常穿著膝蓋上縫有補丁的牛仔褲。
    💡 a patch of shade 一片陰涼處
    patch [pætʃ] v. 補綴，修補
    ▲ I have to patch my jeans; the knees are torn.
    我必須把牛仔褲補一補，膝蓋部分都磨破了。
    💡 patch things up with sb 和⋯重修舊好 | patch up sth
    修補 (物品、關係)

16. **practitioner** [prækˋtɪʃənɚ] n. [C] (醫界等的) 從業人員
    ▲ Dr. Lin is a practitioner of Chinese medicine.
    林醫師是中醫從業人員。
    💡 medical/legal practitioner 醫生 / 律師

17. **racism** [ˋresɪzəm] n. [U] 種族歧視

▲ Many immigrants stood together to fight against racism. 許多移民團結對抗種族歧視。

18. **resemblance** [rɪ`zɛmbləns] n. [C][U] 相似 <to, between>

▲ That boy bears a close resemblance to his father.
那個男孩長得非常像他的父親。

💡 striking resemblance between A and B …和…非常相似之處

19. **scramble** [`skræmbl̩] v. (手腳並用地) 攀爬；爭搶 <for>

▲ Those mountain climbers scrambled along the edge of the cliff. 那些登山者沿著懸崖邊攀行。

💡 scramble to sb's feet 急忙站起來

scramble [`skræmbl̩] n. [sing.] 攀登；爭搶 <for>

▲ It is quite a scramble to get to the top of the mountain. 到山頂得攀爬好一段路。

20. **siege** [sidʒ] n. [C][U] 圍攻；包圍

▲ The town was under siege in the war.
這座城鎮在戰爭中被圍攻。

💡 withstand a siege 抵抗圍攻 | raise/lift a siege 解除圍攻

21. **speculate** [`spɛkjə‚let] v. 推測 <about, on>；做投機買賣 <in, on>

▲ Bob don't want to speculate about the future.
Bob 不想推測未來。

speculation [ˌspɛkjəˈleʃən] **n.** [C][U] 推測 <about>

▲ There has been much speculation about the future.
對未來的推測一直都很多。

💡 pure/mere speculation 毫無根據的臆測

---

22. **straighten** [ˈstretn̩] **v.** 弄直 <out>；整理 <up>

▲ The clerk straightened his tie before entering the
office. 那位職員在進辦公室之前先把領帶弄直。

💡 straighten up 挺直身體 | straighten sth out 弄直…；解
決…

---

23. **theology** [θiˈɑlədʒɪ] **n.** [U] 神學

▲ John wants to study theology and philosophy at
college. John 想在大學研讀神學和哲學。

---

24. **triple** [ˈtrɪpl̩] **adj.** 三倍的；由三部分組成的

▲ The applicant demanded triple pay.
那名應徵者要求三倍的工資。

triple [ˈtrɪpl̩] **v.** (使) 成為三倍

▲ The staff tried their best to triple the profits of the
company. 全體員工努力要使公司的獲利成為三倍。

triple [ˈtrɪpl̩] **n.** [C] 三個一組；(棒球的) 三壘打

▲ Two espressos, no, triples, please.
兩杯濃縮咖啡，喔不，三杯好了。

---

25. **versus** [ˈvɝsəs] **prep.** 與…對抗 , …對… ；與…對比
(abbr. vs.) [同] against

▲ Tonight's match is Brazil versus Uruguay.
今晚的比賽是巴西與烏拉圭對打。

Unit 3

1. **attorney** [ə`tɜnɪ] n. [C] 律師 [同] lawyer
   ▲ The attorney advised her client to remain silent.
   那名律師建議她的當事人保持沉默。
   💡 defense attorney 辯護律師

2. **bulk** [bʌlk] n. [C] 巨大的東西，龐然大物 (usu. sing.)；
   [sing.] 大部分 (the ～) <of>
   ▲ The elephant heaved its bulk out of the river.
   大象挪動龐大的軀體從河裡站起來。
   💡 in bulk 大量地

3. **coherent** [ko`hɪrənt] adj. (論述等) 條理清楚的，合乎邏
   輯的，連貫的；(人) 說話有條理的
   ▲ The witness gave a coherent account of the accident.
   目擊者為那起意外提供了條理清楚、合乎邏輯的描述。

4. **comprise** [kəm`praɪz] v. 包含，包括；組成 [同] make up
   ▲ The U.S. comprises 50 states. 美國包含五十個州。

5. **correlation** [ˌkɔrə`leʃən] n. [C][U] 相互關係，相關性，
   關聯 <with, between>
   ▲ There is a close correlation between smoking and
   many diseases such as lung cancer and heart attack.

抽菸和很多疾病都密切相關，例如肺癌和心臟病。

6. **delegate** [ˋdɛləˏget] n. [C] 代表
   ▲ My cousin is the Australian delegate to the United Nations. 我表哥是澳洲駐聯合國代表。

   delegate [ˋdɛləˏget] v. 委任，委派 <to>
   ▲ Susan was delegated to attend the conference.
   Susan 被委派為代表去參加會議。

7. **disclose** [dɪsˋkloz] v. 揭露，透露 [同] reveal
   ▲ The CEO disclosed that she will retire next month.
   那名執行長透露她將在下個月退休。

8. **entrepreneur** [ˏɑntrəprəˋnɝ] n. [C] 企業家
   ▲ The young entrepreneur made his money in the stock market. 那名年輕的企業家靠股市賺錢。

9. **faculty** [ˋfæklˏtɪ] n. [C][U] 全體教職員；[C] (感官、心智等的) 機能，能力 (usu. pl.) <of>
   ▲ We had a party to welcome the new members of our school's faculty.
   我們辦了一個派對歡迎我們學校的新進教職員。
   ♥ the faculty of sight/hearing 視覺 / 聽覺 | critical faculties 判斷能力

10. **grant** [grænt] n. [C] (政府或機構的) 補助金
    ▲ The girl was awarded a student grant from the government to complete her education. 那名女孩獲得一筆來自政府的獎助學金，讓她完成學業。

💡 research grant 研究補助金

grant [grænt] v. 准予，給與；承認，同意

▲ The journalist was granted permission to take pictures. 這個記者獲准拍照。

💡 take sth for granted 視…為理所當然

---

11. **illusion** [ɪˈluʒən] n. [C] 錯誤的想法或認知，幻想 <about>

▲ I had no illusions about my chances of success. 我對我成功的機會不抱幻想。

💡 be under the illusion that... 存有…的幻想

---

12. **investigator** [ɪnˈvɛstəˌgetɚ] n. [C] 調查者，調查員

▲ The investigators are examining the crime scene. 調查員正在勘查案發現場。

💡 private investigator 私家偵探

---

13. **meantime** [ˈminˌtaɪm] n. [U] 期間

▲ My car is under repair; in the meantime, I take the bus to work. 我的車送修，在此期間我搭公車上班。

meantime [ˈminˌtaɪm] adv. 在此期間，同時 [同] meanwhile

▲ Tom is going to college. Meantime, he will work part-time to support his family.

Tom 要上大學了，同時他將會打工賺錢貼補家用。

---

14. **nominate** [ˈnɑməˌnet] v. 提名 <as, for>

▲ The film was nominated for 11 Academy Awards.

這部電影獲得奧斯卡十一項提名。

💡 be nominated as sth 被提名為…

15. **patent** [ˋpætn̩t] n. [C][U] 專利 (權) <on, for>

▲ The inventor took out a patent on her invention.
那位發明家取得了她發明的專利。

💡 apply for a patent on/for sth 為…申請專利 | sth be
protected by patent …受專利保護

patent [ˋpætn̩t] adj. 專利 (權) 的；明顯的 [同] obvious

▲ My boss needs a patent lawyer to help her with
patent applications.
我的老闆需要一位專利權律師幫她處理專利申請。

💡 patent medicine 專利藥品，成藥

patent [ˋpætn̩t] v. 取得…的專利 (權)

▲ This product is patented by the company.
這個產品的專利為這家公司所有。

16. **predator** [ˋprɛdətɚ] n. [C] 掠食者，肉食性動物

▲ Most frogs are natural predators of insects.
大部分的青蛙是昆蟲的天敵。

17. **rack** [ræk] n. [C] 架子

▲ I put my bag onto the luggage rack.
我把袋子放到行李架上。

rack [ræk] v. 折磨，使痛苦 <by, with>

▲ Sam's head was racked with pain. Sam 頭疼得厲害。

💡 rack sb's brain(s) 絞盡腦汁

18. **resident** [ˋrɛzədənt] n. [C] 居民；住院醫師
   ▲ Many residents of the town travel by boat.
      那個城鎮的許多居民以船作為交通工具。
   resident [ˋrɛzədənt] adj. 居住的 <in>
   ▲ My friend is resident in Venice. 我朋友住在威尼斯。

---

19. **scrap** [skræp] n. [C] (紙、布等的) 小片，小塊，碎片；
   (資訊等的) 少量，一點點
   ▲ The boy wrote the message on a scrap of paper.
      男孩把消息寫在碎紙片上。
   scrap [skræp] v. 放棄，捨棄 (scrapped | scrapped |
   scrapping)
   ▲ Our plan was scrapped for lack of support.
      我們的計畫因為缺乏支持被取消了。

---

20. **slam** [slæm] n. [C] 砰的一聲 (usu. sing.)
   ▲ The door shut with a slam. 門砰的一聲關上了。
   slam [slæm] v. 砰地關上或放下；嚴厲批評，猛烈抨擊
   (slammed | slammed | slamming)
   ▲ Josh slammed his book down on the desk.
      Josh 把他的書砰地摔在桌上。
   💡 slam the door in sb's face 當…的面摔門；悍然拒絕…

---

21. **sphere** [sfɪr] n. [C] 球體；範圍，領域
   ▲ The Earth is a sphere. 地球是個球體。

---

22. **strand** [strænd] v. 使進退不得，使陷於困境；使 (船、
   魚等) 擱淺

▲ Because of the typhoon, many people were left stranded at the airport. 因為颱風，很多人被困在機場。

strand [strænd] n. [C] (繩子、頭髮等的) 一縷，一綹

▲ The detective found a strand of red hair on the carpet. 警探在地毯上發現一綹紅髮。

---

23. **therapist** [ˋθɛrəpɪst] n. [C] 治療師

▲ My cousin works as a physical therapist in a hospital. 我的表姊在醫院當物理治療師。

---

24. **trophy** [ˋtrofɪ] n. [C] 獎盃；戰利品

▲ The tennis player finally won a trophy in the tournament. 那名網球選手終於在錦標賽中贏得獎盃。

---

25. **vertical** [ˋvɝtɪkl] adj. 垂直的

▲ The tower is not completely vertical to the ground. 那座塔並沒有完全和地面垂直。

vertical [ˋvɝtɪkl] n. [C] 垂直的線或平面 (the ～)

▲ The engineer will figure out how many degrees the post is off from the vertical. 工程師會弄清楚那根柱子傾斜了幾度。

Unit 4

1. **auction** [ˋɔkʃən] n. [C][U] 拍賣

▲ A couple bought the antique vase at auction yesterday.

一對夫妻在昨天的拍賣買了這個古董花瓶。

💡 put sth up for auction 將…交付拍賣

auction [`ɔkʃən] v. 拍賣 <off>

▲ The auctioneer tried to auction off the antiques.
拍賣會主持人試著拍賣掉這些古董。

---

2. **bureaucracy** [bjuˈrɑkrəsɪ] n. [C][U] 官僚的體制或作風

▲ Dealing with bureaucracy can sometimes be annoying. 跟官僚體制應對有時可能很討厭。

---

3. **coincidence** [koˈɪnsədəns] n. [C][U] 巧合

▲ George and Mary met again by coincidence.
George 和 Mary 碰巧又見面了。

coincide [ˌkoɪnˈsaɪd] v. 同時發生 <with>；相符 <with>

▲ The incident coincided with the mayor's arrival.
那事件恰巧在市長到達時發生。

coincident [koˈɪnsədənt] adj. 同時發生的 <with>

▲ Poverty tends to be coincident with disease.
貧困和疾病常常伴隨而生。

coincidental [koˌɪnsəˈdɛntl] adj. 巧合的

▲ It was purely coincidental that Jeff and his ex-girlfriend both showed up at the party.
Jeff 和他前女友同時出現在此派對上純屬巧合。

---

4. **compulsory** [kəmˈpʌlsərɪ] adj. 強制性的

▲ Military service is compulsory in some countries.
服兵役在某些國家是強制性的。

💡 compulsory education 義務教育

---

5. **corridor** [ˋkɔrədɚ] n. [C] 走廊
   ▲ The children ran down the corridor.
   孩子們沿著走廊奔跑。

6. **delegation** [ˌdɛləˋgeʃən] n. [C] 代表團
   ▲ The government sent a delegation to the United Nations to attend a conference.
   政府派了一個代表團去聯合國參加會議。

7. **disconnect** [ˌdɪskəˋnɛkt] v. 切斷 (水、電或瓦斯等)；切斷 (電話、網路等的連線)
   ▲ Disconnect the computer from the electricity supply before fixing it. 修理電腦前要先切斷電源。

8. **envious** [ˋɛnvɪəs] adj. 羨慕的，嫉妒的 <of>
   ▲ My friends are envious of my good fortune.
   我的朋友們都羨慕我的好運。

9. **fascinate** [ˋfæsəˌnet] v. 使著迷
   ▲ The idea of sailing around the world fascinated John.
   駕船環遊世界的想法使 John 著迷。

   fascinated [ˋfæsəˌnetɪd] adj. 著迷的 <by>
   ▲ Everyone was fascinated by the beautiful music.
   這美妙的音樂使每個人都著迷。

   fascinating [ˋfæsəˌnetɪŋ] adj. 迷人的
   ▲ Some young girls find romance novels fascinating.

有些年輕女孩覺得浪漫小說很迷人。

10. **gravity** [ˋɡrævətɪ] n. [U] (地心) 引力，重力；重大，嚴重性
   ▲ Objects fall to the ground because the force of gravity pulls them down.
   物體落地是因為地心引力把它們往下拉。

11. **implication** [ˌɪmplɪˋkeʃən] n. [C] 可能的影響或後果 (usu. pl.) <for>；[C][U] 含意，暗示
   ▲ The proposal will have far-reaching implications for our future. 這項提案將對我們的未來有深遠的影響。

12. **irony** [ˋaɪrənɪ] n. [U] 嘲諷；[C][U] 出人意料或啼笑皆非的事
   ▲ "Thank you so much," the angry man said with irony.
   那個生氣的男人語帶嘲諷地說：「真是謝謝你啊！」

13. **mentor** [ˋmɛntɚ] n. [C] 指導者
   ▲ Judy's college professor is her mentor and close friend. Judy 的大學教授是她的良師益友。

14. **nomination** [ˌnɑməˋneʃən] n. [C][U] 提名 <for>
   ▲ The movie got 6 nominations for the Academy Awards. 這部電影榮獲奧斯卡六項提名。

15. **pathetic** [pəˋθɛtɪk] adj. 悲慘的；差勁的
   ▲ Eric looked pathetic after the serious illness.

Eric 大病一場之後看起來很悲慘。

---

16. **premier** [prɪ`mɪɚ] adj. 首要的，最重要的
   ▲ South Africa is one of the premier producers of diamonds. 南非是最重要的鑽石產地之一。
   premier [prɪ`mɪɚ] n. [C] 首相，總理 [同] prime minister
   ▲ The premier attended the conference.
   首相出席了那場會議。

---

17. **radiation** [ˌredɪ`eʃən] n. [U] 輻射
   ▲ Exposure to high levels of radiation can cause some forms of cancer.
   暴露於高強度的輻射可能會導致某些癌症。

---

18. **residential** [ˌrɛzə`dɛnʃəl] adj. 住宅的，有住宿設施的
   ▲ No factories should be built in the residential areas.
   住宅區不應蓋工廠。
   💡 residential college 提供住宿的大學

---

19. **script** [skrɪpt] n. [C] 劇本，講稿；[C][U] 文字
   ▲ Who wrote the script for this movie?
   這部電影的劇本是誰寫的？
   script [skrɪpt] v. 為 (電影、廣播、演講等) 寫劇本或講稿
   ▲ This movie is scripted and directed by Ang Lee.
   這部電影由李安編寫劇本並導演。

---

20. **slot** [slɑt] n. [C] 溝槽；時段
   ▲ After putting a coin in the slot, the kid pressed the button to get a can of soda from the vending machine.

那個孩子把硬幣放入投幣口後按下按鈕，從自動販賣機取得一罐汽水。

💡 slot machine 吃角子老虎機

slot [slɑt] v. 將…插入或投入溝槽中

▲ The clerk helped me slot the SIM card into my new smartphone.

店員幫我把 SIM 卡插入我的新智慧型手機裡。

---

21. **spine** [spaɪn] n. [C] 脊椎 [同] backbone；(仙人掌、豪豬等的) 刺

▲ The poor man injured his spine in a car accident.

那個可憐的男子在一場車禍中傷到了他的脊椎。

---

22. **strategic** [strə`tidʒɪk] adj. 戰略的

▲ The enemy occupied an important strategic location.

敵軍占據了一個戰略要地。

---

23. **thereby** [ðɛr`baɪ] adv. 因此，藉此

▲ Brian signed the document, thereby gaining control of the firm.

Brian 在文件上簽名，藉此取得公司的控制權。

---

24. **tuition** [tju`ɪʃən] n. [U] 學費；家教 <in>

▲ College tuition can be very expensive.

大學學費可能會很貴。

💡 tuition fee 學費

---

25. **veteran** [`vɛtərən] n. [C] 老手，經驗豐富者；退伍軍人

▲ My uncle is a veteran of several political campaigns.

我叔叔參與過數次政治運動，是經驗豐富的老手。

Unit 5

1. **authorize** [ˋɔθəˌraɪz] v. 授權，認可

   ▲ The president authorized the foreign minister to negotiate with the U.S.
   總統授權外交部長與美國進行交涉。

   authorized [ˋɔθəˌraɪzd] adj. 經授權的，獲得授權的

   ▲ Ms. Liu is the only authorized dealer in Asia.
   劉女士是亞洲唯一獲得授權的經銷商。

---

2. **butcher** [ˋbʊtʃɚ] n. [C] 肉販，肉店；屠夫

   ▲ Some local butchers do not sell bacon.
   當地有些肉販沒賣培根。

   ● butcher's 肉店，肉鋪

   butcher [ˋbʊtʃɚ] v. 屠殺

   ▲ Hundreds of thousands of innocent Chinese were butchered by the Japanese soldiers during World War II. 第二次世界大戰時數十萬無辜的中國人民被日本軍人屠殺。

---

3. **collaboration** [kəˌlæbəˋreʃən] n. [C][U] 合作 <with, between>

   ▲ Jack is working in collaboration with Alice on a book. Jack 和 Alice 合作編寫一本書。

---

4. **concede** [kən`sid] v. 承認；讓出，讓與 <to>

▲ I concede that I am wrong. 我承認我錯了。

💡 concede defeat 認輸

5. **corrupt** [kə`rʌpt] adj. 墮落的；貪汙腐敗的

▲ The drug dealer leads a corrupt life.
那個毒販過著墮落的生活。

corrupt [kə`rʌpt] v. 使墮落，使腐化

▲ Power tends to corrupt those who hold it.
權力容易使掌權者腐化。

6. **deliberate** [dɪ`lɪbərɪt] adj. 刻意的 [同] intentional [反] unintentional；慎重的

▲ That kid told a deliberate lie to cover his mistake.
那孩子刻意撒謊以掩飾過錯。

deliberate [dɪ`lɪbə͵ret] v. 仔細考慮 <on, over, about>

▲ We deliberated on possible solutions to the problem.
我們仔細思考問題可能的解決之道。

deliberately [dɪ`lɪbərɪtlɪ] adv. 刻意地，故意 [同] intentionally

▲ Witnesses said that the fire was started deliberately.
目擊者說有人故意縱火。

7. **discourse** [`dɪskors] n. [C] 演講，論文 <on>

▲ Mr. Wang delivered a discourse on critical thinking.
王先生發表了一場關於批判性思考的演講。

8. **envision** [ɪn`vɪʒən] v. 預想，設想

▲ We can envision the future by learning from the past.
我們可以透過了解過往來預想未來。

9. **filter** [`fɪltɚ] n. [C] 過濾器
▲ We bought a water filter to purify the drinking water.
我們買了濾水器來淨化飲用水。

💡 coffee filter paper 咖啡濾紙

filter [`fɪltɚ] v. 過濾，穿透；(消息) 走漏，逐漸傳開
▲ I enjoy seeing sunlight filter through branches and leaves. 我喜歡看陽光穿透枝葉間的縫隙灑落而下。

💡 filter out sth 將…過濾掉，濾除

10. **greed** [grid] n. [U] 貪心 <for>
▲ In Shakespeare's play, Macbeth's greed for power cost him his life. 在莎士比亞的戲劇中，馬克白對權力的貪婪使他喪失了生命。

11. **indulge** [ɪn`dʌldʒ] v. 縱容；沉迷，沉溺 <in>
▲ Some parents indulge their children dreadfully.
有些父母太過縱容孩子。

💡 indulge oneself in sth 沉迷於…

indulgence [ɪn`dʌldʒəns] n. [U] 縱容；沉迷，沉溺 <in>
▲ Some grandparents treated their grandchildren with indulgence. 有些祖父母會縱容寵溺孫子孫女。

indulgent [ɪn`dʌldʒənt] adj. 縱容的，溺愛的
▲ The father is indulgent toward his daughter.
那名父親溺愛他的女兒。

12. **journalism** [`dʒɝnə,lɪzəm] n. [U] 新聞業，新聞工作
   ▲ Susan plans to begin her career in journalism after graduation. Susan 打算畢業後要投身新聞工作。

13. **merge** [mɝdʒ] v. 合併 <into, with>；融入，融合 <into, with>
   ▲ The two lanes merge into one. 兩線道合併成一線。
   merger [`mɝdʒɚ] n. [C] 合併 <of, with, between>
   ▲ The merger of the two companies is big news.
     那兩家公司合併是大新聞。

14. **nominee** [,nɑmə`ni] n. [C] 被提名人 <for>
   ▲ Many celebrities attended the party, including several Oscar nominees. 許多名流出席了那場宴會，其中包括了幾位獲得奧斯卡獎提名的人。

15. **patron** [`petrən] n. [C] 贊助者 <of>；顧客，常客 [同] customer
   ▲ This lady is well-known as a patron of the arts.
     這位女士是知名的藝術贊助者。
   patronage [`petrənɪdʒ] n. [U] 贊助；光顧
   ▲ The principal's patronage has made the performance possible. 校長的贊助促成了這次的表演。
   patronize [`petrə,naɪz] v. 以施恩或高人一等的態度對待；光顧
   ▲ This program focuses on children's interests, instead of patronizing them.

這節目注重兒童的興趣，而不是對他們高高在上。

16. **premise** [ˋprɛmɪs] n. [C] 前提
   ▲ The detective's reasoning is based on the premise that the crime scene was not actually a locked room.
   那位偵探的推理是以案發現場並非密室為前提。

17. **raid** [red] n. [C] 突擊，突襲 <on, against>；警方的突擊搜查 <on>
   ▲ The enemy launched air raids on the capital.
   敵軍對首都發動空襲。
   raid [red] v. 突擊，突襲；(警方) 突擊搜查
   ▲ The enemy raided our military base.
   敵人突襲我們的軍事基地。

18. **respondent** [rɪˋspɑndənt] n. [C] (問卷調查等的) 受訪者
   ▲ A majority of respondents agreed with the plan.
   大多數受訪者贊同這項計畫。

19. **sector** [ˋsɛktɚ] n. [C] (國家經濟或商業活動的) 領域，產業；戰區
   ▲ Salaries in the public sector can be quite different from those in the private sector.
   國營產業的薪資與民間業界的可能不太一樣。
   💡 the manufacturing/financial/service sector 製造業 / 金融業 / 服務業

20. **smash** [smæʃ] v. 打碎，打破；猛擊

▲ The boy accidentally smashed the mirror to pieces.
男孩不小心把鏡子砸得粉碎。

smash [smæʃ] n. [sing.] 破碎聲，碎裂聲；[C] 大受歡迎的歌曲或影片等 [同] smash hit

▲ The plate fell to the floor with a smash.
盤子掉在地上啪啦一聲碎了。

---

21. **sponsorship** [`spɑnsɚʃɪp] n. [C][U] 資助，贊助

▲ We are looking for sponsorship for our school team.
我們在為校隊找贊助。

---

22. **submit** [səb`mɪt] v. 呈遞，提交 <to>；服從，順從，屈服 <to> [同] give in (submitted │ submitted │ submitting)

▲ I'll submit my homework to the teacher on Monday.
我星期一會交作業給老師。

💡 submit oneself to sth 服從⋯，接受⋯

submission [səb`mɪʃən] n. [C][U] 呈交；[U] 服從，屈服，投降 [同] surrender

▲ Submission of applications is due at noon on Friday.
呈交申請書的最後期限是星期五中午。

💡 be forced into submission 被迫屈服

---

23. **thesis** [`θisɪs] n. [C] 學位論文，畢業論文

▲ My sister is writing a thesis on Taiwanese cuisine.
我姊正在寫畢業論文，是有關臺灣料理的。

---

24. **tumor** [`tumɚ] n. [C] 腫瘤

▲ The patient had an operation to remove a brain tumor. 病人接受移除腦部腫瘤的手術。

💡 benign/malignant tumor 良性 / 惡性腫瘤

25. **viewer** [`vjuɚ] n. [C] 觀眾

▲ The TV program is popular and attracts many viewers. 這個電視節目很受歡迎，吸引很多觀眾。

Unit 6

1. **autonomy** [ɔ`tɑnəmɪ] n. [U] 自治 (權) [同] independence；自主 (權)

▲ The local government enjoys a high degree of autonomy. 地方政府享有高度的自治權。

💡 local/economic autonomy 地方自治 / 經濟自主

2. **canal** [kə`næl] n. [C] 運河

▲ Venice has a complex system of canals.
威尼斯有著複雜的運河系統。

3. **collective** [kə`lɛktɪv] adj. 集體的，共同的，集合的

▲ All of us take collective responsibility for the environment. 我們全都對環境負有共同責任。

💡 collective noun 集合名詞

collective [kə`lɛktɪv] n. [C] 集體經營的農場或企業

▲ In the old communist society, most people worked in collectives.
在舊共產主義社會中，大部分的人在集體農場工作。

collectively [kə`lɛktɪvlɪ] adv. 集體地，共同地，集合地

▲ A group of students taught together can be collectively referred to as a class.

一群一起上課的學生可以集體統稱為一個班級。

---

4. **conceive** [kən`siv] v. 想出，想像 <of>；懷孕

▲ The writer conceived the plot for her novel when she visited London.

作者在探訪倫敦時構想出小說的情節。

🔮 conceive of sb/sth (as sth) 想像…(為…)

conceivable [kən`sivəbḷ] adj. 可想像的，可想見的，可能的 [反] inconceivable

▲ It is conceivable that the absentee will be flunked.

可以想見缺勤者會被當掉。

---

5. **corruption** [kə`rʌpʃən] n. [U] 貪汙腐敗

▲ The government officer was accused of corruption and bribery. 那位政府官員被指控貪汙及收賄。

---

6. **democrat** [`dɛmə͵kræt] n. [C] 民主主義者；美國民主黨員 (D-)

▲ Democrats oppose dictators. 民主主義者反對獨裁者。

---

7. **disrupt** [dɪs`rʌpt] v. 擾亂

▲ Protesters stormed the building and disrupted the meeting. 抗議者攻占建築物，擾亂了會議。

---

8. **episode** [ˋɛpəˏsod] n. [C] 事件;(連載小說、連續劇等的) 一集,一回

▲ The first landing on the moon was an important episode in human history.
首次登陸月球是人類史上的一大事件。

9. **fiscal** [ˋfɪskḷ] adj. 財政稅收的,金融的

▲ The government needs sound fiscal policies to combat inflation.
政府需要健全的財稅政策來抑制通貨膨脹。

10. **grieve** [griv] v. (因為某人去世而) 悲痛 <for, over>

▲ The old woman grieved for her son.
老婦因為喪子而悲痛。

11. **inevitable** [ɪnˋɛvətəbḷ] adj. 不可避免的,必然的 [同] unavoidable

▲ It is inevitable that all living creatures will die.
所有的生物都會死亡,這是不可避免的。

inevitably [ɪnˋɛvətəblɪ] adv. 不可避免地,必然地

▲ According to the economist, a recession inevitably leads to high unemployment rates. 根據那位經濟學家所說,經濟不景氣必然會導致高失業率。

12. **judicial** [dʒuˋdɪʃəl] adj. 司法的

▲ People in that country don't quite trust the judicial system. 該國人民不太相信司法系統。

💡 judicial review 司法審查

13. **metropolitan** [,mɛtrə`pɑlətn̩] adj. 大都會的，大都市的
   ▲ The metropolitan area is notorious for its terrible air pollution.
   這個大都會區以嚴重的空氣汙染而惡名昭彰。

   metropolitan [,mɛtrə`pɑlətn̩] n. [C] 都市人
   ▲ Many people think that metropolitans are sophisticated. 不少人認為都市人比較世故。

---

14. **notify** [`notə,faɪ] v. 正式告知，通知 <of> [同] inform
   ▲ Notifying your supervisor of your resignation in advance is necessary.
   提早告知上司你要辭職是必要的。

   notification [,notəfə`keʃən] n. [C][U] 通知 <of>
   ▲ All the residents have received prior notification of the power outage.
   所有居民都已經提前收到停電通知。

   💡 written notification 書面通知

---

15. **pedal** [`pɛdl̩] n. [C] 腳踏板
   ▲ One of the pedals came off my bike.
   我的腳踏車有一個踏板掉下來了。

   pedal [`pɛdl̩] v. 騎腳踏車
   ▲ The girl pedaled her bicycle up the hill.
   女孩騎腳踏車上坡。

---

16. **premium** [`primɪəm] n. [C] 保險費，保費；額外的費用，附加費

▲ I hope that the monthly premium for my health insurance will not go up again.

希望我每月的健康保險費不會再上漲。

17. **rally** [ˈrælɪ] n. [C] 大會；(價格、景氣等) 止跌回升，復甦 (pl. rallies)

▲ The group held an antiwar rally appealing for peace.

該團體舉行了訴求和平的反戰大會。

rally [ˈrælɪ] v. 召集，集合；復甦，重振

▲ The general rallied the scattered troops.

將軍把離散的軍隊集合起來。

💡 rally to sb's support 集結起來支持⋯

18. **resume** [rɪˈzum] v. (中斷後) 繼續，重新開始；回到，重返 (座位、職位等)

▲ The speaker resumed his talk after a long silence.

演講者在沉默許久後才繼續演說。

resume [ˈrɛzəˌme] n. [C] 履歷表 (also résumé)

▲ Alex sent his resume to about 30 companies and got several interviews. Alex 向大約三十家公司投遞履歷表，得到一些面試機會。

19. **seminar** [ˈsɛməˌnɑr] n. [C] 研討會

▲ Dr. Chen will attend a seminar on juvenile crime tomorrow.

陳博士明天要參加一場有關青少年犯罪的研討會。

💡 hold/conduct a seminar 舉辦研討會

20. **smog** [smɑg] n. [C][U] 煙霧，霧霾，霾害
   ▲ Vehicle exhaust is one major source of smog in the cities.
   車輛排放的廢氣是城市裡霧霾的一個主要來源。

21. **spouse** [spaʊs] n. [C] 配偶
   ▲ Please bring your spouse to the party.
   請帶您的配偶一起參加派對。

22. **subsidy** [ˋsʌbsəˌdɪ] n. [C] 補助金，補貼，津貼 (pl. subsidies)
   ▲ The government is criticized for abolishing subsidies to farmers. 政府因為取消對農民的補貼而遭受批評。
   💡 housing/agricultural subsidy 住房津貼 / 農業補助

23. **thigh** [θaɪ] n. [C] 大腿
   ▲ Many girls want to have slender thighs.
   很多女孩子希望擁有纖瘦的大腿。

24. **tuna** [ˋtunə] n. [C][U] 鮪魚 (pl. tuna, tunas)
   ▲ Mom bought some bread and several cans of tuna to make sandwiches for us.
   媽媽買了一些麵包和幾罐鮪魚來幫我們做三明治。

25. **viewpoint** [ˋvjuˌpɔɪnt] n. [C] 觀點 (pl. viewpoints)
   ▲ From an economic viewpoint, the plan has no merits.
   從經濟的觀點來看，這項計畫並無優點。

Unit 7

1. **backyard** [ˌbæk`jɑrd] n. [C] 後院
   ▲ Mom grew flowers and vegetables in our backyard.
   媽媽在我們的後院種了花和菜。

---

2. **canvas** [`kænvəs] n. [U] 帆布;[C] 油畫 (pl. canvases)
   ▲ We bought a tent that is made of canvas.
   我們買了一頂帆布做的帳篷。
   canvas [`kænvəs] v. 用帆布覆蓋

---

3. **collector** [kə`lɛktɚ] n. [C] 收藏家;收取或收集⋯的人
   ▲ My father is an avid coin collector.
   我爸是狂熱的錢幣收藏家。
   💡 tax/garbage/stamp collector 收稅員 / 收垃圾的人 / 集郵者

---

4. **conception** [kən`sɛpʃən] n. [C][U] 想法,概念,觀念 <of> [同] concept, notion;懷孕
   ▲ Many young children have no conception of money management. 很多小孩對金錢管理毫無概念。

---

5. **counsel** [`kaʊnsl̩] n. [U] 建議,勸告 [同] advice
   ▲ The young man listened to his parents' wise counsel and remained patient.
   那位年輕人聽從父母明智的勸告,保持耐心。
   💡 seek/reject counsel 尋求建議 / 不聽勸告
   counsel [`kaʊnsl̩] v. 建議,勸告 [同] advise

▲ My doctor counseled me to take a long vacation.
我的醫生建議我休個長假。

---

6. **denial** [dɪˈnaɪəl] n. [C][U] 否認 <of>；拒絕 <of>
 ▲ The official issued a strong denial of all the charges against her. 那名官員堅決否認所有的指控。
 💡 in denial (對事實等) 拒絕接受，拒絕承認

---

7. **doctrine** [ˈdɑktrɪn] n. [C][U] 教義，信條
 ▲ The missionary believes in Christian doctrine.
 那位傳教士信奉基督教教義。

---

8. **equity** [ˈɛkwətɪ] n. [U] 公平，公正 [反] inequity
 ▲ Many people want a society in which equity and justice prevail.
 許多人都想要充滿公平和正義的社會。

---

9. **fleet** [flit] n. [C] 艦隊；(同家公司的) 車隊或船隊等
 ▲ The war finally ended after the Spanish fleet was defeated. 西班牙艦隊被擊敗後，戰爭終於結束了。
 fleet [flit] adj. 能快速移動的，跑得快的
 ▲ The runner is fleet of foot. 這位跑者跑得飛快。
 fleeting [ˈflitɪŋ] adj. 短暫的，飛逝的 [同] brief
 ▲ We caught only a fleeting glimpse of the superstar.
 我們只瞬間瞥見了那位巨星。

---

10. **grill** [grɪl] n. [C] 烤肉架，燒烤架；烤肉，燒烤的食物
 ▲ My neighbor cooked pork on the grill.
 我鄰居用烤肉架烤豬肉。

grill [grɪl] v. 用烤肉架燒烤 [同] barbecue；長時間審問，盤問 <about>
▲ I grilled some fish for dinner. 我烤了些魚當晚餐。

---

11. **inherent** [ɪn`hɪrənt] adj. 本質上的，固有的 <in>
▲ Competition is an inherent part of the free market economy. 自由市場經濟本質上就會有競爭。

---

12. **jug** [dʒʌg] n. [C] 罐，壺 [同] pitcher；一壺的量 (also jugful)
▲ Please rinse the bottles and jugs before placing them in the trash can. 瓶罐放進垃圾桶之前請先沖洗。
jug [dʒʌg] v. 將…裝入罐或壺中；用陶罐燉煮 (兔肉等)

---

13. **minimal** [`mɪnɪml] adj. 極少或極小的，最低限度的
▲ We only made minimal changes when renovating the old temple. 我們整修這間古廟時，只做了最少的改變。

---

14. **notion** [`noʃən] n. [C] 概念 <of>；(心血來潮或異想天開的) 想法
▲ I didn't have the slightest notion of the answer.
我完全不知道答案是什麼。
💡 abstract notion 抽象概念 | dispel the notion that... 摒除…的想法

---

15. **pedestrian** [pə`dɛstrɪən] n. [C] 行人
▲ This area used to be open to pedestrians only.
這個區域以前只開放給行人。

💡 pedestrian <u>area</u>/<u>walkway</u>/<u>crossing</u> <u>步行區</u> / <u>人行道</u> /
<u>行人穿越道</u>

pedestrian [pə`dɛstrɪən] `adj.` 平淡無奇的，缺乏想像力
的

▲ This novel is pedestrian and unimaginative.
這本小說平淡無奇，缺乏想像力。

16. **prescribe** [prɪ`skraɪb] `v.` 開藥，開處方 <for>；(法律等)
規定

▲ The doctor prescribed medicine for the patient's
stomachache after diagnosis.
醫生診斷後幫那位病人開了治胃痛的藥。

17. **ranch** [ræntʃ] `n.` [C] 大牧場，大農場

▲ My brother is going to work part-time on a ranch
during the summer vacation.
我弟暑假要去一座大農場打工。

💡 cattle/sheep ranch 牧牛 / 羊場 | ranch house 牧場主
人所住的房子；(屋頂平緩的) 平房

ranch [ræntʃ] `v.` 經營大牧場或大農場

▲ My aunt ranches in Australia.
我阿姨在澳洲經營大農場。

rancher [`ræntʃɚ] `n.` [C] 大牧場或大農場的經營者或工
作者

▲ My uncle works as a cattle rancher.
我舅舅是牧牛場主。

18. **retail** [`ritel] `n.` [U] 零售

▲ The sportswear is for retail only.
這款運動服僅供零售。

retail [ˋritel] adj. 零售的

▲ The recommended retail price is 20 dollars.
建議零售價為二十美元。

💡 retail trade/business 零售業

retail [ˋritel] adv. 零售地

▲ It is usually cheaper to buy wholesale than retail.
買東西通常是批發比零售便宜。

retail [ˋritel] v. 零售 <at, for>

▲ The dress retails at 30 dollars.
這款洋裝零售每件三十美元。

retailer [ˋritelɚ] n. [C] 零售商

▲ This company is a major clothing retailer.
這家公司是一大服飾零售商。

---

19. **senator** [ˋsɛnɪtɚ] n. [C] 參議員；評議委員

▲ This young man is a senator from the state of California. 這位年輕人是來自加州的參議員。

senate [ˋsɛnɪt] n. [C] (美國) 參議院 (usu. the S-)；(大學的) 評議會

▲ Will the Senate approve the bill?
參議院會批准這項法案嗎？

20. **snatch** [snætʃ] v. 一下子搶走，一把抓起，奪取；抓住機會 (做)⋯，趁機抽空 (做)⋯

▲ The thief snatched the old lady's purse and ran.

小偷一把搶過老太太的手提包就跑。

snatch [snætʃ] n. [C] 奪取；片段，小量 <of>

▲ There are reports of several bag snatches.

有幾起包包搶奪案的報導。

💡 in snatches 斷斷續續地

---

21. **squad** [skwɑd] n. [C] 分隊，小隊，小組

▲ A bomb squad soon arrived to defuse the time bomb.

防爆小組迅速抵達拆除定時炸彈。

💡 flying/drugs/rescue squad 霹靂 / 緝毒 / 救援小組

---

22. **substantial** [səb`stænʃəl] adj. (在數量、重要性等方面)
大的，可觀的；堅固的

▲ The billionaire has donated a substantial amount of
money to charity.

那位億萬富翁捐了很多錢給慈善機構。

💡 substantial change/improvement/contribution/salary/
meal 重大的改變 / 大幅的進步 / 重大的貢獻 / 優渥的
薪水 / 豐盛的餐點

---

23. **threshold** [`θrɛʃold] n. [C] 門檻；閾，界限

▲ You shall never cross the threshold of this house
again! 你永遠別想再跨進這房子的門檻！

💡 pain threshold 忍痛力 | on the threshold of sth 即
將⋯

---

24. **uncover** [ʌn`kʌvɚ] v. 打開⋯的蓋子；揭發，揭露

▲ The waiter uncovered the dish.

服務生打開餐盤的蓋子。

25. **vinegar** [ˈvɪnɪgɚ] n. [C][U] 醋
▲ The dish is so sour. You could have added too much vinegar. 這道菜好酸，你可能放太多醋了。

Unit 8

1. **ballot** [ˈbælət] n. [C][U] 無記名投票，投票表決；[C] 選票 [同] ballot paper
▲ We elected the president of the club by ballot.
我們投票選出社長。
💡 count the ballots 計算選票，計票 | ballot box 投票箱，票匭
ballot [ˈbælət] v. 要求⋯投票表決 <on>
▲ The union is considering balloting its members on the issue.
工會在考慮要讓會員就這件事進行投票表決。

2. **carnival** [ˈkɑrnəvl] n. [C][U] 嘉年華會
▲ Judy and Jack met each other when they went to the carnival in Rio de Janeiro, Brazil. Judy 和 Jack 是在參加巴西的里約熱內盧嘉年華會時認識彼此的。

3. **columnist** [ˈkɑləmnɪst] n. [C] 專欄作家
▲ Ann Landers was a famous American columnist in the 20th century.

安夫人是二十世紀的知名美國專欄作家。

---

4. **condemn** [kən`dɛm] v. 公開譴責 <as, for>；將…判刑 <to>

   ▲ Most countries condemned Russia for its invasion of Ukraine. 大多數國家都對俄羅斯入侵烏克蘭表示譴責。

---

5. **counselor** [`kaunsələ] n. [C] 諮商師，顧問；(兒童夏令營的) 輔導員

   ▲ The couple talked to a marriage counselor about their problem. 那對夫妻找婚姻諮商師討論他們的問題。

---

6. **deploy** [dɪ`plɔɪ] v. 部署，調度 (軍隊、武器等)；運用 (資源等)

   ▲ Troops and weapons were deployed in this area.
   這個地區以前有部署軍隊和武器。

---

7. **documentary** [ˌdɑkjə`mɛntərɪ] n. [C] 紀錄片 <on, about>

   ▲ We saw a documentary on the aboriginal peoples in Taiwan. 我們看了一部有關臺灣原住民的紀錄片。

   documentary [ˌdɑkjə`mɛntərɪ] adj. 文件的，書面的；(電影等) 紀實的

   ▲ Investigators are looking for documentary evidence or proof of torture. 調查員正在找刑求的書面證據。

---

8. **erect** [ɪ`rɛkt] v. 建立；使直立，豎起 [同] put up

   ▲ The villagers erected a statue in memory of the great poet. 村民們建立了一座雕像來紀念這位偉大的詩人。

💡 erect a tent 搭帳篷

erect [ɪ`rɛkt] adj. 筆直的

▲ The soldier was standing erect. 士兵筆直地站著。

---

9. **fluency** [`fluənsɪ] n. [U] 流利，流暢

▲ The professor speaks English with fluency.
教授講英語很流利。

---

10. **grip** [grɪp] n. [C] 抓牢，抓緊，緊握 (usu. sing.) <on>；
[sing.] 掌握，控制 <on>

▲ Olive kept a grip on my hands.
Olive 緊握住我的手。

💡 get a grip (on oneself) 控制自己的情緒，鎮定自制，
自我克制

grip [grɪp] v. 抓牢，抓緊，緊握；吸引，使感興趣
(gripped | gripped | gripping)

▲ Victor gripped May's arm. Victor 抓住 May 的手臂。

---

11. **inherit** [ɪn`hɛrət] v. 繼承 <from>；遺傳 <from>

▲ My friend inherited a million dollars from her father.
我朋友從她父親那裡繼承了一百萬元。

💡 inherited disease 遺傳病

inheritance [ɪn`hɛrətəns] n. [C][U] 遺產 (usu. sing.)

▲ Ada has recently received a large inheritance from a
distant relative.
Ada 最近從一個遠親那邊繼承了一大筆遺產。

---

12. **jury** [ˋdʒʊrɪ] n. [C] 陪審團；(競賽等的) 評審團 (pl. juries)

▲ After full discussion, the jury found the defendant not guilty. 經過充分討論，陪審團裁決被告無罪。

💡 be/sit/serve on a jury 擔任陪審員 | the jury is (still) out on sth …仍未確定，尚無定論

---

13. **minimize** [ˋmɪnəˌmaɪz] v. 將…減到最低

▲ Make preparations in advance of the typhoon to minimize the damage.
在颱風來襲之前事先做準備，以便將災害減到最低。

---

14. **nutrient** [ˋnjutrɪənt] n. [C] 營養，養分，營養素，營養物質

▲ Vegetables and fruits provide many essential nutrients. 蔬果提供許多必要的營養。

nutrient [ˋnjutrɪənt] adj. 營養的

▲ A person on a strict diet may suffer from a nutrient deficiency. 嚴格控制飲食的人可能會營養不良。

---

15. **perspective** [pɚˋspɛktɪv] n. [C] 觀點 <on, from> [同] viewpoint；[U] 理性客觀的判斷力

▲ What's your perspective on life? 你的人生觀為何？

💡 from a different/historical/female perspective 從不同 / 歷史 / 女性的觀點來看 | from sb's perspective 從…的觀點來看

perspective [pɚˋspɛktɪv] adj. 透視畫法的

---

16. **presume** [prɪ`zum] v. 以為，認為，認定，假定 [同] assume；冒昧，膽敢，擅自

▲ I presumed that we could reason with the salesman.
我以為我們能跟業務員講理。

presumption [prɪ`zʌmpʃən] n. [C] 假定，推測，以為，認為

▲ The duchess made a presumption that her servant stole her ring. 公爵夫人認為僕人偷了她的戒指。

17. **rational** [`ræʃənḷ] adj. 合理的 [反] irrational；理性的 [反] irrational

▲ You must give rational arguments to be persuasive.
你必須提出合理的論點才有說服力。

18. **rhetoric** [`rɛtərɪk] n. [U] (煽動或浮誇的) 言詞，華麗的詞藻，花言巧語；修辭學

▲ The politician's speech was full of empty rhetoric.
那個政客的演講全是空虛的花言巧語。

rhetorical [rɪ`tɔrɪkl] adj. 修辭學的，修辭上的

▲ "Who cares?" is one of the so-called rhetorical questions. 「誰在乎？」是一種所謂的修辭性問句。

19. **sensor** [`sɛnsɚ] n. [C] 感應器，感應裝置

▲ I'm looking for a sensor that can detect smoke or fire. 我想找一個可以偵測煙霧或火災的感應器。

20. **sniff** [snɪf] v. 嗅，聞 <at>；吸鼻子

▲ The dog sniffed at the stranger. 狗嗅了嗅陌生人。

💡 sniff at sth 對…嗤之以鼻 | sniff out sth 嗅出… ; 察覺… | sniff around 四處探查

sniff [snɪf] n. [C] 嗅聞或吸鼻子

▲ The cook took a sniff of the soup. 廚師聞了聞湯。

21. **squash** [skwɑʃ] n. [C][U] 南瓜屬的植物或其果實 (pl. squashes, squash) ; [U] 壁球

▲ I planted some squash in the field.
我在田裡種了一些南瓜。

squash [skwɑʃ] v. 塞進,擠進 <in, into> [同] squeeze ; 壓扁,壓壞,壓爛 [同] flatten

▲ My roommate squashed the clothes into a small suitcase. 我室友把衣服塞進小小的行李箱中。

22. **successor** [sək`sɛsɚ] n. [C] 繼任者 <to>

▲ Ted was chosen to be the successor to the current president. Ted 被選為現任董事長的繼任者。

23. **thrill** [θrɪl] n. [C] 激動,興奮刺激,戰慄

▲ It gave us a thrill to meet the superstar.
和那位巨星碰面令我們興奮激動。

thrill [θrɪl] v. (使) 興奮,激動

▲ The good news thrilled me.
那個好消息令我感到興奮。

24. **undergraduate** [ˌʌndɚ`grædʒuɪt] n. [C] 大學生

▲ A group of Harvard undergraduates threw a party at the bar last night.

昨晚有一群哈佛大學生在這家酒吧開派對。

25. **visa** [ˋvizə] n. [C] 簽證

▲ My visitor's visa expired. I need to extend it.
我的觀光簽證過期了。我需要延長簽證。

♥ entry/exit/transit visa 入境 / 出境 / 過境 簽證 |
tourist/student/work visa 觀光 / 學生 / 工作簽證

Unit 9

1. **banner** [ˋbænɚ] n. [C] 橫幅標語

▲ The protesters carried banners which said, "No More
Chernobyls."
抗議者拿著上面寫了「拒絕車諾比事件重演」的標語。

♥ under the banner of sth 以…為由，打著…的口號

---

2. **casino** [kəˋsino] n. [C] 賭場 (pl. casinos)

▲ Las Vegas is known for many casinos.
拉斯維加斯以賭場眾多聞名。

---

3. **combat** [ˋkɑmbæt] n. [C][U] 戰鬥

▲ Many soldiers were killed in combat.
很多士兵在戰鬥中被殺。

combat [ˋkɑmbæt] v. 打擊 (combated, combatted |
combated, combatted | combating, combatting)

▲ One of the responsibilities of the police is to combat
crime. 警察的職責之一是打擊犯罪。

4. **confession** [kənˋfɛʃən] n. [C][U] 坦白，供認

▲ The killer was relieved after making a full confession. 那名凶手全盤招供了之後如釋重負。

💡 I have a confession (to make)... 我要坦白承認一件事…

5. **credibility** [ˌkrɛdəˋbɪlətɪ] n. [U] 可信度，信用

▲ The bribery has undermined that man's credibility as a judge. 行賄案已破壞了那個男人身為評審的信用。

6. **depress** [dɪˋprɛs] v. 使沮喪

▲ Failing to get into his ideal college depressed Jimmy. 無法進入理想的大學讓 Jimmy 很沮喪。

depressed [dɪˋprɛst] adj. 沮喪的

▲ Some people feel depressed about the election results. 有些人對選舉的結果感到沮喪。

depressing [dɪˋprɛsɪŋ] adj. 令人沮喪的

▲ Such bad news was really depressing. 這樣的壞消息真的很令人沮喪。

7. **domain** [doˋmen] n. [C] 領域，範圍

▲ Is this issue outside or within the domain of medicine? 這個議題算不算在醫學的領域範圍內呢？

8. **erupt** [ɪˋrʌpt] v. (火山) 爆發 <from>；(動亂、戰爭、抗議等) 突發 [同] break out

▲ The volcano erupted and left several tourists injured. 火山爆發造成數名觀光客受傷。

eruption [ɪˈrʌpʃən] n. [C][U] (火山) 爆發；(動亂、戰爭、抗議等) 突發
▲ The ancient Roman city of Pompeii was destroyed by a volcanic eruption.
羅馬古城龐貝毀於一場火山爆發。

---

9. **forum** [ˈforəm] n. [C] 討論會，研討會 <on, for>；網路論壇，討論區 (pl. forums, fora)
▲ There will be a forum for discussion on economic development. 將會有一場探討經濟發展的研討會。

---

10. **guideline** [ˈgaɪd͵laɪn] n. [C] 指導方針 (usu. pl.) <on, for>
▲ The government issued guidelines on the stock market for would-be investors.
政府發行了股市指南給有意投資者。

---

11. **initiative** [ɪˈnɪʃɪətɪv] n. [sing.] 主動，自主性，主導權 (the ~)
▲ We took the initiative in starting diplomatic relationships with that country.
我們主動與那個國家建立外交關係。
🔅 on sb's own initiative 主動地
initiative [ɪˈnɪʃɪətɪv] adj. 開始的，發起的

---

12. **landlord** [ˈlænd͵lɔrd] n. [C] 房東或地主
▲ Few landlords would lower their tenants' rents; some landlords even raise the rents.

很少房東會幫租客調降租金；有些房東甚至會調漲租金。

13. **missionary** [ˈmɪʃəˌnɛrɪ] n. [C] 傳 教 士 (pl. missionaries)

▲ The missionaries built buildings for their religious work. 那些傳教士建造用於宗教工作的房屋。

missionary [ˈmɪʃəˌnɛrɪ] adj. 傳教士的，傳教的

▲ Bill did missionary work in Africa.

Bill 以前在非洲當過傳教士。

💡 missionary zeal 傳教士般的狂熱，極度的熱忱

14. **observer** [əbˈzɝvɚ] n. [C] 觀察者，觀察員；觀察家，評論家

▲ UN observers will also attend the conference.

聯合國觀察員也將會出席這場會議。

15. **pessimism** [ˈpɛsəˌmɪzəm] n. [U] 悲 觀 ，悲 觀 主 義 <about, over> [反] optimism

▲ Because of the pandemic, pessimism about the economy could remain for a while.

因為疫情的關係，對經濟的悲觀可能會持續一陣子。

pessimist [ˈpɛsəmɪst] n. [C] 悲觀的人，悲觀主義者 [反] optimist (pl. pessimists)

▲ The old man is a pessimist; he believes the worst things will happen to him. 那個老人是個悲觀的人，他認為最壞的事都會發生在他身上。

16. **prevail** [prɪ`vel] v. 流行，盛行 <in, among>；占上風，占優勢，勝過 <over>

▲ Internet slang prevails among the younger generation. 網路用語在年輕一代中很盛行。

💡 prevail on/upon sb 說服…

prevailing [prɪ`velɪŋ] adj. 普遍的，流行的 [同] current

▲ The prevailing attitudes toward abortion are polarized. 對於墮胎，大眾普遍的態度兩極化。

17. **rattle** [`rætl̩] v. 嘎嘎作響，發出卡嗒聲；使緊張，使惶恐不安

▲ The windows were rattling in the violent wind. 窗戶在暴風中嘎嘎作響。

💡 rattle on 喋喋不休

rattle [`rætl̩] n. [C] (硬物碰撞等發出的) 嘎嘎聲，卡嗒聲 (usu. sing.)

▲ A rattle of dishes from the kitchen caught our attention. 廚房傳來的一陣碗盤碰撞聲吸引了我們的注意。

18. **rib** [rɪb] n. [C] 肋骨；排骨

▲ The thief fell off a ladder and broke a rib. 那個小偷從梯子上摔下來而斷了一根肋骨。

rib [rɪb] v. 揶揄，調侃，取笑 <about> [同] tease (ribbed | ribbed | ribbing)

▲ My friends ribbed me about my silly mistake. 我的朋友揶揄我愚蠢的錯誤。

19. **sentimental** [ˌsɛntə`mɛntl̩] adj. 情感的；多愁善感的，感傷的 <about>

▲ For sentimental reasons, the old man came back to his hometown.
基於情感上的理由，那位老人回到了家鄉。

20. **soar** [sor] v. 暴增；高聳，高飛翱翔

▲ The temperature soared to 46°C, and many people died from the heat.
溫度飆升到攝氏四十六度，很多人因高溫而熱死。

21. **squat** [skwɑt] adj. 矮胖的

▲ The squat guy over there is a lawyer.
那邊那個矮胖的傢伙是位律師。

squat [skwɑt] n. [C] 蹲，蹲著的姿勢

▲ The coach stood up from a squat and then bent to a squat again.
教練從蹲著的姿勢站起來，然後又蹲下去。

squat [skwɑt] v. 蹲；擅自非法占用 (房屋或土地)
(squatted | squatted | squatting)

▲ The boy squatted down to pick up his pen.
男孩蹲下來撿筆。

22. **suite** [swit] n. [C] (旅館等的) 套房

▲ I want to reserve a suite. 我想預約一間套房。

🔆 honeymoon suite 蜜月套房

23. **thriller** [`θrɪlɚ] n. [C] 驚悚片或驚悚小說等文藝作品

▲ This movie is the best thriller I have ever seen.
這部電影是我看過最棒的驚悚片。

24. **underline** [ˌʌndɚˋlaɪn] v. 在 (字句等) 之下劃線，(為了強調而) 將⋯劃底線；強調，突顯 [同] highlight

▲ I underlined the important words in red.
我在重要的字下面劃了紅色底線。

underline [ˋʌndɚˌlaɪn] n. [C] 底線

▲ You can see a wavy red underline appear under a word that is spelled wrongly.
在拼錯的字下面可以看到有波浪狀的紅色底線。

25. **vomit** [ˋvɑmɪt] n. [U] 嘔吐物

▲ The nurse made sure that the unconscious patient didn't choke on his own vomit. 護士確保那名失去意識的病人不被他自己的嘔吐物嗆到。

vomit [ˋvɑmɪt] v. 嘔吐

▲ The smell was so terrible that all of us wanted to vomit. 那味道臭得讓我們都想吐。

Unit 10

1. **batch** [bætʃ] n. [C] 一批 <of>

▲ The dealer delivered the goods in batches.
商家分批送貨。

♥ a batch of letters 一批信件 | a fresh batch of bread 一爐剛烤好的麵包

2. **cemetery** [ˋsɛməˌtɛrɪ] n. [C] (常指非附屬於教會的) 墓地 (pl. cemeteries)

▲ They buried their mother in a public cemetery.
他們把母親葬在公墓。

3. **comedian** [kəˋmidɪən] n. [C] 喜劇演員

▲ Chaplin is one of the most famous comedians in the 20th century.
卓別林是二十世紀最著名的喜劇演員之一。

4. **confine** [kənˋfaɪn] v. 限制，使侷限於 <to> [同] restrict；關住，困住，使離不開

▲ During the lockdowns, many people were confined to their homes. 封城期間，許多人都被限制待在家裡。

5. **creek** [krik] n. [C] 小溪

▲ When I was little, I used to catch tadpoles in the creek. 我小時候常在這條小溪裡抓蝌蚪。

6. **deputy** [ˋdɛpjəˌtɪ] n. [C] 代理人，副手 (pl. deputies)

▲ Who'll be your deputy while you are away?
你不在時誰是你的代理人？

♥ deputy governor/mayor/chairman 副州長 / 副市長 / 副主席

7. **dome** [dom] n. [C] 半球形屋頂，圓頂，穹頂

▲ The dome of the cathedral was painted gold.
這座大教堂的圓頂被漆上金色。

♥ the dome of the sky 蒼穹

dome [dom] v. 以圓頂覆蓋；使成半球形

---

8. **escalator** [`ɛskə,letɚ] n. [C] 電扶梯，自動手扶梯
   ▲ We took the escalator down to the lower level.
   我們搭電扶梯到下一層樓。
   💡 up/down escalator 向上 / 向下的電扶梯
   escalate [`ɛskə,let] v. 上升，增加；擴大，惡化 <into>
   ▲ The inflation rate could escalate sharply during a time of war. 通貨膨脹率在戰時很可能急劇上升。

---

9. **foster** [`fɔstɚ] adj. 寄養的，(暫時) 收養的
   ▲ This child will be placed with a nice foster family.
   這個孩子將被安置在一個良好的寄養家庭。
   💡 foster children/parents 寄養孩童 / 父母 ∣ foster family/home 寄養家庭
   foster [`fɔstɚ] v. 培養，助長，促進 [同] encourage, promote；養育 (非親生子女)，收養
   ▲ The establishment of industrial parks helped to foster the growth of the domestic industries.
   工業園區的建立幫助促進了國內工業的成長。
   💡 foster an interest in sth 培養對…的興趣

---

10. **gut** [gʌt] n. [C] 腸道 [同] intestine；[pl.] 內臟 (～s)
    ▲ To help food pass through the gut smoothly, consume enough water.
    要讓食物順利通過腸道就要攝取足夠的水分。
    💡 have the guts (to do sth) 有做…的膽識或勇氣 ∣ it takes guts to do sth 做…需要膽識或勇氣

gut [gʌt] v. 清除 (魚等) 的內臟 (gutted │ gutted │ gutting)

▲ I gutted the fish and then cooked it for dinner.
我清除魚的內臟，然後把牠煮了當晚餐。

---

11. **inject** [ɪn`dʒɛkt] v. 注射 <into, with>；注入，增添 (活力、資金等) <into>

▲ The doctor injected the patient with antibiotics.
醫生為病人注射抗生素。

💡 inject money/capital into the business 為企業挹注資金

---

12. **laser** [`lezɚ] n. [C] 雷射

▲ Lasers can be used to perform eye surgery or to read bar codes on products. 雷射可以用於眼睛手術，也可以用來讀取商品上的條碼。

💡 laser printer 雷射印表機 │ laser surgery 雷射手術

---

13. **moan** [mon] n. [C] 呻吟聲

▲ The rescue team heard a moan from under the rubble.
搜救隊伍聽見瓦礫堆下傳來的呻吟聲。

moan [mon] v. 呻吟 [同] groan；發牢騷 <about> [同] complain

▲ The wounded soldier moaned with pain.
受傷的士兵痛苦地呻吟。

---

14. **odds** [ɑdz] n. [pl.] 可能性

▲ The odds are against us. 我們的勝算不大。

💡 the odds are in favor of/against sth …可能 / 不可能發生 | the odds are in sb's favor/against sb …可能 / 不可能成功

---

15. **petty** [ˈpɛtɪ] adj. 微不足道的，瑣碎的 [同] trivial (pettier | pettiest)
▲ Some adolescents are involved in shoplifting or other petty crimes. 有些青少年會順手牽羊或犯其他輕罪。

---

16. **proclaim** [proˈklem] v. 宣布，聲明，宣稱
▲ The famous actor proclaimed that he would run for president. 那位知名演員宣布將參選總統。
💡 proclaim sb/sth/oneself sth 宣布或宣稱…為…

---

17. **realism** [ˈriəˌlɪzəm] n. [U] 務實，實際；(文學、藝術等的) 逼真，寫實 (主義)
▲ There is a mood of realism at the conference.
這場會議有務實的氛圍。

---

18. **ridge** [rɪdʒ] n. [C] 山脊；(屋脊等) 狹長的隆起
▲ The mountain climber walked carefully along the ridge. 登山者小心地沿著山脊行走。
ridge [rɪdʒ] v. 使隆起成脊狀
▲ The soles of the shoes are ridged to help prevent you from slipping. 鞋底有突起的紋路可以防滑。

---

19. **server** [ˈsɝvɚ] n. [C] 伺服器；服務生 [同] waiter, waitress；(大湯匙等) 分菜用具；(網球、排球等的) 發球者

▲ "Did the server crash?" "Yes, the server is down again!" 「伺服器當機了嗎？」「對，伺服器又當了！」

20. **sob** [sɑb] n. [C] 啜泣 (聲)，抽噎 (聲)，嗚咽 (聲)

▲ Tess asked her father for forgiveness with sobs.
Tess 啜泣著求她父親原諒。

sob [sɑb] v. 啜泣，抽噎，嗚咽 (sobbed | sobbed | sobbing)

▲ We heard someone sobbing in the room.
我們聽到有人在那個房間裡啜泣。

21. **stability** [stə`bɪlətɪ] n. [U] 安定 (性)，穩定 (性) [反] instability

▲ The job offers stability and a good salary.
這份工作提供穩定性及不錯的薪水。

💡 economic/political/emotional stability 經濟 / 政治 / 情緒的穩定

22. **supervise** [`supə‚vaɪz] v. 監督

▲ The teacher supervised the students taking their final exam. 老師監督學生們考期末考。

23. **throne** [θron] n. [C] 王位 (usu. the ～)

▲ The incident happened when the old king was still on the throne. 那件事發生在老國王還在位的時候。

💡 succeed to the throne 繼承王位 | seize the throne 篡奪王位 | come to/ascend the throne 登上王位，即位

24. **undertake** [ˌʌndɚˈtek] v. 從事，進行，承擔 (任務等)；承諾，答應 (undertook | undertaken | undertaking)

▲ The directors of the company were reluctant to undertake a risky venture.
公司的董事們不願從事有風險的事業。

---

25. **voucher** [ˈvaʊtʃɚ] n. [C] 抵用券，兌換券

▲ This voucher is valid till May and entitles you to 10% off all books. 這張抵用券到五月都有效，你憑券可享所有書籍都九折的優惠。

💡 gift/travel voucher 禮券 / 旅遊券 | voucher for a free meal/swim 免費用餐券 / 游泳券

Unit 11

1. **betray** [bɪˈtre] v. 背叛，出賣 <to>；洩漏 (祕密、情感等)

▲ The general betrayed his country to the enemy.
將軍向敵人出賣祖國。

betrayal [bɪˈtreəl] n. [C][U] 背叛

▲ Ruining the natural environment is an act of betrayal of our ancestors.
破壞自然環境是一種背叛我們祖先的行為。

betrayer [bɪˈtreɚ] n. [C] 背叛者

▲ Those who sell out their friends are called betrayers.
那些出賣朋友的人被稱為背叛者。

2. **certainty** [ˈsɝtn̩tɪ] n. [C] 確定的事；[U] 確切，確實
   ▲ It's a certainty that we will win.
   我們會贏是可以確定的事。

3. **commentary** [ˈkɑmənˌtɛrɪ] n. [C][U] 實況報導 <on>；
   [C] 評論 <on>
   ▲ The reporter's vivid commentary on the election
   caught everyone's attention. 這名記者對於這場選舉
   生動的實況報導吸引了所有人的注意。

4. **confront** [kənˈfrʌnt] v. 與…面對面或對峙；針對…提出
   質疑 <with>；面臨 <with>
   ▲ They confronted each other across the table.
   他們隔著桌子對峙。

5. **cripple** [ˈkrɪpl̩] v. 使跛腳
   ▲ The old man is crippled with severe joint pain.
   這個老人因為關節劇痛而跛腳。
   cripple [ˈkrɪpl̩] n. [C] 跛子
   ▲ Although I'm a cripple, I still walk fast with the aid
   of crutches.
   我雖然是個跛子，但在拐杖的幫助下還是走得快。

6. **descend** [dɪˈsɛnd] v. 下降 <to>；傳承 <from>
   ▲ The passengers fastened their seat belts when the
   plane was descending.
   乘客們在飛機下降期間繫好安全帶。
   💡 be descended from sb 是…的後代

descendant [dɪˋsɛndənt] n. [C] 子孫 <of> [反] ancestor
▲ They are descendants of the original Chinese immigrants. 他們是中國最初移民的後裔。

---

7. **donate** [ˋdonet] v. 捐贈 <to>
▲ The billionaire donated one thousand U.S. dollars to charity. 這名億萬富翁捐贈一千美元給慈善機構。

---

8. **estate** [əˋstet] n. [C] 地產
▲ Because of the global financial crisis, he had to sell his ancestral estate.
因為全球金融危機，他不得不賣掉祖傳的地產。

---

9. **fraction** [ˋfrækʃən] n. [C] 分數；極小部分
▲ 1/2 and 2/4 are fractions of the same amount.
1/2 和 2/4 是數量一樣的分數。

---

10. **haul** [hɔl] v. 拖拉；運送
▲ The tow truck hauled the damaged car away.
拖車把這輛損壞的車輛拖走了。
🕯 haul sb up 傳喚…(出庭)
haul [hɔl] n. [C] 運送的距離
▲ It's a long haul from Taipei to Pingtung.
從臺北到屏東是一段很長的運送距離。

---

11. **injection** [ɪnˋdʒɛkʃən] n. [C][U] 注射
▲ Sue was given an injection for flu.
Sue 因為流感而被打一針。

---

12. **lawmaker** [ˈlɔˏmekɚ] n. [C] 立法者，立法委員 [同] legislator

▲ People in Taiwan have the right to elect lawmakers.
臺灣的人民有權選舉立法委員。

13. **mode** [mod] n. [C] 模式

▲ Lesley turned the camera to manual mode.
Lesley 把照相機調成手動模式。

14. **operational** [ˌɑpəˈreʃənḷ] adj. 運作的

▲ The security system will be fully operational within two months. 安全系統將在兩個月內全面運作。

operationally [ˌɑpəˈreʃənəlɪ] adv. 操作上地

▲ The machine must be operationally feasible.
機器在操作上必須是可行的。

15. **phase** [fez] n. [C] 階段

▲ The negotiations have entered into a new phase.
談判已進入一個新階段。

🔹 in phase 同步地，一致地

phase [fez] v. 分段實施

▲ The Ministry of Education is phasing in a new examination system.
教育部正分段實施新的考試制度。

16. **profound** [prəˈfaʊnd] adj. 深奧的；深切的

▲ The book is too profound for me to understand.
這本書太深奧我無法理解。

profoundly [prə`faʊndlɪ] adv. 深切地

▲ Aaron's writing style was profoundly influenced by his teacher.

Aaron 的寫作風格深切地受到他老師的影響。

---

17. **realm** [rɛlm] n. [C] 領域

▲ The author's book opened a new realm of thoughts and ideas. 這名作者的書開啟了新的思想領域。

---

18. **rifle** [`raɪfl] n. [C] 來福槍

▲ The rifle was used in the murder.

那把來福槍被用在謀殺案。

rifle [`raɪfl] v. (尤指為了行竊而) 迅速翻找 (書頁、櫃子等) <through>

▲ The thief rifled through the drawers, but didn't find anything valuable.

小偷很迅速地翻找抽屜，可是沒有找到值錢的東西。

---

19. **session** [`sɛʃən] n. [C] 會議；(活動、授課的) 期間

▲ The congress is now in session. 國會現在開會中。

🔘 hold a session on sth 開有關⋯的會

---

20. **soften** [`sɔfən] v. (使) 變軟，(使) 軟化；(使) 變得溫和，(使) 態度軟化

▲ Oil softens leather. 油使皮革軟化。

🔘 soften sb up 減低⋯的防備 | soften the blow 減低衝擊

21. **stack** [stæk] n. [C] 一堆 <of>

▲ Paul quit his job last month because he inherited stacks of money from his grandfather! Paul 上個月辭職了，因為他從他祖父那繼承了一大筆錢！

stack [stæk] v. 堆疊，堆積 <up>；使充滿 <with>

▲ Addison stacked up the books on the table.
Addison 把書堆在桌上。

💡 stack up against sb/sth 與⋯相比 | the odds are stacked against sb ⋯處於不利的處境 | stack the deck 暗中做手腳

---

22. **supreme** [sə`prim] adj. 最高的，至高無上的

▲ Zeus is the supreme god in Greek mythology.
宙斯是希臘神話裡最至高無上的神。

💡 the Supreme Court 最高法院

---

23. **thrust** [θrʌst] v. 猛推或猛塞；刺；迫使 (thrust | thrust | thrusting)

▲ Mr. Brown thrust his hand at the wall because he was angry. Brown 先生因為生氣而用手猛推牆壁。

thrust [θrʌst] n. [C] 猛力一推；批評，抨擊

▲ My thrust burst the door open. 我猛力一推把門撞開。

---

24. **undo** [ʌn`du] v. 解開；使回復原狀，消除 (影響等) (undid | undone | undoing)

▲ Alan undid the buttons of his shirt.
Alan 解開他襯衫上的鈕扣。

25. **vow** [vaʊ] n. [C] 誓言
   ▲ My father made a vow to quit smoking.
   我父親發誓戒菸。
   💡 make/take a vow 發誓 | keep/break a vow 遵守 / 違背誓言

   vow [vaʊ] v. 發誓 <to, that>
   ▲ The son vowed to avenge his father's death.
   兒子立誓要為死去的父親報仇。

Unit 12

1. **bias** [`baɪəs] n. [C][U] 偏見 <against, toward, in favor of>
   ▲ The woman has a bias against her neighbor.
   這名女人對她的鄰居有偏見。
   💡 racial/religious/political bias 種族 / 宗教 / 政治偏見 | root out a bias 根除偏見

   bias [`baɪəs] v. 使有偏見 <against, toward, in favor of>
   [同] prejudice
   ▲ The old man's background biased him against Christianity. 這位老人的背景使他對基督教有偏見。

---

2. **chapel** [`tʃæpl̩] n. [C] (基督教的) 小教堂
   ▲ The couple got married at a chapel in Las Vegas last summer.
   這對夫妻去年夏天在拉斯維加斯的小教堂結婚。

3. **commentator** [ˋkɑmənˏtetɚ] n. [C] 評論員

▲ Danny's dream is to be a sports commentator.
Danny 的夢想是當一個體育節目評論員。

---

4. **consensus** [kənˋsɛnsəs] n. [sing.] 共識

▲ The committee has reached a general consensus on this issue.
關於這個議題，委員會已經達成一致的共識。

---

5. **criterion** [kraɪˋtɪrɪən] n. [C] 衡量標準 (usu. pl.) <for> (pl. criteria)

▲ What are the criteria for judging a work of art?
評斷藝術品的標準為何？

---

6. **despair** [dɪˋspɛr] n. [U] 絕望

▲ Finding her little son died in the fire, the lady uttered a cry of despair.
發現小兒子命喪火場，那個女人發出絕望的哭喊。

💡 be the despair of sb 成為…的心病 | to sb's despair 令…絕望的

despair [dɪˋspɛr] v. 絕望，死心 <of>

▲ Many young couples despair of finding an affordable house in the capital.
許多年輕夫妻放棄在首都找到負擔得起的房子。

---

7. **donor** [ˋdonɚ] n. [C] 捐贈者

▲ The donor took it as natural to help others and refused to receive any reward.

那位捐贈者認為幫助別人是很平常的事並拒絕接受報酬。

💡 blood donor 捐血者 | organ donor 器官捐贈者

---

8. **ethic** [ˈɛθɪk] n. [C] 倫理，道德標準 (usu. pl.)

▲ The issue of expired medicine has raised public concern about medical ethics.
過期藥品的議題引發大眾對於醫療道德的關心。

---

9. **fragment** [ˈfrægmənt] n. [C] 碎片 <of>

▲ The vase broke into fragments. 花瓶打碎了。

fragment [ˈfræɡˌmɛnt] v. (使) 破碎 <into>

▲ The huge rock fragmented into smaller pieces.
這塊大岩石碎成小片。

---

10. **hazard** [ˈhæzɚd] n. [C] 危害物 <of, to>

▲ Smoking is a major health hazard.
吸菸是健康的主要危害物。

💡 take the hazard 承受風險 | at/in hazard 冒著危險地 | at all hazards 不顧一切危險地 | occupational hazard 職業性危害

hazard [ˈhæzɚd] v. 使遭受危險；冒險猜測

▲ The new law hazards the safety of pedestrians.
這個新的法律危及行人的安全。

hazardous [ˈhæzɚdəs] adj. 危險的

▲ Traveling alone in a foreign country can be hazardous. 獨自在國外旅遊可能很危險。

11. **inning** [ˋɪnɪŋ] n. [C] (棒球中的) 回合，局
   ▲ The player hit a home run in the extra inning.
   這名球員在延長賽中擊出全壘打。

12. **league** [lig] n. [C] 聯盟
   ▲ During the war, several countries formed a league to fight against their common enemies. 在戰爭期間，部分國家為了對抗共同的敵人而組織聯盟。
   💡 in league with sb 與⋯勾結
   league [lig] v. 結盟，聯合 <together>
   ▲ Several women's groups leagued together against sex discrimination.
   幾個婦女團體聯合起來對抗性別歧視。

13. **molecule** [ˋmɑləˌkjul] n. [C] 分子
   ▲ A molecule is the smallest unit of a substance.
   分子是物質的最小單位。
   molecular [məˋlɛkjələ] adj. 分子的
   ▲ Heating a protein will change its molecular structure.
   加熱蛋白質會改變其分子結構。

14. **optimism** [ˋɑptəˌmɪzəm] n. [U] 樂觀 [反] pessimism
   ▲ Even in a desperate situation, he is full of optimism.
   即使情況很糟，他仍然保持樂觀。
   optimist [ˋɑptəˌmɪst] n. [C] 樂觀的人 [反] pessimist
   ▲ An optimist looks at the bright side of things.
   樂觀的人看到事物的光明面。

15. **photographic** [ˌfotəˈgræfɪk] adj. 攝影的
   ▲ Photographic images can be stored on a CD.
   攝影圖像可以儲存在光碟上。

16. **prohibit** [proˈhɪbɪt] v. (以法律、規定等) 禁止 <from>
   ▲ Smoking is strictly prohibited in this area.
   在此區域吸菸是被嚴格禁止的。

17. **reassure** [ˌriəˈʃʊr] v. 使安心
   ▲ After the doctor's examination, I felt reassured about
   my father's health.
   經過醫生的檢查，我對於我父親的健康感到安心。

18. **rim** [rɪm] n. [C] 邊緣
   ▲ The glass is filled to the rim.
   這個杯子被裝滿到了邊緣。
   rim [rɪm] v. 環繞 (rimmed | rimmed | rimming)
   ▲ A low fence rimmed the swimming pool.
   一道矮圍籬把游泳池環繞起來。

19. **shareholder** [ˈʃɛrˌholdɚ] n. [C] 股東 [同] stockholder
   ▲ As a shareholder of this company, Jack will attend
   the annual conference this Wednesday.
   身為這家公司的股東，Jack 將會出席本週三的年會。

20. **sole** [sol] adj. 唯一的；獨占的，獨有的
   ▲ Mike lost his sole son in a car crash.
   Mike 在一場車禍中失去了他唯一的兒子。
   sole [sol] n. [C] 腳底；鞋底

▲ The sand on the beach was so hot that burnt the soles of my feet.

海灘上的沙子太燙以致於燙傷了我的腳底。

sole [sol] v. 把鞋子配上底

▲ The shoemaker had the shoes soled.

鞋匠把鞋子配上底。

solely [`sollɪ] adv. 僅，只

▲ My mom cooks three meals every day solely for the sake of our health.

我母親每天煮三餐僅只是為了我們的健康。

---

21. **stain** [sten] n. [C] 汙漬；(名聲等的) 汙點

▲ Fruit stains are difficult to remove.

水果汙漬很難去除。

stain [sten] v. 弄髒 <with>；染色

▲ The rug was stained with ink. 地毯被墨水弄髒了。

---

22. **surplus** [`sɝplʌs] n. [C][U] 剩餘

▲ Let's divide the surplus equally.

我們把剩餘的平均分了吧。

surplus [`sɝplʌs] adj. 過剩的

▲ The man wants to invest his surplus cash in real estate. 男子想把過剩的錢投資在房地產上。

---

23. **tick** [tɪk] n. [C] 滴答聲

▲ Hearing the ticks of the clock in a pitch-black room is scary.

在一片漆黑的房裡聽見時鐘的滴答聲讓人感到害怕。

tick [tɪk] v. 滴答響

▲ The little girl stood there, listening to the clock ticking. 小女孩站在那兒聽時鐘滴答滴答響。

24. **unemployment** [ˌʌnɪmˈplɔɪmənt] n. [U] 失業 (率)；失業救濟金

▲ Unemployment is on the rise in the country.
這個國家的失業率正在上升。

💡 eliminate/reduce unemployment 消除 / 減少失業率

unemployed [ˌʌnɪmˈplɔɪd] adj. 失業的，沒有工作的

▲ My aunt has been unemployed for two months.
我阿姨已經失業兩個月了。

💡 the unemployed 失業人口

---

25. **warehouse** [ˈwɛrˌhaʊs] n. [C] 倉庫

▲ There are lots of warehouses near the harbor.
港口附近有很多倉庫。

warehouse [ˈwɛrˌhaʊz] v. 存入倉庫

▲ After the fire, this company warehoused their goods into their new building.
火災過後，這間公司改將商品存入他們的新大樓。

Unit 13

1. **bizarre** [bɪˈzɑr] adj. 怪異的

▲ The movie was scary because many bizarre things happened.

這部電影很嚇人，因為有很多怪異的事情發生。

2. **characterize** [ˋkærɪktə͵raɪz] v. 描述特點 <as>；是…的特徵

▲ The play is characterized as a black comedy.
這部劇被描述為有黑色喜劇的特點。

characterization [͵kærɪktərəˋzeʃən] n. [C][U] (對劇中、書中人物的) 描寫或塑造

▲ The characterization of the vampire is very unique in this film. 這部電影對吸血鬼的描寫非常特別。

3. **commuter** [kəˋmjutə] n. [C] 通勤者

▲ The buses are always packed with commuters during rush hour. 公車在尖峰時段總是擠滿了通勤者。

4. **constitutional** [͵kɑnstəˋtjuʃn̩l] adj. 憲法允許的

▲ We have a constitutional right to speak freely.
我們能自由言論是憲法允許的權利。

💡 constitutional monarchy 君主立憲制

constitutional [͵kɑnstəˋtjuʃn̩l] n. [C] 健身散步

▲ My grandma takes a constitutional after dinner every day. 我祖母每天晚飯過後都會健身散步。

5. **crude** [krud] adj. 粗略的；粗俗的

▲ This is just a crude idea, which may even not be put into practice.
這只是粗略的想法，可能根本不會付諸實行。

💡 crude oil/sugar/rubber 原油 / 粗糖 / 生橡膠

6. **destiny** [`dɛstənɪ] n. [C] 命運

▲Robin believed it was his destiny to fight for justice.
Robin 相信為正義而戰是他的命運。

7. **doorway** [`dɔr,we] n. [C] 門口

▲Ann stood in the doorway. Ann 站在門口。

8. **ethical** [`ɛθɪkl] adj. 道德的 [同] moral [反] unethical

▲It is not ethical for a doctor to reveal the patient's
confidences. 醫生洩漏病人的祕密是不道德的。

9. **framework** [`frem,wɜ·k] n. [C] 架構

▲We need to set up the framework of the project
before we begin.
在我們開始之前，必須先建立好企劃的架構。

10. **heir** [ɛr] n. [C] 繼承人

▲Samuel fell heir to the great estate.
Samuel 繼承了那筆龐大的財產。

💡 heir apparent 法定繼承人

11. **innovation** [,ɪnə`veʃən] n. [C] 新事物；[U] 創新

▲The smartphone is one of the most important
innovations of the past 20 years.
智慧型手機是近二十年來重大的新事物之一。

innovate [`ɪnə,vet] v. 創新

▲It's harder but also more rewarding to innovate.
創新比較難但得到的回報也比較多。

12. **legacy** [ˋlɛgəsɪ] n. [C] 遺產 [同] inheritance
   ▲ The billionaire had left her son a legacy of a billion dollars. 這名億萬富翁留給她兒子十億美元的遺產。

13. **morality** [məˋrælətɪ] n. [U] 正當性 <of>；[C][U] 道德觀 (pl. moralities)
   ▲ We had a debate over the morality of euthanasia.
   我們就安樂死的正當性進行辯論。

14. **orchard** [ˋɔrtʃəd] n. [C] 果園
   ▲ The farmer brought us to see his plum orchard.
   農夫帶我們去看他的梅子園。
   💡 apple/cherry orchard 蘋果 / 櫻桃園

15. **pickup** [ˋpɪk͵ʌp] n. [C] 小卡車，皮卡 (also pickup truck)
   ▲ Although the pickup is second-hand, it is still in good condition. 雖然小卡車是二手的，它仍然狀態良好。

16. **projection** [prəˋdʒɛkʃən] n. [U] 放映；[C] 預測
   ▲ The teacher showed us some slides in the projection room. 老師在放映室放幻燈片給我們看。

17. **rebellion** [rɪˋbɛljən] n. [C][U] 叛亂 <against>；叛逆 <against>
   ▲ The people finally raised a rebellion against the tyrant. 人民終於發動對暴君的叛亂。
   💡 suppress/crush a rebellion 鎮壓叛亂

rebellious [rɪˋbɛljəs] adj. 反叛的；叛逆的

▲ Teenagers tend to be rebellious.
   青少年有叛逆的傾向。

💡 rebellious streak 叛逆的傾向 ｜ rebellious troops 反叛軍

rebelliously [rɪˋbɛljəslɪ] adv. 叛逆地

▲ The boy spoke rebelliously, challenging his teacher.
   那男孩說話叛逆向老師挑戰。

---

18. **rip** [rɪp] v. 撕裂，撕碎；劃破 (ripped ｜ ripped ｜ ripping)

▲ The letter was ripped into pieces. 信被撕碎了。

rip [rɪp] n. [C] 裂口

▲ I sewed up a rip in the sleeve.
   我把袖子上的裂口縫起來。

---

19. **shatter** [ˋʃætɚ] v. 粉碎；破壞 <into>

▲ The ball shattered the window. 這球把窗戶打得粉碎。

shattering [ˋʃætərɪŋ] adj. 令人震驚的，毀滅性的

▲ The failure of the project was a shattering blow to his pride. 計畫失敗讓他的自尊受到毀滅性的打擊。

---

20. **solo** [ˋsolo] n. [C] 獨奏 (pl. solos)

▲ Judy played a piano solo. Judy 彈奏了鋼琴獨奏。

solo [ˋsolo] adv. 單獨地

▲ Charles Lindbergh became the very first person to fly solo across the Atlantic Ocean.
   林白是第一個單獨飛越大西洋的人。

solo [ˋsolo] adj. 單獨的

▲ Vic wants to try a solo flight across the world.
Vic 想試試單獨飛越全世界。

---

21. **stake** [stek] n. [C] 椿；利害關係 <in>

▲ The cowboy tied his horse to a stake.
牛仔把馬拴在椿上。

🏵 at stake 有失去的危險｜pull up stakes 移居他處；離職｜go to the stake for sth 為⋯不惜赴湯蹈火

stake [stek] v. 用椿撐起 <up>；投注 <on>

▲ The farmer staked up the tomato plants.
農夫用椿撐起番茄苗。

🏵 stake out 標出界線；祕密監視｜stake a claim 宣布所有權

---

22. **suspend** [səˋspɛnd] v. 垂掛 <from>；暫緩，暫停；停學 <from>

▲ Chandeliers are suspended from the ceiling.
天花板上垂掛著吊燈。

---

23. **tile** [taɪl] n. [C] 瓦片；磁磚

▲ The strong winds loosened many tiles on the roof.
強風使屋頂上的許多瓦片鬆動。

tile [taɪl] v. 鋪上磁磚

▲ The workers spent a whole day tiling the floor.
工人花了一整天把地板鋪上磁磚。

---

24. **unfold** [ʌn`fold] v. 展開；顯露，揭露 [反] fold

▲ Louise unfolded the napkin and put it on her lap.
　Louise 展開餐巾放在大腿上。

25. **warrior** [`wɔrɪɚ] n. [C] 戰士

▲ It took much training to be a good warrior.
　成為一名好戰士需要接受很多訓練。

Unit 14

1. **blur** [blɝ] n. [C] 模糊不清的事物

▲ Without glasses, everything is a blur to me.
　沒有了眼鏡，所有的東西對我來說都模糊不清。

blur [blɝ] v. 變得模糊 (blurred | blurred | blurring)

▲ Tina was so sleepy that her vision blurred.
　Tina 非常地想睡，以致於視線變得模糊。

2. **chord** [kɔrd] n. [C] 和絃

▲ With proper chords, you can also make a beautiful song of your own.
　配上適當的和絃，你也可以創作出你自己的美妙歌曲。

💡 strike/touch a chord (with sb) 得到 (⋯的) 共鳴或贊同

3. **compact** [kəm`pækt] adj. 小巧的

▲ My office is compact and well-equipped.
　我的辦公室小巧而配備齊全。

compact [ˈkɑmpækt] n. [C] 協定

▲ They made a compact to cooperate.
他們訂定合作的協定。

compact [kəmˈpækt] v. 壓縮

▲ We compacted all the trash into one garbage bag.
我們把所有的垃圾壓縮到一個垃圾袋裡。

---

4. **constraint** [kənˈstrent] n. [C] 束縛，限制 (usu. pl.) <on> [同] restriction；[U] 拘束

▲ To solve the financial constraints, the company decides to lay off half of the employees.
為了解決財務的束縛，這家公司決定裁掉一半的員工。

💡 economic/legal/political constraints 經濟 / 法律 / 政治束縛

---

5. **crystal** [ˈkrɪstl̩] n. [C][U] 水晶

▲ My husband bought me a pair of crystal earrings as an anniversary gift.
我丈夫買給我一對水晶耳環當作紀念日禮物。

crystal [ˈkrɪstl̩] adj. 清澈的，透明的

▲ My grandparents live by a river with crystal water.
我的祖父母住在一條清澈的河旁邊。

💡 crystal clear 清澈晶瑩的；清楚明瞭的

---

6. **diagnose** [ˌdaɪəgˈnos] v. 診斷 <as, with>

▲ The patient's condition was diagnosed as a stroke.
這名病患的病況被診斷為中風。

💡 sb be diagnosed as having depression/diabetes/flu/cancer 被診斷患有憂鬱症 / 糖尿病 / 流感 / 癌症 | sb be diagnosed with depression/diabetes/flu/cancer 被診斷患有憂鬱症 / 糖尿病 / 流感 / 癌症

7. **dough** [do] n. [C][U] 麵團

▲ The baker is rolling the dough. 麵包師傅在揉麵團。

8. **exclaim** [ɪk`sklem] v. 突然大叫

▲ "Would you please shut up," Jessica exclaimed angrily.

「拜託你閉嘴行不行，」Jessica 生氣地叫了出來。

9. **fraud** [frɔd] n. [C][U] 詐欺；[C] 騙子

▲ The young man was accused of fraud.

這個年輕人被控詐欺。

💡 commit fraud 詐欺

10. **herb** [ɝb] n. [C] 香料

▲ Beef stew can be flavored with herbs.

燉牛肉可加香料調味。

herbal [`ɝbl] adj. 草本的

▲ Herbal medicine has been replaced by synthetic medicine. 草本的藥物已被合成藥物所取代。

11. **inquiry** [ɪn`kwaɪrɪ] n. [C][U] 詢問，查詢 <about>；調查 <into> [同] investigation (pl. inquiries)

▲ The tourist made an inquiry about the opening hours of the museum.

那位觀光客詢問博物館的開放時間。

12. **legislative** [`lɛdʒɪsˌletɪv] adj. 立法的
▲ The government decided to take legislative action over the problem.
政府決定就這個問題採取立法行動。

13. **mortality** [mɔr`tælətɪ] n. [U] 死亡數量；不免一死
▲ Cancer mortality among young people has been on the increase. 年輕族群的癌症死亡數量一直在增加。
♥ mortality rate 死亡率

14. **originality** [əˌrɪdʒə`nælətɪ] n. [U] 獨創性
▲ Carl's work lacks originality. Actually, he just copies other people's work. Carl 的作品缺乏獨創性。事實上，他只是模仿別人的作品。

15. **pier** [pɪr] n. [C] 碼頭
▲ As the storm came, huge waves swept over the pier and struck the boats docked there. 隨著暴風雨的到來，巨大的海浪席捲碼頭並襲擊了停在那邊的船隻。

16. **prone** [pron] adj. 容易⋯的，有⋯的傾向 <to>；俯臥的，趴著的
▲ People are prone to illness when they are tired.
人們疲勞時容易生病。

17. **recipient** [rɪ`sɪpɪənt] n. [C] 收受者

▲ You should write the name of the recipient in the middle of the envelope.

你應該把收信者的姓名寫在信封中央。

18. **rod** [rɑd] n. [C] 釣竿

▲ The old man fished with a rod and line.

老人用釣竿垂釣。

19. **sheer** [ʃɪr] adj. 全然的；陡峭的

▲ My parents felt sheer delight when they heard the good news.

我父母在聽到這個好消息時，感到全然的喜悅。

sheer [ʃɪr] adv. 垂直地

▲ The cliff falls sheer to the river below.

懸崖陡降直到下面的河川。

20. **sophomore** [`sɑf,mor] n. [C] (高中、大學的) 二年級學生

▲ Nancy is now a sophomore in college.

Nancy 現在是名大學二年級學生。

21. **stall** [stɔl] n. [C] 攤位；隔欄，欄舍，小隔間

▲ My dad bought the magazine from the news stall.

我父親從報紙攤位買了這本雜誌。

stall [stɔl] v. (把家畜) 關入畜舍中；拖延；(車、引擎等) 熄火，拋錨

▲ Can you stall that pig? 你可以把那隻豬關入豬舍嗎？

22. **sustainable** [sə`stenəbl] adj. 可持續的

▲ Wind energy is a type of sustainable energy, which can be used continuously without polluting the environment. 風力發電是一種可持續的能源，可以在不汙染環境的情況下持續使用。

23. **tin** [tɪn] n. [C] (裝餅乾等的) 有蓋金屬盒或罐頭；[U] 錫

▲ Iris put a tin of peas on the table.
Iris 把豌豆罐頭放在桌上。

24. **unlock** [ʌn`lɑk] v. 打開門鎖

▲ Rick unlocked the door and entered the house.
Rick 打開門鎖然後進到屋裡。

💡 unlock the mystery/secret of sth 解開…之謎

25. **wary** [`wɛrɪ] adj. 小心的 <of>

▲ Be wary of strangers. 當心陌生人。

Unit 15

1. **blush** [blʌʃ] n. [C] 臉紅

▲ Martin walked away from me to hide his blushes.
Martin 為了不想讓我看到他臉紅而走開。

blush [blʌʃ] v. 臉紅 <with>

▲ The little girl blushed with embarrassment.
小女孩尷尬地臉紅了。

2. **chore** [tʃor] n. [C] 雜務

▲ Cynthia helps her mother do the household chores every day. Cynthia 每天幫母親做家務。

3. **compassionate** [kəm`pæʃənɪt] adj. 有同情心的
   ▲ The kind woman is very compassionate toward the orphans and often brings some food to them. 這位善心的女士對孤兒富有同情心，經常帶食物給他們。

4. **consultation** [ˌkɑnsl̩`teʃən] n. [U] 商議 <with>；諮詢 <with>
   ▲ The president is in consultation with his advisers. 董事長正與他的顧問群商議中。

5. **custody** [`kʌstədɪ] n. [U] 監護權；拘留
   ▲ After divorce, the mother lost custody of her children. 離婚之後，那位母親失去了孩子的監護權。
   💡 joint custody 共同監護權 | take sb into custody 拘留⋯

6. **dialect** [`daɪəˌlɛkt] n. [C][U] 方言
   ▲ Chinese has a great variety of dialects. 漢語有非常多種不同的方言。

7. **driveway** [`draɪvˌwe] n. [C] (連接公用道路與車庫或民宅等的) 車道
   ▲ Don't park your car on the driveway. Park it in the garage. 不要把你的車停在車道上。停在車庫裡。

8. **exclude** [ɪk`sklud] v. 排除，不包含 <from> [反] include

▲ Grandmother asked us to exclude sugar from our diet. 祖母叫我們不要吃含糖的飲食。

excluding [ɪk`skludɪŋ] prep. 除去

▲ Your bill comes to $25, excluding tax.
你的帳款除去稅是二十五美元。

---

9. **freight** [fret] n. [U] 貨運；貨物

▲ You can send the goods by air, sea, or rail freight.
你可以將這些貨物空運、海運或是陸運。

♥ freight train 貨運列車

freight [fret] v. 運送 (貨物) <with>

▲ The ship was freighted with coal. 這艘船運送著煤炭。

---

10. **hockey** [`hɑkɪ] n. [U] 冰上曲棍球 [同] ice hockey

▲ Samuel played hockey every day to improve his game. Samuel 為了提升球技每天打冰上曲棍球。

---

11. **insane** [ɪn`sen] adj. 瘋狂的

▲ It was insane of you to jump from such a height.
你從這麼高的地方跳下來是一件瘋狂的事。

♥ go insane 發瘋，瘋了 | the insane 精神病患者

---

12. **liability** [ˌlaɪə`bɪlətɪ] n. [C] 負債 (usu. pl.)；[U] 責任，義務 <for>

▲ The man has liabilities of nearly a million dollars.
這個男人有將近百萬美元的負債。

---

13. **mortgage** [`mɔrgɪdʒ] n. [C] (房屋) 貸款或抵押

▲ The couple have a twenty-year mortgage on their new house. 這對夫妻的新家有二十年期的房屋貸款。

💡 take out/pay off a mortgage 取得／清償房貸 | mortgage interest rate 房貸利率

mortgage [`mɔrgɪdʒ] v. 抵押

▲ Rex mortgaged his house to pay off his debts. Rex 抵押房子以還清債款。

---

14. **outfit** [`aʊt‚fɪt] n. [C] (整套) 服裝

▲ Tracy had that outfit made in Paris. Tracy 那套服裝是在巴黎訂做的。

outfit [`aʊt‚fɪt] v. 提供裝備，配置 <with> (outfitted | outfitted | outfitting)

▲ The expedition team was outfitted with the latest equipment. 探險隊配置了最新裝備。

---

15. **pillar** [`pɪlɚ] n. [C] 柱子，柱狀物；(團體中的) 核心人物，臺柱 <of>

▲ The roof is supported by four huge pillars. 屋頂由四根大柱子支撐。

💡 from pillar to post 到處奔走，四處奔波 | pillar of strength 中流砥柱

---

16. **propaganda** [‚prɑpə`gændə] n. [U] (政治等的) 宣傳

▲ People's opinions are greatly influenced by political propaganda. 民意深受政治宣傳的影響。

---

17. **recruit** [rɪ`krut] v. 招募 <to, for>

▲ The golf club recruited a few new members.
高爾夫俱樂部招募了幾個新會員。

recruit [rɪˋkrut] n. [C] 新兵；新進人員，新手

▲ How many raw recruits are enlisted and trained?
有多少新兵入伍受訓？

💡 draft/drill/seek recruits 徵募 / 訓練 / 尋求新兵或新手

recruitment [rɪˋkrutmənt] n. [U] 招募

▲ We will start our annual recruitment of college graduates in June.
我們六月將展開年度招募大學畢業生的工作。

---

18. **sacred** [ˋsekrɪd] adj. 神聖的

▲ The Bible is sacred to all Christians.
《聖經》對所有基督徒而言是神聖的。

---

19. **sheriff** [ˋʃɛrɪf] n. [C] (縣、郡的) 治安官，警長

▲ The local sheriff has already come to the scene.
地方的治安官已到現場。

---

20. **sovereignty** [ˋsɑvrɪntɪ] n. [U] 主權 <over>

▲ People should learn to protect national sovereignty.
人民應該學習保護國家主權。

---

21. **stance** [stæns] n. [C] 立場 <on>

▲ What is your stance on the presidential election?
你對於總統大選的立場為何？

---

22. **swap** [swɑp] v. 交換 <for, with> [同] exchange
(swapped | swapped | swapping)

▲ Thomas swapped his camera for a watch.
Thomas 用相機來換手錶。

swap [swɑp] n. [C] 交換 (usu. sing.)

▲ The boss asked us to arrange a job swap.
老闆要求我們安排交換工作。

💡 do a swap 作交換

23. **torch** [tɔrtʃ] n. [C] 火炬；手電筒 [同] flashlight

▲ The Olympic torch is now carried by a famous runner. 奧林匹克聖火現在由一位知名的跑者傳遞。

💡 carry a torch for sb 暗戀…

torch [tɔrtʃ] v. 縱火

▲ The drunk man torched the building to take revenge on society. 這名酒醉的男子縱火燒大樓來報復社會。

24. **upgrade** [ʌpˋgred] v. 升級 [反] downgrade

▲ Medical facilities are being upgraded.
醫療設施正在升級中。

upgrade [ˋʌpˏgred] n. [C] 改進

▲ We need upgrades in our security system.
在保安系統上我們需要改進。

25. **weird** [wɪrd] adj. 怪異的 [同] strange

▲ The man is very weird. He is wearing a T-shirt on such a cold day.
這男人很奇怪。他在這麼冷的天氣穿著一件 T 恤。

Unit 16

1. **bolt** [bolt] n. [C] 門閂；閃電

    ▲ Sam slowly slid the bolt open and left the house quietly. Sam 慢慢地把門閂打開，悄悄地離開了房子。

    💡 make a bolt for sth 往…急忙逃走

    bolt [bolt] v. 奔逃，逃跑 <for>；囫圇吞嚥 <down> [同] gobble

    ▲ The audience bolted for the exit. 觀眾急忙往出口逃。

2. **chronic** [`krɑnɪk] adj. 慢性的 [反] acute

    ▲ The old man has suffered from a chronic heart disease for years.
    那位老人受慢性心臟病之苦已經很多年了。

3. **compel** [kəm`pɛl] v. 迫 使 <to> (compelled | compelled | compelling)

    ▲ The illness compelled the student to give up his studies. 這疾病迫使那位學生放棄他的學業。

4. **contempt** [kən`tɛmpt] n. [U] 輕蔑 <for>

    ▲ He showed contempt for the poor.
    他對窮人表現出輕蔑的態度。

    💡 hold sb/sth in contempt 輕視… | beneath contempt 令人不齒 | with contempt 輕蔑地

5. **customs** [`kʌstəmz] n. [pl.] 海關

    ▲ It took me a long time to go through the customs.

我花了很多時間才通過海關。

---

6. **diameter** [daɪˋæmətɚ] n. [C][U] 直徑
   ▲ The circle is five inches in diameter.
   這個圓的直徑為五英寸。

---

7. **ego** [ˋigo] n. [C] 自我 (意識) 或自負 (pl. egos)
   ▲ Nelson has such a big ego that he regards himself as the champion in the contest.
   Nelson 很自負,認為自己是這場比賽的冠軍。
   💡 boost sb's ego 增強⋯的自信心

---

8. **exclusive** [ɪkˋsklusɪv] adj. 獨有的,專用的,專有的
   ▲ The scholar has the exclusive right to use the private library. 這位學者有使用這個私人圖書館的專有權。
   💡 exclusive report/interview 獨家報導 / 採訪

---

9. **frontier** [frʌnˋtɪr] n. [C] 國界;[sing.] (尤指十九世紀美國西部的) 邊疆
   ▲ Music has no frontiers. 音樂無國界。

---

10. **honorable** [ˋɑnərəbl̩] adj. 值得尊敬的
    ▲ In my country, serving in the military is considered an honorable profession.
    在我的國家,從軍被認為是值得尊敬的職業。

---

11. **installation** [ˌɪnstəˋleʃən] n. [U] 安裝
    ▲ Tim was blamed for the installation of unnecessary software on the company's computer.

Tim 因為在公司的電腦上安裝不必要的軟體而被責
罵。

12. **lounge** [laʊndʒ] n. [C] (飯店、機場等的) 休息室
▲ The staff can take a break in the staff lounge, such as chatting and having some snacks.
員工可以在員工休息室小憩，像是聊天和吃零食。
♥ the departure lounge 候機室
lounge [laʊndʒ] v. 閒晃 <around>
▲ My cousin likes to lounge around during the weekend. 我表哥週末喜歡四處閒晃。

13. **motive** [`motɪv] n. [C] 動機 <for>
▲ Before scolding Julie, you should find out her motive for telling a lie.
你在責備 Julie 之前，應該找出她說謊的動機。

14. **outlet** [`aʊt,lɛt] n. [C] 宣洩方法 <for>；零售店
▲ Painting is her outlet for stress.
繪畫是她宣洩壓力的方法。

15. **pipeline** [`paɪp,laɪn] n. [C] (石油、瓦斯等的) 輸送管
▲ The government needs to build a gas pipeline here immediately. 政府必須立即在這裡建造瓦斯輸送管。
♥ in the pipeline 正在進行中

16. **prophet** [`prɑfɪt] n. [C] 預言家，先知
▲ Listen to the words of the prophet carefully.

仔細聽先知的話。

17. **regime** [rɪ`ʒim] n. [C] 政權
   ▲ The country is prospering under the new regime.
   那個國家在新政權下蓬勃發展。

18. **saddle** [`sædḷ] n. [C] 馬鞍
   ▲ Put a saddle on the horse before riding it.
   騎馬前先裝上馬鞍。
   💡 in the saddle 掌權；騎馬
   saddle [`sædḷ] v. 使承擔 (責任) <with>
   ▲ Ann is saddled with too many jobs.
   Ann 擔負太多工作。
   saddler [`sædlɚ] n. [C] 馬具商
   ▲ The saddler sells the best saddles and leather objects
   for horses in town.
   這位馬具商賣鎮上最好的馬鞍和皮製馬具。

19. **shield** [ʃild] n. [C] 盾牌 (等保護物) <against>
   ▲ The bank robber used one of the bank clerks as a
   human shield.
   銀行搶匪挾持一名銀行行員當作人體盾牌。
   shield [ʃild] v. 保護 <from>
   ▲ Motorcyclists wear helmets to shield their heads
   from injury. 機車騎士戴安全帽保護頭部以免受傷。

20. **spacious** [`speʃəs] adj. 寬敞的 [同] roomy
   ▲ It is really a spacious hall. 這真是個寬敞的大廳。

21. **startle** [ˋstɑrtl̩] v. 吃驚

▲ I was startled by the horrible sight of the car crash.
那場車禍的駭人景象使我大吃一驚。

startling [ˋstɑrtl̩ɪŋ] adj. 令人吃驚的

▲ The startling news spread quickly.
這令人吃驚的消息很快地傳開。

22. **symptom** [ˋsɪmptəm] n. [C] 症狀 <of>；徵兆 <of> [同] indication

▲ A cough and a sore throat are the usual symptoms of a cold. 咳嗽和喉嚨痛是感冒常有的症狀。

23. **tournament** [ˋtɝnəmənt] n. [C] 錦標賽

▲ Peter won the championship in the tournament.
Peter 贏得錦標賽冠軍。

💡 tennis/badminton/golf tournament 網球 / 羽球 / 高爾夫球錦標賽

24. **utility** [juˋtɪlətɪ] n. [C] 設施

▲ The rent includes utilities such as gas, water, and electricity. 租金包含公共設施費用，像瓦斯、水和電。

25. **whine** [waɪn] n. [C] 哀鳴聲 (usu. sing.)

▲ A high-pitched whine came out from an empty house. 尖銳的哀鳴聲從無人的房子傳出。

whine [waɪn] v. 哀鳴

▲ The old man heard his dog whining outside the door.
老人聽到他的狗在門外哀鳴著。

Unit 17 📝

1. **bonus** [ˋbonəs] n. [C] 獎金，紅利
   ▲ The workers received their Christmas bonuses.
   員工收到他們的耶誕節獎金。

2. **chunk** [tʃʌŋk] n. [C] 厚塊
   ▲ The butcher cut a chunk of meat for my mom.
   肉販切一大塊肉給我的母親。
   💡 a chunk of meat/bread/wood/ice 一大塊肉 / 麵包 / 木頭 / 冰塊
   chunky [ˋtʃʌŋkɪ] adj. 厚重的，厚實的，沉甸甸的
   ▲ The chunky pair of earrings hurt my ears.
   這副沉甸甸的耳環讓我的耳朵很痛。

3. **compensation** [͵kɑmpənˋseʃən] n. [U] 賠償金
   ▲ The electricity company promised to give compensation for losses caused by the power outage.
   電力公司承諾會賠償停電造成的損失。
   💡 in compensation for sth 作為⋯的賠償

4. **continental** [͵kɑntəˋnɛntl̩] adj. 大陸 (性) 的
   ▲ A continental climate is much drier than an oceanic one. 大陸性氣候比海洋性氣候乾燥多了。

5. **debut** [deˋbju] n. [C] 首次亮相
   ▲ The ballet dancer made her debut in *The Nutcracker* at the age of 18.

這位芭蕾舞者在十八歲時於《胡桃鉗》中首次亮相。

6. **diaper** [ˈdaɪəpɚ] n. [C] 尿布
   ▲ Eco-friendly parents use cloth diapers instead of disposable diapers on their babies.
   環保的父母讓他們的小孩使用布尿布而不是紙尿布。

7. **emission** [ɪˈmɪʃən] n. [C] (氣體、熱量、光線等的) 排放
   ▲ It has been proven that driving hybrid cars can cut vehicle emissions.
   駕駛油電混合車已經被證實能減少車輛廢氣的排放。

8. **execution** [ˌɛksɪˈkjuʃən] n. [U] 實行
   ▲ The execution of the project went well.
   這個計畫進行順利。

9. **galaxy** [ˈgæləksɪ] n. [C] 星系 (pl. galaxies)
   ▲ Scientists have discovered a giant galaxy.
   科學家發現一個巨大的星系。

10. **hormone** [ˈhɔrmon] n. [C] 荷爾蒙
    ▲ When women are getting old, the hormones in their bodies decrease.
    當女人逐漸年長，她們體內的荷爾蒙會減少。

11. **integrate** [ˈɪntəˌgret] v. 融合，融入 <into, with>
    ▲ Simon is trying hard to integrate himself into the new school. Simon 很努力融入新的學校。

12. **lump** [lʌmp] n. [C] 腫塊；方糖

▲ My classmate banged his head against a shelf and got a big lump. 我同學的頭撞到架子腫了一個大包。

💡 have a lump in sb's throat 哽咽

lump [lʌmp] v. 把…湊在一起，歸攏在一起 <together>

▲ We lumped our money together to buy her a birthday present. 我們湊錢為她買生日禮物。

---

13. **mumble** [ˈmʌmbl] v. 含糊地說，咕噥

▲ Jack mumbled to himself while he was doing the housework. Jack 一邊做家事一邊喃喃自語。

mumble [ˈmʌmbl] n. [C] 喃喃自語 (usu. sing.)

▲ Helen spoke in a low mumble, and I could hardly hear what she had said.
Helen 喃喃自語低聲說話，我幾乎聽不到她在說什麼。

---

14. **outsider** [aʊtˈsaɪdɚ] n. [C] 外人，局外人 [反] insider

▲ Even though I have been living in Japan for 10 years, I still feel like an outsider here. 即使我已在日本住了長達十年，我仍覺得自己在這裡是外人。

---

15. **pirate** [ˈpaɪrət] n. [C] 海盜

▲ According to the news report, some pirates attacked a liner. 根據新聞報導，一些海盜攻擊一艘郵輪。

pirate [ˈpaɪrət] v. 盜版，剽竊

▲ It is illegal to pirate CDs. 盜版光碟是違法的。

---

16. **proportion** [prəˈporʃən] n. [C] 部分；比例 [同] ratio

▲ A large proportion of the trainees drop out in the first month. 大部分的受訓者在第一個月就退出了。

💡 in proportion to sth 與…成比例 | out of (all) proportion to sth 與…不成比例 | keep a sense of proportion 辨別輕重緩急

proportion [prə`porʃən] v. 使成比例，使協調 <to>

▲ The furniture is well proportioned to the room. 家具與房間很相稱。

---

17. **reinforce** [ˌrɪm`fors] v. 加強

▲ The police reinforce law enforcement because the crime rate is increasing.
因為犯罪率增加，所以警方加強執法。

reinforcement [ˌrɪm`forsmənt] n. [U] 加強

▲ The bridge needs reinforcement before the rainy season. 在雨季前這座橋梁需要補強。

---

18. **salmon** [`sæmən] n. [C] 鮭魚 (pl. salmon)

▲ Salmon return to the rivers where they were born.
鮭魚會洄游至出生的河流。

---

19. **shiver** [`ʃɪvɚ] n. [C] 顫抖

▲ A shiver ran down my back. 我背上感到一陣寒顫。

shiver [`ʃɪvɚ] v. (因寒冷或恐懼而) 顫抖 <with> [同] tremble

▲ I was shivering with cold. 我冷得直發抖。

---

20. **sparkle** [`spɑrk!] v. 閃閃發光

▲ The icy road sparkled in the sunlight.
結冰的路面在陽光下閃閃發光。

sparkle [ˋspɑrkl̩] n. [C][U] 光芒

▲ I know that Jenny is in love from the sparkle in her eyes. 我從 Jenny 眼中的閃耀光芒知道她戀愛了。

21. **steer** [stɪr] v. 駕駛；引導

▲ The captain steered the ship out of the harbor.
船長將船駛離港口。

💡 steer the conversation away 轉移話題

steer [stɪr] n. [C] 建議

▲ My father gave me a steer on my studies.
我的父親在我的學業方面給予我建議。

22. **tackle** [ˋtækl̩] v. 處理或解決 (難題等)

▲ The firefighters finally tackled the blaze, but the building had burned to ashes.
消防隊員終於控制火勢，但房子已經燒成灰燼。

tackle [ˋtækl̩] n. [U] 工具

▲ Alan took his fishing tackle with him to the lake.
Alan 攜帶著他的釣魚工具去湖邊。

23. **traitor** [ˋtretɚ] n. [C] 背叛者，叛徒

▲ Alex was a traitor to his country. Alex 是賣國賊。

24. **utilize** [ˋjutə‚laɪz] v. 使用

▲ Human beings utilize nuclear energy not only for generating electricity but also for making weapons.

人們使用核能不僅是為了生產電力，還為了製造武器。

25. **wig** [wɪg] n. [C] 假髮

▲ Leo wears a wig to cover his bald head.
Leo 戴假髮掩蓋他的禿頭。

Unit 18

1. **booth** [buθ] n. [C] 小隔間 (pl. booths)

▲ The detective sat in the back booth, observing the bar. 警探坐在後面的隔間觀察這個酒吧。

💡 a phone booth 電話亭 | a polling/voting booth 投票間

2. **cite** [saɪt] v. 引用 [同] quote

▲ The poem cited in my report was written by Shakespeare. 我報告中所引用的詩是莎士比亞寫的。

3. **competent** [`kɑmpətənt] adj. 勝任的 <at> [反] incompetent

▲ Bill is hard-working but he is not competent at his job. Bill 很努力，但他無法勝任工作。

4. **contractor** [`kɑntræktɚ] n. [C] 承包商

▲ The contractor promised to control the water leaks and repair the water damage in the office building within a week. 承包商允諾會在一週內控制辦公大樓的漏水及修復漏水造成的損壞。

5. **decay** [dɪ`ke] n. [U] 腐敗;衰退,衰微

▲ The deserted wooden cottage smelled of decay.
這間被遺棄的木造小屋有腐敗的味道。

decay [dɪ`ke] v. 腐敗 [同] rot;衰退 [同] decline

▲ The meat began to decay without refrigeration.
肉類在沒有冷藏之下開始腐敗。

6. **digestion** [daɪ`dʒɛstʃən] n. [U] 消化

▲ A cow's stomach is divided into 4 chambers, which
helps it store food for later digestion. 牛的胃分為四
個腔室,幫助牠儲存食物以便稍後消化。

7. **endorse** [ɪn`dɔrs] v. (公開) 贊同,支持

▲ We totally endorse what the leader said.
我們完全贊同領袖所說的話。

endorsement [ɪn`dɔrsmənt] n. [C][U] 支持,認可

▲ We need some endorsements to launch the campaign.
我們需要一些支援來展開這項活動。

8. **exile** [`ɛgzaɪl] n. [U] 流放,放逐

▲ The criminal was sent into exile. 犯人被流放到國外。

exile [`ɛgzaɪl] v. 流放,放逐

▲ Napoleon was exiled to Saint Helena in 1815.
拿破崙於 1815 年時被流放到聖赫勒拿島。

9. **gasp** [gæsp] n. [C] 喘氣或倒抽一口氣

▲ Craig gave a gasp of horror when he saw a snake in
the bedroom.

Craig 看到房間裡有蛇，嚇得倒抽一口氣。

💡 the last gasp 最後一口氣，奄奄一息

gasp [gæsp] v. 喘氣 <for>；(因驚訝等) 倒抽一口氣，屏息
▲ The swimmer raised his head and gasped for air.
泳者抬起頭來喘氣。

---

10. **hostage** [`hɑstɪdʒ] n. [C] 人質
▲ The girl was taken hostage by the bank robber.
女孩被銀行搶匪扣為人質。

---

11. **integration** [ˌɪntə`greʃən] n. [U] 整合，結合
▲ The integration of the bus and the MRT systems saves passengers a lot of time.
公車與捷運系統的整合節省乘客不少時間。

---

12. **mandate** [`mændet] n. [C] (政黨等經選舉獲得的) 授權
▲ This party has a mandate for reform after the election victory. 選舉獲勝後，這政黨有改革的權力。

---

13. **municipal** [mju`nɪsəpl] adj. 市政的
▲ The municipal authorities have to manage 20 administrative areas.
市政府當局必須管理二十個行政區。

💡 municipal government 市政府 | municipal election 市政選舉 | municipal library 市立圖書館

---

14. **overhead** [ˌovɚ`hɛd] adv. 在頭上方，在空中
▲ A flock of seagulls flew overhead.
一群海鷗從頭頂上飛過。

overhead [`ovɚ,hɛd] adj. 在頭上方的，高架的

▲ There are many overhead power lines in my village.
在我的村莊裡，有很多高架輸電線。

overhead [`ovɚ,hɛd] n. [C][U] (公司的) 經常性支出，營運成本

▲ The overhead is extremely high since the office is in New York.
因為辦公室在紐約，所以營運成本非常地高。

15. **placement** [`plesmənt] n. [C][U] 臨時工作或實習工作

▲ Anna's father found a placement for her in his company right after she graduated from university.
Anna 從大學畢業後，她父親馬上幫她在自己公司找到一份臨時工作。

16. **prosecution** [,prɑsɪ`kjuʃən] n. [C][U] 起訴

▲ The suspect will face prosecution only when there is enough evidence to prove that he or she was involved in the crime. 嫌疑犯只在有足夠的證據證明他或她與犯罪有關時才會遭到起訴。

17. **render** [`rɛndɚ] v. 使變成 [同] make；給與

▲ The defendant's insulting remarks rendered the judge speechless. 被告侮辱的話讓法官啞口無言。

18. **scan** [skæn] n. [C] 掃描

▲ The pregnant woman was rushed to the hospital for a scan after she fell down.

那名孕婦跌倒後被緊急送往醫院做掃描。

scan [skæn] v. 審視；瀏覽 [同] skim (scanned | scanned | scanning)

▲ Peter scanned her face for a sign of hope.
　Peter 審視她的臉龐，盼有一絲希望。

---

19. **shove** [ʃʌv] v. 猛推，推擠；隨便放，亂塞

▲ The girl shoved through the crowd.
　女孩推擠著穿越人群。

shove [ʃʌv] n. [C] 猛推，推擠

▲ My friend gave me a hard shove. 我朋友猛推我一下。

---

20. **specialize** [`spɛʃə,laɪz] v. 專攻 <in>

▲ My company specializes in making handcrafted furniture and cooking utensils.
　我的公司專門製作手工家具和炊具。

---

21. **stereotype** [`stɛrɪə,taɪp] n. [C] 刻板印象

▲ Some people have stereotypes about different races and cultures.
　有些人對於不同的種族和文化有刻板印象。

stereotype [`stɛrɪə,taɪp] v. 以刻板印象看待…，把…定型 <as>

▲ Asians are stereotyped as hard workers.
　亞洲人被定型為辛勤的工作者。

---

22. **tangle** [`tæŋgl] n. [C] 纏結的一團

▲ The wool was in a tangle. 毛線纏結成一團。

tangle [ˈtæŋgl̩] v. 纏結，纏住

▲ The fishing line tangles every time he throws a cast.
他每次甩竿時釣魚線都纏結在一起。

---

23. **transit** [ˈtrænzɪt] n. [U] 通過；運送

▲ They granted us safe transit across the country.
他們允許我們安全通過該國。

💡 transit lounge 轉機候機室 | transit visa 過境簽證

transit [ˈtrænzɪt] v. 通過，穿越

▲ We are transiting the Straits of Gibraltar.
我們現在正穿越直布羅陀海峽。

---

24. **variable** [ˈvɛrɪəbl̩] n. [C] 變數 [反] constant

▲ I can't tell you the exact cost beforehand because there are so many variables.
我不能事先告訴你確切的成本，因為有很多變數。

variable [ˈvɛrɪəbl̩] adj. 多變的

▲ Willy is a man of variable moods.
Willy 是一位心情多變的男子。

---

25. **wilderness** [ˈwɪldənɪs] n. [C] 荒地 (usu. sing.)

▲ The Sahara is one of the largest wildernesses in the world. 撒哈拉沙漠是世界上最大的荒地之一。

Unit 19

1. **boredom** [ˈbordəm] n. [U] 無聊

▲ My classmates started to play cards to relieve the boredom.
為了解悶，我的同學們玩起牌來。

2. **citizenship** [ˈsɪtəznˌʃɪp] n. [U] 公民身分
▲ Iris is applying for American citizenship.
Iris 正在申請美國公民身分。

3. **compliance** [kəmˈplaɪəns] n. [U] 遵守 <with>
▲ All the experiments in the laboratory must be conducted in compliance with safety regulations.
這個實驗室進行的所有實驗都必須遵守安全規範。

4. **contradiction** [ˌkɑntrəˈdɪkʃən] n. [C][U] 矛盾
▲ There is a contradiction between the man's testimony and the clues found in the house.
那個男子的證詞和屋中找到的線索有矛盾之處。

💡 in contradiction to sth 與…相反

contradictory [ˌkɑntrəˈdɪktərɪ] adj. 矛盾的 <to>
▲ The result of the study is contradictory to the previous ones. 這個研究的結果與先前的相矛盾。

5. **deceive** [dɪˈsiv] v. 欺騙 <into>
▲ The dishonest businessman deceived the old lady into signing the contract.
那個不誠實的商人欺騙老太太簽合約。

6. **dimension** [dəˈmɛnʃən] n. [C] 尺寸 (usu. pl.) [同] measurement；規模

▲ Please tell me the dimensions of the room.
請告訴我這房間的尺寸。

7. **enterprise** [`ɛntə‚praɪz] n. [C] 事業
   ▲ The ambitious young man dreams of starting a new enterprise of his own.
   這位有抱負的年輕人夢想開創自己的新事業。

8. **exploit** [ɪk`splɔɪt] v. 開發 (資源)；剝削
   ▲ Most of the natural resources in that country have been exploited.
   那個國家大部分的天然資源都已被開發利用。
   exploit [ɪk`splɔɪt] n. [C] 英勇的行為 (usu. pl.)
   ▲ The soldier's exploits in the war brought honor to his family. 那位士兵在戰場上英勇的行為帶給家人榮耀。

9. **generator** [`dʒɛnə‚retə] n. [C] 發電機
   ▲ The generator will be on automatically if there is a power outage. 若有停電，發電機會自動開啟。

10. **hostility** [hɑs`tɪlətɪ] n. [U] 敵意 <to, toward>
    ▲ As a newcomer to this town, I constantly feel the hostility toward me from the locals. 身為這城鎮的新來者，我一直感受到當地人對我的敵意。
    hostilities [hɑs`tɪlətɪs] n. [pl.] 戰爭，戰鬥
    ▲ Hostilities will break out one day between the two sides. 雙方之間終有一天會爆發戰爭。

11. **integrity** [ɪn`tɛgrətɪ] n. [U] 正直；完整性 [同] unity

▲ As a man of integrity, Mr. Gilbert is not likely to betray his team. 身為一個正直的人，Gilbert 先生不太可能背叛他的團隊。

12. **masculine** [ˋmæskjəlɪn] adj. 男性的
▲ Cathy has a deep masculine voice.
Cathy 有深沉的男性嗓音。

masculine [ˋmæskjəlɪn] n. [C] 陽性 (the ～)
▲ The Spanish word for "color" is the masculine.
在西班牙語中「顏色」一詞是陽性。

masculinity [ˏmæskjəˋlɪnətɪ] n. [U] 男子氣概
▲ Tom tried to prove his masculinity by excelling in sports. Tom 試著利用精通運動來證明他的男子氣概。

13. **mustard** [ˋmʌstɚd] n. [U] 芥末醬
▲ I always put mustard on my hot dogs.
我總是在熱狗上放芥末醬。

14. **overwhelm** [ˏovɚˋhwɛlm] v. (在情感等方面) 使深受影響 [同] overcome
▲ Jenny was overwhelmed while listening to the orchestra playing her favorite symphony. 聽到管弦樂團演奏她最喜愛的交響樂曲令 Jenny 激動不已。

overwhelming [ˏovɚˋhwɛlmɪŋ] adj. 無法抗拒的
▲ Drug addicts have an overwhelming desire to take drugs. 吸毒成癮者對吸食毒品有無法抗拒的慾望。

overwhelmingly [ˏovɚˋhwɛlmɪŋlɪ] adv. 壓倒性地
▲ The performance is overwhelmingly successful.

演出壓倒性地成功。

---

15. **plural** [ˋplʊrəl] adj. 複數的
   ▲ Some nouns such as "family" and "couple" can take both singular and plural verbs. 一些名詞像是 family 和 couple 可接單數或複數動詞。
   plural [ˋplʊrəl] n. [C][U] 複數
   ▲ The word "sheep" remains the same in the plural. sheep 這個字複數形也是 sheep。

---

16. **province** [ˋprɑvɪns] n. [C] 省
   ▲ Ontario is the second largest province in Canada. 安大略是加拿大第二大省。

---

17. **rental** [ˋrɛntḷ] n. [C][U] 租金
   ▲ How much is the monthly rental for that apartment? 那間公寓每月的租金是多少錢？

---

18. **scar** [skɑr] n. [C] 傷疤；(心靈、精神上的) 創傷
   ▲ Shelly has a scar on her forehead. Shelly 的額頭上有一個傷疤。
   scar [skɑr] v. 留下傷疤 (scarred | scarred | scarring)
   ▲ The pirate's cheek was scarred by a sword cut. 這個海盜的臉頰上有一道刀疤。

---

19. **shrug** [ʃrʌg] n. [C] 聳肩 (usu. sing.)
   ▲ Watson said, "I don't know," with a shrug. Watson 聳肩地說：「不知道。」
   shrug [ʃrʌg] v. 聳肩 (shrugged | shrugged | shrugging)

▲ When I asked Ben where his sister was, he just replied by shrugging his shoulders.

當我詢問 Ben 他的姊姊在哪裡，他只以聳肩答覆。

20. **specify** [`spɛsə,faɪ] v. 詳細說明，明確指出

▲ Please specify the time and place for our next meeting. 請詳述下次集會的時間和地點。

21. **stew** [stju] n. [C] 燉煮的食物

▲ My favorite dish is beef stew.

我最喜歡的菜肴是燉牛肉。

stew [stju] v. 燉煮

▲ Stew the meat for 2 hours. 把肉燉兩個小時。

22. **tempt** [tɛmpt] v. 引誘，吸引 <to>

▲ Customers are tempted to buy more because of special offers. 顧客因為特惠而被引誘買得更多。

23. **transition** [træn`zɪʃən] n. [C][U] 轉變

▲ The transition from a feudal society to a modern one took years.

封建社會轉變成現代社會需要好幾年的時間。

💡 in transition 在過渡期

24. **vein** [ven] n. [C] 靜脈

▲ Veins carry blood toward the heart while the arteries are quite the opposite.

靜脈往心臟輸送血液，而動脈正好相反。

25. **windshield** [`wɪnd,ʃild] n. [C] 擋風玻璃
▲ Last Monday morning, William found that the windshield of his car had been crushed by a falling rock. 上週一早上，William 發現他車子的擋風玻璃被掉下來的石頭砸壞了。

Unit 20

1. **boundary** [`baʊndərɪ] n. [C] 邊界 (pl. boundaries)
▲ Many Mexicans illegally crossed the boundary between Mexico and America.
許多墨西哥人非法跨越墨西哥及美國邊界。

2. **civic** [`sɪvɪk] adj. 市民的
▲ Being the host city for this international sports event has created civic pride in this area. 擔任此國際運動賽事的主辦城市已是這裡市民的驕傲。

3. **complication** [,kɑmplə`keʃən] n. [C][U] 使更複雜或困難的事物
▲ Bad weather added complication to the rescue of the crash victims.
惡劣的天氣讓失事受害者的救援增加更多的困難。

4. **controversy** [`kɑntrə,vɝsɪ] n. [C][U] 爭議 <over, about> (pl. controversies)
▲ The educational reform has caused much controversy.

教育改革引起很多爭議。

5. **dedicate** [`dɛdə͵ket] v. 奉獻 <to>

▲ George has dedicated his youth and passion to the company. George 對公司奉獻出他的青春和熱情。

6. **diplomatic** [͵dɪplə`mætɪk] adj. 有手腕的 <with> [同] tactful

▲ The salesperson is diplomatic with all of his customers. 推銷員對他所有的顧客都很有手腕。

7. **enthusiastic** [ɪn͵θjuzɪ`æstɪk] adj. 熱中的 <about>

▲ My best friend became enthusiastic about modern drama. 我最好的朋友熱中於現代戲劇。

8. **exploration** [͵ɛksplə`reʃən] n. [C][U] 探索

▲ The travelers hired experienced tour guides to help with the exploration of the mountain so that they wouldn't get lost. 這些旅客僱用有經驗的領隊協助探索這個山區，這樣他們就不會迷路了。

9. **genetics** [dʒə`nɛtɪks] n. [U] 遺傳學

▲ Genetics is the study of how genes are passed down from one generation to their offspring.
遺傳學是研究基因如何由一代傳給後代子孫。

10. **icon** [`aɪkɑn] n. [C] 圖示；偶像

▲ I clicked on the icon to log in, but nothing happened. 我點擊圖示登入，但沒有反應。

11. **intensify** [ɪn`tɛnsə‚faɪ] v. 加強 [同] heighten

▲ The coming final exams intensified the pressure on the students.

即將到來的期末考加大了學生們的壓力。

12. **massage** [mə`sɑʒ] n. [C][U] 按摩

▲ My daughter gave me a massage to relieve my back pain. 我的女兒幫我按摩來減輕我背部的疼痛。

massage [mə`sɑʒ] v. 按摩

▲ You can ease your headache by massaging your temples. 你可以按摩太陽穴來減輕頭痛。

13. **myth** [mɪθ] n. [C][U] 神話

▲ According to Greek myth, Athena represents wisdom, craft, and war.

根據希臘神話，雅典娜代表智慧、工藝和戰爭。

mythical [`mɪθɪkḷ] adj. 虛構的

▲ The unicorn is a mythical creature.

獨角獸是虛構的生物。

mythology [mɪ`θɑlədʒɪ] n. [C][U] 神話 (pl. mythologies)

▲ Thomas is interested in the stories of Greek mythology. Thomas 對希臘神話故事有興趣。

14. **particle** [`pɑrtɪkḷ] n. [C] 微粒；極少量

▲ The vibration of particles in the air makes sound travel. 空氣微粒的震動讓聲音傳播。

15. **poke** [pok] v. 戳 <into>；伸出 <out of, through>

▲ He poked a hole in the wallpaper.

他在壁紙上戳了一個洞。

poke [pok] n. [C] 戳

▲ Jimmy's classmate gave him a poke in the ribs in class. Jimmy 的同學在班上戳了他的肋骨一下。

16. **quiver** [`kwɪvɚ] n. [C] 顫抖 <of>

▲ The teacher felt a quiver of excitement when he was told the good news.

被告知好消息時，老師因興奮而顫抖。

quiver [`kwɪvɚ] v. 顫抖 <with> [同] tremble

▲ Betrayed by her beloved, Molly was quivering with anger. 因被摯愛背叛，Molly 憤怒地顫抖。

17. **repay** [rɪ`pe] v. 報答 <for> (repaid | repaid | repaying)

▲ I don't know how to repay you for your kindness.

我不知要如何報答你的好意。

repayment [rɪ`pemənt] n. [C][U] 償還

▲ The bank demands mortgage repayments in 30 days.

銀行要求在三十天內償還抵押貸款。

18. **scenario** [sɪ`nɛrɪˌo] n. [C] 情況，設想 (pl. scenarios)

▲ As a leader, you had better consider all the possible scenarios to guide your team in the right direction.

身為領導人，你必須考慮所有可能的情況，引導你的團隊朝向正確的方向。

19. **shuttle** [`ʃʌtl] n. [C] (往返兩地的) 接駁車
▲ The hotel offers a free shuttle service.
飯店提供免費的接駁巴士。

shuttle [`ʃʌtl] v. 往返
▲ To avoid traffic jams, I prefer to shuttle between Boston and New York by train.
為了避免塞車，我較喜歡搭火車往返波士頓與紐約。

20. **spectator** [`spɛktetɚ] n. [C] 觀眾
▲ More than 60,000 spectators were watching the football match. 超過六萬名觀眾在看這場足球賽。

21. **stimulus** [`stɪmjələs] n. [C][U] 刺激 <to> (pl. stimuli)
▲ Bonus payments can be a stimulus to higher production. 獎金可以刺激產量的提高。

22. **terrify** [`tɛrə,faɪ] v. 驚嚇
▲ The lion's roar terrified the little kids.
獅子的吼聲嚇壞了這些小孩。

terrifying [`tɛrə,faɪɪŋ] adj. 嚇人的
▲ Bungee jumping is a terrifying experience for most people.
高空彈跳對大多數的人而言是一個嚇人的體驗。

23. **treaty** [`tritɪ] n. [C] 條約 (pl. treaties)
▲ The prime minister signed a peace treaty yesterday.
首相昨天簽署和平條約。

24. **venue** [ˋvɛnju] n. [C] (活動) 場地 <for>
▲ This conference room is the alternative venue for our annual convention.
這間會議室是我們年度大會的替代場地。

25. **wither** [ˋwɪðɚ] v. 枯萎；消失 <away>
▲ The grass withered in the heat. 草因天熱枯萎了。

26. **worthwhile** [ˋwɝθˋhwaɪl] adj. 值得的
▲ It was worthwhile to learn Spanish when I was a high school student.
當我是高中生時，我學了西班牙文，這是值得的。

27. **yacht** [jɑt] n. [C] 遊艇
▲ Look at that beautiful yacht on the river.
看那河上美麗的遊艇。
yacht [jɑt] v. 駕遊艇
▲ Let's yacht! 我們駕遊艇吧！

Unit 1

1. **admiral** [`ædmərəl] n. [C] 海軍上將
   ▲ Admirals are highest ranking navy officers who direct military operations.
   海軍上將是海軍最高階軍官，負責指揮軍事行動。

2. **annoyance** [ə`nɔɪəns] n. [U] 惱怒 [同] irritation
   ▲ To my annoyance, my brother took my digital camera without telling me and broke it. 令我惱怒的是，弟弟擅自拿走我的數位相機，而且把它弄壞了。

3. **arithmetic** [ə`rɪθmə,tɪk] n. [U] 算術
   ▲ If my arithmetic is correct, you have been playing the video game for 48 hours. 如果我的算術是正確的，你已經打電動打了四十八小時了。
   arithmetic [,ærɪθ`mɛtɪk] adj. 算術的
   ▲ We have an arithmetic test tomorrow.
   我們明天有算術測驗。

4. **bilateral** [baɪ`lætərəl] adj. 雙邊的，雙方的
   ▲ We have signed a bilateral agreement to help economic growth.
   我們已經簽訂一項雙邊協定以幫助經濟成長。

5. **broth** [brɔθ] n. [U] 高湯
   ▲ If you make corn soup with chicken broth, it will be tastier. 若你用雞肉高湯來做玉米湯會更美味。

6. **Celsius** [ˈsɛlsɪəs] n. [U] 攝氏

▲ To kill all the bacteria, the water is heated to 100 degrees Celsius. 為了殺菌，水被加熱至攝氏一百度。

---

7. **colloquial** [kəˈlokwɪəl] adj. 口語的

▲ Some colloquial expressions are not suitable for academic essays.

有些口語的用詞不適合用在學術論文。

---

8. **consonant** [ˈkɑnsənənt] n. [C] 子音

▲ Ben has difficulty pronouncing the consonant "z." Ben 覺得發出子音 z 很難。

---

9. **coral** [ˈkɔrəl] n. [U] 珊瑚

▲ The Great Barrier Reef attracts many tourists coming to explore the colorful coral reefs.

大堡礁吸引許多觀光客前來探索五顏六色的珊瑚礁。

coral [ˈkɔrəl] adj. 珊瑚色的

▲ Ann is wearing coral lipstick to go with her pink dress. Ann 擦珊瑚色口紅來搭配她粉紅色的洋裝。

---

10. **courtyard** [ˈkortˌjɑrd] n. [C] 中庭

▲ My parents are used to taking a walk in the courtyard. 我父母習慣在中庭散步。

---

11. **crossing** [ˈkrɔsɪŋ] n. [C] 穿越道

▲ Drivers should stop at the crossing and yield to pedestrians. 駕駛在穿越道應該要停車並禮讓行人。

💡 zebra/railroad crossing 斑馬線 / 平交道

---

12. **detach** [dɪ`tætʃ] v. 拆開 <from> [同] remove [反] attach；使分離 <from>
   ▲ Some workers detached the engine from the rest of the train. 一些工人把火車頭和火車廂拆開。

---

13. **enrich** [ɪn`rɪtʃ] v. 使 (心靈、生活等) 豐富
   ▲ Pursuing some hobbies such as cooking and gardening has enriched the retired man's life. 從事一些像是烹飪和園藝的嗜好豐富了這位退休男子的生活。
   enrichment [ɪn`rɪtʃmənt] n. [U] 豐富
   ▲ The old man was seeking spiritual enrichment in religion. 這位老先生在宗教中尋求靈性的富足。

---

14. **eternity** [ɪ`tɜnətɪ] n. [U] 永恆；[sing.] 漫長的時間
   ▲ On the wedding ceremony, Matt told his wife that he would love her for eternity.
   在婚禮上，Matt 告訴妻子他永遠愛她。

---

15. **hospitable** [`hɑspɪtəbl] adj. 友好熱情的，好客的 <to> [同] welcoming
   ▲ Mr. and Mrs. Smith are always hospitable to their guests. Smith 先生和太太總是對他們的客人十分的友好熱情。

---

16. **liberate** [`lɪbə,ret] v. 解放，使自由 <from> [同] release
   ▲ The prisoner of war was liberated from the prison camp.

Level 6 Unit 1　**117**

那名戰俘從集中營被釋放出來。

17. **merchandise** [`mɝtʃən͵daɪz] n. [U] 貨品 [同] product
   ▲ Keep the receipt in case you want to return the merchandise. 保留收據以防你想退貨。

   merchandise [`mɝtʃən͵daɪz] v. 銷售
   ▲ The CEO emphasized that the company would apply itself to merchandising this new product this year.
   執行長強調今年公司會盡全力促銷這一項新產品。

18. **nickel** [`nɪkl] n. [U] 鎳
   ▲ Though some people are allergic to nickel, the British government still uses it as the material for making coins. 即便有些人對鎳金屬過敏，英國政府還是用它作為製作硬幣的原料。

   nickel [`nɪkl] v. 將…鍍上鎳

19. **notorious** [no`torɪəs] adj. 惡名昭彰的 <for> [同] infamous
   ▲ The king is notorious for his cruelty to his people.
   那個國王因對人民殘暴而惡名昭彰。

   notoriously [no`torɪəslɪ] adv. (因惡名) 眾人皆知
   ▲ It is notoriously difficult to drive in the city.
   眾人皆知在市區開車是有難度的。

20. **radius** [`redɪəs] n. [C] 半徑 (pl. radii, radiuses)
   ▲ Please draw a circle with a radius of 10 cm.
   請用十公分的半徑來畫一個圓。

21. **solidarity** [ˌsɑləˋdærətɪ] n. [U] 團結

▲ Supporters will march to show their solidarity tomorrow. 支持者明天將遊行表明他們的團結。

💡 express solidarity with sb 表示和…的團結

---

22. **strangle** [ˋstræŋgl] v. 勒死;扼殺,壓制

▲ That man strangled his wife with a necktie. 那個男人用領帶勒死了他的妻子。

---

23. **trek** [trɛk] n. [C] (徒步) 長途跋涉

▲ Tony is on a trek through the Sahara Desert. Tony 正步行穿越撒哈拉沙漠。

trek [trɛk] v. 徒步旅行 (trekked | trekked | trekking)

▲ We are going trekking in the Himalayas this year. 我們今年要去喜馬拉雅山旅行。

---

24. **vanilla** [vəˋnɪlə] n. [U] 香草

▲ Vanilla ice cream is my favorite dessert. 香草冰淇淋是我最喜歡的點心。

---

25. **veil** [vel] n. [C] 面紗;[sing.] 覆蓋物

▲ The widow wore a black veil at the funeral. 寡婦在喪禮上戴著黑色面紗。

💡 draw a veil over sth 避而不談…

veil [vel] v. 戴面紗;隱藏,遮掩

▲ Muslim women often veil their faces in public. 穆斯林婦女通常在公開場合戴面紗。

Unit 2

1. **advisory** [əd`vaɪzərɪ] adj. 顧問的

   ▲ John acts in an advisory role in our company.
   John 在我們的公司扮演顧問的角色。

2. **antibiotic** [ˌæntɪbaɪ`ɑtɪk] n. [C] 抗生素

   ▲ The doctor prescribed some antibiotics for my sore throat. 醫生開了一些抗生素治療我的喉嚨痛。
   antibiotic [ˌæntɪbaɪ`ɑtɪk] adj. 抗生素的

   ▲ Penicillin is one kind of antibiotic drug.
   盤尼西林是一種抗生素藥物。

3. **ascend** [ə`sɛnd] v. 上升，登上，攀登 [反] descend

   ▲ My grandfather panted heavily after ascending the stairs. 上樓梯後，我的祖父氣喘吁吁。

4. **beforehand** [bɪ`for͵hænd] adv. 預先，事先

   ▲ We reserved a table at the restaurant two days beforehand. 我們兩天前就在這家餐廳訂位。

5. **blaze** [blez] n. [C] 火焰，大火

   ▲ Within minutes the firemen controlled the blaze.
   消防員在幾分鐘內就控制了火勢。

   💡 a blaze of publicity 眾所周知的事
   blaze [blez] v. 熊熊燃燒；發光，閃耀

   ▲ The living room was warm with a fire blazing in the fireplace. 客廳有壁爐的火熊熊燃燒而變得溫暖。

💡 blaze down (太陽) 炎炎照耀，閃耀

---

6. **brotherhood** [ˈbrʌðɚˌhʊd] n. [U] 手足情誼，親善友愛

▲ The Statue of Liberty is a symbol of brotherhood between France and the U.S.
自由女神像是法國與美國親善關係的象徵。

---

7. **cement** [səˈmɛnt] n. [U] 水泥

▲ Concrete is made of cement, stones, sand, and water.
混凝土是水泥、石頭、沙子及水製成的。

cement [səˈmɛnt] v. 加強，鞏固

▲ We are planning to cement the link with other communities. 我們正計畫加強與其他社區的聯繫。

---

8. **comet** [ˈkɑmɪt] n. [C] 彗星

▲ Do you know when Halley's Comet will come back?
你知道哈雷彗星何時回來嗎？

---

9. **conspiracy** [kənˈspɪrəsɪ] n. [C][U] 共謀或密謀策劃 <to, against> (pl. conspiracies)

▲ The woman was found guilty of conspiracy in the murder of her husband.
這個女子被發現共謀殺害她丈夫。

conspire [kənˈspaɪr] v. 共謀 <to, against> [同] plot

▲ John conspired with other directors against the president. John 和其他董事共謀反對董事長。

---

10. **crutch** [krʌtʃ] n. [C] (夾在腋下用的) 拐杖 <on>

▲ Allen broke his leg and has been on crutches for two months. Allen 摔斷腿並用了兩個月的拐杖。

11. **cumulative** [ˋkjumjələtɪv] adj. 累積的
  ▲ Your cumulative grade in class depends on homework, test scores, and attendance. 你這堂課的累積成績靠回家作業、考試成績和出席率決定。

12. **defect** [ˋdifɛkt] n. [C] 毛病，缺陷
  ▲ The mechanic checked the machine for defects.
  技師檢查機器以找出毛病。
  💡 birth/speech/hearing/heart/sight defect 先天性 / 言語 /
  聽覺 / 心臟 / 視力缺陷
  defect [dɪˋfɛkt] v. 投奔，叛離 <from, to>
  ▲ A Cuban diplomat defected to the United States.
  一名古巴外交官投奔美國。

13. **detain** [dɪˋten] v. 羈押，拘留；耽擱 [同] delay
  ▲ The suspect was detained at the police station for 24 hours. 嫌犯被羈押在警局中二十四個小時。

14. **examinee** [ɪg͵zæməˋni] n. [C] 應試者，考生
  ▲ There are thousands of examinees at school today.
  今天在學校有數以千計的考生。

15. **examiner** [ɪgˋzæmənɚ] n. [C] 主考官
  ▲ Lucas sat facing three examiners, who took turns asking him questions.

Lucas 坐在三位主考官面前，被他們依序問問題。

---

16. **hybrid** [ˋhaɪbrɪd] adj. 混合的
    ▲ Ken just bought a hybrid car yesterday as his birthday present for himself.
    昨天 Ken 買給自己一輛油電混合車當作生日禮物。
    hybrid [ˋhaɪbrɪd] n. [C] 混合物 [同] mixture
    ▲ The dance is a hybrid of modern dance and street dance. 這舞蹈融合了現代舞和街舞。

---

17. **liberation** [ˌlɪbəˋreʃən] n. [U] 解放 (運動)
    ▲ Lara is a spokesperson for the women's liberation movement. Lara 是這次婦女解放運動的發言人。

---

18. **mimic** [ˋmɪmɪk] v. 模仿 [同] imitate (mimicked | mimicked | mimicking)
    ▲ This comedian can mimic the way other people talk.
    這位喜劇演員可以模仿其他人說話的方式。
    mimic [ˋmɪmɪk] n. [C] 模仿者 [同] imitator
    ▲ In my class, Kelly is the greatest mimic.
    在我班上，Kelly 是最棒的模仿者。

---

19. **nourish** [ˋnɝɪʃ] v. 提供營養或養育；懷有，培養
    ▲ Teenagers need lots of fresh food to nourish them.
    青少年們需要許多新鮮食物來提供營養。
    nourishment [ˋnɝɪʃmənt] n. [U] 營養
    ▲ Children must get enough nourishment to grow up properly. 孩童需要攝取足夠的營養才能好好長大。

nourishing [ˋnɝɪʃɪŋ] adj. 有營養的

▲ Fresh vegetables are very nourishing.
新鮮蔬菜很有營養。

---

20. **orient** [ˋɔrɪənt] n. [U] 東方國家 (the ～)

▲ Many westerners are curious about the cultures of the Orient. 很多西方人對東方文化感到好奇。

orient [ˋɔrɪˏɛnt] v. 使適應 <to>

▲ The new immigrants need some time to orient themselves to the new surroundings.
新移民需要些時間來適應新環境。

---

21. **rap** [ræp] n. [U] 饒舌音樂

▲ Sue wants to be a rap artist. Sue 想當饒舌歌手。

---

22. **soothe** [suð] v. 安慰，撫慰 [同] calm；舒緩，減輕 (疼痛)

▲ The mother soothed her crying baby.
母親安慰哭鬧的嬰兒。

---

23. **stride** [straɪd] n. [C] 大步，闊步

▲ Tom has a long stride that is hard to keep up with. Tom 的步伐很大，不容易跟上。

💡 make giant strides 突飛猛進 | get into sb's stride (工作) 漸入情況 | take sth in sb's stride 從容處理

stride [straɪd] v. 大步行走或跨越 <over> (strode | stridden | striding)

▲ Leo strode over a ditch. Leo 跨越一條水溝。

---

24. **underneath** [ˌʌndɚˈniθ] prep. 在…之下 [同] under, below, beneath
   ▲ The criminal hid the weapon underneath his coat.
   那個罪犯將武器藏在他的大衣底下。

   underneath [ˌʌndɚˈniθ] adv. 在下面，在底下
   ▲ Mary seems hard, but she is very generous underneath. Mary 看似苛刻，但她其實非常慷慨。

   underneath [ˌʌndɚˈniθ] n. [sing.] 底部，下面
   ▲ The underneath of the bread is terribly burnt.
   麵包的底部被烤焦了。

   underneath [ˌʌndɚˈniθ] adj. 底下的，下面的
   ▲ The underneath part of the bed is very dirty.
   床底下的部分很髒。

25. **versatile** [ˈvɝsətl] adj. 多才多藝的；多功能的
   ▲ Alex is a versatile actor. Alex 是個多才多藝的演員。

Unit 3

1. **affiliate** [əˈfɪlɪet] n. [C] 隸屬機構，分支機構
   ▲ Our company is an affiliate of A&Q Corp.
   我們公司隸屬於 A&Q 公司。

2. **applicable** [ˈæplɪkəbl] adj. 適用的 <to>
   ▲ The new law is applicable to all motorcycle riders.
   新法律適用於所有摩托車騎士。

3. **aspire** [ə`spaɪr] v. 渴望

▲ The baseball team aspired to win the championship so much. 那支棒球隊非常渴望贏得冠軍。

4. **bleach** [blitʃ] n. [U] 漂白劑

▲ Shelly used bleach to remove the stain on the white shirt. Shelly 用漂白劑去除白襯衫上的汙漬。

bleach [blitʃ] v. (藉化學作用或因陽光) 漂白，褪色

▲ The label on the skirt says it cannot be bleached.
裙子上的標籤說明不可漂白。

5. **bureaucrat** [`bjʊrə,kræt] n. [C] 官僚

▲ The newly elected legislator turned out to be a nasty bureaucrat.
新選上的立法委員結果變成令人討厭的官僚。

6. **census** [`sɛnsəs] n. [C] 人口普查 (pl. censuses)

▲ It is important to have a census every ten years.
十年一度的人口普查是重要的。

7. **commonwealth** [`kɑmən,wɛlθ] n. [sing.] 聯邦，國協

▲ Australia is a member of the British Commonwealth.
澳洲是大英國協的成員國。

8. **contention** [kən`tɛnʃən] n. [C] 論點，看法；[U] 爭議，爭吵

▲ Our main contention is that the project would be too expensive. 我們主要的論點是這計畫會花費太大。

9. **cub** [kʌb] n. [C] (狼、獅、熊等肉食性動物的) 幼獸
   ▲ The bear took care of its cub. 大熊照顧牠的小孩。

---

10. **cynical** [`sɪnɪkl̩] adj. 憤世嫉俗的
    ▲ Lily became so cynical after her job application was rejected. Lily 在求職遭拒後變得十分憤世嫉俗。

---

11. **detention** [dɪ`tɛnʃən] n. [U] 羈押，拘留
    ▲ The criminal was held in detention before a date was set for his trial.
    這個罪犯在決定審判日期之前被拘留。

---

12. **drastic** [`dræstɪk] adj. 嚴厲的或激烈的
    ▲ The mayor took drastic measures to sweep away the sex industry. 市長採取嚴厲的措施要消滅性產業。
    drastically [`dræstɪklɪ] adv. 急劇地
    ▲ Never drastically change your diet without a doctor's instruction.
    未經醫生的指示，不要急劇地改變你的飲食。

---

13. **excerpt** [`ɛksɚpt] n. [C] 摘錄 <from>
    ▲ An excerpt from the government's latest report on domestic violence will appear in tomorrow's newspapers. 明天的報紙將刊登一段政府有關家庭暴力最新報告的摘錄。
    excerpt [ɪk`sɚpt] v. 摘錄
    ▲ Parts of Tina's speech were excerpted in the magazine. Tina 的部分演說被引用在雜誌中。

14. **fable** [ˋfebl] n. [C] 寓言

▲ There are some moral values in fables.
在寓言故事中有一些道德觀念。

15. **glacier** [ˋgleʃ⋅] n. [C] 冰河

▲ We planned to see the glaciers in New Zealand.
我們計畫去紐西蘭看冰河。

16. **hygiene** [ˋhaɪdʒin] n. [U] 衛生

▲ My dentist always emphasizes the importance of good oral hygiene.
我的牙醫總是強調良好口腔衛生的重要性。

💡 food/personal/dental hygiene 食物 / 個人 / 口腔衛生

17. **linger** [ˋlɪŋɡⅇ] v. 留連 <on>

▲ The audience still lingered in their seats, hoping the singer would come back onstage for an encore. 觀眾還留連在座位上不走，希望歌手會回到舞臺再唱一曲。

18. **navigate** [ˋnævə‚get] v. 導航，向駕駛指示行車路線

▲ You should drive, and I can navigate.
你來開車，我可以跟你指示行車路線。

19. **oath** [oθ] n. [C] (在法庭上的) 宣誓，誓言 (pl. oaths)

▲ You have to take the oath before you give testimony in court. 在法庭作證前必須先宣誓。

💡 under/on oath (尤指在法庭上) 發誓是真的

20. **orphanage** [ˋɔrfənɪdʒ] n. [C] 孤兒院

▲The orphanage devoted itself to caring for the orphans. 孤兒院致力於照顧孤兒。

21. **realization** [ˌriələ`zeʃən] n. [sing.] 領悟，意識到 [同] awareness

▲Judy felt sad after the realization of her failure.
Judy 意識到失敗後感到傷心。

22. **sorrowful** [`sɑrəfəl] adj. 悲傷的，傷心的 [同] sad

▲Bill told us a sorrowful story about the death of his younger brother.
Bill 告訴我們一個關於他弟弟去世的悲慘故事。

23. **subjective** [səb`dʒɛktɪv] adj. 主觀的 [反] objective

▲Most of our likes and dislikes are subjective.
我們的好惡多是主觀的。

subjective [səb`dʒɛktɪv] n. [C][U] 主詞，主格 (the ～)；
主觀事物

24. **vigorous** [`vɪgərəs] adj. 活力充沛或強而有力的 [同] energetic

▲Stretch after you do vigorous exercise. Otherwise, your muscles would be sore the next day.
做完劇烈運動後要伸展一下，否則隔天會肌肉痠痛。

25. **villain** [`vɪlən] n. [C] 惡棍，歹徒，流氓

▲The police caught the villain who robbed the convenience store. 警察抓到了搶劫便利商店的歹徒。

Unit 4

1. **accumulate** [ə`kjumjə‚let] v. 累積 [同] build up
   ▲ Daisy worked diligently to accumulate wealth, hoping to pay off her student loan soon. Daisy 勤奮地工作以累積財富，希望可以盡快還清她的學生貸款。

2. **affirm** [ə`fɝm] v. 斷言，確定 [同] confirm
   ▲ Mr. Brown affirmed that everything was fine.
   Brown 先生肯定地說一切都很好。

3. **assassinate** [ə`sæsə‚net] v. 暗殺
   ▲ Mr. Smith fought for freedom but was assassinated one day. Smith 先生為自由而戰，但某一天被暗殺了。
   assassination [ə‚sæsə`neʃən] n. [C][U] 暗殺
   ▲ The assassination of Mr. Wilson shocked many people. Wilson 先生的暗殺震驚了許多人。

4. **astronaut** [`æstrə‚nɔt] n. [C] 太空人
   ▲ Astronauts require a high level of physical fitness.
   太空人需要具備很好的體適能。

5. **blond** [blɑnd] n. [C] (尤指) 金髮男子
   ▲ Who is the blond that is talking to Ann?
   那位跟 Ann 說話的金髮男子是誰？
   blonde [blɑnd] n. [C] (尤指) 金髮女子
   ▲ Look at the blonde over there. She is so charming.
   看在那裡的金髮女子。她真的很迷人。

blond [blɑnd] adj. 金髮的 (男性常用 blond， 女性常用 blonde)

▲ Simon's blond hair shines in the sun.
Simon 的金髮在陽光中閃耀。

6. **bypass** [ˋbaɪ͵pæs] n. [C] (繞過城市或城鎮的) 旁道，外環道路

▲ Contractors are building a new bypass around the town. 承包商正在城鎮周圍建造新的外環道路。

bypass [ˋbaɪ͵pæs] v. 繞過；越過，不顧

▲ To avoid traffic jams, we bypassed the busy downtown area and took a side road. 為了避開交通阻塞，我們繞過繁忙的市中心，走旁邊的小路。

7. **ceramic** [səˋræmɪk] adj. 陶器的，瓷器的

▲ They decorated the walls with colorful ceramic tiles. 他們用彩色瓷磚裝飾牆壁。

ceramic [səˋræmɪk] n. [C] 陶器，瓷器 (usu. pl.)

▲ Ceramics have been used by human beings since prehistoric times. 人類從史前時代就開始使用陶器。

8. **communicative** [kəˋmjunə͵ketɪv] adj. 健談的

▲ Salespeople need to be patient and very communicative. 推銷員必須有耐心且健談。

9. **contestant** [kənˋtɛstənt] n. [C] 競爭者，參賽者

▲ Hundreds of contestants from all over the country fought for first place in the boxing championship.

數百名來自全國各地的競賽者爭取拳擊錦標賽的冠軍。

---

10. **cucumber** [ˋkjukʌmbɚ] n. [C][U] 黃瓜

▲ Cucumbers are often made into pickles.
黃瓜常被做成醬菜。

---

11. **dedication** [ˌdɛdəˋkeʃən] n. [U] 奉獻，盡心盡力 [同] commitment

▲ Tom's dedication to his work impressed his boss.
Tom 對工作的盡心盡力令老闆印象深刻。

---

12. **deter** [dɪˋtɝ] v. 阻止，使打消念頭 <from> (deterred | deterred | deterring)

▲ The installation of cameras in the store is aimed at deterring people from shoplifting. 店裡裝置攝影機的目的在於打消人們順手牽羊的念頭。

---

13. **excess** [ˋɛksɛs] adj. 多餘的，過多的，過度的

▲ For the sake of health, Thomas wants to lose the excess weight.
為了健康，Thomas 想要減去多餘的體重。

excess [ɪkˋsɛs] n. [sing.] 過度 <of>

▲ An excess of alcohol will damage your body.
過度飲酒會傷害你的身體。

---

14. **fragrance** [ˋfregrəns] n. [C][U] 芳香，香氣

▲ The fragrance of coffee filled the kitchen.

廚房裡瀰漫著咖啡香。

15. **illuminate** [ɪˋlumə͵net] v. 照亮
▲ These trees were illuminated at night during the Christmas and New Year holidays.
耶誕新年期間的夜晚，這些樹被打上燈光。

illumination [ɪ͵luməˋneʃən] n. [C][U] 照明
▲ During the blackout, the only illumination came from emergency lights along the corridor.
停電時，唯一的照明來自於走廊的緊急照明燈。

16. **imperial** [ɪmˋpɪrɪəl] adj. 帝國的，皇帝的
▲ The imperial palace is being renovated.
皇宮正在修復中。

imperialism [ɪmˋpɪrɪəlɪzəm] n. [U] 帝國主義
▲ Small nations feel threatened by the cultural and economic imperialism of world powers. 來自世界強國的文化和經濟帝國主義使小國家感受到威脅。

17. **lizard** [ˋlɪzə-d] n. [C] 蜥蜴
▲ Tony's new pet is a lizard. Tony 的新寵物是蜥蜴。

18. **odor** [ˋodə-] n. [C][U] (常指難聞的) 氣味，臭味 <of>
▲ When smelling a gas odor, never turn on or off any electrical equipment around you. 當聞到瓦斯味時，絕對不要打開或關上身邊任何電器。
💡 body odor 體臭

19. **offspring** [ˋɔf͵sprɪŋ] n. [C] 子女，孩子 (pl. offspring)

▲ Many parents have trouble getting along with their teenage offspring.

許多父母與青少年子女相處上有困難。

---

20. **outbreak** [ˋaʊt͵brek] n. [C] 爆發

▲ An outbreak of food poisoning led to dozens of school children being hospitalized earlier today.

今天稍早發生一起食物中毒事件，造成數十名學童住院治療。

---

21. **outward** [ˋaʊtwɚd] adj. 表面的

▲ To all outward appearances, this couple seem to be fine and happy. 從表面看來，這對情侶似乎和睦快樂。

outward [ˋaʊtwɚd] adv. 向外地 (also outwards)

▲ This door can open outward and inward.

這扇門可以向外或向內開。

outwardly [ˋaʊtwɚdlɪ] adv. 表面上 [反] inwardly

▲ Outwardly, Sue may appear serious, but she is actually humorous.

表面上，Sue 可能看起來很嚴肅，但她其實很幽默。

---

22. **reckless** [ˋrɛkləs] adj. 魯莽的 <of> [同] rash

▲ David was fined for reckless driving.

David 因魯莽駕駛而遭罰款。

recklessly [ˋrɛkləslɪ] adv. 魯莽地

▲ I have to break the bad habit of spending money recklessly. 我必須改掉亂花錢的壞習慣。

---

23. **spacecraft** [`spes,kræft] n. [C] 太空船 [同] spaceship (pl. spacecraft)

▲ An unmanned spacecraft has been successfully launched into deep space.

一艘無人駕駛的太空船已經成功發射至遙遠的宇宙。

24. **surname** [`sɝ,nem] n. [C] 姓氏

▲ We guess the man may come from Japan because his surname is Suzuki.

我們猜這個人可能來自日本，因為他的姓氏是鈴木。

25. **vitality** [vaɪ`tælətɪ] n. [U] 活力 [同] vigor

▲ The young person is always full of vitality.

這個年輕人總是充滿了活力。

Unit 5

1. **aboriginal** [,æbə`rɪdʒənl] adj. 原始的，土生土長的，原住民的

▲ Many aboriginal people used to make a living by farming and hunting.

許多原住民以前靠農耕及狩獵維生。

aboriginal [,æbə`rɪdʒənl] n. [C] 原住民

▲ Many aboriginals were persecuted by colonizers.

許多原住民遭到殖民者迫害。

aborigine [,æbə`rɪdʒəni] n. [C] 原住民

▲ The government is trying hard to preserve the culture of the aborigines. 政府正努力保存原住民的文化。

2. **airway** [ˈɛr͵we] n. [C] 氣道

▲ Before giving the patients artificial respiration, you have to make sure their airways are clear. 為病人們做人工呼吸前，你必須確定他們的氣道是暢通的。

3. **apprentice** [əˈprɛntɪs] n. [C] 學徒

▲ Mr. Twain was an apprentice in a printing factory when he was young.
吐溫先生年輕時曾在印刷工廠當學徒。

4. **asthma** [ˈæzmə] n. [U] 氣喘

▲ Sandra suffers from asthma. Sandra 患有氣喘。

5. **attendant** [əˈtɛndənt] n. [C] 接待員

▲ The museum attendant told me not to bring any food into the building.
博物館接待員告訴我不可攜帶食物入內。

6. **blot** [blɑt] v. (用紙或布) 吸乾 (blotted | blotted | blotting)

▲ Eric tried to blot the stains on the tablecloth.
Eric 試著把桌布上的汙漬吸乾。

💡 blot sth out 抹掉 (記憶)

blot [blɑt] n. [C] 汙漬；(人格、名聲等的) 汙點 <on>

▲ I don't know how to get rid of the ink blots on my shirt. 我不知道如何去除我襯衫上的墨水漬。

💡 a blot on the landscape 破壞風景的東西

---

7. **calculator** [`kælkjə,letə] n. [C] 計算機
▲ The teacher asked the students not to use the calculators in class.
老師要求學生在課堂上不要使用計算機。

---

8. **certify** [`sɝtə,faɪ] v. 證實，證明
▲ The authorities certified that the proposal had been rejected. 當局證實此提議已被否絕。
certified [`sɝtə,faɪd] adj. 有證書的
▲ Tim is a certified lawyer and works as a legal consultant.
Tim 是有證書的律師，以擔任法律顧問為業。

---

9. **compile** [kəm`paɪl] v. 彙編
▲ The encyclopedia took ten years to compile.
這套百科全書花了十年彙編而成。

---

10. **continuity** [,kɑntə`nuətɪ] n. [U] 連續性
▲ Several episodes in the novel lack continuity.
小說中的一些片段缺乏連續性。

---

11. **cultivate** [`kʌltə,vet] v. 耕種 [同] grow；培養或塑造
▲ The settlers cultivated the wilderness.
拓荒者耕種荒地。

---

12. **dental** [`dɛntl] adj. 牙科的

▲ Although dental treatment costs a lot of money, it will save future problems.
雖然牙科治療很貴，可是會省去未來的問題。

---

13. **detergent** [dɪˋtɝdʒənt] n. [C][U] 清潔劑
   ▲ It is important to use the detergent to do the dishes.
   用清潔劑洗碗是很重要的。

---

14. **exclusion** [ɪkˋskluʒən] n. [C][U] 排除，除外 <from, of>
   ▲ Mason spent all his time with his girlfriend to the exclusion of his other friends. Mason 把所有時間花在和女友在一起，無暇顧及其他的朋友。

---

15. **frantic** [ˋfræntɪk] adj. 忙亂的
   ▲ The rescuers made frantic attempts to save people from the earthquake rubble.
   救援人員拼命努力要救出困在地震碎石中的人們。

---

16. **indifference** [ɪnˋdɪfərəns] n. [U] 漠不關心 <to, toward>
   ▲ Many people showed indifference to the political issue. 許多人對這個政治議題漠不關心。

---

17. **literacy** [ˋlɪtərəsɪ] n. [U] 知識，能力
   ▲ Computer literacy is crucial to surviving in the workplace.
   電腦知識對於在職場生存可說是非常重要。

---

18. **longevity** [lɑnˋdʒɛvətɪ] n. [U] 長壽；壽命
   ▲ What's the secret to your grandfather's longevity?

你祖父長壽的訣竅是什麼？

19. **oriental** [ˌorɪˈɛntl̩] adj. 東方的
▲ Oriental cuisine is getting popular in western countries. 東方料理在西方國家漸受歡迎。

oriental [ˌorɪˈɛntl̩] n. [C] 東方人
▲ Some of Leo's classmates called him a dark oriental. Leo 的一些同學說他是黝黑的東方人。

20. **outnumber** [ˌaʊtˈnʌmbɚ] v. 在數量上超過
▲ The enemy greatly outnumbered us. Our chance of winning was slim.
敵軍的數量超過我們很多，我們要贏的機會渺茫。

21. **outright** [ˈaʊtˌraɪt] adj. 徹底的
▲ Helen gave me an outright refusal.
Helen 斷然地拒絕我。

outright [ˌaʊtˈraɪt] adv. 當場地
▲ The driver was killed outright in the accident.
駕駛人在車禍中當場死亡。

22. **recreational** [ˌrɛkrɪˈeʃənl̩] adj. 休閒娛樂的
▲ The hotel compiled a list of its top ten recreational activities. 這家旅館編了一份最受歡迎的十項休閒娛樂活動清單。

23. **spontaneous** [spɑnˈtenɪəs] adj. 自發的或不由自主的
▲ There was spontaneous applause from the audience after the performance. 表演結束後，觀眾自發地鼓掌。

spontaneously [spɑn`tenɪəslɪ] adv. 自發地或不由自主地
▲ On hearing the lively music, the girl spontaneously started to dance.
一聽到這活潑的音樂，那女孩情不自禁地開始跳舞。

24. **symbolize** [`sɪmbə,laɪz] v. 象徵 [同] represent
▲ Generally, doves symbolize peace.
一般來說，鴿子象徵和平。

25. **wardrobe** [`wɔrdrob] n. [C] 衣櫥
▲ Judy has many new dresses in the wardrobe.
Judy 衣櫃裡有很多新洋裝。

Unit 6

1. **algebra** [`ældʒəbrə] n. [U] 代數
▲ My best subject in high school was algebra.
代數是我高中時最拿手的科目。

2. **astray** [ə`stre] adv. 迷路地；誤入歧途地
▲ The child went astray in the woods.
這孩子在樹林裡迷了路。
♥ go astray 誤入歧途
astray [ə`stre] adj. 迷路的；誤入歧途的

3. **awesome** [`ɔsəm] adj. 很棒的
▲ The concert last night was awesome.
昨晚的音樂會很棒。

4. **banquet** [ˋbæŋkwɪt] n. [C] (正式的) 宴會
   ▲ Many heads of government and industry are invited to the state banquet.
   許多政府首腦及業界龍頭被邀請至國宴。

5. **blunt** [blʌnt] adj. 鈍的 [反] sharp；直率的
   ▲ The knife is too blunt to cut anything.
   這把刀太鈍了什麼都切不下。
   💡 blunt instrument 鈍器
   blunt [blʌnt] v. 使 (情感等) 減弱
   ▲ Alcohol blunted the man's grief for his dead son.
   酒減弱了那個男人的喪子之痛。

6. **calligraphy** [kəˋlɪgrəfɪ] n. [U] 書法
   ▲ Chinese calligraphy is the art of writing with a brush.
   中國書法是用毛筆書寫的藝術。

7. **champagne** [ʃæmˋpen] n. [U] 香檳
   ▲ I like to watch the small bubbles rise to the surface when champagne is poured into a glass. 我喜歡看著香檳倒入杯中時細小泡泡浮升到表面的樣子。

8. **complement** [ˋkɑmpləˏmɛnt] v. 使完善，補足，與⋯互補或相配
   ▲ The necklace complements your dress perfectly.
   這條項鍊與你的洋裝相得益彰。
   complement [ˋkɑmpləmənt] n. [C] 補充或襯托的事物

▲ Leo's fine appearance is a nice complement to his gentle personality.

Leo 的俊秀外表與溫和個性十分相襯。

complementary [ˌkɑmpləˈmɛntərɪ] adj. 互補的 <to>

▲ These two arguments are complementary to each other. 這兩個論點是互補的。

---

9. **contradict** [ˌkɑntrəˈdɪkt] v. 與…矛盾;反駁

▲ Eric's behavior contradicts his principles.

Eric 的行為與原則相矛盾。

---

10. **curb** [kɝb] n. [C] 抑制 <on>

▲ If you cannot put a curb on spending, you will not be able to make both ends meet.

你若無法抑制花費,將入不敷出。

curb [kɝb] v. 抑制

▲ The government needs to curb inflation.

政府必須抑制通貨膨脹。

---

11. **destined** [ˈdɛstɪnd] adj. 命中注定的 ; 預定前往…的 <for>

▲ Eddie was destined for the medical profession.

Eddie 命中注定要從事醫療工作。

---

12. **devour** [dɪˈvaʊr] v. 狼吞虎嚥地吃光 [同] gobble

▲ It is so impressive that such a petite girl can devour all the dishes on the table. 真是讓人印象深刻,這嬌小的女孩可以吃光滿桌的菜。

♥ be devoured by sth 被 (焦慮等) 吞噬，內心充滿 (焦慮等)

---

13. **fascination** [ˌfæsəˈneʃən] n. [C][U] 魅力，吸引力；著迷 <with, for>

▲ Venice holds a fascination for me.
威尼斯對我很有吸引力。

---

14. **graze** [grez] v. (牛、羊等) 吃草 <on>；擦傷，擦破

▲ The cattle grazed on the hillside. 牛在山坡上吃草。

---

15. **induce** [ɪnˈdjus] v. 誘使 <to>；導致

▲ Nothing will induce me to change my mind.
沒有任何事可誘使我改變心意。

---

16. **lullaby** [ˈlʌləˌbaɪ] n. [C] 催眠曲，搖籃曲 (pl. lullabies)

▲ The mother was humming a lullaby in a low voice.
那位母親低聲哼著催眠曲。

---

17. **lunar** [ˈlunɚ] adj. 月球的

▲ Lunar eclipses usually last for a few hours or so.
月蝕通常持續幾個小時。

♥ lunar calendar 陰曆

---

18. **originate** [əˈrɪdʒəˌnet] v. 創始；開始 <in, from>

▲ That style of dancing was originated in Ireland.
那種舞步創始於愛爾蘭。

---

19. **oyster** [ˈɔɪstɚ] n. [C] 牡蠣

▲ Ken doesn't dare to eat raw oysters.

Ken 不敢吃生牡蠣。

💡 the world is sb's oyster … 可以隨心所欲

20. **paradox** [ˋpærə͵dɑks] n. [C][U] 矛盾的人或事物
   ▲ The paradox is that the more one owns, the more one wants. 矛盾的是，人擁有的愈多，想要的反而愈多。

21. **rehearse** [rɪˋhɝs] v. 預演
   ▲ The stage actors will rehearse the play the day before the performance.
   舞臺劇演員們會在戲劇演出的前一天預演。

22. **solitary** [ˋsɑlə͵tɛrɪ] adj. (喜歡) 獨處的
   ▲ Rather than going out with friends, Arthur likes to be solitary. 比起和朋友出去玩，Arthur 喜歡一個人獨處。
   solitary [ˋsɑlə͵tɛrɪ] n. [U] 單獨監禁 (also solitary confinement)
   ▲ The savage prisoner spent 500 days in solitary.
   這名凶殘的犯人被單獨監禁了五百天。

23. **spotlight** [ˋspɑt͵laɪt] n. [C] 大眾關注的焦點；聚光燈
   ▲ The actor's romance is in the spotlight.
   這名男演員的羅曼史成為大眾關注的焦點。
   💡 under the spotlight 被徹底剖析 | in the spotlight 備受矚目的
   spotlight [ˋspɑt͵laɪt] v. 以聚光燈照亮；使大眾關注 [同] highlight (spotlighted, spotlit | spotlighted, spotlit | spotlighting)

▲ The singer slowly walks out onto the spotlighted stage. 歌手緩緩出場走上被聚光燈照亮的舞臺。

24. **telecommunications** [ˌtɛləkəˌmjunəˈkeʃənz] n. [pl.] 電信 (科技)

▲ Bad management has led to this telecommunications company going bankrupt.
經營不善導致這家電信公司破產。

25. **weary** [ˈwɪrɪ] adj. 疲倦的 (wearier | weariest)，

▲ After working all day, Linda lies in bed and rests her weary eyes.
工作整天後，Linda 躺在床上讓她疲倦的雙眼休息。

💡 weary of 對⋯感到厭倦的

weary [ˈwɪrɪ] v. (使) 感到疲倦

▲ Andy doesn't dare to admit how much his son wearies him. Andy 不敢承認他的兒子多麼使他疲倦。

Unit 7

1. **alienate** [ˈeljənˌet] v. 使疏遠 <from>

▲ Mike is alienated from his friends.
Mike 遭到朋友疏遠。

alienation [ˌeljənˈeʃən] n. [U] 疏離感

▲ The sense of alienation is growing in modern society.
疏離感正在現代社會中蔓延。

2. **anthem** [ˈænθəm] n. [C] (團體組織的) 頌歌
   ▲ After the game, the team members sang the national anthem to celebrate their victory.
   比賽結束後，團隊成員唱國歌慶祝他們的勝利。
   💡 national/school anthem 國歌 / 校歌

3. **astronomer** [əˈstrɑnəmɚ] n. [C] 天文學家
   ▲ The astronomers discovered a planet that was similar to the Earth.
   那些天文學家發現了一顆和地球相似的行星。

4. **bachelor** [ˈbætʃələ˞] n. [C] 單身漢；學士
   ▲ The poet remained a bachelor all his life.
   這個詩人終身都是單身漢。
   💡 confirmed bachelor 單身且想保持此狀態的男子

5. **bodily** [ˈbɑdɪlɪ] adj. 身體的
   ▲ The virus spreads through contact with infected blood, other bodily fluids, or dead patients. 這病毒通過接觸受感染的血液、其他體液或死亡的患者而傳播。
   bodily [ˈbɑdɪlɪ] adv. 整體地，整個地
   ▲ The temple will have to be moved bodily to the new site because of the urban renewal program. 由於都市更新計畫，寺廟將不得不整體地移動到新的地點。

6. **cape** [kep] n. [C] 岬，海角
   ▲ The boat sailed around the cape before it entered the harbor. 在進入港口前，那艘船繞過海岬。

💡 the Cape of Good Hope 好望角

---

7. **captive** [`kæptɪv] adj. 被俘虜的；受制於人的，無選擇權的

▲ The man was held captive as a political prisoner.
那個男人被當作政治犯被俘虜起來。

💡 hold/take sb captive 俘虜…

captive [`kæptɪv] n. [C] 俘虜

▲ Soldiers bound and chained the captives.
士兵綑綁並用鏈條拴住俘虜。

---

8. **chemist** [`kɛmɪst] n. [C] 化學家

▲ A chemist spends a lot of time working in a laboratory. 化學家花很多時間在實驗室裡工作。

---

9. **complexion** [kəm`plɛkʃən] n. [C] 臉色

▲ The little girl has a pale complexion.
小女孩的臉色蒼白。

💡 pale/rosy/fair complexion 蒼白 / 紅潤 / 白皙的臉色

---

10. **convene** [kən`vin] v. 召開

▲ Henry convened a meeting of the students to discuss an issue of dress code. Henry 召開了一次學生會議，討論關於穿著規範的議題。

---

11. **curfew** [`kɝfju] n. [C][U] 宵禁

▲ The government announced to impose a curfew because of a state of political turmoil.
因為政治動盪，政府宣布實施宵禁。

💡 impose/lift a curfew 實施 / 解除宵禁

12. **dictate** [`dɪktet] v. 口述;命令 <to>

▲ The president of the company dictated a letter to his secretary. 公司的董事長口述一封信要祕書記下。

13. **differentiate** [ˌdɪfə`rɛnʃɪˌet] v. 辨別 <between, from>;使不同 <from>

▲ Children at this age still can't differentiate between right and wrong. 這個年紀的孩子仍無法辨別是非。

14. **fertility** [fɚ`tɪlətɪ] n. [U] 肥沃;生育能力 [反] infertility

▲ The farmer uses animal waste to maintain the fertility of his farm soil.
這農夫使用動物的排泄物來維持農田土壤的肥沃。

15. **grease** [gris] n. [U] 油

▲ The car mechanic had a lot of grease on his hands.
汽車修理工的手上有很多油。

grease [gris] v. 用油塗

▲ Grease the pan if you want to keep the omelet from sticking.
如果你想要防止歐姆蛋黏鍋,用油塗在平底鍋上。

💡 grease sb's palm 向…行賄;收買

16. **infer** [ɪn`fɚ] v. 推論 <from> (inferred | inferred | inferring)

▲ Mandy inferred from John's statement that he was not satisfied with his present situation.

Mandy 從 John 的話推論他對現況不滿。

---

17. **lush** [lʌʃ] adj. 茂盛的；豪華的
    ▲ The villa is surrounded by lush meadows.
    這間別墅被茂盛的草地環繞。

18. **ornament** [ˋɔrnəmənt] n. [C] 裝飾品；[U] 裝飾
    ▲ My mom is putting ornaments on the Christmas tree.
    我媽正在把裝飾品掛到耶誕樹上。
    ornament [ˋɔrnəˌmɛnt] v. 裝飾，點綴 <with>
    ▲ The shelf was ornamented with a vase and several pictures. 架上裝飾著一只花瓶和幾張照片。

19. **outgoing** [ˋautˌɡoɪŋ] adj. 外向的
    ▲ Ken's outgoing personality makes it easy for him to make friends. Ken 外向的個性使他很容易交到朋友。

20. **peacock** [ˋpiˌkɑk] n. [C] 孔雀
    ▲ A peacock is eating the peas in front of a rooster.
    一隻孔雀正在吃公雞面前的豌豆。

21. **pianist** [pɪˋænɪst] n. [C] 鋼琴家
    ▲ The concert hall was filled with sweet music as the pianist moved his fingers swiftly on the keyboard.
    當鋼琴家的手指快速地在琴鍵上移動時，音樂廳裡便充滿美妙的音樂。

22. **relentless** [rɪˋlɛntlɪs] adj. 持續的

▲ Many people blamed the death of Princess Diana on paparazzi's relentless pursuit.
許多人把黛安娜王妃的死歸咎於狗仔隊持續的追蹤。

23. **stimulation** [ˌstɪmjə`leʃən] n. [U] 刺激
   ▲ Reading a book can act as great stimulation of the mind. 閱讀書籍可以用來作為心智上很好的刺激。

24. **vice** [vaɪs] n. [C] 壞習慣，惡習；[U] 罪行，惡行
   ▲ Mr. Chen's only vice is smoking.
   陳先生唯一的惡習就是抽菸。

25. **woodpecker** [`wʊdˌpɛkɚ] n. [C] 啄木鳥
   ▲ A woodpecker is making holes on the trunks with its beak, finding insects for food.
   啄木鳥用牠的喙在樹幹上啄洞找蟲子吃。

Unit 8

1. **abundance** [ə`bʌndəns] n. [sing.] 大量 <of>；[U] 充足，富足
   ▲ Our garden produced an abundance of cabbages last year. 去年我們家院子種出了大量的甘藍菜。

2. **align** [ə`laɪn] v. (使) 成一直線，(使) 對齊
   ▲ The librarian carefully aligned the books on the shelf.
   圖書館管理員小心地將書架上的書排成一直線。
   💡 align oneself with sb/sth 與…結盟

3. **attain** [ə`ten] v. 獲得 [同] achieve
   ▲ Van Gogh attained no fame during his lifetime.
      梵谷在生前沒有獲得名聲。
   attainment [ə`tenmənt] n. [U] 獲得 <of>
   ▲ The attainment of happiness depends on your attitude
      toward life. 快樂的獲得取決於你對生活的態度。

4. **beverage** [`bɛvrɪdʒ] n. [C] 飲料 (usu. pl.)
   ▲ The restaurant doesn't serve alcoholic beverages.
      這家餐廳不供應含酒精的飲料。

5. **bosom** [`buzəm] n. [C] 前胸
   ▲ The mother held the baby to her bosom.
      母親將小嬰兒抱在胸前。
   💡 in the bosom of sth 在 (家庭等) 的關懷裡

6. **capsule** [`kæpsl̩] n. [C] 膠囊
   ▲ Medicine in capsules is easier to swallow.
      藥裝在膠囊裡比較容易吞嚥。
   💡 time capsule 時光膠囊

7. **caretaker** [`kɛr,tekɚ] n. [C] 管理員 [同] custodian
   ▲ The school caretakers clean up the campus every
      day. 每天學校管理員都會清理校園。

8. **chestnut** [`tʃɛsnət] n. [C] 栗子
   ▲ Lisa made a birthday cake with the flavor of
      chestnut. Lisa 做了一個栗子口味的生日蛋糕。
   💡 old chestnut 老掉牙的話題

chestnut [ˋtʃɛsnət] adj. 栗色的，紅棕色的
▲ Mary dyed her hair chestnut.
Mary 把頭髮染成紅棕色。

9. **compute** [kəmˋpjut] v. 計算 [同] calculate
▲ It's easy to compute such a complicated math problem by computer.
以電腦計算這種複雜的數學題相當容易。

10. **corpse** [kɔrps] n. [C] 屍體
▲ The police found the old man's corpse in the room.
警方在房間裡找到這個老人的屍體。

11. **curry** [ˋkɝɪ] n. [C][U] 咖哩 (pl. curries)
▲ Nick gave us a cooking demonstration; he taught us how to cook beef curry.
Nick 為我們做烹飪示範，他教我們如何煮牛肉咖哩。
💡 curry powder 咖哩粉

12. **dictation** [dɪkˋteʃən] n. [U] 聽寫
▲ The secretary can take dictation in shorthand.
這位祕書能速記聽寫。

13. **disastrous** [dɪˋzæstrəs] adj. 災難性的 [同] catastrophic
▲ This decision will have a disastrous impact on the economy. 這決定將會給經濟帶來災難性的衝擊。

14. **eccentric** [ɪkˋsɛntrɪk] adj. 古怪的 [同] odd, weird, bizarre

▲ Carrying an open umbrella indoors is just one of his eccentric acts. 在室內撐傘不過是他古怪的行徑之一。

eccentric [ɪkˋsɛntrɪk] n. [C] 怪人

▲ People who stay from social norms are often described as eccentric.
遠離社會規範的人常常被描述為怪人。

---

15. **fertilizer** [ˋfɝtəˌlaɪzɚ] n. [C][U] 肥料

▲ Ammonium nitrate is commonly used to make fertilizers and explosives.
硝酸銨普遍用於製造肥料和炸藥。

---

16. **harness** [ˋhɑrnɪs] n. [C] 馬具

▲ The horseman is putting a harness on a horse.
馬術師正在幫馬套上馬具。

💡 in harness with 與⋯合作

harness [ˋhɑrnɪs] v. (用馬具) 套牢，拴繫 <to>；利用 (太陽能等自然力)

▲ A horse was harnessed to a cart loaded with luggage.
一匹馬被套牢在一輛滿載行李的馬車上。

---

17. **inflict** [ɪnˋflɪkt] v. 施加 (痛苦等)，使遭受 (傷害等) <on>

▲ These bullies take delight in inflicting pain on their classmates. 這些霸凌者以折磨他們的同學為樂。

---

18. **maiden** [ˋmedn̩] adj. 初次的

▲ It's the singer's maiden appearance on TV.
這是這位歌手在電視上初次亮相。

♥ maiden name 娘家的姓 | maiden voyage/flight 處女航 / 首次飛行

maiden [`medn̩] n. [C] 少女

▲ Different from what we used to read, the story is about the adventure of a maiden. 和我們以往所讀到的不同，這是篇關於少女的冒險故事。

19. **overflow** [`ovɚ͵flo] n. [sing.] 容納不下 (的人或物) <of>

▲ There are enough wards to accommodate the overflow of patients from the other hospitals.
有足夠的病房容納其他醫院容納不下的病人。

♥ overflow of population 人口過剩

overflow [͵ovɚ`flo] v. 溢出，滿出來，爆滿 <with>

▲ Torrential rain has made the ditches overflow and turned the roads into rivers.
豪雨讓水溝滿溢，把道路變成了河流。

♥ be filled to overflowing 多到滿出來，滿溢的

20. **persistent** [pɚ`sɪstənt] adj. 堅持的，固執的；持續的

▲ Mark is persistent in seeing you.
Mark 堅持要見你。

♥ persistent offender 慣犯

21. **pimple** [`pɪmpl] n. [C] 青春痘，面皰

▲ Many people try to hide their pimples by wearing makeup. 許多人藉由化妝掩飾他們的青春痘。

22. **remainder** [rɪ`mendə] n. [sing.] 剩餘的部分 (the ～) <of>

▲ My mom gave the remainder of the meal to my dog.
我媽把剩餘的飯菜給我的狗吃。

23. **subscription** [səb`skrɪpʃən] n. [C][U] 訂閱

▲ Don't forget to renew your subscription to the magazine. 不要忘了延長雜誌的訂閱期限。

💡 renew/cancel a subscription 延長 / 取消訂閱

24. **suspension** [sə`spɛnʃən] n. [C][U] (作為處罰的) 暫令停止活動；(車輛等的) 懸吊系統，懸吊裝置

▲ The athlete received a two-year suspension.
那個運動員遭受暫停活動兩年的處分。

💡 suspension bridge 吊橋

25. **workforce** [`wɝk,fɔrs] n. [sing.] 勞動人口

▲ Two-thirds of the workforce is affected by the financial crisis.
三分之二的勞動人口受到金融危機的影響。

Unit 9

1. **abbreviate** [ə`brivɪ,et] v. 縮寫 <to>

▲ People abbreviate Sunday to "Sun."
人們將 Sunday 縮寫成 Sun.。

abbreviation [ə,brivɪ`eʃən] n. [C] 縮寫 <for>

▲ "Dr." is an abbreviation for "doctor."
Dr. 是 doctor 的縮寫。

---

2. **acclaim** [ə`klem] n. [U] (公開的) 讚賞
   ▲ The writer's novel received acclaim.
   這位作家的小說獲得讚賞。
   acclaim [ə`klem] v. (公開) 讚賞
   ▲ The director's latest movie was acclaimed as a masterpiece. 這位導演最新的電影被讚賞為傑作。

---

3. **allege** [ə`lɛdʒ] v. (未經證實地) 宣稱
   ▲ A man alleged that the U.S. government had covered up an alien visit to the Earth.
   一名男子宣稱美國政府掩蓋了外星人到訪地球的事。

---

4. **audit** [`ɔdɪt] n. [C] 審計，查帳
   ▲ Our company's annual audit will take place next Friday. 我們公司的年度審計將會在下週五舉行。

---

5. **booklet** [`buklət] n. [C] 小冊子
   ▲ Everyone will get a booklet before entering the meeting room.
   在進入會議室之前，每個人都會拿到一本小冊子。

---

6. **boulevard** [`bulə,vard] n. [C] 林蔭大道；大道 (abbr. Blvd.)
   ▲ It is nice to explore the city by taking a stroll along its tree-lined boulevards.

沿著林蔭大道漫步是探索這個城市的好方法。

---

7. **caption** [`kæpʃən] n. [C] (照片、圖畫的) 說明文字

▲ Captions underneath the photos explain the details of the pictures.

照片下的說明文字解釋了那些照片的細節。

caption [`kæpʃən] v. 圖片說明

▲ The photograph captioned "The End of the World" is really eye-catching.

那張圖說寫著「世界末日」的照片很吸睛。

---

8. **chant** [tʃænt] n. [C] 反覆呼喊或吟唱的詞語

▲ When Jackie arrived at the airport, he was greeted by the chant of "Jackie! We love you!"

當 Jackie 抵達機場時，迎接他的是反覆的呼喊聲：「Jackie！我們愛你！」

💡 Buddhist chant 佛教誦經

chant [tʃænt] v. 唱聖歌

▲ The choir was chanting psalms. 唱詩班唱著聖歌。

---

9. **chili** [`tʃɪlɪ] n. [C][U] 辣椒 (pl. chilies, chiles, chilis) (also chile, chili pepper)

▲ Mexican dishes are usually very spicy, as they contain a lot of chilies and other spices. 墨西哥菜通常很辣，因為它們含有大量的辣椒和其他調味香料。

💡 chili sauce 辣椒醬

---

10. **computerize** [kəm`pjutə͵raɪz] v. 電腦化

▲ To increase efficiency, they computerized their office. 他們將辦公室電腦化以提升效率。

computerization [kəmˌpjutərəˋzeʃən] n. [U] 電腦化

▲ The computerization of the library makes data searching much faster.
圖書館的電腦化使資料搜尋加快許多。

---

11. **cosmetic** [kɑzˋmɛtɪk] adj. 美容的；表面的 [同] superficial

▲ This best-selling cosmetic cream uses natural ingredients. 這款暢銷的美容霜使用天然成分。

💡 cosmetic surgery 整形手術

---

12. **customary** [ˋkʌstəˌmɛrɪ] adj. 慣例的 [同] usual

▲ In Japan, it is customary to wear kimonos on formal occasions. 在日本，正式場合中穿和服是慣例。

---

13. **dictator** [ˋdɪktetɚ] n. [C] 獨裁者

▲ This country has been ruled by the military dictator for two decades.
這個國家已被這軍事獨裁者統治了二十年。

---

14. **discharge** [ˋdɪsˌtʃɑrdʒ] n. [C][U] 釋放；排放

▲ The prisoner got his discharge from jail last week.
這囚犯上星期從監獄獲釋了。

discharge [dɪsˋtʃɑrdʒ] v. 准許…離開；排放

▲ Emily went back to work right after she was discharged from the hospital.

Emily 一獲准出院就回去上班了。

---

15. **firecracker** [ˈfaɪrˌkrækɚ] n. [C] 鞭炮
▲ People in Taiwan like to set off firecrackers during Chinese New Year.
臺灣人喜歡在農曆過年期間放鞭炮。

---

16. **fortify** [ˈfɔrtəˌfaɪ] v. (在防禦、體力等方面) 增強，加強；強化 (食物) 的營養成分 <with>
▲ The soldiers are fortifying the town for the coming battle.
為了即將來臨的戰役，士兵們正在增強小鎮的防禦力。

---

17. **haunt** [hɔnt] v. (幽靈等) 時常出沒於；使困擾
▲ That house is said to be haunted by its former occupant's ghost.
據說前任屋主的幽靈時常在那棟房子裡出沒。
haunt [hɔnt] n. [C] 常去的地方
▲ The bar is a favorite haunt of actors.
這家酒吧是演員常去的地方。

---

18. **inhabit** [ɪnˈhæbɪt] v. 居住於
▲ The tribes inhabit the desert all the year round.
這些部族終年居住於沙漠裡。

---

19. **majestic** [məˈdʒɛstɪk] adj. 雄偉的
▲ A majestic monument stands at the center of the city.
一座雄偉的紀念碑矗立在市中心。
majestically [məˈdʒɛstɪklɪ] adv. 雄偉地

▲ The 60-foot statue of a saint stands majestically on top of the hill.
這座六十呎的聖人雕像雄偉地站立在山頂上。

20. **patriot** [ˈpetrɪət] n. [C] 愛國者
▲ Three patriots sacrificed themselves for their country.
三位愛國者為了國家而犧牲自己。

21. **polar** [ˈpolə] adj. 極地的
▲ The scientists were sent out to the polar region for research. 那些科學家們被派往極區做研究。

22. **preventive** [prɪˈvɛntɪv] adj. 預防的
▲ Preventive measures must be taken to avoid influenza. 必須採取預防措施以防止流感。

preventive [prɪˈvɛntɪv] n. [C] 預防藥
▲ Some experts said that this herb is a useful anti-viral preventive.
一些專家說，這種藥草是對抗病毒有效的預防藥。

23. **reproduce** [ˌriprəˈdjus] v. 重現；複製；繁殖
▲ The scene was vividly reproduced in the film.
那個景象栩栩如生地在影片中重現。

reproduction [ˌriprəˈdʌkʃən] n. [C] 複製品；[U] 複製；[U] 繁殖
▲ My father bought a reproduction of the famous painting. 我父親買了這幅名畫的複製品。

24. **synonym** [ˈsɪnəˌnɪm] n. [C] 同義字

▲ Vick wants to find synonyms for "love" in a thesaurus. Vick 想在同義字字典中查 love 的同義字。

25. **yoga** [ˋjogə] n. [U] 瑜伽

▲ Practicing yoga helps me relax my muscles.
練習瑜伽幫助我放鬆肌肉。

Unit 10

1. **abide** [əˋbaɪd] v. 忍受；遵守 <by>

▲ The woman cannot abide the mess in her son's room.
那個女人無法忍受她兒子房間的髒亂。

abiding [əˋbaɪdɪŋ] adj. 永久不變的

▲ Beethoven had an abiding passion for music even after he had lost his hearing.
即使在失聰後，貝多芬對音樂仍有著永久不變的熱情。

2. **accordance** [əˋkɔrdn̩s] n. [U] 遵照

▲ People must act in accordance with the rules.
人們必須遵照規則行動。

3. **alligator** [ˋæləˏgetɚ] n. [C] 短吻鱷

▲ Many people don't know how to distinguish alligators from crocodiles.
許多人不知道如何區別短吻鱷和長吻鱷。

4. **anchor** [ˋæŋkɚ] n. [C] 錨

▲ The captain decided to lift the anchor right away.

船長決定立刻起錨。

💡 at anchor 停泊 | cast/drop anchor 下錨 | weigh anchor 起錨

anchor [`æŋkɚ] v. 停泊；使固定

▲ The boat anchored in the harbor for regular maintenance. 船隻為了定期檢修而停泊港灣。

---

5. **auditorium** [ˌɔdə`torɪəm] n. [C] 禮堂 (pl. auditoriums, auditoria)

▲ The graduation ceremony will take place in the auditorium. 畢業典禮將在禮堂舉行。

---

6. **boxing** [`bɑksɪŋ] n. [U] 拳擊

▲ The woman is the youngest world boxing champion ever. 這名女子是有史以來最年輕的世界拳擊冠軍。

---

7. **breadth** [brɛdθ] n. [U] 寬度 <in>

▲ A standard basketball court is 28 meters in length and 15 meters in breadth.
標準籃球場的大小是長二十八公尺、寬十五公尺。

---

8. **captivity** [kæp`tɪvətɪ] n. [U] 監禁

▲ After two years of captivity, the prisoner was finally released. 經過兩年的監禁，那名囚犯終於被釋放。

💡 in captivity 被囚禁

---

9. **cholesterol** [kə`lɛstəˌrol] n. [U] 膽固醇

▲ More and more people choose foods that are low in cholesterol.

越來越多人選擇低膽固醇的食品。

10. **cigar** [sɪ`gɑr] n. [C] 雪茄
   ▲ The merchant offers cigars imported directly from Cuba. 商人提供直接從古巴進口的雪茄。

11. **comrade** [`kɑmræd] n. [C] 戰友
   ▲ The veteran visited several of his comrades from wartime. 這個退伍軍人拜訪了幾個他在戰時的戰友。

12. **cosmetics** [kɑz`mɛtɪks] n. [pl.] 化妝品
   ▲ The actress uses cosmetics to cover up her wrinkles. 這名女演員用化妝品來遮掩皺紋。

13. **dazzle** [`dæzl] v. 使目眩；使驚嘆
   ▲ Nancy was dazzled by the headlights of an approaching car.
   Nancy 被來車的車頭燈照得目眩眼花。

   dazzle [`dæzl] n. [U] 耀眼
   ▲ Ben put on his sunglasses to protect his eyes from the dazzle of the sun.
   Ben 戴上太陽眼鏡擋住耀眼的陽光。

   dazzling [`dæzlɪŋ] adj. 耀眼的；令人驚嘆的
   ▲ The lady's dazzling jewels attracted everyone's attention. 那位女士耀眼的珠寶吸引了每個人的注意。

14. **dictatorship** [dɪk`tetɚ‚ʃɪp] n. [C] 獨裁統治的國家；[U] 獨裁統治
   ▲ Myanmar became a military dictatorship in 1962.

緬甸在 1962 年成為軍事獨裁統治國家。

---

15. **dispensable** [dɪ`spɛnsəbl̩] adj. 非必要的 [反] indispensable

▲ The company will get rid of any dispensable workers. 公司將裁掉非必要的員工。

---

16. **flake** [flek] n. [C] (雪的) 小薄片;碎片

▲ Flakes of snow are falling. 雪片正在飄落。

flake [flek] v. (成薄片) 剝落 <off>

▲ The paint on the door was beginning to flake off. 門上的油漆開始剝落。

---

17. **healthful** [`hɛlθfəl] adj. 有益健康的

▲ It is necessary for a pregnant woman to have a healthful diet. 孕婦需要有益健康的飲食。

---

18. **inquire** [ɪn`kwaɪr] v. 詢問,查詢 <about>

▲ The tourist called the museum and inquired about the opening hours.

這位觀光客致電博物館詢問開放時間。

💡 inquire after sb/sth 問候⋯的健康狀況等

---

19. **martial** [`mɑrʃəl] adj. 戰鬥的,軍事的

▲ Bruce Lee was known for his mastery of martial arts. 李小龍因為他嫻熟的武術技巧而聞名。

💡 martial law 戒嚴法,軍事法

---

20. **marvel** [`mɑrvl̩] n. [C] 奇蹟

▲ That new invention is truly a marvel of modern technology. 那項新發明真是現代科技的一個奇蹟。

marvel [`mɑrvl] v. 對…感到驚嘆

▲ My family marveled at the golfer's skills.
我的家人對這位高爾夫球員的球技驚嘆不已。

---

21. **pharmacy** [`fɑrməsɪ] n. [C] 藥房，藥局；[U] 藥劑學 (pl. pharmacies)

▲ John went to a pharmacy to have his prescription filled. John 去藥局配藥。

---

22. **prose** [proz] n. [U] 散文

▲ Mr. Lee started his literary career writing prose.
李先生從寫散文開啟他的文學生涯。

---

23. **prototype** [`protə,taɪp] n. [C] 原型 <for, of>

▲ The company has developed the prototype of the modern car. 這家公司製造出了現代車的原型。

---

24. **reside** [rɪ`zaɪd] v. 居住，定居 <in>

▲ Mrs. Wang longs to reside in the U.K.
王太太渴望能定居在英國。

---

25. **synthetic** [sɪn`θɛtɪk] adj. 合成的，人造的

▲ Are synthetic nutrients as healthy as natural vitamins that come from food?
合成營養素是否像來自食物的天然維生素一樣健康？

synthetic [sɪn`θɛtɪk] n. [C] 合成物 (usu. pl.)

▲ Is this cloth made of natural fibers or synthetics?

這塊布是天然纖維製成的還是合成物？

synthesize [ˋsɪnθəˏsaɪz] v. 合成

▲ No one has ever succeeded in synthesizing gold.
從來沒有人成功地合成金。

synthesis [ˋsɪnθəsɪs] n. [C] 綜合體 (pl. syntheses)

▲ The band's new album is a synthesis of rap and jazz.
這個樂團的新專輯是饒舌和爵士樂的綜合體。

Unit 11

1. **abound** [əˋbaʊnd] v. 為數眾多，有很多，多得很；盛產，充滿 <in, with>

▲ Game birds abound in this area.
此地充滿可獵捕的鳥。

2. **accountable** [əˋkaʊntəbl] adj. 負有責任的，有義務做說明的 <for, to>

▲ Henry must be accountable for his own actions.
Henry 必須對他的行為負責。

3. **aluminum** [əˋlumənəm] n. [U] 鋁

▲ Take a large piece of aluminum foil, put some onions and potatoes on it, and place it in the oven. 取一大張的鋁箔紙，放些洋蔥和馬鈴薯在上面，然後放進烤箱。

4. **astronomy** [əˋstrɑnəmɪ] n. [U] 天文學

▲ Jenny majored in astronomy at Penn State.

Jenny 曾經在賓州州立大學主修天文學。

---

5. **avert** [ə`vɝt] v. 轉移 <from>
   ▲ Mark averted his eyes from the horrible sight.
   Mark 把他的目光從這可怕的景象轉移。

---

6. **boycott** [`bɔɪ,kɑt] n. [C] 抵制 <on, against>
   ▲ The citizens called for a boycott against the company's new products to protest animal testing.
   市民們發起抵制這公司的新產品以抗議動物試驗。
   boycott [`bɔɪ,kɑt] v. 抵制
   ▲ The consumers boycotted the company's overpriced products. 消費者抵制這家公司索價過高的產品。

---

7. **bulky** [`bʌlkɪ] adj. 龐大的 (bulkier | bulkiest)
   ▲ This refrigerator was so bulky that we couldn't get it through the door.
   這臺冰箱太龐大以致於我們無法從門搬過去。

---

8. **cardboard** [`kɑrd,bord] n. [U] 厚紙板
   ▲ My dad made a toy out of cardboard.
   我爸爸用厚紙板做了一個玩具。

---

9. **civilize** [`sɪvə,laɪz] v. 教化
   ▲ They tried to civilize the barbarians.
   他們試圖教化野蠻人。
   civilized [`sɪvə,laɪzd] adj. 文明的 [反] uncivilized
   ▲ All civilized countries have laws against domestic violence and murder.

所有文明國家都有法律反對家庭暴力和謀殺。

---

10. **collision** [kə`lɪʒən] n. [C][U] 碰撞 <with>

▲ The man's car was completely wrecked in a collision with a big truck.
這男人的車與大卡車互相碰撞結果全毀。

♥ head-on collision 迎頭相撞 | on a collision course 勢必發生衝突

collide [kə`laɪd] v. 抵觸 <with>

▲ Our ideas collided with theirs.
我們的意見和他們的相抵觸。

---

11. **concession** [kən`sɛʃən] n. [C][U] 讓步 <to>

▲ The labor union has made it clear that no concessions will be made to the employers.
工會已清楚表明不會對資方做出讓步。

♥ make concessions to sb 對…讓步

---

12. **counterpart** [`kaʊntɚ‚pɑrt] n. [C] 相對應的人或事物

▲ Tokyo Disneyland is much smaller than its American counterpart. 東京迪士尼樂園比美國的小多了。

---

13. **deafen** [`dɛfən] v. 使聽不見

▲ The fireworks deafened us, so we couldn't hear each other. 煙火震耳欲聾，所以我們聽不見彼此在說什麼。

---

14. **diesel** [`dizl] n. [U] 柴油 (also diesel fuel)

▲ The diesel engine is reliable and long-lasting.

柴油引擎可靠又持久。

---

15. **dispense** [dɪ`spɛns] v. 分發 <to>

▲ The nuns dispensed food to the poor.
修女們分發食物給窮人。

💡 dispense a prescription 按處方配藥 | dispense with sth 免除⋯

---

16. **folklore** [`fok͵lor] n. [U] 民間傳說

▲ According to folklore, the ghosts in the mountains would make people get lost.
根據民間傳說，山中的鬼怪會讓人迷失方向。

---

17. **imperative** [ɪm`pɛrətɪv] adj. 迫切的 [同] vital

▲ It is imperative that we finish the urgent task today.
我們迫切需要在今天完成緊急的任務。

imperative [ɪm`pɛrətɪv] n. [C] 必須做的事

▲ It is a moral imperative for me to help people in need. 對我來說幫助有需要的人是道德上必須做的事。

---

18. **intruder** [ɪn`trudɚ] n. [C] 侵入者

▲ The smart dog secured the house against the intruder.
聰明的狗保護房子不讓侵入者闖入。

---

19. **mingle** [`mɪŋɡl̩] v. 混合 <with> [同] mix；交際 <with> [同] circulate

▲ Allie's excitement about college life mingled with some fear. Allie 對大學生活的興奮混合著一些恐懼。

20. **permissible** [pɚˋmɪsəbl] adj. (法律) 可容許的 [反] impermissible

▲ Smoking in public places is not permissible under the new law.

在新的法律下在公共場合抽菸是不可容許的。

21. **playwright** [ˋpleˌraɪt] n. [C] 劇作家 [同] dramatist

▲ Shakespeare is regarded as the greatest playwright in English literature.

莎士比亞被認為是英國文學上最偉大的劇作家。

22. **radiate** [ˋredɪˌet] v. 放射 <from>；散發情感

▲ Light and heat radiate from the sun.

太陽放射出光和熱。

radiate [ˋredɪət] adj. 有射線的；輻射狀的

23. **respective** [rɪˋspɛktɪv] adj. 各自的

▲ The girls returned to their respective homes as night fell. 隨著夜幕降臨，女孩們回到各自的家。

respectively [rɪˋspɛktɪvlɪ] adv. 分別地

▲ The prize for first place and the prize for second place went to Joe and Sam respectively.

第一、二名獎項分別由 Joe 和 Sam 獲得。

24. **retrieve** [rɪˋtriv] v. 檢索；取回 <from>

▲ Enter the password and then you can retrieve information from the computer.

輸入密碼後就可以檢索電腦裡的資料。

retrieval [rɪ`trivl̩] n. [U] 挽回

▲ Bygone days are beyond retrieval.
過去的日子無法挽回。

---

25. **tenant** [`tɛnənt] n. [C] 租客

▲ The landlord sued the tenant for not paying the rent.
房東控告租客未繳房租。

tenant [`tɛnənt] v. 租

▲ The old house is tenanted by a poor couple.
這間老房子租給一對貧窮的夫妻。

Unit 12

1. **abstraction** [æb`strækʃən] n. [C][U] 抽象

▲ Tim often talks in empty abstractions without real
examples. Tim 說話常空洞抽象，沒有真實的例子。

2. **accumulation** [ə,kjumjə`leʃən] n. [C] 累積物；[U] 累積

▲ An accumulation of rubbish ruined the beautiful
view. 垃圾累積物破壞了這美景。

3. **amid** [ə`mɪd] prep. 在…之間 (also mid, amidst) [同]
among

▲ The hikers moved along a narrow trail amid trees.
登山者沿著樹木之間的狹窄小徑移動。

4. **aviation** [,evɪ`eʃən] n. [U] 航空

▲ The Boeing Company is the major and most influential company in aviation industry.

波音公司是航空業界最主要且最有影響力的公司。

💡 aviation academy 航空學校｜aviation badge 飛行徽章

---

5. **brace** [bres] n. [C] 牙齒矯正器

▲ John wore braces to straighten his crooked teeth.

John 戴牙齒矯正器來矯正他歪的牙齒。

brace [bres] v. 支撐 <against>；使做好準備

▲ The bridge is braced with a temporary pillar to prevent it from collapsing.

這座橋以臨時支柱支撐以防崩塌。

---

6. **broaden** [ˋbrɔdn̩] v. 拓展

▲ Both reading and travel broaden the mind.

閱讀與旅行皆有助於拓展眼界。

💡 broaden sb's mind/horizons 拓展眼界，增廣見聞

---

7. **caffeine** [kæˋfin] n. [U] 咖啡因

▲ A study found that caffeine consumed 6 hours before bedtime had a significant effect on sleep disturbance.

一項研究發現睡前六小時攝取咖啡因會嚴重干擾睡眠。

---

8. **cardinal** [ˋkɑrdn̩əl] n. [C] 紅衣主教

▲ The man has received a clear directive from the cardinal. 那男人收到了來自紅衣主教的明確指示。

cardinal [ˋkɑrdṇəl] adj. 基本的

▲ Sour, sweet, bitter, salty, and umami are the 5 cardinal tastes.

酸、甜、苦、鹹和鮮是五個基本的味覺。

💡 cardinal number 基數

9. **clam** [klæm] n. [C] 蛤，蚌

▲ For real Japanese clam miso soup, just follow the recipe.

要做道地的日式味噌蛤蜊湯，只要遵照這份食譜即可。

💡 clam up/shut up like a clam 沉默不語

10. **comparative** [kəmˋpærətɪv] adj. 比較的

▲ With double income, they now live in comparative comfort.

有了雙份薪水後，他們現在的生活比較舒適了。

11. **concise** [kənˋsaɪs] adj. 簡潔的

▲ The report is concise and to the point.

這份報告簡明扼要。

12. **coupon** [ˋkupɑn] n. [C] 優待券

▲ With this coupon, you can get one free cheeseburger.

有了這張優待券，你就可以得到一個免費的起司漢堡。

13. **deduct** [dɪˋdʌkt] v. 扣除 <from>

▲ When you buy something with your debit card, the amount of money will be deducted from your account.

當你用簽帳金融卡買東西時，金額將會從你的戶頭中扣除。

---

14. **diplomacy** [dɪ`ploməsɪ] n. [U] 外交手腕

▲ Skillful diplomacy was needed to prevent a war.
要避免戰爭，巧妙的外交手腕是必要的。

---

15. **diversify** [də`vɝsə,faɪ] v. 使多樣化 <into>

▲ The radio station diversified its programs to attract more listeners.
廣播電臺使節目多樣化來吸引到更多聽眾。

---

16. **gay** [ge] adj. 男同性戀的；鮮豔的

▲ The celebrities spoke up for the gay and lesbian community through the song. 這些名人透過這首歌為男同性戀與女同性戀族群發聲。

gay [ge] n. [C] 男同性戀者

▲ The girl knew some gays and lesbians, and she didn't view it as something special. 女孩認識一些男同性戀者和女同性戀者，而她並不覺得那是什麼特別的事。

---

17. **inclusive** [ɪn`klusɪv] adj. 包含的 <of> [反] exclusive

▲ The list is inclusive of 3 girls.
這份名單包含了三個女孩。

---

18. **invaluable** [ɪn`væljəbl] adj. 無價的，無比貴重的，非常寶貴的 [同] priceless

▲ Thank you for your invaluable comments on my essay.

感謝你對我的文章所提供的寶貴意見。

---

19. **miraculous** [mə`rækjələs] adj. 奇蹟似的
   ▲ The magician made a miraculous escape from the prison. 魔術師做了一個奇蹟似的監獄逃脫。

20. **pneumonia** [nju`monjə] n. [U] 肺炎
   ▲ People could take precautions to prevent pneumonia, such as washing hands regularly.
   人們可以採取預防措施來預防肺炎，比如勤洗手。
   💡 catch/get pneumonia 得肺炎

21. **refresh** [rɪ`frɛʃ] v. 使恢復活力；喚起記憶
   ▲ Mike felt refreshed after the bath.
   Mike 洗過澡後恢復活力。

22. **resistant** [rɪ`zɪstənt] adj. 抗拒的 <to>
   ▲ Oliver likes handwritten letters. He is resistant to change. Oliver 喜歡手寫信。他抗拒改變。

23. **robust** [ro`bʌst] adj. 強健的；堅固的 [同] sturdy
   ▲ The boxer is very robust. 那拳擊手很強健。

24. **screwdriver** [`skru,draɪvɚ] n. [C] 螺絲起子
   ▲ The worker tightened a screw with a screwdriver.
   工人用螺絲起子鎖緊螺絲。

25. **tentative** [`tɛntətɪv] adj. 暫定的，不確定的
   ▲ Margot and Tom have a tentative plan for their honeymoon. Margot 和 Tom 有暫定的蜜月計畫。

💡 tentative smile 遲疑或靦腆的微笑

Unit 13

1. **academy** [ə`kædəmɪ] n. [C] 學院
   ▲ Mr. Black graduated from a military academy.
   Black 先生畢業於一所軍校。

2. **adolescence** [ˌædə`lɛsn̩s] n. [U] 青春期 [同] puberty
   ▲ During adolescence, most boys and girls are strongly influenced by their peers.
   大多數的男孩和女孩在青春期都很受同儕影響。

3. **analytical** [ˌænə`lɪtɪkl̩] adj. 分析的 (also analytic)
   ▲ Students can learn more by applying an analytical learning strategy.
   藉著運用分析的學習方法，學生可以學得更多。

4. **awhile** [ə`waɪl] adv. 片刻
   ▲ Let's rest awhile. 我們休息片刻吧。

5. **brassiere** [brə`zɪr] n. [C] 胸罩 (also bra)
   ▲ The shop sells different types of brassieres.
   這間商店販賣不同種類的胸罩。

6. **carefree** [`kɛr͵fri] adj. 無憂無慮的
   ▲ Meg and David live a carefree life in each other's company.

Meg 和 David 在彼此的陪伴中過著無憂無慮的生活。

---

7. **carton** [ˋkɑrtn̩] n. [C] 硬紙盒 <of>

▲ Ted's father asked him to buy a carton of cigarettes at a convenience store.
Ted 的父親請他去便利超商買一盒香菸。

---

8. **chimpanzee** [ˌtʃɪmpænˋzi] n. [C] 黑猩猩 (also chimp)

▲ The intelligent chimpanzee quietly dies at the end of this movie.
在電影最後，那隻聰明的黑猩猩安靜地死去。

---

9. **clasp** [klæsp] v. 抱緊 [同] hold

▲ The mother clasped her baby in her arms.
母親用雙臂抱緊嬰兒。

clasp [klæsp] n. [C] 扣環

▲ My mom bought a leather bag with a silver clasp.
我母親買了一個有銀扣環的皮包。

---

10. **compass** [ˋkʌmpəs] n. [C] 羅盤；圓規 (usu. pl.)

▲ People used to rely on the compass to sail.
人們過去仰賴羅盤航行。

compass [ˋkʌmpəs] v. 達到

▲ Bad guys will do everything to compass their ends.
壞人會盡一切可能來達到目的。

---

11. **condense** [kənˋdɛns] v. 濃縮 <into, to>

▲ My boss's secretary condensed his statement into an abstract.

我老闆的祕書把他說的話濃縮成摘要。

12. **cowardly** [ˋkaʊɚdlɪ] adj. 膽小的
   ▲ The soldiers were ashamed of their cowardly retreat.
   士兵們對於他們膽小的撤退感到羞愧。

13. **deem** [dim] v. 認為 [同] consider
   ▲ The area has been deemed safe by government officials. 政府官員認定此區域是安全的。

14. **directive** [dəˋrɛktɪv] n. [C] 指令，命令
   ▲ The company received a directive from the government. 公司收到了政府的指令。

15. **diversion** [dəˋvɝʒən] n. [C][U] 轉移；[C] 消遣
   ▲ The woman was under investigation because of the illegal diversion of funds into her personal account.
   那個女人因非法轉移資金到個人帳戶而被調查中。

16. **geographical** [ˌdʒiəˋgræfɪk!] adj. 地理的 (also geographic)
   ▲ This supermarket has a good geographical location and is often crowded with customers.
   這間超市有良好的地理位置，常常擠滿了客人。
   geographically [ˌdʒiəˋgræfɪklɪ] adv. 地理上地
   ▲ Geographically speaking, Taiwan is located in the northern hemisphere.
   從地理上來說，臺灣位於北半球。

17. **intellect** [ˈɪntəˌlɛkt] n. [U] 智慧
   ▲ Dr. Lee is a man of great intellect.
   李博士是很有智慧的人。

18. **invariably** [ɪnˈvɛrɪəblɪ] adv. 總是，老是
   ▲ Believe it or not, it invariably rains after I have my car washed. 信不信由你，每次我洗車之後總是會下雨。

19. **mischievous** [ˈmɪstʃɪvəs] adj. 搗蛋的 [同] naughty
   ▲ The little boy had a mischievous grin on his face.
   這個小男孩的臉上露出了搗蛋的一笑。
   mischievously [ˈmɪstʃɪvəslɪ] adv. 惡意地
   ▲ The students teased the boy mischievously.
   學生惡意地嘲笑男孩。

20. **ponder** [ˈpɑndɚ] v. 仔細思考，考慮 <on, over> [同] consider
   ▲ My parents asked me to ponder my future.
   我父母要我仔細思考未來。

21. **renowned** [rɪˈnaʊnd] adj. 著名的 <for, as>
   ▲ The country is renowned for its beautiful scenery.
   這個國家以美麗的景色著名。

22. **royalty** [ˈrɔɪəltɪ] n. [U] 王權；王室成員
   ▲ The crown is a symbol of royalty.
   皇冠是王權的象徵。

23. **serving** [ˈsɝvɪŋ] n. [C] 一份

▲ An adult should eat 3 servings of vegetables and 2 servings of fruit every day.

一個成年人每天應該吃三份蔬菜和兩份水果。

24. **thereafter** [ðɛrˋæftɚ] adv. 從那以後，之後

▲ You will work alone for the first week, but thereafter you will work with a group. 第一個星期你會單獨工作，但之後你會加入一個團體一起工作。

25. **virgin** [ˋvɝdʒɪn] n. [C] 處女

▲ The girl decided to remain a virgin until she got married. 女孩決定在結婚前保持處女之身。

virgin [ˋvɝdʒɪn] adj. 未開發的

▲ This virgin forest is well protected by the government. 這片未開發的森林被政府保護得很好。

Unit 14

1. **accessory** [ækˋsɛsərɪ] n. [C] 裝飾品 (usu. pl.)；幫凶 <to> (pl. accessories)

▲ The actress is wearing a green dress with matching accessories.

這個女演員穿著綠色的洋裝並搭配相襯的裝飾品。

💡 accessory <u>before</u>/<u>after</u> the fact 事前 / 事後幫凶 | <u>auto</u>/<u>car</u> accessory 汽車配件 | <u>fashion</u>/<u>computer</u> accessory 時裝 / 電腦配件

accessory [ækˋsɛsərɪ] adj. 輔助的

▲ The doctor observed the patient's use of accessory muscles. 醫生觀察病人運用輔助肌肉。

2. **accordingly** [əˈkɔrdɪŋlɪ] adv. 照著，相應地
   ▲ Nancy has told you the situation, and you had better behave accordingly.
   Nancy 已經告訴你情況，而你最好能照著做。

3. **aesthetic** [ɛsˈθɛtɪk] adj. 美學的 (also esthetic)
   ▲ This artist's painting has many aesthetic values.
   這位藝術家的畫作有許多美學的價值。

4. **animate** [ˈænəˌmet] v. 使生氣勃勃
   ▲ Vivien's face was animated with joy at the sight of her father.
   當 Vivien 看到她爸爸時，臉上因喜悅而生氣勃勃。

   animate [ˈænəmɪt] adj. 活的，有生命的 [反] inanimate
   ▲ Some scientists believe that animate beings exist on Mars. 有些科學家相信火星上有活的生物存在。

   animated [ˈænəˌmetɪd] adj. 活躍的 [同] lively
   ▲ Tommy and I had an animated discussion about politics. Tommy 和我就政治展開活躍的討論。

   💡 animated cartoon 卡通影片

   animation [ˌænəˈmeʃən] n. [C] 動畫
   ▲ *Toy Story* was the first commercial computer animation, which took 4 years to make. 《玩具總動員》是第一部商業電腦動畫，花了四年的時間製作。

5. **backbone** [`bæk,bon] n. [C] 脊椎 [同] spine；支柱；[U] 勇氣

   ▲ The man fell off his horse and broke his backbone.
   這男子摔下馬而弄斷脊椎。

6. **breakdown** [`brek,daun] n. [C] 故障；崩潰

   ▲ Stop the car on the shoulder and wait for the breakdown service.
   把車停在路肩等待故障維修服務。

7. **cashier** [kæ`ʃɪr] n. [C] 收銀員

   ▲ After graduating from high school, Helen worked as a cashier at a supermarket.
   Helen 高中畢業後在超市當收銀員。

8. **catastrophe** [kə`tæstrəfɪ] n. [C] 大災難

   ▲ Rachel Carson warned us of the upcoming ecological catastrophe.
   Rachel Carson 警告我們即將來臨的生態大災難。

   catastrophic [,kætə`strɑfɪk] adj. 毀滅性的

   ▲ The nuclear bombs dropped on Japan in 1945 caused catastrophic damage to the Japanese people. 於 1945 年投向日本的核彈對日本人造成毀滅性的傷害。

9. **clearance** [`klɪrəns] n. [C][U] 間距；[U] 許可

   ▲ The clearance between the water and the bridge is 4 meters. 水和橋之間的間距是四公尺。

10. **confederation** [kən,fɛdə`reʃən] n. [C][U] 同盟，聯盟

▲ These two countries are celebrating the anniversary of confederation. 這兩個國家在慶祝他們同盟週年。

---

11. **correspondence** [ˌkɔrəˈspɑndəns] n. [U] 通信

▲ Chloe's correspondence with Jim lasted many years.
Chloe 與 Jim 的通信持續多年。

---

12. **cozy** [ˈkozɪ] adj. 舒適的 [同] snug (cozier | coziest)

▲ It was cozy in front of the fireplace.
壁爐前面暖和舒適。

---

13. **default** [dɪˈfɔlt] n. [C][U] 拖欠

▲ This bankrupt company is in default on its loan.
這間破產的公司拖欠貸款。

default [dɪˈfɔlt] v. 拖欠 <on>

▲ If I default on the payment, the bank will repossess my apartment.
如果我拖欠付款，銀行會收走我的公寓。

---

14. **diabetes** [ˌdaɪəˈbitɪz] n. [U] 糖尿病

▲ Work out regularly can prevent diabetes.
定期健身可以預防糖尿病。

diabetic [ˌdaɪəˈbɛtɪk] adj. 糖尿病的

▲ The patient was in a diabetic coma.
病人處於糖尿病引起的昏迷狀態中。

---

15. **disable** [dɪsˈebl̩] v. 使失能，使殘疾

▲ The accident disabled the young worker.
意外使這年輕的員工失能。

disabled [dɪs`ebl̩d] adj. 失能的，殘疾的，有身心障礙的

▲The disabled young man never lets his disability prevent him from doing whatever he wants to do. 這位身有殘疾的年輕人從不讓失能阻礙他做想做的事。

💡 the disabled 身心障礙者

---

16. **downward** [`daʊnwɚd] adj. 向下的

▲Be careful. There's a downward slope ahead.
小心。前方有向下的斜坡。

💡 downward spiral 不斷下降

downward [`daʊnwɚd] adv. 向下地；衰退地 (also downwards)

▲John looked downward in silence.
John 沉默地向下看。

---

17. **geometry** [dʒɪ`ɑmətrɪ] n. [U] 幾何學

▲A basic understanding of geometry can help you learn art and design.
對幾何學的基本認識可以幫助你學習藝術與設計。

geometric [ˌdʒiə`mɛtrɪk] adj. 幾何的 (also geometrical)

▲Many items in nature such as snowflakes and starfish show perfect geometric shapes. 很多自然中的東西呈現完美的幾何圖形，例如雪花和海星。

💡 geometric design 幾何圖案設計

---

18. **intimidate** [ɪn`tɪmə,det] v. 恫嚇 <into>

▲The gangsters intimidated us into agreeing to their demands. 歹徒恫嚇我們答應他們的要求。

intimidated [ɪnˋtɪməˌdetɪd] adj. 感到害怕的

▲ My son felt intimidated on his first day at elementary school. 我兒子上小學的第一天感到害怕。

intimidating [ɪnˋtɪməˌdetɪŋ] adj. 令人害怕的

▲ Many people find public speaking very intimidating. 許多人覺得公開演說非常令人害怕。

---

19. **irritate** [ˋɪrəˌtet] v. 使惱怒

▲ The teacher was a bit irritated by the students' jokes. 老師被學生的玩笑弄得有些惱怒。

---

20. **mobilize** [ˋmobəˌlaɪz] v. 動員 [同] rally

▲ The purpose of the movement is to mobilize public support for women's rights. 這個活動的目的是想動員群眾對女權的支持。

---

21. **preview** [ˋpriˌvju] n. [C] 試映 (會) 或試演

▲ Critics are invited to attend the preview of the film. 影評人受邀參加該片的試映會。

preview [priˋvju] v. 觀看或舉辦⋯的試映會或試演

▲ Journalists and critics are invited to preview the new movie tomorrow. 記者和影評人受邀明天觀賞新片的試映。

---

22. **sanitation** [ˌsænəˋteʃən] n. [U] 衛生 (設備或系統)

▲ The mayor must solve the problem of the city's poor sanitation. 市長必須解決本市環境衛生設備不良的問題。

23. **scenic** [ˋsinɪk] adj. 風景的
   ▲ Naples is famous for its scenic beauty.
   那不勒斯以風景美麗聞名。

24. **skeptical** [ˋskɛptɪkl̩] adj. 懷疑的 <about, of>
   ▲ Penny's mom is skeptical about her chances of success. Penny 的媽媽對她成功的機會存疑。

25. **tornado** [tɔrˋnedo] n. [C] 龍捲風 (pl. tornadoes, tornados)
   ▲ A series of tornadoes ripped through America's heartland. 一連串龍捲風從美國中心地帶橫掃而過。

Unit 15

1. **accusation** [ˌækjəˋzeʃən] n. [C][U] 控訴
   ▲ The singer is under a false accusation.
   這名歌手正面臨不實的控訴。

2. **addiction** [əˋdɪkʃən] n. [C][U] 上癮 <to>
   ▲ The man is trying to cure himself of his addiction to drugs. 那名男子試著要治療自己的毒癮。

3. **affectionate** [əˋfɛkʃənɪt] adj. 深情的 [同] loving
   ▲ My sister gave her baby an affectionate kiss.
   我姊姊給她的寶寶深情的一吻。

4. **anticipation** [ænˌtɪsəˋpeʃən] n. [U] 期盼

▲ The fans waited for the arrival of the singer with eager anticipation. 歌迷們熱切地期盼那位歌手的到來。

💡 in anticipation of 預料到…

5. **badge** [bædʒ] n. [C] 徽章

▲ How will I know you're a policeman if you don't show me your badge?
你若不給我看你的徽章，我怎麼知道你是警察？

💡 badge of sth …的象徵

6. **breakup** [`brek,ʌp] n. [C][U] 瓦解；破裂

▲ The breakup of the Soviet Union led to the unstable condition in Eastern Europe.
蘇聯的解體導致東歐動盪不安的局面。

7. **casualty** [`kæʒuəltɪ] n. [C] 死傷者，傷亡人員 (pl. casualties)

▲ There were many casualties in the plane crash.
這起墜機事件傷亡慘重。

💡 light casualties 輕微的傷亡 | heavy/serious casualties 慘重的傷亡

8. **chairperson** [`tʃɛr,pɝsn̩] n. [C] 主席 [同] chair (pl. chairpersons)

▲ Alma has been appointed as the new chairperson of the committee. Alma 已被委任為委員會的新主席。

chairman [`tʃɛrmən] n. [C] 主席 [同] chair, chairperson (pl. chairmen)

▲ The election for the chairman of the organization will take place on Monday.

該組織的主席選舉將在星期一舉行。

chairwoman [ˋtʃɛr͵wʊmən] n. [C] 女主席 [同] chair, chairperson (pl. chairwomen)

▲ Lisa has the confidence to be re-elected as the chairwoman of the meeting.

Lisa 有信心能連任會議的女主席。

---

9. **climax** [ˋklaɪmæks] n. [C] 高潮

▲ The climax of the movie takes place in the sewer where the buried treasure is found.

這部電影的高潮發生在下水道內埋藏的寶藏被發現。

💡 come to/reach a climax 達到高潮

climax [ˋklaɪmæks] v. 達到高潮 <with, in>

▲ The musical climaxes with a spectacular scene when the crystal chandeliers fall from the ceiling. 水晶吊燈從天花板掉下來時的壯觀場景使音樂劇達到高潮。

---

10. **congressman** [ˋkɑŋgrəsmən] n. [C] 美國國會議員 (pl. congressmen)

▲ The married congressman is having an affair with a celebrity. 這位已婚的美國國會議員和一位明星私通。

congresswoman [ˋkɑŋgrəs͵wʊmən] n. [C] 美國國會女議員 (pl. congresswomen)

▲ Jeannette Rankin became the first congresswoman in 1916.

珍妮特蘭金在 1916 年成為第一位美國國會女議員。

11. **crackdown** [ˋkrækˌdaʊn] n. [C] 鎮壓 (usu. sing.) <on>
   ▲ The president made a public statement in support of the crackdown. 總統發表公開聲明支持鎮壓。

12. **credible** [ˋkrɛdəbl̩] adj. 可信的 [同] believable, convincing [反] incredible
   ▲ Stories on tabloids are hardly credible.
   小報上的故事幾乎不可信。

13. **defiance** [dɪˋfaɪəns] n. [U] 違反
   ▲ In defiance of the school rules, some students smoke in the classrooms.
   一些學生違反學校規定，在教室中吸菸。

14. **disbelief** [ˌdɪsbəˋlif] n. [U] 懷疑，不相信 <in>
   ▲ Ken stared at Luna in disbelief.
   Ken 懷疑地盯著 Luna 看。

15. **eclipse** [ɪˋklɪps] n. [C] (日或月的) 虧蝕
   ▲ A solar eclipse plunged the city into darkness.
   日蝕讓這座城市陷入黑暗。
   💡 solar/lunar eclipse 日蝕 / 月蝕 | partial/total eclipse 偏蝕 / 全蝕
   eclipse [ɪˋklɪps] v. 使相形見絀 <by>
   ▲ The boy has always been eclipsed by his smarter older sister.

這男孩跟他更聰明的姊姊相比總相形見絀。

---

16. **eyelid** [ˋaɪ͵lɪd] n. [C] 眼皮，眼瞼
▲ Both the man's upper and lower eyelids were swollen, so it's hard for him to open his eyes. 這名男子的上下眼瞼都腫起來了，所以他很難張開雙眼。

---

17. **glamorous** [ˋglæmərəs] adj. 有魅力的，迷人的
▲ The glamorous movie star attracted a large crowd wherever she went.
這位有魅力的影星無論走到哪裡都吸引一大群人。

---

18. **jade** [dʒed] n. [U] 玉
▲ My older brother bought a pair of jade earrings as a gift for my mother.
我哥哥買了一對玉耳環給媽媽當作禮物。

---

19. **lifelong** [ˋlaɪf͵lɔŋ] adj. 終身的
▲ I regard Ben as my lifelong friend.
我視 Ben 為終身的朋友。

---

20. **modernization** [͵mɑdənəˋzeʃən] n. [U] 現代化
▲ The government has planned for modernization of the transportation system.
政府預計將交通系統現代化。

---

21. **priceless** [ˋpraɪsləs] adj. 無價的
▲ The childhood memory is priceless to me.
童年回憶對我來說是無價的。

---

22. **scorn** [skɔrn] n. [U] 鄙夷 <for> [同] contempt

▲ Most people have only scorn for the politician's speech. 大多民眾對該政治人物的演說只有鄙夷。

🍎 pour/heap scorn on sb/sth 對…嗤之以鼻

scorn [skɔrn] v. 蔑視

▲ The arrogant man scorns anyone whose position is lower than his.

這個自傲的男人蔑視所有地位比他低的人。

scornful [`skɔrnfəl] adj. 輕蔑的 <of> [同] contemptuous

▲ Don't be scornful of the homeless man.

別輕蔑那個無家可歸的人。

---

23. **sculptor** [`skʌlptɚ] n. [C] 雕刻家，雕塑家

▲ There is going to be an exhibition of that world-famous sculptor's works.

將會有個展覽展出那位世界知名雕刻家的作品。

---

24. **sneeze** [sniz] n. [C] 噴嚏

▲ Coughs and sneezes are classic symptoms of a cold.

咳嗽和噴嚏是感冒的典型症狀。

sneeze [sniz] v. 打噴嚏

▲ "God bless you," said the old man after the boy sneezed.

在這男孩打噴嚏後，老人說：「願上帝保佑你。」

🍎 not to be sneezed at = nothing to sneeze at (金額等)
不可輕忽，非同小可

---

25. **transcript** [`træn,skrɪpt] n. [C] 文本

▲ Do you have a transcript of the speech?
你有這場演講的文本嗎？

Unit 16

1. **accustom** [ə`kʌstəm] v. 使習慣，使適應 <to>
   ▲ It takes one month for John to accustom himself to the new working environment.
   John 花了一個月時間適應新的工作環境。

   •**accustomed** [ə`kʌstəmd] adj. 習慣的 <to>
   ▲ Sara is accustomed to jogging after work. She has been in the habit for one year. Sara 已經習慣下班後慢跑。她已經維持這個習慣一年了。

2. **airtight** [`ɛr,taɪt] adj. 密封的；無懈可擊的
   ▲ Mandy puts the cookies in an airtight container to keep them crispy.
   Mandy 把餅乾存放在密封罐裡讓它們保持酥脆。
   💡 airtight alibi 無懈可擊的不在場證明

3. **antonym** [`æntə,nɪm] n. [C] 反義字 [同] opposite
   ▲ "Up" is the antonym of "down."
   up 是 down 的反義字。

4. **barbarian** [bɑr`bɛrɪən] adj. 野蠻人的
   ▲ The first chapter of this book introduces the barbarian cultures of Europe.

這本書的第一章介紹歐洲野蠻人的文化。

barbarian [bɑrˋbɛrɪən] n. [C] 野蠻人；沒教養的人

▲ In ancient times, people built walls to keep out barbarians. 古時候，人們建牆來防止野蠻人入侵。

barbaric [bɑrˋbærɪk] adj. 野蠻的 [同] barbarous

▲ Some animal activists have indicated that whale hunting tradition is a barbaric ritual. 一些動保人士表示獵捕鯨魚的傳統是一種野蠻的儀式。

---

5. **bribe** [braɪb] n. [C] 賄賂

▲ The official is facing a charge of taking bribes.
這位官員正面臨收賄的指控。

💡 offer/give/pay a bribe 行賄 | take/accept a bribe 收受賄賂

bribe [braɪb] v. 賄賂，行賄 <to>

▲ The candidate attempted to bribe me to vote for him.
這位候選人企圖賄賂我去投票給他。

bribery [ˋbraɪbərɪ] n. [U] 賄賂

▲ The government is taking steps to combat bribery and corruption. 政府正採取措施來打擊賄賂與貪汙。

---

6. **cater** [ˋketɚ] v. 包辦宴席 <for>；迎合 (喜好或需求) <to>

▲ This restaurant can cater for dinner parties of up to 300 people. 這家餐廳可以包辦多達三百人的晚宴。

caterer [ˋketərɚ] n. [C] 承辦宴席的人或業者

▲ The caterer has prepared a wide selection of dishes for the wedding guests.

承辦宴席者準備了各式餐點給婚禮嘉賓。

7. **charitable** [`tʃærətəbl] adj. 慈善的；仁慈的
   ▲ Sam has been giving away most of his savings to the charitable organization.
   Sam 持續將大部分的積蓄捐給慈善機構。
   💡 charitable donation 慈善捐款

8. **clockwise** [`klɑk,waɪz] adv. 順時鐘地 [反] counterclockwise
   ▲ Richard turned the key clockwise to unlock the garage door. Richard 順時鐘轉動鑰匙打開車庫門。
   clockwise [`klɑk,waɪz] adj. 順時鐘的 [反] counterclockwise
   ▲ Ellen twisted the rope around the log in a clockwise direction. Ellen 以順時鐘方向將繩子纏繞在圓木上。

9. **conquest** [`kɑŋkwɛst] n. [U] 征服 <of>；[C] 占領地
   ▲ The conquest of Mount Everest is an amazing achievement. 征服聖母峰是一項了不起的成就。

10. **cracker** [`krækə-] n. [C] 薄脆餅乾；鞭炮
    ▲ Jessie likes to eat crackers with cheese.
    Jessie 喜歡薄脆餅乾搭配起司一起吃。

11. **decisive** [dɪ`saɪsɪv] adj. 決定性的；果斷的 [反] indecisive
    ▲ Dennis played a decisive role in the basketball game by scoring 20 points.
    Dennis 在籃球比賽拿下二十分，扮演決定性的角色。

💡 decisive factor/victory 決定性因素 / 勝利

12. **definitive** [dɪ`fɪnətɪv] adj. 最終的；最完整的

▲ The manager offered a definitive solution to the customer's request.

經理依據顧客的請求提供了一個最終解決方案。

💡 definitive agreement 最終的共識 | definitive work 最完整的作品

13. **discard** [dɪs`kɑrd] v. 丟棄，遺棄 [同] throw away

▲ People who discard garbage into the river will be fined. 丟棄垃圾到河裡會被罰款。

discard [`dɪskɑrd] n. [C] 被遺棄的人或事物

▲ The old broken bike must have been one of Mark's discards.

這臺破舊的腳踏車一定是 Mark 遺棄的東西之一。

14. **discomfort** [dɪs`kʌmfɚt] n. [U] 不適，些微的疼痛；不安；[C] 令人不舒服的事物

▲ When the dentist drilled into my tooth, I felt some discomfort. 當牙醫在鑽我的牙齒時，我感到有些疼痛。

discomfort [dɪs`kʌmfɚt] v. 使不舒服

▲ The constant noise of construction discomforted Louis. 施工持續的噪音使 Louis 不舒服。

15. **dwelling** [`dwɛlɪŋ] n. [C] 住所

▲ Amber lives in a modern dwelling in the center of the city. Amber 住在市中心一間現代化的房子裡。

💡 single-family dwelling 獨戶住宅

16. **flaw** [flɔ] n. [C] 缺陷 <in> [同] defect；瑕疵 <in>

▲ The smartphone has a fatal flaw in design, which leads to the overheating of the battery. 這支智慧型手機在設計上有個致命的缺陷導致電池過熱。

💡 character flaw 性格上的缺陷

flaw [flɔ] v. 使有瑕疵

▲ Uncontrollable jealousy flawed Noah's marriage.
無法控制的嫉妒使 Noah 的婚姻有瑕疵。

17. **gleam** [glim] n. [C] 微光 <of>；光澤，光芒 <of>

▲ The sailors saw the gleam of the lighthouse in the fog. 水手們在霧中看見燈塔的微光。

💡 a gleam of hope 一絲希望

gleam [glim] v. 閃爍，閃閃發光 <with>

▲ Gary's eyes gleamed with joy as he saw the toy car in his father's hands. 當 Gary 看見他父親手中的玩具車時，他的雙眼閃爍著喜悅的光芒。

18. **jingle** [ˋdʒɪŋgl] n. [sing.] 叮噹聲；[C] 廣告歌曲

▲ The jingle of the coins Brian made really irritated me. Brian 弄出來的硬幣叮噹聲令我很惱火。

jingle [ˋdʒɪŋgl] v. (使) 發出叮噹聲

▲ The keys jingled when Pearl walked.
當 Pearl 走路時，鑰匙發出叮噹聲。

19. **lighten** [ˈlaɪtn̩] v. 減輕 [反] increase；緩和 (氣氛、情緒等)

▲ Computers have lightened people's workload.
電腦減輕了人們的工作量。

💡 lighten the burden/load 減輕負擔 | lighten up 放輕鬆

20. **momentum** [moˈmɛntəm] n. [U] 動力

▲ The policy will help gather momentum to improve our current economy.
這項政策將有助於凝聚動力來改善現今的經濟。

💡 lose momentum 失去動力

21. **probe** [prob] n. [C] 探查，調查 <into>

▲ The prosecutors are working on the probe into the suspected bribery.
檢察官正在對涉嫌賄選案件進行調查。

💡 space probe 太空探測器

22. **selective** [səˈlɛktɪv] adj. 選擇 (性) 的；仔細挑選的，精挑細選的 <about>

▲ Emily has a selective memory of her first love.
Emily 對她的初戀有選擇性的回憶。

23. **simplicity** [sɪmˈplɪsətɪ] n. [U] 簡單；簡樸

▲ The project that the professor assigned was not simplicity itself. 這名教授指派的研究非常不簡單。

24. **sociable** [ˈsoʃəbl̩] adj. 好交際的，善於社交的 [反] unsociable

▲ Chad is very sociable. He is good at making new friends. Chad 非常喜歡交際。他擅長結交新朋友。

---

25. **trillion** [ˋtrɪljən] n. [C] 兆

▲ The government has spent a trillion dollars on military defense. 政府已經花費一兆元在軍隊防禦。

Unit 17

1. **acne** [ˋæknɪ] n. [U] 痤瘡，粉刺，青春痘

▲ Helen suffers from acne since she often stays up late watching Korean dramas.

Helen 因為經常熬夜看韓劇而有青春痘的問題。

💡 develop/get acne 長粉刺或青春痘

---

2. **altitude** [ˋæltəˏtjud] n. [C][U] 標高，海拔

▲ Jacob felt dizzy when he reached a higher altitude.

當 Jacob 到一個海拔較高的地方他感到頭暈目眩。

💡 at high/low altitudes 在高 / 低海拔地區

---

3. **applaud** [əˋplɔd] v. 鼓掌 [同] clap；讚賞 <for>

▲ When the concert ended, the audience applauded loudly. 當演唱會結束時，觀眾大聲地鼓掌。

---

4. **bass** [bes] n. [C] 男低音歌手；低音吉他

▲ Sam is determined to be a world-famous bass.

Sam 決心要當一位世界聞名的男低音歌手。

bass [bes] adj. 低音的

▲ Daniel sang for his girlfriend in his deep bass voice.

Daniel 用他低沉的嗓音唱歌給他女朋友聽。

5. **brink** [brɪŋk] n. [sing.] 邊緣 (the ~) <of>

▲ Faced with the sudden death of her dog, Eva was on the brink of a breakdown.

面臨愛犬的驟逝，Eva 處於崩潰邊緣。

6. **caterpillar** [ˋkætɚˌpɪlɚ] n. [C] 毛蟲

▲ It takes a long process for a caterpillar to turn into a beautiful butterfly.

毛蟲蛻變為美麗的蝴蝶需要一段漫長的過程。

7. **checkup** [ˋtʃɛkˌʌp] n. [C] 健康檢查

▲ Having regular checkups helps people find out health problems early.

定期健康檢查幫助人們及早發現健康問題。

8. **clone** [klon] n. [C] 複製 (品)

▲ In the movie, a mad scientist attempted to create many clones of himself to rule the world.

在這部電影裡，一位瘋狂科學家為了掌控世界企圖創造出許多自己的複製人。

clone [klon] v. 複製

▲ Scientists are trying to clone endangered plants to save them from extinction.

科學家們試著複製瀕危植物以防其絕種。

9. **conscientious** [ˌkɑnʃɪˋɛnʃəs] adj. 負責盡職的
   ▲ Kelly is a conscientious employee. She always makes her job a priority.
   Kelly 是一位盡職的員工。她總是以工作為優先。

10. **cram** [kræm] v. 把…塞進 <into> ；死記硬背 <for>
   (crammed | crammed | cramming)
   ▲ Naomi crammed all of her letters into a small box.
   Naomi 把她所有的信塞進一個小盒子裡。

11. **deplete** [dɪˋplit] v. 使大量減少，消耗
   ▲ Working day and night depleted Eason's energy. He fell asleep as soon as he lay down on the sofa.
   日以繼夜地工作耗盡 Eason 的精力。他一躺在沙發上就立刻睡著了。

12. **disciple** [dɪˋsaɪp!] n. [C] 信徒，追隨者 <of>
   ▲ Emily is a disciple of the fashion designer, Vivienne Westwood.
   Emily 是時尚設計師薇薇安魏斯伍德的信徒。

13. **disciplinary** [ˋdɪsəplɪˌnɛrɪ] adj. 懲戒的
   ▲ The teacher took disciplinary measures against students who cheated in the test.
   老師針對考試作弊的學生採取懲戒措施。

14. **distress** [dɪˋstrɛs] n. [U] 痛苦，苦惱
   ▲ The boy was in distress after he confessed his love to a girl and got rejected.

男孩向女孩表白遭拒後感到很苦惱。

distress [dɪ`strɛs] v. 使痛苦，使苦惱

▲ Chester's childhood memories have distressed him greatly. Chester 的童年記憶使他很痛苦。

distressed [dɪ`strɛst] adj. 痛苦的，苦惱的，憂傷的 <at, by>

▲ Many of the actor's fans were deeply distressed at the news of his death.
很多這位演員的影迷為他的死訊深感憂傷。

---

15. **encyclopedia** [ɪn͵saɪklə`pidɪə] n. [C] 百科全書

▲ It took over five years for the publisher to compile this encyclopedia.
出版社花了超過五年時間編纂這本百科全書。

---

16. **garment** [`gɑrmənt] n. [C] (一件) 衣服

▲ The garment factory causes serious pollution to the local environment.
這間成衣工廠帶給當地環境嚴重的汙染。

---

17. **glitter** [`glɪtɚ] n. [U] 閃爍；魅力

▲ The glitter of fireworks attracts many people's attention. 煙火的閃爍吸引了許多人的目光。

glitter [`glɪtɚ] v. 閃閃發光；閃爍 <with>

▲ The diamond necklace glittered under the spotlights.
鑽石項鍊在聚光燈下閃閃發光。

glittering [`glɪtərɪŋ] adj. 閃爍的；成功的

▲ The glittering neon signs brightened the night sky of the big city.

閃爍的霓虹燈招牌照亮了大城市的夜空。

18. **joyous** [`dʒɔɪəs] adj. 喜悅的，歡樂的

▲ Christmas is a joyous day for many families.

耶誕節對許多家庭而言是一個歡樂的日子。

19. **mainland** [`men,lænd] n. [sing.] 國土的主體 (the ~)

▲ There are ferries between the islands and the mainland. 有渡輪往返島嶼和本島之間。

20. **monotony** [mə`nɑtənɪ] n. [U] 單調，無聊 <of>

▲ The monotony of the scenery along the freeway makes driving a tedious task.

高速公路沿途景色單調讓開車變得乏味。

💡 break the monotony 打破單調

monotonous [mə`nɑtənəs] adj. 單調乏味的

▲ Chloe is tired of the monotonous routine of everyday life. Chloe 對每天生活上單調的例行公事感到厭倦。

21. **procession** [prə`sɛʃən] n. [C][U] 行列

▲ The pilgrims marched in procession to a temple of Matsu. 信眾列隊朝向媽祖廟行進。

💡 funeral procession 送葬隊伍

22. **sharpen** [`ʃɑrpən] v. 使鋒利；加強，改善

▲ Mom made me sharpen her fish knife.

媽媽要我幫她磨切魚用刀。

💡 sharpen up 改進，改善

23. **sloppy** [ˋslɑpɪ] adj. 馬虎草率的 [同] careless ；寬鬆的
    (sloppier | sloppiest)
    ▲ John was fired because of his sloppy work.
    John 因為工作馬虎而被解僱。

24. **span** [spæn] n. [C] 一段時間 (usu. sing.)；全長
    ▲ A fruit fly has a short life span. 果蠅的壽命短暫。
    span [spæn] v. 持續，延續 (一段時間)；橫跨，橫越
    (spanned | spanned | spanning)
    ▲ Tom's life spanned nearly a century.
    Tom 活了將近一世紀。

25. **upright** [ˋʌpˌraɪt] adv. 挺直地
    ▲ Leslie sits with her back upright as she does her
    homework.
    當 Leslie 在寫作業時，她背部挺直地坐著。
    upright [ˋʌpˌraɪt] adj. 直立的；正直的
    ▲ For the sake of safety, passengers' seats should be in
    the upright position during takeoff and landing. 為了
    安全，乘客的椅子在飛機起降時都須保持直立狀態。
    upright [ˋʌpˌraɪt] n. [C] 直立之物
    ▲ The uprights of the office chair are made of wood.
    辦公室椅子的支柱是木頭做的。

Unit 18

1. **acre** [ˋekɚ] n. [C] 英畝

   ▲ The field measures more than two acres.

   這塊田面積超過兩英畝。

---

2. **ambiguity** [ˌæmbɪˋgjuətɪ] n. [C][U] 模稜兩可；模稜兩可或含混不清的事物 (pl. ambiguities)

   ▲ When writing a contract, you have to make the statements precise and avoid ambiguity. 在擬合約的時候，你必須讓說明清楚並且避免模稜兩可。

---

3. **approximate** [əˋprɑksəmɪt] adj. 大約的，大概的 [反] exact

   ▲ The approximate population of people over 70 in this city is 10,000.

   這座城市超過七十歲的人口大約是一萬人。

   approximate [əˋprɑksəˌmet] v. 接近 <to>

   ▲ The story approximates to the real history.

   這個故事接近真實歷史。

   approximately [əˋprɑksəmɪtlɪ] adv. 大約，大概 [同] roughly

   ▲ Amy spent approximately 2 days knitting a pair of gloves for her husband.

   Amy 花了大概兩天的時間編織一雙手套給她丈夫。

---

4. **batter** [ˋbætɚ] n. [C] (棒球) 打擊手

   ▲ The pitcher threw a ball at the batter by accident.

這名投手誤將球投向打擊手。

batter [ˋbætɚ] v. 連續猛擊，用力撞擊

▲ The firefighters battered down the door and entered the building. 消防隊員用力撞倒門，進入這棟大樓。

battered [ˋbætɚd] adj. 破舊的

▲ We are going to replace the battered sofa with a new one. 我們將要把破舊的沙發替換成新的。

---

5. **brochure** [broˋʃur] n. [C] 小冊子

▲ Before deciding where to go on vacation, Benton read some travel brochures.
在決定要去哪裡渡假前，Benton 讀了一些旅遊手冊。

---

6. **cavity** [ˋkævətɪ] n. [C] (牙齒) 蛀洞 (pl. cavities)

▲ Mandy went to the dentist's to get her cavities filled.
Mandy 去牙醫診所填補蛀牙。

---

7. **chirp** [tʃɝp] n. [C] 鳥或蟲的叫聲

▲ Chirps of cicadas tell us that summer is coming.
蟬叫聲告訴我們夏天來了。

chirp [tʃɝp] v. 發出啁啾聲，鳴叫，啼叫

▲ Some cuckoos are chirping outside the window.
一些杜鵑鳥正在窗外啼叫。

---

8. **closure** [ˋkloʒɚ] n. [C][U] 關閉，停業 <of>

▲ The closure of the factory resulted in a high unemployment rate in this town.
工廠關閉造成這座城鎮的高失業率。

---

9. **conserve** [kən`sɝv] v. 節約;保護 [同] preserve
   ▲ Replacing the old bulbs with LED lights can help conserve electricity.
   把舊燈泡換成 LED 燈具有助於省電。
   conserve [`kɑnsɝv] n. [C][U] 蜜餞
   ▲ Claire prefers strawberry conserve to lollipops.
   比起棒棒糖,Claire 更喜歡草莓蜜餞。

10. **cramp** [kræmp] n. [C][U] 痙攣,抽筋
   ▲ Hank got a cramp in his foot while swimming.
   Hank 游泳時腳抽筋了。
   cramp [kræmp] v. 限制
   ▲ The lack of education cramped Jill's chances to find a good job. 教育不足限制了 Jill 找到好工作的機會。

11. **deprive** [dɪ`praɪv] v. 從⋯奪去 <of>
   ▲ The accident deprived them of their only son.
   那場意外事故奪去了他們的獨子。

12. **disclosure** [dɪs`kloʒɚ] n. [U] 揭露 <of>;[C] 揭發的事實 <of>
   ▲ The disclosure of Samuel's extramarital affair with his young assistant ruined his political life.
   與年輕助理的婚外情揭露毀了 Samuel 的政治生涯。

13. **disturbance** [dɪ`stɝbəns] n. [C][U] 干擾 <to>;混亂,不安

▲ The construction noise caused a disturbance to Nick when he was studying.

施工噪音在 Nick 讀書時造成了干擾。

---

14. **endeavor** [ɪnˈdɛvɚ] n. [C][U] 努力，嘗試 <to>

▲ All the nations of the world will be at the conference and make every endeavor to establish peace.

世界各國皆會與會並盡一切努力建立和平。

endeavor [ɪnˈdɛvɚ] v. 努力 <to>

▲ The rescue team endeavored to save the victims in the golden 72 hours.

救難團隊盡力在黃金七十二小時內救出受災者。

---

15. **esteem** [əˈstim] n. [U] 敬重

▲ Please accept the small gift as a mark of our esteem.

請接受我們表示敬意的小禮物。

💡 be held in high/low esteem 備受 / 不受敬重

esteem [əˈstim] v. 敬重

▲ The king is greatly esteemed by all his people.

這位國王深受全民敬重。

---

16. **hacker** [ˈhækɚ] n. [C] 電腦入侵者，電腦駭客

▲ The computer hacker, who illegally hacked into the government's computer system, received a harsh sentence.

這個非法入侵政府電腦系統的駭客被判以重刑。

hack [hæk] v. 駭入 <into>；砍，劈 <off, down>

▲ Bill was sent to prison for hacking into several banks' computer systems.
Bill 因為駭入數家銀行的電腦系統而入獄。

---

17. **itch** [ɪtʃ] n. [C] 癢 (usu. sing.)

▲ Don't scratch. Use the herbal cream to stop the itch.
不要抓。用這草藥膏來止癢。

itch [ɪtʃ] v. 發癢

▲ The mosquito bites on my legs itched terribly.
我腿上被蚊子叮咬的包非常癢。

itchy [ˋɪtʃɪ] adj. (令人) 發癢的

▲ As Alex was allergic to seafood, he got an itchy rash after eating some shrimps. 因為 Alex 對海鮮過敏，他吃了一些蝦子後身體出現發癢的疹子。

---

18. **lavish** [ˋlævɪʃ] adj. 奢華的；慷慨大方的 <with, in>

▲ The unwise couple insist on living a lavish life even though they have to borrow money to do so.
這對不明智的情侶即使借錢也堅持要過奢華的生活。

---

19. **marginal** [ˋmɑrdʒɪn!] adj. 些微的 [反] significant

▲ There is only a marginal pay increase while a significant rise in the price.
薪水只有些微增加，而物價卻大幅增長。

💡 of marginal interest 只有少數人感興趣的

marginally [ˋmɑrdʒɪnəlɪ] adv. 些微地 [同] slightly [反] significantly

▲ The two versions of how the explosion happened are about the same; they're only marginally different.
關於爆炸如何發生的兩個版本說法幾乎一樣；它們只有些微地不同。

20. **morale** [mə`ræl] n. [U] 士氣
  ▲ The general made a speech to boost the morale of the soldiers. 將軍發表演說來提升軍人的士氣。
  💡 high/low morale 士氣高昂 / 低落

21. **proficiency** [prə`fɪʃənsɪ] n. [U] 精通，熟練 <in>
  ▲ With proficiency in computer skills, Frank easily found a job as soon as he graduated from the university. 由於 Frank 對於電腦技術很精通，他大學一畢業就輕易找到工作。

22. **slang** [slæŋ] n. [U] 俚語 <for>
  ▲ "Kick the bucket" is slang for "die."
  「踢水桶」是俚語，指「死亡」。

  slang [slæŋ] v. 辱罵
  ▲ The coach slanged me for my poor performance.
  教練因為我表現差而辱罵我。

23. **sparrow** [`spæro] n. [C] 麻雀
  ▲ The chirping of a flock of sparrows woke me up.
  一群麻雀吱吱喳喳的叫聲吵醒我。

24. **supplement** [`sʌpləmənt] n. [C] 補充物；增刊，副刊
  ▲ Tyler takes vitamin supplements every day.

Tyler 每天服用維生素補充劑。

supplement [ˈsʌpləˌmɛnt] v. 補充，增補，補貼 <by, with>

▲ On top of his full-time job, Ralph supplemented his income by working as a freelance writer.

除了全職的工作外，Ralph 自由撰稿補貼收入。

supplemental [ˌsʌpləˈmɛntl̩] adj. 補充的 (also supplementary)

▲ Cindy recommended some supplemental reading materials to Judy.

Cindy 向 Judy 推薦一些補充的閱讀材料。

---

25. **upward** [ˈʌpˌwɚd] adj. 向上的，往上的 [反] downward

▲ The housing prices in the city have been in an upward trend recently.

這座城市的房價近期一直有不斷往上的趨勢。

upward [ˈʌpˌwɚd] adv. 向上地，往上地 (also upwards)

▲ The boy looked upward and saw a helicopter flying over his head.

男孩往上看，見到一架直升機飛過他的頭頂。

Unit 19

1. **adaptation** [ˌædəpˈteʃən] n. [C] 改編 <of>；[U] 適應 <to>

▲ The movie is an adaptation of the novel *The Great Gatsby*.

這部電影改編自小說《大亨小傳》。

---

2. **amplify** [`æmplə,faɪ] v. 擴大，增強；詳述
   ▲ Reading a wide variety of books can amplify our knowledge. 廣泛閱讀各種書籍可以擴充我們的知識。

   amplifier [`æmplə,faɪɚ] n. [C] 擴音器
   ▲ I put my hand on the amplifier to feel the vibration caused by the sound.
   我把手放在擴音器上感受聲音帶來的震動。

   amplification [,æmpləfə`keʃən] n. [U] 闡述
   ▲ Students ask the teacher to provide further amplification of the issue.
   學生們請求老師針對這個議題提供更進一步的闡述。

---

3. **archaeology** [,ɑrkɪ`ɑlədʒɪ] n. [U] 考古學 (also archeology)
   ▲ The unexpected discovery of the emperor's tomb amazed people in the field of archaeology.
   意外發現皇帝的陵寢讓考古學界驚嘆不已。

---

4. **beautify** [`bjutə,faɪ] v. 美化
   ▲ All of my classmates are working together to beautify the campus. 我所有的同學合力美化校園。

---

5. **broil** [brɔɪl] v. 燒烤 [同] grill
   ▲ Turn the chicken over and continue to broil the other side for 20 minutes.
   把雞肉翻面，把另一面繼續烤二十分鐘。

6. **celery** [`sɛlərɪ] n. [U] 芹菜

▲ Julia likes to put some celery on the top of the dish.
Julia 喜歡在菜肴上放些芹菜。

💡 a stalk/stick of celery 一根芹菜

---

7. **coalition** [ˌkoəˋlɪʃən] n. [C][U] 聯盟

▲ These victims of fraud formed a coalition to fight for their rights.
這群詐騙受害者組成聯盟爭取他們的權利。

💡 coalition government 聯合政府

---

8. **commonplace** [`kɑmənˌples] adj. 常見的

▲ It is commonplace for teenagers to have social media accounts. 對於年輕人來說擁有社群帳號是很常見的。

commonplace [`kɑmənˌples] n. [C] 司空見慣的事 (usu. sing.)

▲ Quarrels between the couple have become a commonplace.
夫妻間的爭吵已經是一件司空見慣的事。

---

9. **consolation** [ˌkɑnsəˋleʃən] n. [C][U] 安慰，慰藉 <for, to>

▲ Rock music is Wayne's only consolation after a bad day at school. 搖滾樂是 Wayne 在學校度過了糟糕的一天之後唯一的慰藉。

---

10. **crater** [`kretɚ] n. [C] 火山口；坑洞

▲ This crater lake is a must-see spot in Iceland.

這座火口湖是冰島必看的地點。

crater [`kretɚ] v. 使形成坑洞

▲ The bombing cratered the historic site and caused serious damage.

炸彈襲擊把古蹟炸出坑洞，造成嚴重損失。

---

11. **descent** [dɪ`sɛnt] n. [C][U] 下降 [反] ascent；[U] 血統 <of, from>

▲ The girl was asked to sit still and keep quiet during the plane's descent.

女孩被要求在飛機下降時坐好以及保持安靜。

---

12. **discreet** [dɪ`skrit] adj. 言行謹慎的 [反] indiscreet

▲ The lawyer made discreet inquiries about the witness. 律師謹慎地詢問證人。

---

13. **dwell** [dwɛl] v. 居住 <in> (dwelt, dwelled | dwelt, dwelled | dwelling)

▲ Nomads move from one place to another. They don't dwell in a particular place all the time. 游牧民族從一處移居到另一處。他們不會一直住在某個特定的地方。

💡 dwell on sth 老是想著，一直在說

dweller [`dwɛlɚ] n. [C] 居民

▲ Brian is a typical city dweller and cannot live without department stores. Brian 是一個典型的都市人，生活無法沒有百貨公司。

---

14. **enroll** [ɪn`rol] v. 註冊，登記 <in, on, at>

▲ Steve dreams of enrolling in the best medical school in Taiwan. Steve 夢想註冊就讀臺灣最好的醫學院。

enrollment [ɪn`rolmənt] n. [C][U] 註冊 (人數)

▲ The continuous decline in school enrollments is largely the result of the low birth rate.
學校註冊人數持續減少很大原因是低出生率。

---

15. **hail** [hel] n. [U] 冰雹；[sing.] 一陣

▲ Many cars were badly damaged by heavy showers of hail last night.
許多車輛因為昨夜的大型冰雹雨而嚴重受損。

hail [hel] v. 下冰雹；呼喊；歡呼

▲ It hailed for several hours, causing heavy damage to the crops.
冰雹下了好幾個小時，對農作物造成嚴重損害。

💡 be hailed as sth 被譽為…

---

16. **heighten** [`haɪtn̩] v. 提高，增加 [同] intensify

▲ A series of car bombings have heightened people's fears of terrorists. 一連串的汽車爆炸事件加深了人們對恐怖分子的恐懼。

---

17. **kindle** [`kɪndl̩] v. 點燃，激起 (熱情等)

▲ The bombing kindled their anger at terrorists.
這場爆炸激起了他們對恐怖分子的憤怒。

💡 kindle sb's enthusiasm/interest 激起熱情 / 興趣

---

18. **layman** [`lemən] n. [C] 外行人 [反] expert

▲ This book contains many technical terms that are not easily understood by the layman.

這本書含有許多外行人不易了解的術語。

💡 in layman's terms 以一般用語來說

19. **monetary** [`mʌnə,tɛrɪ] adj. 貨幣的，金融的

▲ The monetary unit of Japan is the yen.

日本的貨幣單位是日圓。

💡 monetary policy 貨幣政策

20. **nationalism** [`næʃənə,lɪzəm] n. [U] 民族主義

▲ The documentary promotes an understanding of the spirit of nationalism.

這部紀錄片促進人們對民族主義精神的了解。

21. **provincial** [prə`vɪnʃəl] adj. 省的；地方的

▲ Each provincial government in this country has its own tax law. 這個國家各個省政府都有自己的稅法。

provincial [prə`vɪnʃəl] n. [C] 鄉下人

▲ Daniel doesn't look like a provincial. He's very familiar with the capital.

Daniel 看起來不像是個鄉下人。他對首都十分熟悉。

22. **slaughter** [`slɔtɚ] n. [U] 屠殺；宰殺

▲ The authorities tried to hide the fact of the mass slaughter of the minority.

當局試圖隱瞞少數民族大屠殺的真實情況。

💡 like a lamb to the slaughter 如同待宰羔羊，任人宰割

slaughter [ˋslɔtɚ] v. 屠殺；宰殺；輕鬆擊敗
▲ The innocent civilians were slaughtered in the war.
無辜的平民在戰爭中被屠殺。

23. **spiral** [ˋspaɪrəl] adj. 螺旋狀的
▲ There is a spiral staircase in the lighthouse.
燈塔中有螺旋狀的樓梯。

spiral [ˋspaɪrəl] n. [C] 螺旋 (狀)
▲ A blue spiral of smoke drifted up from his pipe.
螺旋狀的藍煙自他的菸斗飄出。

spiral [ˋspaɪrəl] v. 呈螺旋狀上升或下墜；上漲
▲ The drone spiraled down and crashed to the ground.
無人機呈螺旋狀下墜，墜毀在地面。

24. **swarm** [swɔrm] n. [C] (昆蟲或人的) 一大群 <of>
▲ A swarm of reporters gathered at the city hall and
waited for the mayor. 大批記者聚在市政府等待市長。

swarm [swɔrm] v. 成群移動；擠滿 <with>
▲ Locusts are swarming across parts of Africa, where
farmers are desperately worried. 在非洲部分地區蝗
蟲正蜂擁而至，那裡的農民倍感擔憂。

25. **underway** [ˌʌndɚˋwe] adv. 進行中，發生中 (also under
way)
▲ Preparations for the school festival are underway.
校慶的準備工作在進行中。

Unit 20

1. **administer** [əd`mɪnəstə] v. 管理；給與，施用，使接受 <to> (also administrate)

   ▲ The mayor administers the affairs of the city.
   市長掌管市內的事務。

   💡 administer first aid/punishment 施行急救 / 懲罰

2. **analogy** [ə`nælədʒɪ] n. [C][U] 類比，比較 <between, with> (pl. analogies)

   ▲ Fred drew an analogy between life and a play.
   Fred 將人生與戲劇做類比。

   💡 by analogy with 以…作比擬

3. **archive** [`ɑrkaɪv] n. [C] 檔案；檔案室

   ▲ My grandma used to store her photos in her family archives. 我的奶奶過去習慣把照片存放在家庭檔案裡。

4. **beep** [bip] n. [C] 嗶聲

   ▲ Josh forgot to leave his message after the beep.
   Josh 忘了在嗶聲後留言。

   beep [bip] v. 發出嗶嗶聲

   ▲ The rice cooker beeps when the rice is ready.
   當米飯煮好後，電飯鍋會發出嗶嗶聲。

5. **brook** [brʊk] n. [C] 小河

   ▲ There is a brook running through the park and into a pond. 有條小河穿過公園，然後流入水池。

6. **cellular** [ˈsɛljələ] adj. 與手機或通訊系統相關的
   ▲ The new cellular phone sells well in European countries. 這支新款手機在歐洲國家很暢銷。

7. **coastline** [ˈkostˌlaɪn] n. [C] 海岸線 <along, around>
   ▲ The travelers enjoyed the views of Taiwan's eastern coastline. 那些遊客享受臺灣東海岸線的風光。
   💡 a stretch of coastline 一段海岸線

8. **comprehensive** [ˌkɑmprɪˈhɛnsɪv] adj. 全面的，詳盡的
   [同] thorough
   ▲ Our company will provide you with a comprehensive training course.
   我們公司將提供你一堂全面的訓練課程。
   💡 comprehensive insurance 綜合保險，全險

9. **console** [ˈkɑnsol] n. [C] (電子設備或機器的) 操控臺
   ▲ Nate saved his pocket money to buy a new game console. Nate 存零用錢打算買一臺新的遊戲機。
   console [kənˈsol] v. 安慰 <with>
   ▲ Patty consoled herself with the thought that she had done her best.
   Patty 以她已經盡力了的想法來安慰自己。

10. **crocodile** [ˈkrɑkəˌdaɪl] n. [C] 鱷魚
    ▲ Crocodiles are considered one of the dangerous animals in the zoo.
    鱷魚被視為是動物園的危險動物之一。

💡 crocodile tears 假慈悲

---

11. **despise** [dɪ`spaɪz] v. 鄙視，厭惡 <for>

▲ The cook didn't despise the vagrants. On the contrary, he cooked a dinner for them. 這名廚師沒有鄙視流浪漢。相反地，他還為他們煮晚餐。

---

12. **disgrace** [dɪs`gres] n. [U] 恥辱；[sing.] 丟臉或不名譽的事

▲ The murderer brought disgrace to his family. 這位殺人犯為他的家庭帶來恥辱。

💡 in disgrace 丟臉地

disgrace [dɪs`gres] v. 使蒙羞

▲ The officer disgraced herself by accepting bribes. 這名官員因為收賄讓自己蒙羞。

disgraceful [dɪs`gresfəl] adj. 可恥的，丟臉的

▲ It is disgraceful that you took home the hotel towels and bathrobes. 你把飯店毛巾和浴衣帶回家，真是太丟臉了。

---

13. **edible** [`ɛdəbl] adj. 可食用的 [反] inedible

▲ If you cannot tell the difference between edible and poisonous plants, don't eat them. 如果你無法分辨可食用和有毒的植物，不要吃它們。

---

14. **escort** [`ɛskɔrt] n. [C][U] 護衛 (者) <under, with>

▲ The visiting heads of state were sent to the meeting under police escort.

來訪的元首們在警察的護送下前往會議。

escort [ɪ`skɔrt] v. 護送；陪同；陪伴 (異性) 參加社交活動

▲ The billionaire is always escorted by several bodyguards. 這位億萬富翁總是由好幾位保鏢保護。

15. **heroin** [`hɛroɪn] n. [U] 海洛因

▲ A flight attendant was under arrest for smuggling heroin. 一名空服員因為走私海洛因而被拘捕。

💡 heroin addict 吸食海洛因成癮者

16. **lengthy** [`lɛŋθɪ] adj. 冗長的，漫長的 (lengthier | lengthiest)

▲ We couldn't help dozing off in the lecturer's lengthy speech.
我們忍不住在講師漫長的演講中打瞌睡。

17. **literal** [`lɪtərəl] adj. 字面的；逐字翻譯的

▲ It's not easy to understand the poem if you only know its literal meaning. 若僅從字面上的意義來理解這首詩，你會發現它不好理解。

literally [`lɪtərəlɪ] adv. 確實地；逐字翻譯地

▲ The dress Ivan bought for his wife cost him literally two million dollars.
Ivan 買給他妻子的洋裝確實值兩百萬元。

18. **medieval** [ˌmidɪ`ivl] adj. 中世紀的

▲ George majored in medieval literature at university.

George 大學時主修中世紀文學。

---

19. **mortal** [ˋmɔrtl̩] adj. 不免一死的 [反] immortal；致命的

▲ Humans are mortal, but their works of art are immortal. 人類不免一死，但作品會留存於世。

mortal [ˋmɔrtl̩] n. [C] 凡人，普通人

▲ In Greek mythology, gods use music and dance to communicate with mortals.

在希臘神話裡，眾神用音樂和舞蹈與凡人交流。

---

20. **notable** [ˋnotəbl̩] adj. 顯著的，著名的 <for>

▲ Taiwan is notable for its local dishes.
臺灣以小吃著稱。

💡 notable achievement 顯著的成就

notable [ˋnotəbl̩] n. [C] 名人，顯要人物

▲ Many notables attended the royal wedding.
皇家婚禮名流薈萃。

notably [ˋnotəblɪ] adv. 明顯地；尤其，特別是

▲ The news report notably biased the public against the company. 這新聞報導明顯使大眾對該公司產生偏見。

---

21. **radiant** [ˋredɪənt] adj. 洋溢著幸福的，容光煥發的 <with>；有射線的，輻射 (狀) 的

▲ Ben's radiant smile shows that he is the happiest man in the world.

Ben 燦爛的笑容透露出他是世上最幸福的男人。

radiant [ˋredɪənt] n. [C] (輻射) 光源或熱源，發光體

▲ Can you see the two radiants in the sky?

你能看見天上那兩個光點嗎？

---

22. **slum** [slʌm] n. [C] 貧民區，貧民窟
   ▲ A nonprofit organization is raising funds to help people living in the slums.
   一個非營利組織在募款幫助住在貧民窟的人。

   slum [slʌm] v. 造訪貧民窟；過簡樸生活，屈就於品質較差的環境 (slummed | slummed | slumming)
   ▲ The kind old lady often goes slumming.
   這位仁慈的老太太常去拜訪貧民區。

---

23. **stationary** [`steʃə,nɛrɪ] adj. 靜止不動的
   ▲ Because of the traffic accident, the cars behind remained stationary for an hour.
   由於交通事故的關係，後方的車子靜止不動一小時了。

---

24. **textile** [`tɛkstaɪl] n. [C] 紡織品；[pl.] 紡織業 (～s)
   ▲ England is famous for its wool textiles.
   英格蘭以羊毛織品聞名。

   textile [`tɛkstaɪl] adj. 紡織的
   ▲ This jacket is made of waterproof textile material.
   這件外套是以防水的紡織原料做成的。

---

25. **urgency** [`ɝdʒənsɪ] n. [U] 緊迫
   ▲ Rescuing those who are trapped inside the collapsed building is a matter of urgency.
   拯救那些受困在傾倒大樓內的人是十分迫切的事。

Unit 21

1. **dismay** [dɪs`me] n. [U] 驚慌
   ▲ The mother looked at her wounded son in dismay.
   母親驚慌地看著受傷的兒子。
   💡 to sb's dismay 令⋯驚慌的是
   dismay [dɪs`me] v. 使驚慌害怕
   ▲ The prime minister's call for reform dismayed many conservative people.
   首相號召改革使許多保守人士感到驚慌。
   dismayed [dɪs`med] adj. 感到震驚的 <by, at>
   ▲ We liked the hotel but were dismayed by the price of the room.
   我們喜歡這間旅館，但房間的價位卻讓我們感到震驚。

2. **editorial** [ˌɛdə`torɪəl] adj. 編輯的
   ▲ Ann is a member of the editorial staff.
   Ann 是編輯部成員。
   editorial [ˌɛdə`torɪəl] n. [C] 社論
   ▲ That editorial is reflective of public opinion.
   那篇社論反映民意。

3. **expire** [ɪk`spaɪr] v. 到期，終止
   ▲ My visa is due to expire next week. I'd better renew it soon.
   我的簽證將在下週到期。我最好趕快更新簽證。

4. **formidable** [`fɔrmɪdəbl̩] adj. 令人敬畏的
   ▲ The president regards the leader of the opposition as a formidable opponent. 總統視在野黨主席為勁敵。
   💡 formidable task/obstacle 令人敬畏的任務 / 障礙

5. **goalkeeper** [`gol,kipɚ] n. [C] 守門員
   ▲ Making a great save, the goalkeeper successfully stopped the other team from scoring.
   那名守門員精采地撲救，成功阻止另一隊射門得分。

6. **hierarchy** [`haɪə,rɑrki] n. [C] （管理）階層 (pl. hierarchies)
   ▲ Fiona has been working so hard, and now she is in the management hierarchy.
   Fiona 努力工作，而現在她位居管理階層。

7. **indignant** [ɪn`dɪgnənt] adj. 憤慨的 <at, about>
   ▲ Shelly was indignant about being laid off.
   Shelly 對於被解僱感到氣憤。
   indignation [,ɪndɪg`neʃən] n. [U] 憤慨
   ▲ The political scandal aroused public indignation.
   這樁政治醜聞引起公憤。

8. **isle** [aɪl] n. [C] 小島
   ▲ My parents have been to some Caribbean isles.
   我父母曾經去過一些加勒比海的島嶼。

9. **lieutenant** [lu`tɛnənt] n. [C] 中尉

▲ Victor was promoted to the rank of lieutenant in the army. Victor 在陸軍被升為中尉。

10. **magnify** [`mæɡnə͵faɪ] v. 擴大

▲ The chairperson used a loudspeaker to magnify her voice so that everyone could hear what she said clearly. 主席用擴音器擴大她的聲音，讓每個人都能清楚地聽到她說什麼。

11. **motto** [`mɑto] n. [C] 座右銘 (pl. mottoes, mottos)

▲ What's your motto? Mine is "Never give up." 你的座右銘是什麼？我的是「永不放棄」。

12. **oblige** [ə`blaɪdʒ] v. 使有義務，迫使

▲ A company is obliged to pay their employees' salaries. 公司有義務支付員工薪水。

13. **outset** [`aʊt͵sɛt] n. [sing.] 開端

▲ At the outset of the film, a man lost his suitcase. 電影一開始，一個男子掉了他的皮箱。

14. **perish** [`pɛrɪʃ] v. 死亡，喪生

▲ Many people perished in the earthquake. 許多人在地震中喪生。

perishable [`pɛrɪʃəbl̩] adj. 易腐敗的

▲ We have to store perishable foods in the refrigerator. 我們必須把易腐敗的食物存放在冰箱。

perishing [ˈpɛrɪʃɪŋ] adj. 非常寒冷的

▲ The winter in Alaska is perishing.
　阿拉斯加的冬天酷寒。

15. **precedent** [ˈprɛsədənt] n. [C][U] 先例，前例

▲ This financial disaster is without precedent.
　這次的財務危機是史無前例的。

💡 set a precedent 開先例 | break with precedent 打破先例
　例

16. **purify** [ˈpjʊrəˌfaɪ] v. 淨化，使純淨

▲ To purify the drinking water, we have to use a filter.
　為了使飲水純淨，我們必須使用濾水器。

17. **reign** [ren] n. [C] (君主的) 統治 (期間)

▲ The reign of Queen Victoria lasted for over sixty
　years. 維多利亞女王的統治超過六十年之久。

reign [ren] v. (君主) 統治

▲ Henry VIII reigned over England from 1509 to 1547.
　亨利八世在 1509 年到 1547 年期間統治英國。

18. **rivalry** [ˈraɪvl̩rɪ] n. [C][U] 競爭 [同] competition (pl.
rivalries)

▲ There is a keen rivalry between the two schools.
　這兩所學校間競爭激烈。

19. **shabby** [ˈʃæbɪ] adj. 破舊的；寒酸的 (shabbier |
shabbiest)

▲ The elderly man lived alone in the shabby apartment.
這年長者獨自住在那棟破舊的公寓裡。

20. **socialism** [ˈsoʃəˌlɪzəm] n. [U] 社會主義
   ▲ Under socialism, the country's industries are owned by the government.
   在社會主義的制度下，該國的產業為政府所有。

21. **statute** [ˈstætʃʊt] n. [C][U] 法規
   ▲ Protection for children is laid down by statute.
   法規中有關於保護兒童的規定。

22. **superiority** [səˌpɪrɪˈɔrətɪ] n. [U] 優越 <of, in, over>
   ▲ We believe in the superiority of our products.
   我們相信我們產品的優越。

23. **tiresome** [ˈtaɪrsəm] adj. 煩人的，令人厭煩的
   ▲ Handling these trivial matters is very tiresome.
   處理這些瑣事很煩人。

24. **unification** [ˌjunəfəˈkeʃən] n. [U] 統一
   ▲ Enemies tried to block the unification of the country.
   敵人試圖阻礙國家統一。

25. **violinist** [ˌvaɪəˈlɪnɪst] n. [C] 小提琴家
   ▲ Vicky is one of the well-known violinists in the world. Vicky 是世界上著名的小提琴家之一。

Unit 22

1. **disposable** [dɪ`spozəbḷ] adj. 用完即丟的
   ▲ Lily always uses reusable containers instead of disposable ones.
   Lily 都用可重複使用而不是用完即丟的容器。

   disposable [dɪ`spozəbḷ] n. [C] 用完即丟的產品 (usu. pl.)
   ▲ Disposables cause much pollution to the environment. 用完即丟的產品造成很多環境汙染。

2. **electrician** [ɪ,lɛk`trɪʃən] n. [C] 電工
   ▲ The electrician tried to repair the electrical equipment. 這位電工試著修理這臺電器設備。

3. **extract** [`ɛkstrækt] n. [C][U] 濃縮物，提取物 <from>
   ▲ I added lemon extract to the soup.
   我把檸檬濃縮汁加入湯裡。

   extract [ɪk`strækt] v. 提取，精煉 <from>；摘錄 <from>
   ▲ The herbalist extracted juice from several plants for medical use.
   藥草商從幾種植物中提煉汁液以作為醫療用途。

4. **formulate** [`fɔrmjə,let] v. 明確地闡述
   ▲ The candidate formulated his political opinions.
   那位候選人明確地闡述了他的政見。

5. **goodwill** [,gʊd`wɪl] n. [U] 友好，友善

▲ They agreed to build houses for the flood victims for free as a gesture of goodwill.

他們同意免費為洪水受災者建造房屋以表示友好。

---

6. **hijack** [`haɪ,dʒæk] v. 劫持 (飛機等)

▲ Several terrorists hijacked an airplane which later crashed into a mountain.

幾名恐怖分子劫持一架飛機，之後飛機撞山墜毀。

hijack [`haɪ,dʒæk] n. [C][U] 劫持事件

▲ There was an airline hijack two hours ago. Fortunately, all the passengers were released safe.

兩小時前有一起劫機事件。幸好，所有乘客平安獲釋。

hijacker [`haɪ,dʒækɚ] n. [C] 劫機犯

▲ One of the suspected hijackers is only a teenager.

其中一位劫機嫌疑犯只是青少年。

hijacking [`haɪ,dʒækɪŋ] n. [C][U] 劫持事件

▲ Drastic measures should be taken to prevent more hijackings.

應該採取嚴厲的措施來預防更多劫機事件。

---

7. **industrialize** [ɪn`dʌstrɪə,laɪz] v. 使工業化

▲ When factories began to industrialize the clothing production, the prices of clothes went down remarkably. 當工廠開始把服裝的生產工業化之後，衣服價格就顯著下降了。

---

8. **ivy** [`aɪvɪ] n. [C][U] 常春藤 (pl. ivies)

▲ The ivy is climbing up the wall.

常春藤沿牆攀附而上。

9. **limp** [lɪmp] n. [C] 跛行
▲ Jane walked with a limp after the car accident.
Jane 在車禍後走路一拐一拐的。

limp [lɪmp] v. 跛行，一拐一拐地行走
▲ The basketball player limped off the court.
那位籃球員一拐一拐地離開球場。

limp [lɪmp] adj. 疲憊無力的
▲ Helen's limp body collapsed on the sofa after the
tiring day. 辛勞的一天結束後，Helen 那疲憊不堪的身
子癱倒在沙發上。

10. **majesty** [ˋmædʒɪstɪ] n. [U] 雄偉
▲ The tourists were awed by the majesty of the Alps.
遊客們對阿爾卑斯山的雄偉嘆為觀止。

11. **mound** [maʊnd] n. [C] 堆
▲ There is a mound of clothes on my bed.
有一堆衣服在我床上。

mound [maʊnd] v. 堆起，堆積
▲ Tony's bowl was mounded with rice.
Tony 的碗堆滿米飯。

12. **obsess** [əbˋses] v. 使著迷
▲ Edward is obsessed with video games. He spends
most of his free time playing them.
Edward 迷上電玩。他閒暇時花許多時間玩。

13. **outskirts** [ˈaʊtˌskɝts] n. [pl.] 郊區 (the ～)
    ▲ Mary lives on the outskirts of the city.
      Mary 住在郊區。

14. **persevere** [ˌpɝsəˈvɪr] v. 堅持 <with, in>
    ▲ Shelly persevered in her fight against sexual discrimination. Shelly 堅持反抗性別歧視。
    perseverance [ˌpɝsəˈvɪrəns] n. [U] 毅力，不屈不撓
    ▲ Perseverance allowed Jack to overcome many hardships. 毅力使 Jack 克服許多困境。
    persevering [ˌpɝsəˈvɪrɪŋ] adj. 不屈不撓的
    ▲ The persevering climber finally reached the top of the mountain. 不屈不撓的登山者終於抵達山頂。

15. **precision** [prɪˈsɪʒən] n. [U] 精確 [同] accuracy
    ▲ Mike chose his words with precision.
      Mike 精確地選擇措辭。

16. **purity** [ˈpjʊrəti] n. [U] 潔淨，純淨；純潔
    ▲ Many people worried about the purity of the water.
      許多人擔心水的純度。

17. **rejoice** [rɪˈdʒɔɪs] v. 高興，喜悅 <at, in, over>
    ▲ We rejoiced at the success of the experiment.
      我們很高興實驗成功。

18. **roam** [rom] v. 閒逛，漫步 <around>
    ▲ Jenny likes to roam around the store to look for discounted items.

Jenny 喜歡逛逛商店，看看有沒有打折商品。
roam [rom] n. [sing.] 漫遊

---

19. **shaver** [ˈʃevɚ] n. [C] 電動刮鬍刀
   ▲ Shavers are fast, safe, and convenient.
   電動刮鬍刀快速、安全又方便。

---

20. **socialist** [ˈsoʃəlɪst] n. [C] 社會主義者
   ▲ There are lots of radical socialists in the meeting room. 會議室裡有許多激進的社會主義者。
   socialist [ˈsoʃəlɪst] adj. 社會主義的
   ▲ Some of the workers come from a socialist country.
   那些工人當中有一些是來自於社會主義的國家。

---

21. **stepchild** [ˈstɛpˌtʃaɪld] n. [C] 繼子，繼女 (pl. stepchildren)
   ▲ Doris lived with her new husband and stepchildren in the country. Doris 跟新丈夫和繼子繼女們住在鄉間。

---

22. **superstitious** [ˌsupɚˈstɪʃəs] adj. 迷信的
   ▲ The islanders are superstitious about old taboos.
   這些島民對古老的禁忌非常迷信。

---

23. **token** [ˈtokən] n. [C] 象徵，代表；代幣
   ▲ Jason bought Lily a gift as a token of appreciation for her help.
   Jason 買了一個禮物給 Lily，表示感謝她的幫忙。

24. **unify** [`junə,faɪ] v. 統一 [反] divide
   ▲ The chairperson wants to unify the political party before the next election.
   主席想在下次選舉之前統一政黨。

25. **vocation** [vo`keʃən] n. [C][U] 職業，志業；使命
   ▲ It is especially important for graduates to find their true vocation.
   找到真正適合自己的職業對畢業生來說格外重要。

Unit 23

1. **disposal** [dɪ`spozl] n. [U] 處理 <of>
   ▲ The disposal of garbage is a problem.
   垃圾處理是一個問題。
   💡 at sb's disposal 供…使用，由…支配

2. **elevate** [`ɛlə,vet] v. 舉起，抬高，提高 [同] raise；提升，晉升 <to> [同] promote
   ▲ The crane elevated the bricks to a higher place.
   起重機舉起磚頭到更高的地方。

3. **extracurricular** [,ɛkstrəkə`rɪkjələ] adj. 課外的
   ▲ Students are encouraged to take part in extracurricular activities. 學生被鼓勵參加課外活動。

4. **forsake** [fə`sek] v. 遺棄 [同] abandon；放棄 [同] give up
   (forsook | forsaken | forsaking)

▲ The poor little girl was forsaken by her parents.
那名可憐的小女孩遭到父母遺棄。

5. **gorilla** [gəˋrɪlə] n. [C] 大猩猩
▲ The breeding season of gorillas has begun this year.
今年大猩猩的繁殖季已到。

6. **hoarse** [hɔrs] adj. (聲音) 沙啞的 (hoarser | hoarsest)
▲ Melissa's voice is hoarse because of a cold.
Melissa 因為感冒而聲音沙啞。

7. **infectious** [ɪnˋfɛkʃəs] adj. 傳染性的
▲ Those who catch infectious diseases should take sick leave. 患有傳染病的人應該要請病假。

8. **janitor** [ˋdʒænətɚ] n. [C] 管理員
▲ A janitor has responsibility for taking care of a building. 管理員有責任看管照料大廈。

9. **liner** [ˋlaɪnɚ] n. [C] 客輪，遊輪
▲ We took a cruise on a luxury liner.
我們搭豪華遊輪去玩。

10. **manuscript** [ˋmænjəˏskrɪpt] n. [C] 手稿，原稿
▲ Alan's manuscripts are currently exhibited in the museum. Alan 的手稿正在博物館展出。

11. **mourn** [mɔrn] v. 哀悼 <for> [同] grieve
▲ Sandra mourned for the death of a friend.
Sandra 哀悼死去的朋友。

mourning [ˋmornɪŋ] n. [U] 哀悼 [同] grief

▲ Everybody wore a black armband as a sign of mourning at the funeral.
喪禮中每個人都戴黑臂紗表示哀悼。

💡 in mourning 服喪

12. **obstinate** [ˋɑbstənɪt] adj. 固執的 [同] stubborn

▲ That man is narrow-minded and obstinate in his opinion. 那個男人心胸狹窄且固執己見。

obstinately [ˋɑbstənɪtlɪ] adv. 固執地

▲ Tony obstinately refused to accept my proposal.
Tony 固執地拒絕我的提議。

13. **overdo** [͵ovɚˋdu] v. 過度 (overdid | overdone | overdoing)

▲ Drinking is enjoyable as long as you don't overdo it.
喝酒很愉快，只要你不過度。

overdone [͵ovɚˋdʌn] adj. 烹煮過久的 [反] underdone

▲ The steak was overdone. It was tough.
牛排煎過頭，太老了。

14. **persistence** [pɚˋsɪstəns] n. [U] 堅持

▲ Their persistence forced the authorities to give in.
他們的堅持迫使當局退讓。

15. **predecessor** [ˋprɛdɪ͵sɛsɚ] n. [C] 前任 ; (機器等改良前的) 舊款，前一代，前身

▲ Will the new president reverse the policies of his predecessor? 新任總統會大改其前任的政策嗎？

---

16. **quake** [kwek] v. 發抖 <with> [同] tremble

▲ The little boy is quaking with fear.
這個小男孩害怕得發抖。

quake [kwek] n. [C] 地震 [同] earthquake

▲ The whole house shook when a quake happened this morning. 今天早上發生地震時，整間房子都在搖晃。

---

17. **relay** [ˋrile] n. [C] 接替的團隊

▲ The rescue teams worked in relays to search for the survivors. 救援隊輪班接力搜尋生還者。

💡 relay race 接力賽 | relay station 中繼站

relay [rɪˋle] v. 轉播

▲ The Olympic Games was relayed worldwide by satellite. 奧運會經由衛星轉播到世界各地。

---

18. **rotate** [ˋrotet] v. 旋轉 [同] revolve；輪流

▲ The Earth rotates on its axis. 地球繞著地軸旋轉。

---

19. **shortcoming** [ˋʃɔrt͵kʌmɪŋ] n. [C] 缺點 (usu. pl.) [同] defect

▲ Please point out my shortcomings so that I can improve myself.
請指出我的缺點，這樣我才能改善自己。

---

20. **socialize** [ˋsoʃə͵laɪz] v. 交際 <with>

▲Gloria doesn't like to go to parties because she dislikes socializing with strangers.

Gloria 不喜歡參加派對，因為她不喜歡跟陌生人交際。

21. **stepfather** [ˋstɛp͵fɑðɚ] n. [C] 繼父

▲Betty was upset when her mother married her stepfather. 當母親與繼父結婚時，Betty 相當沮喪。

22. **suppress** [səˋprɛs] v. 鎮壓 [同] quash；壓抑

▲The revolt was suppressed by the police.
暴動被警察鎮壓了。

23. **torrent** [ˋtɔrənt] n. [C] 急流；(言詞等的) 迸發，連發

▲A mountain torrent lay before us.
我們眼前有一條山谷的急流。

💡 in torrents (雨) 傾盆地 | a torrent of abuse/criticism 恣意地謾罵 / 批評

24. **unveil** [ʌnˋvel] v. (首次) 推出，發表 (新產品等)

▲The company will unveil an innovative product in the exhibition next week.
公司將在下週的展示會發表創新的產品。

25. **vocational** [voˋkeʃənl] adj. 職業的

▲The vocational school is an ideal choice for those who want to learn practical skills. 對那些想要學習實用技能的人而言，職業學校是理想的選擇。

💡 vocational training/education 職業訓練 / 教育

Unit 24

1. **dispose** [dɪ`spoz] v. 丟棄 <of>
   ▲ Nuclear waste must not be disposed of recklessly.
   核廢料絕對不能隨便丟棄。

2. **emigrant** [`ɛməɡrənt] n. [C] (移居他國的) 移民
   ▲ My father left his country as an emigrant at the age
   of ten. 我父親在十歲時，離開他的國家成為移民。

3. **eyelash** [`aɪ,læʃ] n. [C] 睫毛 (usu. pl.) (also lash)
   ▲ With the help of false eyelashes, Meg's eyes looked
   bigger than usual.
   有了假睫毛的幫忙，Meg 的眼睛看起來比平常大。
   ♥ flutter sb's eyelashes 拋媚眼

4. **forthcoming** [,fɔrθ`kʌmɪŋ] adj. 即將到來或出現的
   ▲ This is the catalog of the forthcoming books.
   這是近期將出版圖書的目錄。

5. **gospel** [`gɑspl̩] n. [U] 信條，信念；[sing.] 福音 (usu. the ~)
   ▲ The man took his wife's words as gospel.
   這男人把妻子的話奉為信條。

6. **homosexual** [,homə`sɛkʃʊəl] adj. 同性戀的
   ▲ There is a wide discussion about homosexual
   marriage. 對於同性戀的婚姻有廣泛的討論。
   homosexual [,homə`sɛkʃʊəl] n. [C] 同性戀者

▲ Some people have a strong prejudice against homosexuals. 有些人對同性戀者有強烈的偏見。

7. **inhabitant** [ɪn`hæbətənt] n. [C] 居民；棲息的動物
   ▲ Most of the inhabitants in this area are immigrants from South America.
   這地區大部分的居民是來自南美洲的移民。

8. **jasmine** [`dʒæsmɪn] n. [C][U] 茉莉花
   ▲ My mother enjoys jasmine tea very much.
   我母親非常喜歡茉莉花茶。

9. **lining** [`laɪnɪŋ] n. [C] 內襯
   ▲ Jenny bought this jacket because of its soft lining.
   Jenny 買這件夾克是因為它柔軟的內襯。

10. **maple** [`mepl] n. [C][U] 楓樹
    ▲ There are so many maple trees in the park.
    公園裡有許多楓樹。
    💡 maple syrup 楓糖漿

11. **mournful** [`mornfl] adj. 哀傷的 [同] melancholy
    ▲ The little girl looked at her mother with mournful eyes. 小女孩以哀傷的目光看著她的媽媽。
    mournfully [`mornfəlɪ] adv. 哀傷地
    ▲ Fiona spoke mournfully about her father in the hospital. Fiona 哀傷地說著在醫院的父親。

12. **occurrence** [ə`kɝəns] n. [C] 發生的事

▲ A total solar eclipse is a rare occurrence.
日全蝕是很少發生的事。

---

13. **overhear** [ˌovɚˋhɪr] v. 無意間聽到 (overheard | overheard | overhearing)

▲ I overheard my bosses talking about the financial crisis of our company.
我無意間聽到上司們在談論公司的財務危機。

---

14. **petrol** [ˋpɛtrəl] n. [U] 汽油 [同] gasoline

▲ We need to fill our car up with petrol before going on a road trip around Australia.
在澳洲汽車旅行之前，我們必須給車子裝滿汽油。

---

15. **prehistoric** [ˌprihɪsˋtɔrɪk] adj. 史前時代的

▲ The dinosaur is a giant prehistoric animal.
恐龍是史前時代的巨大動物。

prehistory [priˋhɪstrɪ] n. [U] 史前時代

▲ We can learn about the prehistory of Europe from this book. 我們可以從這本書中得知歐洲的史前時代。

---

16. **qualification** [ˌkwɑləfəˋkeʃən] n. [C][U] 資格，條件

▲ Technology skills and a high level of proficiency in English are necessary qualifications for this job. 運用科技的技能與高水平的英文是這份工作的必備條件。

---

17. **reliance** [rɪˋlaɪəns] n. [U] 依賴，信賴 <on>

▲ Leo placed too much reliance on his friends.

Leo 太信賴他的朋友。

18. **rotation** [ro`teʃən] n. [C][U] 旋轉；輪流

▲ It takes the Earth around 24 hours to complete one rotation on its axis.
地球繞地軸自轉一周大約是二十四小時。

19. **shortsighted** [`ʃɔrt`saɪtɪd] adj. 目光短淺的，缺乏遠見的；近視的 [同] nearsighted

▲ Some politicians are shortsighted and care about nothing but elections.
有些政客缺乏遠見而且只在乎選舉。

20. **sociology** [,soʃɪ`alədʒɪ] n. [U] 社會學

▲ Mary is a student in the department of sociology.
Mary 是社會學系的學生。

21. **stepmother** [`stɛp,mʌðɚ] n. [C] 繼母

▲ Rita became the stepmother of these two girls after she married their father. Rita 在與兩個女孩的父親結婚後，成為了這兩個女孩的繼母。

22. **surge** [sɝdʒ] n. [C] (數量) 急升，遽增 <in>；(人潮) 湧現 <of>

▲ There has been a sudden surge in demand for air conditioners. 冷氣機的需求量遽增。

💡 a surge of excitement/jealousy 一陣興奮 / 嫉妒

surge [sɝdʒ] v. 湧現

▲ Customers surged into the store during the sale.

特價期間，顧客湧入店內。

23. **trademark** [ˋtrɛd͵mɑrk] n. [C] 商標；特徵
▲ This is our registered trademark and cannot be used by any other company without permission. 這是我們的註冊商標，任何其他公司未經允許不得使用。

24. **uprising** [ˋʌp͵raɪzɪŋ] n. [C] 暴動，造反 [同] rebellion
▲ The government tried to put down the popular uprising in the capital.
政府試圖鎮壓首都的人民暴動。

25. **vowel** [ˋvauəl] n. [C] 母音
▲ A vowel is an essential component of a syllable.
母音是音節必要的組成部分。

Unit 25

1. **dissent** [dɪˋsɛnt] n. [U] 不同意，異議
▲ Hearing what the chairman said, Alan made a gesture of dissent. 聽到主席所言，Alan 做出不同意的手勢。

2. **emigrate** [ˋɛmə͵gret] v. 移居他國
▲ We haven't heard from Victor since he emigrated to the United States. 自從 Victor 移民美國後，我們就沒聽到過他的消息了。

3. **eyesight** [ˋaɪ͵saɪt] n. [U] 視力 [同] vision

▲Sandy has good eyesight. She can see objects clearly 20 feet away. Sandy 的視力良好。她可以清楚看見二十呎外的物體。

4. **fowl** [faʊl] n. [C][U] 家禽 (pl. fowl, fowls)
   ▲William raised lots of fowls such as chickens and ducks in his backyard.
   William 養很多家禽在他的後院，像是雞和鴨。

5. **grapefruit** [`grep‚frut] n. [C] 葡萄柚
   ▲Some people start their breakfast with half a grapefruit. 有些人早餐時會先吃半顆葡萄柚。

6. **honorary** [`ɑnə‚rɛrɪ] adj. 榮譽的
   ▲The university gave an honorary degree to Peter in recognition of his many accomplishments.
   這所大學頒授榮譽學位給 Peter，表彰他的許多成就。

7. **injustice** [ɪn`dʒʌstɪs] n. [C][U] 不公平 [反] justice
   ▲Describing him as a second-rate painter, that article did him a great injustice.
   那篇文章把他描述為二流畫家，對他很不公平。

8. **jockey** [`dʒɑkɪ] n. [C] (職業的) 賽馬騎師 (pl. jockeys)
   ▲David is a champion jockey this year.
   David 是今年的職業賽馬冠軍騎師。
   ♥ DJ = disc jockey (電臺音樂節目或舞會等的) 主持人
   jockey [`dʒɑkɪ] v. 運用手段謀取

▲ There were several politicians jockeying for power before the election. 有些政客在選舉前謀求權力。

9. **liter** [ˋlitɚ] n. [C] 公升 (abbr. l)

▲ I drink two liters of water every day.
我每天喝兩公升的水。

10. **mar** [mɑr] v. 弄糟，破壞 [同] spoil, ruin (marred | marred | marring)

▲ The trip was marred by bad weather and the poor service of the hotel.
壞天氣與旅館不好的服務破壞了遊興。

11. **mow** [mo] v. 割草 (mowed | mowed, mown | mowing)

▲ Peter mows the lawn for his neighbors as a part-time job on weekends. Peter 週末兼差幫鄰居修剪草坪。

12. **octopus** [ˋɑktəpəs] n. [C] 章魚 (pl. octopuses, octopi)

▲ An octopus has eight tentacles. 章魚有八隻腳。

13. **overlap** [ˋovɚˌlæp] n. [C][U] 重 疊 或 相 同 之 處 <between>

▲ There are some overlaps between these two dissertations. 這兩篇論文有些相同之處。

overlap [ˌovɚˋlæp] v. 重 疊 或 有 共 同 之 處 <with> (overlapped | overlapped | overlapping)

▲ My vacation doesn't overlap with my husband's so we cannot take a trip together. 我的假期和我先生的沒有重疊，所以我們不能一起去旅行。

overlapping [ˌovɚˈlæpɪŋ] adj. 重疊的或相同的
▲ Those two programs have overlapping functions.
那兩個程式的功能有重疊的地方。

14. **petroleum** [pəˈtrolɪəm] n. [U] 石油
▲ The country is known for producing petroleum.
該國以生產石油聞名。

15. **premiere** [prɪˈmɪr] n. [C] 首映 (會)
▲ All the main actors of the movie attended its world
premiere. 所有這部電影的主要演員都參加了電影的
世界首映會。

16. **radioactive** [ˌredɪoˈæktɪv] adj. 放射性的，有輻射的
▲ Laura is conducting a study of radioactive waste.
Laura 正在做放射性廢料的研究。

17. **reliant** [rɪˈlaɪənt] adj. 依靠的，依賴的 [同] dependent
▲ Sam is still reliant on his parents' support after
graduating from college.
Sam 大學畢業後仍然依靠父母的贊助。

18. **rubbish** [ˈrʌbɪʃ] n. [U] 垃圾；廢話
▲ Please clean out the rubbish in your room.
請清掃出你房裡的垃圾。

19. **shred** [ʃred] n. [C] 碎片 (usu. pl.) [同] scrap
▲ Shelly tore the letter to shreds after breaking up with
her boyfriend.

Shelly 與她的男友分手後，把信撕成碎片。

💡 in shreds 破碎的；嚴重受損的

shred [ʃrɛd] v. 弄碎，使支離破碎 (shredded | shredded | shredding)

▲ My mother shredded the cheese and sprinkled it over the pasta. 我母親把乳酪刨碎，撒在義大利麵上。

---

20. **solemn** [ˋsɑləm] adj. 莊嚴的 [同] serious

▲ All the attendees looked very solemn at the funeral. 參加葬禮的人看起來神情莊嚴肅穆。

💡 solemn promise 鄭重的承諾

---

21. **strait** [stret] n. [C] 海峽

▲ Taiwan is separated from mainland China by the Taiwan Strait. 臺灣和中國大陸由臺灣海峽隔開。

---

22. **surgical** [ˋsɝdʒɪkl̩] adj. 手術的，外科手術的

▲ The doctor explained the details of surgical procedures carefully.

醫師仔細地解釋手術流程的細節。

---

23. **transmit** [trænsˋmɪt] v. 傳送；傳播 (疾病等) (transmitted | transmitted | transmitting)

▲ The message will be transmitted through the computer system. 訊息將藉由電腦系統傳送。

---

24. **usher** [ˋʌʃɚ] v. 引導，接待 <in, into>

▲ Can you usher the guest in?

你可以帶領這位客人入內嗎？

usher [ˋʌʃɚ] n. [C] 帶位員

▲ The usher will show you to your seat.
帶位員會帶你去你的座位。

---

25. **wag** [wæg] v. 搖擺或搖動 (尾巴、手指等) (wagged | wagged | wagging)

▲ My dog will wag its tail and jump on me whenever it greets me home.
我的狗迎接我回家時都會搖尾巴並跳到我身上。

wag [wæg] n. [C] 搖擺，搖動 (usu. sing.)

▲ Rita only responded with a wag of her head.
Rita 只有搖頭回應。

Unit 26

1. **distraction** [dɪˋstrækʃən] n. [C][U] 令人分心或分散注意力的事物；[C] 娛樂，消遣

▲ I like to study in a quiet place free from distractions.
我喜歡在不會分散注意力的安靜場所念書。

💡 drive sb to distraction 使心煩意亂

---

2. **emigration** [ˏɛməˋgreʃən] n. [C][U] 移居他國 <from, to>

▲ The war caused mass emigration of Jews from Germany to the U.S.
戰爭導致大量猶太人從德國移民到美國。

---

3. **faction** [ˈfækʃən] n. [C] 派系

▲ The party leader resigned because of the pressure from different factions within the party.
這位政黨領導人因為黨內不同派系的壓力而辭職。

4. **fracture** [ˈfræktʃɚ] n. [C] 骨折

▲ The rider suffered a skull fracture in the motorcycle accident. 那場摩托車意外事故造成騎士頭骨骨折。

fracture [ˈfræktʃɚ] v. (使) 骨折 ; (使)(團體) 分裂 [同] split

▲ My friend fractured both his legs in the car accident.
我朋友在車禍中雙腿骨折。

5. **groan** [gron] n. [C] (因疼痛、不悅等的) 呻吟聲 [同] moan

▲ The wounded soldier let out a groan.
那名傷兵發出一聲呻吟。

groan [gron] v. (因疼痛、不悅等而) 呻吟 [同] moan ; 發出嘎吱聲 [同] moan

▲ All the students groaned when their teacher assigned them more homework.
老師出了更多功課時，學生們全都叫苦連天。

🍀 moan and groan 抱怨連連

6. **hospitality** [ˌhɑspɪˈtælətɪ] n. [U] 殷勤待客

▲ Taiwan is known for its beautiful scenery and hospitality. 臺灣以風景優美和熱情待客聞名。

7. **inland** [ˋɪnlənd] adj. 內陸的

   ▲ There are some large or famous areas of inland water in the world, such as the Caspian Sea and the Dead Sea.

   世界上有些廣大或知名的內陸水域，例如裏海和死海。

   inland [ˋɪnˏlænd] adv. 向內陸，在內陸

   ▲ The aborigines live further inland.

   這些原住民住在更內陸的地區。

   inland [ˋɪnˏlænd] n. [U] 內陸 (the ～)

   ▲ We are going to move from the coast to the inland.

   我們將要從海岸地區搬家到內陸。

8. **jolly** [ˋdʒɑlɪ] adj. (令人) 愉快的 (jollier | jolliest)

   ▲ The winter vacation is coming, and we are looking forward to a jolly trip.

   寒假快到了，我們期待一趟愉快的旅遊。

   jolly [ˋdʒɑlɪ] adv. 很，非常

   ▲ We have been jolly busy recently. 我們最近很忙。

   jolly [ˋdʒɑlɪ] v. 好言好語地勸說或鼓勵

   ▲ The kindergarten teacher tried to jolly the kids into napping. 幼兒園老師試著哄孩子們睡午覺。

   jolly [ˋdʒɑlɪ] n. [C] 玩樂，歡樂 (pl. jollies)

   ▲ John went out to Thailand on a jolly

   John 跑去泰國玩樂。

   🌢 get sb's jollies (常指從不好的事物中) 得到樂趣

9. **literate** [ˈlɪtərɪt] adj. 有讀寫能力的 [反] illiterate ；精通的，很懂的

▲ Growing up in a slum, the man is barely literate and has trouble writing his name. 那名男子在貧民窟長大，他幾乎不識字，連名字都不太會寫。

💡 be politically/musically literate 很懂政治的 / 很會演奏樂器的

literate [ˈlɪtərɪt] n. [C] 識字的人

▲ There are only ten literates in this village. 這座村莊裡只有十位識字的人。

10. **mastery** [ˈmæstərɪ] n. [U] 精通，熟練 <of>；控制 <of, over>

▲ Students work hard to achieve mastery of English. 學生們為了精通英文而努力用功。

11. **muse** [mjuz] n. [C] 給與靈感的人或事物，靈感的來源 [同] inspiration

▲ My girlfriend is my muse. 我的女朋友是我靈感的來源。

12. **offshore** [ˌɔfˈʃor] adj. 離岸的，海上的；近海的

▲ Do you know how many people working on these offshore oil rigs? 你知道有多少人在這些海上鑽油塔工作嗎？

💡 offshore oil field 海上油田 | offshore/onshore oil reserves 海上 / 陸上石油儲備

13. **overwork** [`ovɚ,wɝk] n. [U] 工作過度

   ▲ We have been exhausted from overwork these days.
   我們這陣子因為工作過度而筋疲力竭。

   overwork [,ovɚ`wɝk] v. (使) 過度工作

   ▲ If you continue to overwork, you're going to fall ill from overwork.
   你如果再這樣過度工作會積勞成疾的。

---

14. **pharmacist** [`fɑrməsɪst] n. [C] 藥劑師

   ▲ The pharmacist soon made up my prescription.
   藥劑師很快就幫我配好藥了。

---

15. **preside** [prɪ`zaɪd] v. 主持，擔任主席 <at, over>

   ▲ Mr. Smith often presides at the company's meetings.
   Smith 先生經常擔任公司會議的主席。

---

16. **radish** [`rædɪʃ] n. [C] 櫻桃蘿蔔

   ▲ I tossed together lettuces, onions, and radishes to make salad.
   我把萵苣、洋蔥和櫻桃蘿蔔拌在一起做成沙拉。

---

17. **relic** [`rɛlɪk] n. [C] 遺跡，遺物；遺風，遺俗

   ▲ The pieces of pottery were relics from prehistoric times. 這些陶器碎片是史前時代的遺物。

---

18. **rugged** [`rʌgɪd] adj. 崎嶇的，起伏不平的；(長相) 粗獷而好看的

   ▲ The trail through the forest is rugged.
   穿越森林的小徑崎嶇不平。

💡 rugged ground 凹凸不平的地面 | rugged features 粗
   獷的容貌

ruggedly [ˈrʌgɪdlɪ] adv. 崎嶇不平地；粗獷地
▲ The hill rises ruggedly ahead of the hikers.
   丘陵在健行者面前越來越陡且崎嶇不平。

---

19. **shriek** [ʃrik] n. [C] 尖叫聲 <of> [同] scream；尖銳刺耳
    的聲音
    ▲ Hearing the good news, Tom hugged Mary with a
       shriek of delight.
       Tom 聽到好消息就興奮尖叫地抱住了 Mary。
    shriek [ʃrik] v. 尖叫 [同] scream；尖叫著說 [同] scream
    ▲ The witch shrieked with laughter. 巫婆尖聲大笑。
    💡 shriek abuse at sb 對…尖聲叫罵

---

20. **solitude** [ˈsɑləˌtjud] n. [U] 獨處
    ▲ I enjoy spending the morning in solitude.
       我喜歡早上獨處。

---

21. **stray** [stre] adj. 走失的，流浪的；偏離的
    ▲ There is a stray dog lying on the sidewalk.
       人行道上躺著一隻流浪狗。
    stray [stre] v. 迷路，走失；偏離
    ▲ The children strayed into the woods.
       那些孩子們迷路走進了森林。
    stray [stre] n. [C] 流浪的動物
    ▲ When the couple found that the cat was a stray, they
       decided to adopt it.

那對情侶發現那是一隻流浪貓而決定領養牠。

---

22. **surpass** [sɚˋpæs] v. 勝過，超過

▲ The new product helped us to surpass our competitors. 這款新產品幫助我們勝過競爭者。

💡 surpass sb's expectations 超過…的預期 | surpass sb's understanding 超過…的理解範圍

---

23. **transplant** [ˋtræns͵plænt] n. [C][U] 移植

▲ The patient had a heart transplant yesterday.
那名病人昨天接受了心臟移植。

💡 kidney/liver/corneal/bone marrow transplant 腎臟 / 肝臟 / 角膜 / 骨髓移植

transplant [trænsˋplænt] v. 移植

▲ I transplanted the flowers from the pots to the garden. 我把花從盆裡移植到庭園中。

---

24. **utensil** [juˋtɛnsl] n. [C] (廚房等家庭) 用具

▲ The couple bought some kitchen utensils, including knives, spoons, spatulas, and whisks. 那對夫妻買了一些廚房用具，包括刀子、湯匙、鏟子和打蛋器。

---

25. **walnut** [ˋwɔlnʌt] n. [C] 胡桃，核桃

▲ The lady added some chopped walnuts in her salad.
那位女士加了一些弄碎的核桃在她的沙拉裡。

Unit 27

1. **divert** [dəˋvɝt] v. 使轉向，使改道 <from>；轉移 (注意力等) <from>
   ▲ The river has been diverted away from the city.
   河流被改道而遠離城市。

2. **endowment** [ɪnˋdaʊmənt] n. [C][U] 資助，捐款，捐贈
   ▲ The hospital received a generous 10 million endowment last year. 醫院去年收到一筆一千萬元的巨額捐款。

3. **Fahrenheit** [ˋfærən͵haɪt] n. [U] 華氏 (溫標)，華氏溫度
   ▲ Please give me the temperature in Fahrenheit.
   請告訴我華氏溫度。
   Fahrenheit [ˋfærən͵haɪt] adj. 華氏的
   ▲ Water freezes at 32° Fahrenheit.
   水在華氏 32 度時會結冰。

4. **fragrant** [ˋfregrənt] adj. 芳香的
   ▲ This island is known for its beautiful scenery and fragrant tea.
   這座島嶼以其美麗的風景和芳香的茶葉聞名於世。

5. **growl** [graʊl] n. [C] 低吼聲，咆哮聲
   ▲ The cat arched its back and exposed its teeth in a threatening growl.
   那隻貓弓背齜牙發出威脅性的低吼聲。
   growl [graʊl] v. 低吼，咆哮 <at>

▲ My neighbor's dog growls at every passing rider.
我鄰居的狗對每位經過的騎士低吼咆哮。

6. **hospitalize** [`hɑspɪtə,laɪz] v. 送醫治療，使住院治療
▲ My neighbor was hospitalized for appendicitis.
我鄰居因盲腸炎被送醫住院治療。

7. **innumerable** [ɪ`njumərəbl] adj. 無數的，數不清的，很多的
▲ The brave girl's story has inspired innumerable people. 那個勇敢女孩的故事激勵了無數人。

8. **junction** [`dʒʌŋkʃən] n. [C] (公路、鐵路、河流等的) 交會點，交叉口 [同] intersection
▲ Formosa Boulevard is one of the biggest metro junctions in Kaohsiung.
美麗島站是高雄最大的捷運交會點之一。

9. **livestock** [`laɪv,stɑk] n. [pl.] 家畜，牲畜
▲ The farmer used to keep livestock on his farm.
那名農夫以前有在他的農場飼養牲畜。

10. **mediate** [`midɪ,et] v. 調停，調解 <between>；藉調解找到解決辦法，達成或促成 (協議等) [同] negotiate
▲ The government tried to mediate between labor and management. 政府試著為勞資雙方調解。
mediation [,midɪ`eʃən] n. [U] 調停，調解
▲ The two conflicting sides finally reached an agreement through the mediation of a third party.

透過第三方的調停，這決裂的兩方終於達成協議。

mediator [`midɪˌetɚ] n. [C] 調停者，調解者

▲ The government is expected to act as a neutral mediator in labor disputes.

政府在勞資糾紛中應該要做中立的調解者。

11. **mustache** [`mʌstæʃ] n. [C] (長在上唇上方的) 鬍子，八字鬍

▲ The general has a mustache, looking very tough.

那名將軍留著八字鬍，看起來很堅韌。

12. **operative** [`ɑpərətɪv] adj. 運作中的，有效的 [同] functional [反] inoperative

▲ When will the agreement become operative?

那份協議什麼時候開始生效？

💡 be fully operative again 全面恢復運作

13. **ozone** [`ozon] n. [U] 臭氧

▲ Ozone protects us from harmful ultraviolet radiation.

臭氧保護我們不受紫外線傷害。

💡 ozone layer 臭氧層

14. **pickpocket** [`pɪkˌpɑkɪt] n. [C] 扒手

▲ I saw a sign of "Beware of Pickpockets" in the crowded market.

我在擁擠的市場中看見「小心扒手」的告示。

15. **prestige** [prɛs`tiʒ] n. [U] 聲望，名聲

▲ The piracy of computer software has damaged the nation's prestige.

盜版電腦軟體已損害了國家的聲望。

prestigious [prɛs`tɪdʒəs] adj. 有聲望的，有名望的

▲ Most senior high school students hope to enter prestigious colleges.

大部分的高中生希望進入有名的大學。

---

16. **rash** [ræʃ] n. [C] 疹子 (usu. sing.)；[sing.] (壞事等的) 接連發生 [同] spate

▲ I break out in a rash if I eat seafood.

我若吃海鮮會起疹子。

💡 diaper/nettle/heat rash 尿布疹 / 蕁麻疹 / 痱子

rash [ræʃ] adj. 輕率的，草率的，魯莽的 [同] reckless

▲ It was too rash of Liz to marry someone she had known for only three days.

Liz 和一個只認識三天的人結婚太草率了。

rashly [`ræʃlɪ] adv. 輕率地，草率地，魯莽地

▲ Don't act rashly. 不要魯莽行事。

rashness [`ræʃnəs] n. [U] 輕率，草率，魯莽

▲ I bitterly regret my rashness.

我非常後悔我的輕率魯莽。

---

17. **reminiscent** [ˌrɛmə`nɪsənt] adj. 令人想起…的 <of>

▲ Old songs can be strongly reminiscent of old days.

老歌很容易令人想起往日時光。

---

18. **ruthless** [`ruθlɪs] adj. 冷酷無情的，殘忍的

▲ The ruthless dictator was finally overthrown.
那個殘忍的獨裁者最終被推翻了。

19. **shrub** [ʃrʌb] n. [C] 灌木
▲ The couple planted evergreen shrubs as well as flowering shrubs in the garden.
那對夫妻在花園裡種了常綠灌木和會開花的灌木。

20. **sovereign** [ˋsɑvrɪn] adj. 有主權的，獨立自主的；至高無上的
▲ Sovereign states enjoy autonomy; they are independent and govern themselves.
主權國家享有自治權，他們獨立自主。

sovereign [ˋsɑvrɪn] n. [C] 君主，元首
▲ Do you know who the first European sovereign to visit this country is?
你知道第一位到訪這個國家的歐洲元首是誰嗎？

21. **stroll** [strol] n. [C] 閒逛，散步
▲ I went for a leisurely stroll in the woods.
我在森林裡悠閒地散步。

stroll [strol] v. 閒逛，散步
▲ My mom and I used to stroll down the riverbank after dinner. 母親和我以前晚餐後都會沿著河岸散步。

22. **suspense** [səˋspɛns] n. [U] 懸疑
▲ The movie kept me in suspense till the end.
這部電影從頭到尾都讓我提心吊膽。

23. **treasury** [ˈtrɛʒərɪ] **n.** [C] 國庫；寶庫

▲ Officials should not steal from the nation's treasury.
官員不應染指國庫。

♥ the Treasury 財政部

---

24. **utter** [ˈʌtɚ] **adj.** 全然的，完全的，極度的

▲ Jason stared at me in utter astonishment.
Jason 極為驚訝地瞪著我。

utter [ˈʌtɚ] **v.** 說；發出聲音

▲ No matter how tired my boyfriend was, he never uttered a word of complaint.
我男友不管多累都沒說過一句抱怨的話。

---

25. **ward** [wɔrd] **n.** [C] 病房；受監護人

▲ There are just a few patients in the emergency wards today. 今天急診病房只有一些病患。

♥ surgical/maternity/isolation ward 外科 / 婦產科 / 隔離病房

ward [wɔrd] **v.** 抵禦，避開 <off>

▲ Infants receive vaccine to ward off some diseases.
嬰兒注射疫苗來抵禦一些疾病。

Unit 28

1. **dividend** [ˈdɪvəˌdɛnd] **n.** [C] 股息，股利

▲ Shareholders can receive dividends from the company once or twice a year.

股東每年可獲該公司配發一次或兩次股利。

---

2. **endurance** [ɪn`djʊrəns] n. [U] 耐力

▲ It requires great endurance to run a marathon.

跑馬拉松需要有極大的耐力。

🌶 beyond endurance 難以忍受，忍無可忍

---

3. **falter** [`fɔltɚ] v. 躊躇，猶豫，動搖；說話結結巴巴，支支吾吾

▲ My faith in my brother never faltered.

我對弟弟的信心從未動搖。

---

4. **freak** [frik] n. [C] 怪人，怪物 [同] weirdo；狂熱的愛好者，…狂，…迷

▲ Wearing that strange heavy makeup, the actor looked like a freak.

那位演員頂著那奇怪的大濃妝，看起來像個怪人。

🌶 fitness/computer/movie freak 健身狂 / 電腦迷 / 電影迷

freak [frik] v. (使) 震驚，(使) 大驚失色，(使) 非常激動 <out>

▲ The horror movie freaked me out.

這部恐怖電影嚇死我了。

freak [frik] adj. 異常的，怪異的，詭異的

▲ A freak storm destroyed half of the buildings in the village.

一場詭異的風暴摧毀了那座村莊一半的建築物。

💡 freak weather conditions 異常的天氣狀況

5. **grumble** [ˋɡrʌmbl̩] **v.** 抱怨 <about, at> [同] moan
   ▲ The students grumbled about having too many exams. 學生們抱怨考試太多。

   grumble [ˋɡrʌmbl̩] **n.** [C] 抱怨 (聲)
   ▲ The teacher ignored students' grumbles about extra homework and exams.
   老師不理會學生對於額外功課和考試的抱怨。

6. **hostel** [ˋhɑstl̩] **n.** [C] (廉價) 旅社
   ▲ To save money, Albert stayed at youth hostels while traveling. 為了省錢，Albert 旅行時都住在青年旅館。

7. **insistence** [ɪnˋsɪstəns] **n.** [U] 堅持 <on>
   ▲ We were surprised by the teacher's insistence on perfection. 那位老師對完美的堅持令我們感到驚訝。
   💡 at sb's insistence 由於⋯的堅持

   insistent [ɪnˋsɪstənt] **adj.** 堅持的 <on>
   ▲ The accused was insistent on his innocence.
   被告堅稱自己無罪。

8. **kin** [kɪn] **n.** [pl.] 親戚，親屬
   ▲ The missing child's kin are all looking for him.
   失蹤孩童的親屬都在找他。
   💡 next of kin (直系血親等) 最近的親屬 | distant/close kin 遠親 / 近親 | be no kin to sb 和⋯不是親屬

   kin [kɪn] **adj.** 有血緣關係的

▲ Susan is kin to the royal family.
Susan 和皇室有血緣關係。

9. **locker** [ˈlɑkɚ] n. [C] (可上鎖的) 儲物櫃，置物櫃
▲ I usually keep my books in my locker at school.
我通常把書放在學校的置物櫃裡。

10. **meditate** [ˈmɛdəˌtet] v. 沉思 <on, upon>
▲ The writer meditated on the theme of his next novel.
作家沉思他下一本小說的主題。

11. **mute** [mjut] adj. 沉默的 [同] silent；啞的 [同] dumb
(muter | mutest)
▲ The accused remained mute about the charges
against him. 被告對於指控保持沉默。
mute [mjut] v. 減弱，減低 (聲音)
▲ Heavy curtains and thick carpets help to mute noises.
厚重的窗簾和地毯有助於減低噪音。
mute [mjut] n. [C] 弱音器；啞巴 (pl. mutes)
▲ The musician played her trumpet with a mute.
那位音樂家演奏裝有弱音器的小喇叭。
💡 mute button (遙控器、電話等的) 靜音鍵

12. **oppress** [əˈprɛs] v. 壓迫；使鬱悶，使心情沉重
▲ The aboriginal people have been oppressed by the
tyrant for years. 這些原住民多年來都受到暴君壓迫。
oppressive [əˈprɛsɪv] adj. 壓迫的，殘暴的；令人鬱悶
的，令人難受的；悶熱的

▲ People are fleeing from the oppressive regime.
人民逃離那個殘暴的政權。

---

13. **packet** [ˋpækɪt] n. [C] 小包，小袋
　▲ Alice poured a packet of sugar into her coffee.
　　Alice 在她的咖啡裡倒了一小包糖。
　🔑 a packet of ketchup/mustard/seeds 一小包番茄醬 / 芥末醬 / 種子

---

14. **pilgrim** [ˋpɪlgrɪm] n. [C] 朝聖者，香客
　▲ Some pilgrims make a long journey to Mecca every year. 有些朝聖者每年長途跋涉去麥加。

---

15. **privatize** [ˋpraɪvə͵taɪz] v. 使 (國營企業等) 民營化 ，使私有化
　▲ Do you agree that the government should privatize education? 你贊成政府應讓教育民營化嗎？

---

16. **ratify** [ˋrɛtə͵faɪ] v. 批准，使正式生效
　▲ The Senate refused to ratify the agreement.
　　參議院拒絕批准那項協議。

---

17. **reptile** [ˋrɛptaɪl] n. [C] 爬蟲類動物；卑鄙的人
　▲ Reptiles, such as snakes and lizards, are cold-blooded animals that lay eggs.
　　蛇、蜥蜴等爬蟲類是會產卵的冷血動物。
　reptile [ˋrɛptaɪl] adj. 爬蟲類的
　▲ The zookeeper found some reptile eggs.

動物園管理員發現一些爬蟲類的卵。

---

18. **salute** [sə`lut] n. [C][U] 敬禮

▲ The general gave the president a salute.

將軍向總統敬禮。

💡 take/return a salute 接受敬禮 / 回禮 | 21-gun salute
二十一響禮炮 | in salute 致敬

salute [sə`lut] v. 敬禮

▲ The soldier always stands to attention and salutes any
officers he meets. 那名士兵遇見軍官都會立正敬禮。

---

19. **shuffle** [`ʃʌfl̩] v. 拖著腳走路；(因厭煩、不安等) 把腳動
來動去，坐立不安

▲ I was so tired that I just shuffled along.

我累到拖著腳走路。

💡 shuffle the cards/deck 洗牌

---

20. **spectacle** [`spɛktəkl̩] n. [C] 奇觀；壯觀

▲ It's a spectacle to see the cat taking care of the
new-born puppies.

看到這隻貓照顧新生的小狗，真是個奇景。

💡 make a spectacle of oneself 使自己出醜

spectacles [`spɛktəklz] n. [pl.] 眼鏡

▲ When did the first pair of spectacles appear?

什麼時候出現了第一副眼鏡？

💡 a pair of spectacles 一副眼鏡

---

21. **stun** [stʌn] **v.** 使不省人事，使昏厥；使震驚，使大吃一驚 <at, by> (stunned | stunned | stunning)

▲ The robber stunned the victim with a blow to the head. 搶匪打受害者的頭，把他打昏了。

stunning [`stʌnɪŋ] **adj.** 驚人的，令人震驚的；非常出色的，令人印象深刻的

▲ Well, well, what stunning news!
哇哦，真是驚人的消息！

---

22. **swamp** [swɑmp] **n.** [C][U] 沼澤，溼地

▲ Alligators usually live in swamps.
短吻鱷通常棲息在沼澤。

swamp [swɑmp] **v.** 使不堪負荷 <by, with>；淹沒 <by>

▲ I was swamped with homework.
我被回家作業給淹沒了。

---

23. **trifle** [`traɪfl] **n.** [C] 瑣事，小事

▲ The couple often quarreled over trifles.
那對夫妻常為一些瑣事爭吵。

trifle [`traɪfl] **v.** 玩弄 <with>；虛度 (光陰)，浪費 (時間)

▲ Don't trifle with anyone's affections.
不要玩弄任何人的感情。

---

24. **vaccine** [vҽk`sin] **n.** [C][U] 疫苗

▲ Is there any vaccine against this virus?
有防治這種病毒的疫苗嗎？

---

25. **warrant** [`wɔrənt] n. [C] (逮捕令、搜索令等) 執行令，
授權令，令狀

▲ The court issued warrants for several suspects' arrest.
法院發出了幾名嫌犯的逮捕令。

💡 arrest/search warrant 逮捕令 / 搜索令

Unit 29

1. **doom** [dum] n. [U] 厄運，劫數

▲ A sense of impending doom hung over the small
island as the hurricane approached.
隨著颶風逐步逼近，一種厄運將臨的感覺籠罩著小島。

💡 doom and gloom 絕望 | meet sb's doom 喪生 | spell
doom for sth 意味著…的滅亡，使滅亡或終結

doom [dum] v. 注定 (失敗等) <to>

▲ Those schemes were doomed to failure.
那些計畫注定要失敗。

2. **enhance** [ɪn`hæns] v. 提升 (品質等)

▲ The company sponsored the music festival to
enhance its image.
這家公司贊助了音樂節以提升形象。

enhancement [ɪn`hænsmənt] n. [C][U] (品質等的) 提
升

▲ The enhancement of the security checks at the airport
will help to prevent terrorist acts.

機場安檢的提升將有助於防止恐怖行動。

---

3. **familiarity** [fəˌmɪlɪˋærətɪ] n. [U] 熟悉 <with>；親切
   ▲ Familiarity with English helped us enjoy our trip to London. 熟悉英語幫助我們享受倫敦之旅。

4. **freeway** [ˋfriˌwe] n. [C] 高速公路
   ▲ Driving on the freeway for the first time can be exciting or frightening for a new driver. 第一次開車上高速公路對新手駕駛來說可能會是刺激或可怕的。

5. **hamper** [ˋhæmpɚ] v. 妨礙，阻礙 [同] hinder
   ▲ Bad weather severely hampered rescue efforts.
   惡劣的天氣嚴重阻礙了救援工作。

6. **hover** [ˋhʌvɚ] v. 盤旋
   ▲ An eagle hovered over the tent.
   一隻老鷹在帳篷上方盤旋。
   hover [ˋhʌvɚ] n. [sing.] 盤旋

7. **instinctive** [ɪnˋstɪŋktɪv] adj. 本能的，直覺的，天生的
   ▲ Animals have an instinctive fear of fire.
   動物天性怕火。
   💡 instinctive reaction 本能反應，直覺反應

8. **knowledgeable** [ˋnɑlɪdʒəbl̩] adj. 知識豐富的 <about>
   ▲ The scholar is knowledgeable about marine life.
   這位學者對海洋生物知識豐富。

9. **lodge** [lɑdʒ] n. [C] 小屋

▲ During the storm, the hikers took refuge in a hunting lodge in the mountains.

在暴風雨期間，那些登山者躲在山中的狩獵小屋裡。

lodge [lɑdʒ] v. 卡住 <in> [反] dislodge；正式提出 (申訴等)

▲ A fish bone lodged in my throat.

一根魚刺卡在我的喉嚨裡。

💡 lodge a protest/claim 提出抗議 / 索賠 | lodge an appeal 提出上訴

lodging [`lɑdʒɪŋ] n. [U] 寄宿 (處)；[C] 出租的房間 (usu. pl.)

▲ Does the price include board and lodging?

這價格有包括食宿費用嗎？

💡 full board and lodging 食宿全包

---

10. **meditation** [ˌmɛdə`teʃən] n. [C][U] 沉思，冥想

▲ The noise interrupted my morning meditations.

噪音打斷了我早晨的冥想。

💡 deep/lost in meditation 陷入沉思

---

11. **nag** [næg] v. 嘮叨，碎碎念 <at> (nagged | nagged | nagging)

▲ Some parents are always nagging their children to clean their rooms.

有些家長總是嘮嘮叨叨地要孩子整理房間。

💡 nag at sb 對⋯嘮叨 | nag sb about sth 嘮叨⋯的⋯

nag [næg] n. [C] 嘮叨的人

▲ An awful nag can drive me crazy.
太嘮叨的人會令我抓狂。

nagging [`nægɪŋ] adj. (問題、病痛等) 煩擾不休的；嘮叨的，喋喋不休的

▲ How can I ease this nagging headache?
我要怎樣才能減緩一直煩擾我的頭痛？

💡 nagging pain/toothache/doubt 煩擾不休的疼痛 / 牙痛 / 疑慮

12. **oppression** [ə`prɛʃən] n. [U] 壓迫

▲ The revolution freed the people from political oppression. 那次革命將人民從政治壓迫中解放出來。

13. **paddle** [`pædl] n. [C] 槳

▲ We found only one paddle inside the canoe.
我們在獨木舟裡只發現了一支槳。

paddle [`pædl] v. 用槳划船

▲ I paddled hard, trying to get the canoe to shore as fast as possible. 我努力用槳划獨木舟，想盡快到達岸邊。

14. **pinch** [pɪntʃ] n. [C] 一小撮，少量 <of>；捏，掐，擰，夾

▲ I put a pinch of salt in the soup and stirred it.
我在湯裡放了一撮鹽攪一攪。

💡 take sth with a pinch of salt 對⋯持保留態度，存疑，半信半疑 | feel the pinch 手頭拮据，手頭緊

pinch [pɪntʃ] v. 捏，掐，擰，夾

▲ I had to pinch myself to make sure that I was not dreaming.

我捏自己一下好確定自己不是在做夢。

15. **prohibition** [ˌproəˈbɪʃən] n. [C] 禁令 <against, on>；
[U] 禁止 <of>

▲ There is a prohibition on the import of weapons.
有針對武器進口的禁令。

16. **reap** [rip] v. 收割 (農作物)；獲得 (報酬等)

▲ The old farmer needs some workers to help him reap
the crops. 那位老農需要一些工人幫他收割作物。

🔮 reap the benefits/rewards of sth 因⋯獲益

17. **resent** [rɪˈzɛnt] v. 憤恨，憎恨，怨恨

▲ The lady resented her husband's ignorance.
那位女士怨恨丈夫的無知。

resentment [rɪˈzɛntmənt] n. [U] 憤恨，憎恨，怨恨

▲ I bear no resentment against you. 我對你毫無怨恨。

18. **salvage** [ˈsælvɪdʒ] v. 搶救 (財物等) <from>

▲ Divers are trying to salvage some cargo from the
sunken ship. 潛水員正試著從沉船中搶救一些貨物。

19. **shutter** [ˈʃʌtɚ] n. [C] (常設有百葉孔的) 護窗板，窗戶的
活動遮板 (usu. pl.)；(照相機的) 快門

▲ Shutters, usually in pairs on the outside of a window,
are wooden or metal covers that can be opened or
closed like a door. 護窗板通常兩片一組裝在窗外，是
木頭或金屬材質、可以像門一樣開關的遮板。

shutter [ˈʃʌtɚ] v. 關上護窗板

▲ During the riot, people barred their doors and shuttered their windows.

在暴動期間，人們把門閂上並把護窗板關上。

---

20. **splendor** [ˈsplɛndɚ] n. [U] 壯麗，輝煌，富麗堂皇

▲ Architects are working hard to restore the decaying palace to as much as possible of its original splendor.

建築師努力整修老舊的宮殿，盡量使它恢復以前的富麗堂皇。

---

21. **stutter** [ˈstʌtɚ] n. [sing.] 結巴，口吃 [同] stammer

▲ The king had a stutter when he was young.

國王年輕時有口吃。

stutter [ˈstʌtɚ] v. 結結巴巴地說 [同] stammer

▲ The nervous student stuttered a reply.

那名緊張的學生結結巴巴地回答。

---

22. **symmetry** [ˈsɪmɪtrɪ] n. [U] 對稱 [反] asymmetry

▲ The perfect symmetry of the leaf is amazing.

這葉子完美的對稱令人驚異。

symmetrical [sɪˈmɛtrɪkl] adj. 對稱的 (also symmetric) [反] asymmetrical

▲ I like patterns that are symmetrical.

我喜歡對稱的圖案。

---

23. **tropic** [ˈtrɑpɪk] n. [C] 回歸線；熱帶 (地區) (usu. pl.)

▲ Taiwan is crossed by the Tropic of Cancer.

臺灣有北回歸線經過。

💡 the Tropic of Capricorn 南回歸線

tropic [ˋtrɑpɪk] adj. 熱帶 (地區) 的 [同] tropical

▲ Have you ever been to tropic rainforests?
你有去過熱帶雨林嗎？

---

24. **vanity** [ˋvænətɪ] n. [U] 虛榮 (心)

▲ The girl bought the diamond necklace for reasons of
vanity. 那個女孩因為虛榮心而買下鑽石項鍊。

---

25. **warranty** [ˋwɔrəntɪ] n. [C] (商品的) 保證書，保固單
(pl. warranties)

▲ This warranty covers the laptop for a year.
這份保證書承諾這臺筆電保固一年。

💡 come with a <u>one-year/three-year</u> warranty 保固<u>一年</u> /
<u>三年</u> | under warranty 在保固期內

Unit 30

1. **dormitory** [ˋdɔrmə,torɪ] n. [C] 學生宿舍 (also dorm)
(pl. dormitories)

▲ Students live in the school's dormitory.
學生們住在學校的宿舍裡。

---

2. **enlighten** [ɪnˋlaɪtn̩] v. 啟發

▲ The essence of education is not only to teach but also
to enlighten students.
教育的本質不僅是教學，也在於啟發學生。

enlightenment [ɪn`laɪtṇmənt] n. [U] 啟發
▲ Good stories provide enlightenment.
好的故事能提供啟發。

3. **feasible** [`fizəbl̩] adj. 可實行的，行得通的，可行的
▲ Your plan may work in a small company, but it is not feasible in a large corporation like this. 你的計畫在小公司也許是可行的，但在像這樣的大企業卻行不通。

4. **friction** [`frɪkʃən] n. [U] (物體的) 摩擦；[C][U] (人際的) 摩擦，不和 <between> [同] tension
▲ Tires wear down because of friction between the tires and the road. 輪胎因和路面摩擦而磨損。
💡 cause/create friction 導致衝突

5. **handicap** [`hændɪ͵kæp] n. [C] 身心障礙 [同] disability；阻礙，障礙 [同] obstacle
▲ The social workers treat people with physical or mental handicaps well.
這些社工們善待身心障礙人士。

handicap [`hændɪ͵kæp] v. 阻礙，妨礙，使處於不利狀況 (handicapped | handicapped | handicapping)
▲ I don't want to be handicapped by poor English.
我不想因為英文不夠好而處於不利狀況。

6. **humiliate** [hju`mɪlɪ͵et] v. 使蒙羞，使丟臉，羞辱
▲ The criminal's actions humiliated his family.
那個罪犯的行為使他的家庭蒙羞。

humiliated [hju`mɪlɪ͵etɪd] adj. 丟臉的，難堪的，屈辱的
▲ Tom said that he had never felt so humiliated in his life. Tom 說他這輩子從沒覺得那麼丟臉過。

humiliation [hju͵mɪlɪ`eʃən] n. [C][U] 丟臉，難堪，屈辱
▲ Most people can't take the humiliation of being criticized in public.
大多數人無法接受被公開批評的屈辱。

---

7. **intake** [`ɪn͵tek] n. [C][U] 攝取 (量)
▲ The doctor told my parents to reduce their daily intake of salt, fat, and sugar. 醫生交代我爸媽要減少每天的鹽分、脂肪和糖分的攝取。
💡 sharp/sudden intake of breath 猛吸一口氣，倒抽一口氣

---

8. **lad** [læd] n. [C] 小伙子，少男
▲ Two lads are fighting outside the shop.
兩個小伙子在店外打架。

---

9. **lofty** [`lɔftɪ] adj. (地位、理想等) 崇高的 (loftier | loftiest)
▲ My teacher is a man of lofty ideals.
我的老師是個有崇高理想的人。

---

10. **melancholy** [`mɛlən͵kɑlɪ] n. [U] 憂鬱，憂傷
▲ Karen sometimes sinks into deep melancholy.
Karen 有時候會陷入憂鬱。

melancholy [`mɛlən͵kɑlɪ] adj. 憂鬱的，憂傷的

▲ Some people feel melancholy in winter because of gloomy weather.
有些人在冬天因為陰暗的天氣而鬱鬱寡歡。

---

11. **narrate** [`næ,ret] v. 敘述 [同] relate
▲ The story is narrated by a nine-year-old boy.
這個故事是由一個九歲的男孩敘述的。
narration [nə`reʃən] n. [C][U] 敘述；旁白
▲ Some stories use first-person narration while others use third-person narration. 有些故事採用第一人稱敘述，有些則是採用第三人稱敘述。

---

12. **ordeal** [ɔr`dil] n. [C] 苦難，磨難 <of>
▲ The refugees went through a terrible ordeal.
這些難民遭受極大的苦難。
💡 face/undergo the ordeal of sth 面對 / 經歷…的磨難

---

13. **paperback** [`pepɚ,bæk] n. [C][U] 平裝書，平裝本
▲ This novel is published both in paperback and hardback. 這本小說平裝本和精裝本都有出。

---

14. **plague** [pleg] n. [C][U] 瘟疫
▲ There was an outbreak of plague in the village.
這個村子爆發瘟疫。
💡 a plague of rats/locusts 鼠害 / 蝗災

---

15. **propel** [prə`pɛl] v. 推動，推進；驅使，促使 <to, into>
(propelled | propelled | propelling)
▲ This boat is propelled by a motor.

這艘船是由馬達推動。

propeller [prə`pɛlɚ] n. [C] 螺旋槳

▲ The propellers are spinning. The helicopters are going to take off. 螺旋槳正在轉動，直升機即將起飛。

---

16. **reckon** [`rɛkən] v. 猜想，覺得；認為，視為

▲ I reckon that there will be an afternoon thunderstorm soon. 我覺得就要下午後雷陣雨了。

💡 be reckoned (to be) sth 被認為是… ，被視為… | reckon on sth 指望… ，盼望… | reckon with/without sth 有將 / 未將…列入考慮

reckoning [`rɛkənɪŋ] n. [C][U] 計算，估計

▲ By my reckoning, ten thousand people attended the rally. 據我估計，有一萬人參與集會。

---

17. **restoration** [ˌrɛstə`reʃən] n. [C][U] 恢復 <of> ；修復 <of>

▲ We are hoping for the restoration of peace.
我們希望能恢復和平。

---

18. **savage** [`sævɪdʒ] adj. 猛烈的 [反] mild；凶殘的，野蠻的

▲ The speaker made a savage attack on the government's policies.
那位發言者猛烈抨擊政府的政策。

💡 savage dog 惡犬 | savage tribe 野蠻部落

savage [`sævɪdʒ] n. [C] 凶殘的人，野蠻的人

▲ The terrorist attack was regarded as the work of savages. 那起恐怖攻擊被認為是凶殘野蠻人的行徑。

savage [`sævɪdʒ] v. 攻擊

▲ The victim was savaged to death by a fierce animal.
受害者被一隻凶惡的動物攻擊致死。

19. **simplify** [`sɪmplə,faɪ] v. 簡化，使變簡單

▲ The introduction of the computer into the workplace has simplified many jobs.
引進電腦到工作場所中簡化了許多工作。

20. **spokesperson** [`spoks,pɜsṇ] n. [C] 發言人 <for>

▲ A government spokesperson denied the rumors.
政府發言人否認了傳言。

spokesman [`spoksmən] n. [C] (男) 發言人 <for>

▲ This gentleman used to be the spokesman for Buckingham Palace.
這位紳士曾是白金漢宮的發言人。

spokeswoman [`spoks,wumən] n. [C] (女) 發言人

▲ A police spokeswoman confirmed the news.
警方發言人證實了這項消息。

21. **stylish** [`staɪlɪʃ] adj. 時髦的

▲ You can find a variety of stylish clothes in that shop.
你可以在那家店裡找到各式各樣時髦的服飾。

22. **sympathize** [`sɪmpə,θaɪz] v. 同情 <with>

▲ We sympathize with the orphan. 我們同情這名孤兒。

23. **trout** [traʊt] n. [C][U] 鱒魚 (pl. trout, trouts)

▲ We had trout for lunch yesterday.

我們昨天吃鱒魚當午餐。

---

24. **vapor** [ˋvepɚ] n. [C][U] 蒸氣

▲ Dense clouds of vapor rise from the hot spring.
一陣陣濃密的蒸氣從溫泉升起。

💡 water vapor 水蒸氣

---

25. **waterproof** [ˋwɔtɚˏpruf] adj. 防水的

▲ Jessica bought a new waterproof jacket.
Jessica 買了一件新的防水外套。

💡 waterproof <u>watch</u>/<u>boots</u> 防水手錶 / 靴子

waterproof [ˋwɔtɚˏpruf] v. 使防水，將 (布料等) 作防水
處理

▲ The workers are waterproofing the roof.
工人正在為屋頂作防水處理。

Unit 31

1. **doze** [doz] v. 小睡

▲ Mom usually dozes for half an hour in the afternoon.
媽媽通常會在下午小睡半小時。

💡 doze off 打盹，打瞌睡

doze [doz] n. [sing.] 小睡

▲ I had a doze after lunch. 我吃完午餐後小睡了一下。

---

2. **equalize** [ˋikwəˏlaɪz] v. 使平等，使均等，使相等

▲ The company tried to equalize the workload among
the staff.

公司試著均分員工們的工作量。

---

3. **feeble** [`fibl] adj. 虛弱的；微弱的 (feebler | feeblest)

▲ The patient was too feeble to utter a word.
這位病人虛弱到連聲音都發不出來。

💡 feeble excuse/joke 站不住腳的藉口 / 乾巴巴的笑話

---

4. **fume** [fjum] v. 發怒，發火，發脾氣 <at, about, over>

▲ The customer fumed at the clumsy waiter.
那名顧客對笨手笨腳的服務生發火。

fume [fjum] n. [C] 廢氣，臭氣 (usu. pl.)

▲ Car exhaust fumes made me sick.
汽車廢氣的臭味令我作嘔。

---

5. **handicraft** [`hændɪ,kræft] n. [C] 手工藝 (usu. pl.)；手工
藝品 (usu. pl.)

▲ Jenny has been learning handicrafts, and her favorite
handicraft is pottery. Jenny 一直都有在學手工藝，而
她最喜歡的手工藝是陶藝。

---

6. **hunch** [hʌntʃ] n. [C] 直覺

▲ I have a hunch (that) you will pass the exam.
我直覺認為你會通過考試。

💡 act on/follow/play a hunch 憑直覺行動

hunch [hʌntʃ] v. 弓背，弓著身子，彎腰駝背，拱肩縮
背

▲ Mom always tells me to stand up straight and not to
hunch my back. 媽媽總是叫我要站直、不要彎腰駝背。

---

7. **interpreter** [ɪnˈtɝprɪtɚ] n. [C] 口譯員

   ▲ My friend was the interpreter when we were in Poland. 我們在波蘭時由我朋友擔任口譯員。

---

8. **landlady** [ˈlændˌledɪ] n. [C] 女房東，女地主

   ▲ The landlady promised to redecorate the house before we move in.
   女房東答應在我們搬進去之前先把房子重新裝潢。

---

9. **logo** [ˈlogo] n. [C] 商標 (pl. logos)

   ▲ The athlete wore a T-shirt with her sponsor's logo.
   那位運動員穿著一件帶有贊助者商標的 T 恤。

---

10. **mentality** [mɛnˈtælətɪ] n. [C] 心態 (usu. sing.) (pl. mentalities)

    ▲ Can you understand the mentality of those people?
    你能理解那些人的心態嗎？

    💡 criminal/get-rich-quick mentality 犯罪 / 一步登天的心態

---

11. **narrator** [ˈnæretɚ] n. [C] 敘述者

    ▲ The narrator of that film is a pig.
    那部電影的敘述者是一隻豬。

---

12. **orderly** [ˈɔrdɚlɪ] adj. 井然有序的，有規律的 [反] disorderly

    ▲ After retirement, Sam lives a simple and orderly life.
    退休後，Sam 過著簡單規律的生活。

    💡 in an orderly fashion 井然有序地

orderly [`ɔrdəlɪ] n. [C] (醫院病房) 雜役，勤務員 (pl. orderlies)

▲ My friend works part-time as a hospital orderly.
我朋友在醫院打工當醫院病房雜工。

---

13. **paralyze** [`pærə,laɪz] v. 使癱瘓

▲ The accident paralyzed traffic in the downtown area.
這起交通事故使得市中心區的交通癱瘓。

paralyzed [`pærə,laɪzd] adj. 癱瘓的

▲ The stroke left the patient permanently paralyzed.
那名病人因為中風而終身癱瘓。

💡 paralyzed from the waist/neck down 腰部 / 頸部以下
癱瘓 | paralyzed with/by fear 嚇得無法動彈，嚇呆了

---

14. **plantation** [plæn`teʃən] n. [C] (熱帶地區的) 大農場，種植園，種植場

▲ In the past, many people who worked on plantations
were slaves. 以前在熱帶大農場工作的人很多是奴隸。

💡 coffee/rubber/sugar/cotton plantation 咖啡 / 橡膠 / 蔗糖 / 棉花園

---

15. **prosecute** [`prɑsɪ,kjut] v. 起訴 <for>；繼續進行 (戰爭等)，將…執行到底

▲ That man was prosecuted for murder.
那名男子因謀殺被起訴。

prosecutor [`prɑsɪ,kjutə] n. [C] 檢察官

▲ The prosecutor has begun an investigation into the
bribery scandal.

檢察官對這起賄賂醜聞展開調查。

16. **reconcile** [`rɛkən,saɪl] v. 使和解 <with>；調和，使一致 <with>

▲ The couple was reconciled with each other after a brief separation. 這對夫妻在短暫分居後和解了。

💡 reconcile oneself to sth 與 (現實等) 妥協，接受 (現實等)

---

17. **restrain** [rɪ`stren] v. 抑制，克制，制止 <from>

▲ I could barely restrain myself from striking him.
我幾乎無法克制自己去揍他。

---

18. **scrape** [skrep] v. 擦傷，刮壞；刮除，削去

▲ The kid scraped his knee on a stone.
那孩子的膝蓋被石頭擦傷。

💡 scrape through sth 勉強通過 (考試等) | scrape by (on sth) (靠⋯) 糊口，勉強維持生計

scrape [skrep] n. [C] 擦傷；(自己造成的) 困境，麻煩；[sing.] 摩擦聲

▲ Fortunately, my sister only suffered a few scrapes in the car crash.
很幸運地，我姊在車禍中只受了一點擦傷。

---

19. **simultaneous** [,saɪml̩`tenɪəs] adj. 同時的

▲ Betty works as a simultaneous interpreter.
Betty 從事同步翻譯的工作。

simultaneously [,saɪml̩`tenɪəslɪ] adv. 同時地

▲ The two accidents happened simultaneously.
兩件意外同時發生。

20. **sportsman** [`sportsmən] n. [C] 運動員

▲ Charles is considered a talented all-round sportsman.
Charles 被認為是極具天賦的全能運動員。

sportswoman [`sports͵wumən] n. [C] 女運動員

▲ Jessica is the most talented sportswoman I have ever met. Jessica 是我遇過最有天賦的女運動員。

21. **subordinate** [sə`bɔrdn̩ɪt] adj. 次 要 的 <to> [同] secondary

▲ Some people think environmental protection is subordinate to economic growth.
有些人認為環保沒有經濟成長重要。

💡 subordinate clause 從屬子句

subordinate [sə`bɔrdn̩ɪt] n. [C] 下屬

▲ The boss asked one of her subordinates to carry out that project.
老闆叫她的其中一個下屬來完成那項計畫。

subordinate [sə`bɔrdn̩͵et] v. 使居於次要地位

▲ Most parents subordinate their wishes to their children's.
大多數父母將他們的願望置於他們孩子的願望之下。

22. **symphony** [`sɪmfənɪ] n. [C] 交響樂 (pl. symphonies)

▲ Grace is impressed with Beethoven's Fifth Symphony.

Grace 對貝多芬的五號交響曲印象深刻。

---

23. **trustee** [trʌsˋti] n. [C] 受託人

▲ Who will act as the trustee for the estate until this child grows up?

誰會在這孩子長大之前擔任遺產受託人？

---

24. **velvet** [ˋvɛlvɪt] n. [U] 天鵝絨

▲ The lady dressed in dark purple velvet over there is my teacher.

那邊那一位穿著深紫色天鵝絨的女士是我的老師。

velvet [ˋvɛlvɪt] adj. 天鵝絨 (製) 的

▲ Judy bought some velvet cushions for her new house.

Judy 為她的新房子買了一些天鵝絨坐墊。

---

25. **wharf** [wɔrf] n. [C] 碼頭 (pl. wharfs, wharves)

▲ The sailor unloaded the crates onto the wharf.

水手把箱子卸下放在碼頭上。

wharf [wɔrf] v. 將 (船) 停靠於碼頭

Unit 32

1. **draught** [dræft] n. [C] (吹過房間的) 冷風 [同] draft

▲ The candle on the table flickered in a draught.

桌上的蠟燭在一陣冷風中閃爍。

---

2. **equate** [ɪˋkwet] v. 將⋯視為同等，等同視之，相提並論 <with>

▲ People tend to equate wealth with happiness.
人們容易將財富與幸福視為同等。

---

3. **feminine** [ˋfɛmənɪn] adj. 女性的，女性特有的，有女性
特質的
▲ Decorated with many flowers, my cousin's room is
very feminine.
我表姊的房間用許多花裝飾，很有女孩味。
💡 traditional feminine role 傳統的女性角色
feminine [ˋfɛmənɪn] n. [sing.] 女性 (the ～)；[C] (某些
語言中的) 陰性詞彙
▲ The distinction between the masculine and feminine
used to be emphasized. 以前很強調男女有別。

---

4. **fury** [ˋfjʊrɪ] n. [U][sing.] 狂怒，暴怒 [同] rage
▲ Learning his friend's betrayal, the businessman flew
into a fury. 得知朋友的背叛，那名企業家勃然大怒。
💡 in a fury 盛怒之下

---

5. **harass** [həˋræs] v. 煩擾，騷擾
▲ The singer was harassed by the repeated questions
from the reporters.
這位歌手被記者不斷重複的質問煩擾。
💡 sexually harass sb 對…性騷擾
harassment [həˋræsmənt] n. [U] 煩擾，騷擾
▲ Cases of sexual harassment are increasing rapidly.
性騷擾案例快速地增加。

💡 racial harassment 種族騷擾

---

6. **hurdle** [ˋhɝdḷ] n. [C] 障礙，困難 [同] obstacle；(跨欄等的) 欄架
   ▲ We overcame a lot of hurdles. 我們克服了許多困難。
   💡 clear a hurdle 克服困難 ； 成功跨欄｜the 100-meter/
      400-meter hurdles 一百 / 四百公尺跨欄賽跑
   hurdle [ˋhɝdḷ] v. (奔跑著) 跨越，跳越 (欄架、籬笆等)
   ▲ The boy hurdled the fence with a dog going after
      him. 男孩被狗追著跑跳過圍欄。

---

7. **intersection** [ˏɪntɚˋsɛkʃən] n. [C][U] 交叉 (口) ，交叉
   (點)
   ▲ The station is at the intersection of Zhongxiao E. Rd.
      and Fuxing S. Rd.
      這個車站位在忠孝東路和復興南路的交叉口。
   💡 at a busy intersection 在繁忙的交叉路口

---

8. **landslide** [ˋlændˏslaɪd] n. [C] 山崩，坍方
   ▲ Miraculously, the family survived the landslide.
      這一家人奇蹟似地在山崩中倖免於難。

---

9. **lonesome** [ˋlonsəm] adj. 寂寞的 [同] lonely
   ▲ Alice felt lonesome without her friends around her.
      沒有朋友在身邊，Alice 感到很寂寞。

---

10. **mermaid** [ˋmɝˏmed] n. [C] 美人魚
    ▲ The sailor mistook manatees for mermaids while
       sailing in the sea.

這水手在海上航行時將海牛誤認為美人魚。

11. **navigation** [ˌnævəˈgeʃən] n. [U] 導航；航行
   ▲ Usually, George drives, and Mary does the navigation. 通常是 George 開車而 Mary 導航。

12. **organizer** [ˈɔrgəˌnaɪzɚ] n. [C] 組織者，籌辦者，主辦者 (pl. organizers)
   ▲ The event organizers should provide enough seats for the guests. 活動籌辦者應提供來賓足夠的座位。

13. **parliament** [ˈpɑrləmənt] n. [C][U] 國會，議會
   ▲ In this country, laws are made by parliament.
   在該國，法律是國會制定的。
   💡 dissolve parliament 解散國會

14. **plow** [plaʊ] n. [C] 犁
   ▲ The local farmers use horses to pull heavy plows.
   當地的農夫利用馬匹來拉沉重的犁。
   💡 under the plow (田地) 用於耕作的
   plow [plaʊ] v. 犁 (田)，耕 (地)
   ▲ Farmers usually start to plow fields in spring.
   農夫通常在春天開始耕作。
   💡 plow through sth 費力地穿越或通過… ；費力地閱讀… | plow into sb/sth (車等) 撞上…

15. **prospective** [prəˈspɛktɪv] adj. 可能的，有望的 [同] potential

▲ The personnel manager is interviewing prospective employees. 人事經理正在和未來可能的員工面試。

16. **redundancy** [rɪˋdʌndənsɪ] n. [U] 冗贅

▲ Redundancy should be avoided in writing.
寫作應該避免贅詞。

17. **restraint** [rɪˋstrent] n. [C][U] 克制，抑制，限制

▲ My anger was beyond restraint. 我無法克制怒火。

💡 be placed/kept under restraint 受到限制 | without restraint 自由地，無所顧忌地 | impose restraints on sth 對…加以限制

18. **scroll** [skrol] n. [C] 卷軸；渦卷形的圖案或裝飾

▲ The ancient scrolls were found in caves by the desert.
那些古代卷軸在沙漠旁的洞穴中被找到。

💡 roll up/unroll a scroll 捲起 / 展開卷軸

scroll [skrol] v. 使電腦頁面上下轉動 <up, down, through>

▲ Julia scrolled down to find more information.
Julia 往下轉動頁面找尋更多資訊。

19. **skim** [skɪm] v. 撈掉，撇去 <off, from>；擦過，掠過；瀏覽 <over, through> [同] scan (skimmed | skimmed | skimming)

▲ I skimmed the cream off the milk.
我撈掉牛奶上的浮油。

skim [skɪm] n. [sing.] 瀏覽;(從液體表面撈掉的) 浮油等薄層

▲ Leo did a quick skim through the list to find his own name. Leo 快速瀏覽了一下名單想找他自己的名字。

💡 skim milk 脫脂牛奶

20. **sportsmanship** [ˋsportsmənˏʃɪp] n. [U] 運動家精神

▲ The coach tried to teach these children good sportsmanship after they lost the game. 在輸掉比賽後，這教練試著教導孩子良好的運動家精神。

21. **subscribe** [səbˋskraɪb] v. 訂閱 <to>;贊同 <to>

▲ My classmates have subscribed to the online music service. 我的同學們訂閱了那個線上音樂服務。

22. **syrup** [ˋsɪrəp] n. [C][U] 糖漿

▲ Ann's parents like to eat pancakes with maple syrup. Ann 的父母喜歡鬆餅配著楓糖漿吃。

💡 cough syrup 止咳糖漿

23. **tuck** [tʌk] v. 把…塞入

▲ Jeff tucked his handkerchief into his pocket.
Jeff 把手帕塞入口袋。

tuck [tʌk] n. [C] (衣物上的) 褶子

▲ The tailor made a tuck in the dress.
裁縫師在洋裝上打了一個褶子。

24. **veterinarian** [ˏvɛtrəˋnɛrɪən] n. [C] 獸醫 (also vet)

▲ If your pet has a skin problem, you'd better bring it to a veterinarian.

如果你的寵物有皮膚病，你最好帶牠去看獸醫。

25. **whiskey** [ˋwɪskɪ] n. [C][U] 威士忌 (also whisky) (pl. whiskeys, whiskies)

▲ Some people like to mix whiskey with Coke.

有些人喜歡把威士忌和可樂調在一起。

Unit 33

1. **dresser** [ˋdrɛsɚ] n. [C] 有抽屜的衣櫃 [同] chest of drawers；衣著…的人

▲ Open the top drawer of the dresser, and you will find the pink sweater.

打開衣櫃的上層抽屜，你就會找到那件粉紅色毛衣了。

💡 smart/stylish/sloppy dresser 衣著時髦有型／邋遢的人

2. **evacuate** [ɪˋvækjʊ‚et] v. (使) 撤離 <from>

▲ Hundreds of people were evacuated from the theater because of a fire. 數百人因火災被疏散出戲院。

3. **fiancé** [fiˋɑnse] n. [C] 未婚夫 (also fiance)

▲ Emily introduced her fiancé to us yesterday.

Emily 昨天介紹她的未婚夫讓我們認識。

4. **fuse** [fjuz] n. [C] 保險絲；導火線，引信 (also fuze)

▲ The fuse blew and the room became dark.

保險絲燒斷，房間一片漆黑。

fuse [fjuz] v. 融合，結合 <into>

▲ Several minor parties were fused into the most powerful one. 幾個小政黨結合成一個最大黨。

---

5. **harden** [ˋhɑrdn̩] v. (使) 變硬，(使) 硬化 [反] soften；(使) 變得強硬或冷酷 [反] soften

▲ The concrete hardened after several hours.
混凝土在幾個小時後變硬了。

---

6. **hypocrite** [ˋhɪpəˏkrɪt] n. [C] 偽善者，偽君子

▲ You are a hypocrite! You tell us to care about the weak and the poor but you do the opposite.
你是個偽善者！你要我們關心弱者、貧者，但你自己卻不這樣做。

hypocrisy [hɪˋpɑkrəsɪ] n. [C][U] 偽善，虛偽 [反] sincerity (pl. hypocrisies)

▲ Saying one thing but doing another is hypocrisy.
說一套做一套就是虛偽。

---

7. **intervene** [ˏɪntɚˋvin] v. 干涉，干預，介入 <in>

▲ The teacher intervened before the boys started fighting. 老師在男孩們開打前介入。

---

8. **latitude** [ˋlætəˏtjud] n. [C][U] 緯度 (abbr. lat.)；[U] 自由

▲ I need a map that shows lines of longitude and latitude. 我需要一份有標示經緯線的地圖。

💡 at a latitude of 23 degrees north/23 degrees north latitude 在北緯 23 度 | high/low/northern/southern latitudes 高緯度 / 低緯度 / 北緯 / 南緯地區

9. **longitude** [ˋlɑndʒəˏtjud] n. [C][U] 經度 (abbr. long.)

▲ The current position of the typhoon is at 130 degrees east longitude and 20 degrees north latitude.
颱風現在位置在東經 130 度、北緯 20 度。

10. **migrant** [ˋmaɪɡrənt] n. [C] 移居者，移民；候鳥等遷徙動物

▲ There are more migrants looking for work in the major cities. 大城市中有較多尋找工作的移民。

migrant [ˋmaɪɡrənt] adj. 遷徙的，移居的

▲ Some migrant workers suffer unfair treatment.
有些移工遭受到不公平的對待。

💡 migrant bird 候鳥

11. **nearsighted** [ˏnɪrˋsaɪtɪd] adj. 近視的

▲ It is reported that 80% of high school students in this country are nearsighted.
據報導，該國 80% 的高中生近視。

12. **orthodox** [ˋɔrθəˏdɑks] adj. 被普遍接受的，傳統的，正統的，正規的 [反] unorthodox

▲ Some people prefer alternative medicine to orthodox medicine. 有些人偏好另類療法勝於傳統的正規醫療。

13. **pastime** [ˋpæsˏtaɪm] n. [C] 消遣，娛樂

▲ Dancing is my favorite pastime.
我最喜歡的消遣是跳舞。

---

14. **pony** [ˋponɪ] n. [C] 小型馬，矮種馬 (pl. ponies)

▲ A pony is a small horse that is generally friendly and intelligent.
矮種馬是一種矮小的馬，通常很友善和聰明。

---

15. **proverb** [ˋprɑvɝb] n. [C] 諺語

▲ As the proverb goes, "Haste makes waste." I made mistakes when I did things too quickly. 正如諺語所說：「欲速則不達。」我做事太急就犯錯了。

---

16. **reef** [rif] n. [C] 暗礁，礁石

▲ Have you ever been to the Great Barrier Reef?
你有去過大堡礁嗎？

💡 coral reef 珊瑚礁

---

17. **retort** [rɪˋtɔrt] n. [C] 回嘴，反駁

▲ Hearing May's criticism, Tim made an amusing retort.
Tim 聽到 May 的批評而做出了詼諧的反駁。

retort [rɪˋtɔrt] v. 回嘴，反駁

▲ "It's none of my business," my sister retorted.
我妹回嘴說：「那不關我的事」。

---

18. **scrutiny** [ˋskrutənɪ] n. [U] 仔細檢查，嚴格審查，詳細調查

▲ All applications are under scrutiny.

所有的申請書都受到嚴格審查。

---

19. **slash** [slæʃ] v. 揮砍，劈砍，將…劃出深長的切口；大幅削減

▲ Don't try to commit suicide by slashing your wrists.
不要試圖割腕自殺。

slash [slæʃ] n. [C] 深長的切口

▲ The cook made deep slashes in the meat.
廚師在肉上劃了幾刀深長的切口。

💡 slash (mark) 斜線

---

20. **spur** [spɝ] v. 用馬刺驅策馬；激勵 <on> (spurred | spurred | spurring)

▲ The riders spurred their horses (on).
騎士們策馬快跑。

spur [spɝ] n. [C] 馬刺；激勵 <to>

▲ The cowboy wore boots and spurs.
那牛仔穿著有馬刺的靴子。

💡 on the spur of the moment 一時興起 | win/earn sb's spurs 功成名就，揚名立萬

---

21. **subsidize** [ˋsʌbsəˌdaɪz] v. 補貼，補助，資助

▲ Is this project subsidized by the government?
這項計畫有受政府補助嗎？

---

22. **tan** [tæn] n. [C][U] 日曬後的膚色，古銅色，棕褐色 (usu. sing.) [同] suntan

▲ My friend came back from Miami with a beautiful tan. 我朋友從邁阿密曬了一身美麗的古銅膚色回來。

💡 get a tan 將皮膚曬成古銅色或棕褐色

tan [tæn] adj. 古銅色的，棕褐色的 (tanner | tannest)

▲ The girl wore tan shoes.
那個女孩穿著棕褐色的鞋子。

tan [tæn] v. (使) 曬黑，(使) 曬成古銅色或棕褐色 (tanned | tanned | tanning)

▲ Some people have pale skin that does not tan easily.
有些人有不容易曬黑的白皮膚。

---

23. **turmoil** [ˋtɝmɔɪl] n. [U][sing.] 混亂

▲ The death of the king threw the country into turmoil.
國王駕崩使國家陷入混亂之中。

💡 in (a) turmoil 處於混亂狀態

---

24. **veto** [ˋvito] n. [C][U] 否決 (權) <on> (pl. vetoes)

▲ Who has a veto on this project?
誰對這項提案有否決權？

💡 exercise the veto 行使否決權

veto [ˋvito] v. 否決

▲ The bill was vetoed by the Parliament.
那項法案遭議會否決。

---

25. **wholesale** [ˋhol͵sel] adj. 批發的

▲ Wholesale prices are usually cheaper.
批發價通常比較便宜。

💡 wholesale dealer 批發商

wholesale [ˋholˏsel] adv. 批發地

▲ That store only sells wholesale. 那家店只賣批發。

wholesale [ˋholˏsel] n. [U] 批發

▲ There's a sharp increase in food prices at wholesale.
食物的批發價急遽上漲。

wholesale [ˋholˏsel] v. 批發販售

▲ The merchant wholesales clothing to retailers.
這名商人將服飾批發販售給零售商。

wholesaler [ˋholˏselɚ] n. [C] 批發商

▲ My aunt is a furniture wholesaler.
我阿姨是一名家具批發商。

Unit 34

1. **dressing** [ˋdrɛsɪŋ] n. [C][U] (沙拉等的) 調味醬 (also salad dressing)；[C] (保護傷口的) 敷料

▲ Helen had a salad with Thousand Island dressing.
Helen 吃了一份加千島醬的沙拉。

💡 dressing room 後臺更衣室

2. **evergreen** [ˋɛvɚˏgrin] adj. (植物) 常綠的

▲ Evergreen plants have green leaves all year.
常綠植物全年都有綠葉。

evergreen [ˋɛvɚˏgrin] n. [C] 常綠植物

▲ Ivy is an evergreen. 常春藤是一種常綠植物。

3. **fin** [fɪn] n. [C] 鰭

▲ We don't have soup made of sharks' fins anymore because we think it's cruel.

我們不再吃魚翅湯了，因為我們覺得殘忍。

---

4. **fuss** [fʌs] n. [sing.] 過度緊張，小題大作，大驚小怪

▲ Don't make such a fuss. 別這樣小題大作。

💡 make a fuss about sth 對…小題大作 | make a fuss over sb 對…關愛備至或過分關愛 | a fuss about nothing 無謂的小題大作，庸人自擾

fuss [fʌs] v. 過度緊張，小題大作，大驚小怪

▲ My colleague was fussing about a little cockroach.

我同事對一隻小蟑螂大驚小怪。

💡 fuss over sb 對…關愛備至或過分關愛

---

5. **harmonica** [hɑr`mɑnɪkə] n. [C] 口琴

▲ Harry likes to play the harmonica. Harry 愛吹口琴。

---

6. **iceberg** [`aɪs,bɝg] n. [C] 冰山

▲ The *Titanic* struck an iceberg and sank.

鐵達尼號撞到冰山而沉了。

💡 the tip of the iceberg 冰山一角

---

7. **intimacy** [`ɪntəməsɪ] n. [C][U] 親密，親近

▲ I feel great intimacy with my elder sister.

我和姊姊特別親近。

---

8. **layout** [`le,aʊt] n. [C] (建築等的) 設計，格局；(書籍等的) 版面設計

▲ The couple liked the layout of the apartment.

那對夫妻喜歡那間公寓的格局。

9. **lotion** [`loʃən] n. [C][U] 乳液
   ▲ Apply some lotion or cream after a bath.
   洗完澡後擦些乳液或乳霜。

10. **miscellaneous** [ˌmɪsə`lenɪəs] adj. 各式各樣的
    ▲ You can find miscellaneous goods in a grocery store.
    你可以在雜貨店找到各式各樣的貨品。

11. **nostril** [`nɑstrəl] n. [C] 鼻孔
    ▲ One of John's nostrils is stuffed up.
    John 有一邊鼻孔塞住了。

12. **ounce** [auns] n. [C] 盎司 (abbr. oz.)
    ▲ There are about 28 grams in one ounce.
    一盎司大約為二十八公克。
    💡 An ounce of prevention is worth a pound of cure.
    【諺】 預防勝於治療。 | an ounce of common
    sense/truth 一點點常識 / 事實 | every ounce of
    courage/strength 全部的勇氣 / 力氣

13. **patriotic** [ˌpetrɪ`ɑtɪk] adj. 愛國的
    ▲ The soldiers are singing a patriotic song.
    士兵們正在唱一首愛國歌曲。

14. **populate** [`pɑpjəˌlet] v. 居住於，生活於
    ▲ New York City is densely populated.
    紐約市人口密度很高。

15. **provisional** [prə`vɪʒən!] adj. 暫時的，臨時的 [同] temporary

▲ In most states in the U.S., teens between 15 and 18 must have a provisional license to learn how to drive. 在美國大多數的州，十五到十八歲的青少年必須有臨時駕照才能學開車。

16. **referee** [ˌrɛfə`ri] n. [C] 裁判

▲ Don't argue with the referee, or you may be sent off. 不要跟裁判發生爭執，不然可能會被罰出場。

referee [ˌrɛfə`ri] v. 當裁判

▲ Who will referee the final? 誰會是決賽的裁判？

17. **revelation** [ˌrɛvə`leʃən] n. [C][U] (出乎意料的) 發現或揭露

▲ It was a revelation to me that my brother can cook so well. 發現我弟很會做菜讓我很意外。

18. **seagull** [`sigəl] n. [C] 海鷗 (also gull)

▲ Hearing the cries of seagulls, I know the beach is not far away. 我聽見海鷗的叫聲，就知道沙灘不遠了。

💡 a flock of seagulls 一群海鷗

19. **slay** [sle] v. 殺 (slew | slain | slaying)

▲ President Kennedy was slain in Dallas. 甘迺迪總統在達拉斯遇刺身亡。

20. **stabilize** [`stebəˌlaɪz] v. (使) 穩定

▲ The government has a plan to stabilize prices.

政府有穩定物價的計畫。

---

21. **succession** [səkˋsɛʃən] n. [U] 繼承 <to>；[sing.] 連續，
一連串

   ▲ The prince will be the first in succession to the
   throne. 這位王子將是王位的第一繼承人。

   🕯 in succession 連續地，接連地

---

22. **tedious** [ˋtidɪəs] adj. 冗長乏味的 [同] boring

   ▲ The speech was incredibly tedious! I could not help
   dozing off. 這演講真是有夠無聊！我忍不住打瞌睡了。

---

23. **twilight** [ˋtwaɪ͵laɪt] n. [U] 黃昏，薄暮；[sing.] 衰退期，
晚期 (the ～)

   ▲ We enjoyed watching the stars come out in the
   twilight. 我們享受在薄暮中看著星星出來。

   🕯 the twilight years 晚年，暮年

---

24. **vibrate** [ˋvaɪbret] v. 震動

   ▲ Someone's smartphone is vibrating in the drawer.
   有人的手機在抽屜裡震動。

---

25. **wholesome** [ˋholsəm] adj. 有益 (身心) 健康的

   ▲ Teresa made a wholesome dish with many vegetables
   and fruits.

   Teresa 用很多蔬菜和水果做了一份有益健康的餐點。

   🕯 wholesome entertainment 有益身心健康的娛樂 |
   wholesome food 健康食品

Unit 35 📝

1. **dual** [ˋdjuəl] adj. 雙重的，兩個的
   ▲ With her dual role as principal and mother, my cousin is a busy career woman. 我的表姊有著校長與母親的雙重角色，是一名忙碌的職業婦女。
   🔮 dual citizenship/nationality 雙重國籍 | dual purpose 雙重用途或目的

2. **evoke** [ɪˋvok] v. 喚起或引起 (記憶、感情等)，使人想起
   ▲ This song evoked memories of my childhood.
   這首歌使我想起童年回憶。
   🔮 evoke sympathy 引起同情

3. **finite** [ˋfaɪnaɪt] adj. 有限的 [反] infinite
   ▲ The length of a human life is finite.
   人類的壽命是有限的。
   🔮 finite resources 有限的資源 | a finite number of possibilities/choices 為數有限的可能 / 選擇

4. **gallop** [ˋgæləp] n. [sing.] 奔馳，飛奔
   ▲ Hearing the gunshot, most horses will break into a gallop. 聽到槍聲，大部分的馬會飛奔起來。
   🔮 at a gallop 快速地
   gallop [ˋgæləp] v. 騎馬奔馳；飛奔，疾馳
   ▲ The cowboy galloped across the field.
   牛仔騎馬疾馳過原野。

5. **headphones** [ˋhɛdˌfonz] n. [pl.] (頭戴式) 耳機

▲ I usually listen to music on my headphones.
我聽音樂通常會戴耳機。

💡 a pair/set of headphones 一副耳機

---

6. **imminent** [ˋɪmənənt] adj. (尤指壞事) 即將發生的,即將
來臨的

▲ We took precautions because of an imminent storm.
因為暴風雨即將來臨,我們採取預防措施。

💡 imminent disaster/threat 迫在眉睫的災難 / 威脅 | in
imminent danger of extinction/collapse 瀕臨滅絕 / 崩
潰的危險

---

7. **intonation** [ˌɪntoˋneʃən] n. [C][U] 語調

▲ Some foreign language learners have difficulty
learning intonation.
有些外語學習者覺得語調很難學。

---

8. **lease** [lis] n. [C] 租約 <on>

▲ The couple signed a one-year lease on the apartment.
那對夫妻簽下那間公寓一年的租約。

💡 take out a lease on sth 租下… | the lease runs
out/expires 租約到期

---

9. **lottery** [ˋlɑtərɪ] n. [C] 彩券 (pl. lotteries)

▲ Many people hope to win the lottery.
很多人希望彩券中獎。

💡 a lottery ticket 彩券 | play the lottery/buy lottery tickets 買彩券

10. **mistress** [ˈmɪstrɪs] n. [C] 女主人;情婦

▲ The unqualified servant got fired by the mistress of the house. 那位不稱職的僕人被女主人解僱了。

11. **novice** [ˈnɑvɪs] n. [C] 初學者,新手 <at, in> [同] beginner

▲ George and Mary are complete novices at skiing. George 和 Mary 完全是滑雪新手。

💡 novice driver/writer/pilot/teacher 新手駕駛 / 作家 / 飛行員 / 教師

12. **outing** [ˈautɪŋ] n. [C] 出遊,遠足 <to>

▲ Sue and her friends went on an outing to the wetland park. Sue 和朋友去溼地公園遠足。

💡 school/class/family outing 校外教學 / 班遊 / 家庭遠足

13. **pebble** [ˈpɛbl] n. [C] 小圓石,鵝卵石

▲ The little girl is picking up pebbles at the beach. 小女孩在海灘撿小石頭。

14. **porter** [ˈportɚ] n. [C] 行李員,搬運工

▲ I tipped the porter because he carried my baggage to the car. 我給行李員小費,因為他幫我把行李拿到車上。

15. **psychiatry** [saɪ`kaɪətrɪ] n. [U] 精神病學
    ▲ The doctor has a degree in psychiatry.
    這位醫生有精神病學的學位。

---

16. **referendum** [ˌrɛfə`rɛndəm] n. [C][U] 公民投票 <on>
    (pl. referenda, referendums)
    ▲ Environmental groups have gathered enough
    signatures to initiate the referendum.
    環保團體已收集到足以發起公投的連署簽名。
    💡 hold a referendum on sth 就⋯舉行公民投票

---

17. **revival** [rɪ`vaɪv!] n. [C][U] 復興，再度流行
    ▲ Recently there seems to be a revival of herbal
    medicine. 最近草藥似乎再度流行了起來。

---

18. **seduce** [sɪ`djus] v. 引誘，誘惑；誘姦，勾引
    ▲ How can you seduce the little boy into smoking?
    你怎麼可以引誘那個小男孩抽菸？
    seduction [sɪ`dʌkʃən] n. [C][U] 誘惑
    ▲ I can't resist the seductions of the articles in shop
    windows. 我無法抗拒櫥窗商品的誘惑。
    seductive [sɪ`dʌktɪv] adj. 誘人的
    ▲ The roast chicken has a very seductive aroma.
    烤雞的香味非常誘人。

---

19. **slump** [slʌmp] n. [C] 暴跌 <in>；(經濟不景氣、運動員
    低潮等) 表現低落的時期
    ▲ The slump in prices depressed merchants.

價格暴跌令商人沮喪。

💡 in a slump 處於蕭條期或低潮期

slump [slʌmp] v. 沉重地落下或倒下；暴跌

▲ The drunken man slumped to the floor.
那個喝醉的男人重重地倒在地上。

---

20. **stagger** [`stægɚ] v. 搖搖晃晃，蹣跚，踉蹌 [同] stumble；
使震驚，使驚愕

▲ The wounded soldier staggered to his feet.
那名傷兵搖搖晃晃地站起來。

stagger [`stægɚ] n. [C] 搖晃，蹣跚 (usu. sing.)

▲ The old lady walked with a stagger.
那位老婦人步履蹣跚。

staggered [`stægɚd] adj. 震驚的，驚愕的 [同] amazed

▲ We were all staggered to hear the bad news.
我們聽到這個壞消息都很震驚。

💡 staggered at/by sth 對…感到震驚

staggering [`stægərɪŋ] adj. 令人吃驚的，驚人的 [同]
amazing

▲ The result turned out to be quite staggering.
結果變得很令人吃驚。

---

21. **successive** [sək`sɛsɪv] adj. 連續的，接連的 [同]
consecutive

▲ It has rained for five successive days.
已經連續下雨下了五天。

💡 three/four successive victories 三／四連勝｜the third/fourth successive victory 第三／四次連勝｜successive governments 歷屆政府

22. **teller** [ˋtɛlɚ] n. [C] 銀行出納員；選舉計票員；講述者
   ▲ My neighbor is a bank teller.
   我的鄰居是一名銀行出納員。

23. **twinkle** [ˋtwɪŋkl] n. [C] 閃爍，閃耀，發亮 (usu. sing.)
   ▲ There was a mischievous twinkle in the kid's eye.
   那孩子的眼神中閃爍著惡作劇的光芒。
   twinkle [ˋtwɪŋkl] v. 閃爍，閃耀，發亮
   ▲ Stars were twinkling in the night sky.
   星星在夜空中閃閃發亮。
   💡 sb's eyes twinkle with excitement/amusement 興奮／開心地雙眼發亮

24. **vibration** [vaɪˋbreʃən] n. [C][U] 震動
   ▲ The strong winds caused vibrations of the windows.
   強風造成窗戶的震動。

25. **widow** [ˋwɪdo] n. [C] 寡婦
   ▲ The soldier was killed, leaving a widow and a child.
   那名士兵被殺，身後留下寡婦和一個孩子。
   widower [ˋwɪdəwɚ] n. [C] 鰥夫
   ▲ The man became a widower after his wife got killed in an accident.
   那名男子在妻子意外身亡之後成了鰥夫。

1. **dubious** [`djubɪəs] adj. 可疑的，不可靠的 [同] suspicious；懷疑的 <about> [同] doubtful
   ▲ Frank's excuse for being late sounded highly dubious. Frank 遲到的理由聽起來很可疑。
   💡 dubious character 可疑人物

2. **excel** [ɪk`sɛl] v. 擅長 <in, at> (excelled | excelled | excelling)
   ▲ Angela excels in math. Angela 擅長數學。
   💡 excel oneself 超越自我，勝過平時

3. **fireproof** [`faɪr,pruf] adj. 防火的
   ▲ I saw a firefighter in her fireproof suit standing by a fire engine.
   我看到一位消防員穿著防火衣站在消防車旁邊。

4. **gangster** [`gæŋstɚ] n. [C] 犯罪集團成員，幫派分子
   ▲ Carl read a book about Chicago gangsters last week.
   Carl 上週讀了一本跟芝加哥的幫派分子有關的書。
   💡 gangster movie 幫派電影

5. **hearty** [`hɑrtɪ] adj. 熱情的，熱誠的，誠摯的；豐盛的 (heartier | heartiest)
   ▲ The family received a hearty welcome.
   這一家人受到熱情的歡迎。

💡 hearty greeting/handshake 熱情的問候 / 握手 | hearty congratulations 真誠的祝賀 | hearty laugh 開懷大笑 | hearty meal/appetite/eater 豐盛的餐點 / 好胃口 / 吃很多的人

6. **implicit** [ɪm`plɪsɪt] adj. 不言明的，含蓄的 [反] explicit；毫無疑問的，絕對的 [同] absolute
   ▲ When popping the question, Eric interpreted Ann's smile as implicit consent to marry him.
   求婚時，Eric 把 Ann 的微笑解讀為默許同他結婚。
   💡 have implicit faith/trust in sth 對⋯絕對信任

7. **intrigue** [ɪn`trig] n. [C][U] 密謀，陰謀
   ▲ The story is about political intrigue, betrayal, and murder. 這個故事跟政治陰謀、背叛和謀殺有關。
   intrigue [ɪn`trig] v. 激發興趣或好奇心
   ▲ We were all intrigued by the mystery.
   我們都被那個謎團激發了好奇心。

8. **legislator** [`lɛdʒɪsˌletɚ] n. [C] 立法者，立法委員
   ▲ Will legislators in both parties support the idea?
   兩黨的立法委員都會支持這個想法嗎？

9. **lotus** [`lotəs] n. [C] 蓮花，荷花 (pl. lotuses, lotus)
   ▲ In the pond, lotuses float on the surface of the water.
   水池中有蓮花漂浮在水面上。

10. **modernize** [`madɚˌnaɪz] v. (使) 現代化

▲ The mayor planned to modernize the transportation system. 市長計畫將運輸系統現代化。

11. **nucleus** [ˋnjuklɪəs] n. [C] 核心 <of>；原子核 (pl. nuclei)

   ▲ These players form the nucleus of our school team. 這些球員組成我們校隊的核心。

12. **outlaw** [ˋaʊtˏlɔ] n. [C] 不法之徒

   ▲ Robin Hood is probably the most famous outlaw in legend. 羅賓漢大概是傳說中最有名的不法之徒。

   outlaw [ˋaʊtˏlɔ] v. 禁止，宣布為非法 [同] ban

   ▲ The sale of alcohol in vending machines is outlawed. 自動販賣機禁止賣酒。

13. **peek** [pik] n. [C] 一瞥 (usu. sing.)

   ▲ The kid sneaked a peek inside the envelope.
   那孩子偷偷瞥了一眼信封裡面。

   💡 have/take a peek 看一眼 | a quick peek 匆匆一瞥

   peek [pik] v. 偷看

   ▲ The thief peeked through the keyhole.
   小偷從鑰匙孔偷看。

14. **posture** [ˋpɑstʃɚ] n. [C][U] 姿勢，姿態；態度，立場 (usu. sing.)

   ▲ Those who have bad posture are very likely to have back pain. 姿勢不良的人很可能會背痛。

   posture [ˋpɑstʃɚ] v. 裝模作樣

▲ Don't mind the yelling man. He is just posturing.
別理那個大吼大叫的人。他只是在裝模作樣。

💡 political posturing 政治作秀

---

15. **psychic** [ˋsaɪkɪk] adj. 有特異功能的，通靈的

▲ I have no idea. I'm not psychic!
我不知道啦，我又不會通靈！

💡 psychic powers 特異功能

---

16. **refine** [rɪˋfaɪn] v. 精煉；使精進，改良，改善

▲ Crude oil must be refined before it can be used as a fuel. 原油必須先經精煉才能當作燃料。

refinement [rɪˋfaɪnmənt] n. [C][U] 改良，改善，改進；[U] 文雅，有教養

▲ Refinements are needed to improve the performance of the car. 這輛車需要改良來提升性能。

refined [rɪˋfaɪnd] adj. 文雅的，有教養的；精煉的，精製的 [反] unrefined

▲ The queen's speech and manners are always refined.
女王的言行舉止總是很文雅。

💡 refined oil/sugar 精煉油 / 精製糖

refinery [rɪˋfaɪnərɪ] n. [C] 精煉廠，精製廠 (pl. refineries)

▲ The beach is polluted by a nearby refinery.
海灘被附近的一座精煉廠汙染了。

💡 oil/sugar refinery 煉油廠 / 製糖廠

---

17. **revive** [rɪ`vaɪv] v. (使) 復興；(使) 甦醒，(使) 復甦
   ▲ The old custom is reviving.
   這個古老的風俗正在復興。

18. **serene** [sə`rin] adj. 平靜的，寧靜的
   ▲ The nun leads a serene life.
   那位修女過著平靜的生活。
   serenity [sə`rɛnətɪ] n. [U] 平靜，寧靜
   ▲ Joanne looked at her baby with complete serenity.
   Joanne 十分平靜地看著她的寶貝。

19. **sly** [slaɪ] adj. 狡猾的 [同] cunning (slyer, slier | slycst, sliest)
   ▲ That dishonest man is as sly as a fox.
   那個不誠實的男人像隻狐狸一樣地狡猾。
   💡 on the sly 偷偷地

20. **staple** [`stepl̩] n. [C] 主要產物；主食或基本食物；釘書針
   ▲ Coffee is one of the staples of Brazil.
   咖啡是巴西的主要產物之一。
   staple [`stepl̩] v. 用釘書針固定
   ▲ The teacher stapled the handouts together.
   老師用釘書針把講義釘在一起。
   stapler [`steplɚ] n. [C] 釘書機
   ▲ Put some staples in the stapler.
   把釘書針裝到釘書機裡。

21. **suffocate** [`sʌfə͵ket] v. (使) 窒息而死，(使) 悶死；呼吸困難，難以呼吸
▲ The murderer suffocated the victim by placing a bag over her head.
凶手用一個袋子套在被害人的頭上來悶死她。

22. **tempo** [`tɛmpo] n. [C][U] (樂曲的) 速度，節拍 (pl. tempos, tempi)；(生活等的) 節奏，步調 (pl. tempos)
▲ Can you keep up with the tempo of the music?
你跟得上音樂的節拍嗎？

23. **unanimous** [ju`nænəməs] adj. 一致同意的，無異議的
▲ Did the judges make a unanimous ruling?
法官們有做出一致同意的裁決嗎？

24. **victor** [`vɪktə] n. [C] 優勝者
▲ Ben was the victor of the tournament.
Ben 是錦標賽的優勝者。

25. **withhold** [wɪθ`hold] v. 拒絕給與，拒絕提供 <from> (withheld | withheld | withholding)
▲ You can't withhold information from the police.
你不能拒絕提供消息給警方。

◆

Unit 37

1. **duration** [dju`reʃən] n. [U] 持續期間
▲ The summer camp is of one week's duration.

= The duration of the summer camp is one week.
夏令營為期一週。

💡 for the duration of sth 在…期間

2. **exempt** [ɪgˋzɛmpt] adj. 被免除的，被豁免的 <from>

▲ Some books are exempt from tax in that country.
在該國有些書籍免稅。

💡 exempt from <u>military service/certain exams</u> 免役 / 免試

3. **fishery** [ˋfɪʃərɪ] n. [C] 漁場 (pl. fisheries)

▲ The environmental organization raised public awareness of protecting the fisheries.
該環保組織提高大眾保護漁場的意識。

💡 <u>tuna/salmon</u> fishery <u>鮪魚</u> / <u>鮭魚</u> 漁場 | <u>freshwater/saltwater</u> fishery <u>淡水</u> / <u>鹹水</u> 漁場 | <u>coastal/inshore/deep-sea</u> fishery <u>沿海</u> / <u>近海</u> / <u>深海</u> 漁場

4. **gauge** [gedʒ] n. [C] (燃油、瓦斯等的) 計量表，測量儀器

▲ Does the fuel gauge read full or empty?
油表顯示滿的還是空的？

💡 <u>temperature/rain</u> gauge <u>溫度</u> / <u>雨量</u> 計

gauge [gedʒ] v. 評估，判斷；測量

▲ Francis tried to gauge whether his boss was angry or not. Francis 試著判斷他的老闆是不是在生氣。

💡 gauge sb's <u>mood/reaction</u> 評估…的<u>心情</u> / <u>反應</u>

5. **hedge** [hɛdʒ] n. [C] 樹籬；避免經濟損失等的方式，防範措施 <against>

▲ Tim is trimming the hedge. Tim 正在修剪樹籬。

hedge [hɛdʒ] v. 迴避問題，閃爍其詞；(以樹籬) 圍住

▲ My boyfriend often hedges when I ask him questions. 我男友常在我問他問題時閃爍其詞。

6. **imposing** [ɪmˋpozɪŋ] adj. 宏偉的

▲ The imposing building is a landmark in the city. 這棟宏偉的建築物是這個城市的地標。

7. **intrude** [ɪnˋtrud] v. 侵入，侵擾 <on, into>

▲ How many planes intruded into our airspace yesterday? 昨天有多少飛機侵入我方領空？

💡 intrude on/into sb's private life/personal freedom 侵犯…的私生活 / 個人自由

8. **lesbian** [ˋlɛzbɪən] adj. 女同性戀者的

▲ Sappho is an ancient Greek female poet, especially admired by lesbian communities. 莎芙是特別受到女同性戀團體尊崇的古希臘女詩人。

9. **loudspeaker** [ˋlaʊd͵spikɚ] n. [C] 擴音器

▲ The students listened to the principal's speech over the loudspeaker. 學生透過擴音器聽校長的演講。

10. **monarch** [ˋmɑnɚk] n. [C] 君主

▲ A monarch is a king or queen who rules a country. 君主是統治一國的國王或女王。

monarchy [`mɑnə-kɪ] n. [U] 君主政體；[C] 君主國家 (pl. monarchies)

▲ People sometimes discuss whether to abolish the monarchy. 人們有時會討論要不要廢除君主政體。

---

11. **nude** [njud] adj. 裸體的 [同] naked

▲ There are some nude scenes in this movie.
這部電影有一些裸體的畫面。

🍃 nude model 裸體模特兒

nude [njud] n. [C] 裸體畫

▲ There are several nudes in the exhibition.
展覽中有幾幅裸體畫。

🍃 in the nude 裸體地，一絲不掛地

---

12. **outlook** [`aʊt͵lʊk] n. [C] 景觀，景色；前景，展望 (usu. sing.) <for>；[C][U] 看法，觀點 (usu. sing.) <on>

▲ From the top of the mountain, the outlook over the forest was beautiful. 從山頂上眺望森林的景色很美。

---

13. **pending** [`pɛndɪŋ] adj. 未定的，待決的，即將發生的

▲ The result of the election is still pending.
選舉的結果仍然未定。

🍃 pending case 懸案

---

14. **potent** [`potn̩t] adj. 強大的，強效的，強而有力的

▲ Some potent drugs have unpleasant side effects.
有些強效藥物有不好的副作用。

💡 potent painkiller/weapon/argument 強效止痛藥 / 強大的武器 / 有力的論點

---

15. **psychotherapy** [ˌsaɪko`θɛrəpɪ] n. [U] 心理治療

⚠ A psychotherapist practices psychotherapy by discussing problems with patients rather than by giving them drugs. 心理治療師藉由與病人討論問題，而不是藉由給與病人藥物，來進行心理治療。

---

16. **reflective** [rɪ`flɛktɪv] adj. 反射的，反光的；反映出…的 <of>；深思的，沉思的 [同] thoughtful

⚠ It is safer to wear a reflective jacket when you go jogging at night. 晚上出門慢跑穿反光外套比較安全。

---

17. **revolt** [rɪ`volt] n. [C][U] 反抗 <against> [同] rebellion

⚠ The people rose in revolt against the military government. 人民奮起反抗軍政府。

revolt [rɪ`volt] v. 反抗 <against> [同] rebel；使反感，使厭惡

⚠ The people revolted against tyranny. 人民反抗暴政。

revolting [rɪ`voltɪŋ] adj. 令人反感的，令人作嘔的 [同] disgusting

⚠ It is a revolting habit to take off your shoes and scratch the toes in public.
在公共場合脫掉鞋子抓腳趾頭是令人作嘔的習慣。

---

18. **sergeant** [`sɑrdʒənt] n. [C] 中士

⚠ The soldier saluted the sergeant. 士兵向中士敬禮。

---

19. **smuggle** [ˋsmʌg!] v. 走私

▲ Some people smuggled cocaine into the country.
有些人走私古柯鹼進入這個國家。

smuggler [ˋsmʌglɚ] n. [C] 走私者

▲ The drug smuggler was arrested at the airport.
毒品走私者在機場被逮捕。

20. **starvation** [stɑrˋveʃən] n. [U] 挨餓，飢餓

▲ There are still many people in the world facing
starvation. 世上仍有許多人面臨挨餓。

21. **suitcase** [ˋsutˌkes] n. [C] 行李箱

▲ I packed my suitcase for the trip.
我把旅行的用品裝進行李箱。

22. **terrace** [ˋtɛrɪs] n. [C] 平臺

▲ A girl is sitting on the sea-facing terrace.
一名女孩坐在面海的平臺上。

terrace [ˋtɛrɪs] v. 使成梯田，使成階地

▲ Farmers terraced the hillside to grow rice.
農夫將那片山坡整成梯田來種稻。

terraced [ˋtɛrɪst] adj. 梯田形的，階地狀的

▲ There are some terraced fields by the hill.
山丘旁有些梯田。

23. **unconditional** [ˌʌnkənˋdɪʃən!] adj. 無條件的，無限制的

▲ The enemy finally made an unconditional surrender.
敵軍最終無條件投降了。

💡 unconditional love 毫無保留的愛

24. **vigor** [ˋvɪgɚ] n. [U] 活力，精力 [同] vitality
▲ The students learned English with renewed vigor after a brief break.
學生們在短暫休息後繼續精力充沛地學習英文。

25. **woe** [wo] n. [U] 悲痛；[pl.] 苦難 (~s)
▲ The poor widow's life was full of misery and woe.
那名可憐寡婦的人生充滿了不幸與悲痛。

Unit 38

1. **dusk** [dʌsk] n. [U] 黃昏 [同] twilight
▲ As dusk fell, the farmer went home.
隨著黃昏降臨，那位農夫回家了。
💡 at dusk 在黃昏時刻

2. **exert** [ɪgˋzɝt] v. 運用或行使 (權力等)，施加 (影響力等)
▲ Several politicians exerted great pressure on the committee to pass the proposal.
數名政客向委員會大力施壓以通過提案。
💡 exert oneself 盡力，努力

3. **flourish** [ˋflɝɪʃ] v. 繁榮，興盛 [同] thrive；茁壯成長，茂盛 [同] thrive
▲ My business is flourishing. 我的生意興隆。

flourish [ˈflɝɪʃ] n. [C] 誇張或引人注目的動作 (usu. sing.)

▲ The magician opened the box with a flourish.
魔術師動作誇張地打開箱子。

4. **glamour** [ˈglæmɚ] n. [U] 魅力

▲ The couple couldn't resist the glamour of staying in a five-star hotel.
那對情侶無法抗拒住宿五星級飯店的魅力。

5. **hemisphere** [ˈhɛməsˌfɪr] n. [C] (地球等天體的) 半球；腦半球

▲ The equator divides the Earth into the southern and northern hemispheres. 赤道把地球分成南北半球。

💡 the left/right hemisphere 左 / 右半腦

6. **imprison** [ɪmˈprɪzn̩] v. 使入獄，關押，監禁

▲ The two men were imprisoned for drug dealing.
那兩個男人因為販毒而被關押入獄。

imprisonment [ɪmˈprɪzn̩mənt] n. [U] 入獄，關押，監禁

▲ The drug dealers were sentenced to 25 years' imprisonment. 那些毒犯被判處二十五年徒刑。

💡 life imprisonment 終身監禁

7. **inventory** [ˈɪnvənˌtorɪ] n. [C][U] 存貨，庫存 [同] stock (pl. inventories)

▲ The store keeps a large inventory of kitchen utensils.
這家店有大量廚房用具的存貨。

inventory [ˈɪnvənˌtorɪ] v. 列出清單

▲ The storekeeper is inventorying the stock.
店主正在列出存貨的清單。

---

8. **lessen** [ˈlɛsn̩] v. 減少，減輕，減低 [同] diminish, reduce

▲ Eating vegetables can lessen the risk of cancer.
多吃蔬菜可減低罹患癌症的危險。

---

9. **lucrative** [ˈlukrətɪv] adj. 有利潤的，賺錢的，有利可圖
的 [同] profitable

▲ The entrepreneur is looking for a more lucrative
market. 那名企業家在尋找更有利可圖的市場。

---

10. **monstrous** [ˈmɑnstrəs] adj. (像怪獸般) 龐大而駭人的，
巨大的；凶殘或醜惡的，駭人聽聞的

▲ The lost child was frightened by monstrous shadows
of the trees in the forest.
這迷路的孩子被森林中彷彿大怪獸的樹影嚇壞了。

💡 monstrous crime/lie 凶殘或駭人聽聞的罪行 / 彌天大
謊

---

11. **nurture** [ˈnɝtʃɚ] v. 培養

▲ Parents should nurture their children's special talents.
父母親應該培養孩子的特殊天分。

nurture [ˈnɝtʃɚ] n. [U] 培養，養育，教養

▲ I believe both nature and nurture greatly influence a
child's development.
我相信本性和養育對孩子的發展都有很大的影響。

---

12. **outrage** [`aʊt͵redʒ] n. [U] 憤怒，憤慨

▲ The release of the murderer provoked public outrage.
謀殺犯被釋放這件事激起公憤。

outrage [`aʊt͵redʒ] v. 激怒

▲ Mike shouted at his sister because he was outraged by her insult.
Mike 對他的姊姊大吼，因為他被她的侮辱給激怒。

---

13. **peninsula** [pə`nɪnsələ] n. [C] 半島

▲ Vivian bought a house on the Florida Peninsula.
Vivian 在佛羅里達半島買了一棟房子。

🔖 the Korean/Arabian Peninsula 朝鮮／阿拉伯半島

---

14. **poultry** [`poltrɪ] n. [pl.] 家禽；[U] 家禽的肉

▲ The farmer keeps poultry such as chicken, ducks, and geese. 那名農夫養了雞、鴨、鵝等家禽。

🔖 poultry farming 家禽養殖業

---

15. **publicize** [`pʌblɪ͵saɪz] v. 宣傳，宣揚

▲ The author gave speeches to publicize her latest book. 這位作家以演講來宣傳新書。

🔖 be much/well/highly/widely publicized 廣為宣傳的

---

16. **refreshments** [rɪ`frɛʃmənts] n. [pl.] 點心，茶點 (also refreshment)

▲ Let's take some refreshments at the café.
我們到咖啡館吃些點心吧。

---

17. **revolve** [rɪˋvɑlv] v. (使) 旋轉，(使) 轉動 <around>；圍繞著…打轉，以…為中心或重心 <around>
  ▲ Many planets, including the Earth, revolve around the Sun. 很多行星，包括地球，繞著太陽轉動。
  💡 revolving door 旋轉門

18. **serial** [ˋsɪrɪəl] adj. 連續的，連環的，一連串的
  ▲ Jack saw a thriller about a serial killer.
    Jack 看了一部有關連續殺人魔的驚悚片。
  💡 serial novel/number 連載小說 / 編號或序號

19. **sneaker** [ˋsnikɚ] n. [C] (膠底) 運動鞋 (usu. pl.)
  ▲ The athlete wore a pair of black sneakers.
    那位運動員穿著一雙黑色的運動鞋。

20. **statesman** [ˋstetsmən] n. [C] 政治家
  ▲ There are many politicians, but few statesmen.
    政客很多，但政治家很少。
  statesmanship [ˋstetsmənˏʃɪp] n. [U] 政治才能
  ▲ People praise the leader for his statesmanship.
    人們讚賞那位領導者的政治才能。

21. **summon** [ˋsʌmən] v. 召喚，傳喚；鼓起 (勇氣等) <up>
  ▲ The driver was summoned to appear in court as a witness. 那位駕駛被傳喚出庭作證。
  💡 summon a meeting/conference 召開會議

22. **thermometer** [θɚˋmɑmətɚ] n. [C] 溫度計
  ▲ The thermometer reads 36°C.

溫度計顯示為攝氏三十六度。

23. **underestimate** [ˌʌndɚˈɛstəˌmet] v. 低估

▲ We failed because we underestimated the difficulty of the task.
我們因為低估了這項工作的困難性而失敗了。

underestimate [ˌʌndɚˈɛstəmɪt] n. [C] 低估

▲ Those figures might be underestimates.
那些數據可能都是低估。

24. **villa** [ˈvɪlə] n. [C] 別墅

▲ Let's rent a seaside villa for our honeymoon.
我們租一棟海濱別墅來度蜜月吧。

25. **wrestle** [ˈrɛsl] v. 摔角，將…摔倒或壓制在地 <with>；奮力對付，努力處理 <with>

▲ Michael wrestled the attacker to the ground.
Michael 把襲擊者摔倒並壓制在地上。

wrestle [ˈrɛsl] n. [sing.] 奮鬥，掙扎

▲ After a brief wrestle with her conscience, Ruby decided to take the money she found on the road to the police station. 經過一番天人交戰，Ruby 決定將路上撿到的錢送交警察局。

Unit 39

1. **dwarf** [dwɔrf] n. [C] (童話中的) 小矮人；侏儒 (pl. dwarfs, dwarves)

   ▲ In the story, the princess Snow White lives with seven dwarfs in the forest.
   在故事中，白雪公主和七個小矮人住在森林裡。

   dwarf [dwɔrf] v. 使顯得矮小

   ▲ I was dwarfed by the sumo wrestler's gigantic figure.
   相撲選手龐大的身軀使我顯得矮小。

   dwarf [dwɔrf] adj. 矮小的

   ▲ Jason grows dwarf trees in pots in the living room.
   Jason 在客廳種矮小的樹木盆栽。

2. **expenditure** [ɪk`spɛndɪtʃɚ] n. [C][U] 花費，支出，開銷 <on>

   ▲ The government tried to reduce annual expenditure on education. 政府試圖縮減年度教育支出。

3. **flunk** [flʌŋk] v. 考試不及格

   ▲ I flunked math. 我數學考不及格。

   ♥ flunk a test/an exam 考試不及格 | flunk out (因課業成績不及格) 遭到退學

   flunk [flʌŋk] n. [C][U] 不及格 (的成績)

4. **glide** [glaɪd] v. 滑動，滑行；滑翔

   ▲ Skaters glided over the frozen lake.
   溜冰的人在結冰的湖面上滑行。

glide [glaɪd] n. [sing.] 滑行或滑翔

▲ The airplane will go into a glide. 飛機將開始滑行。

5. **heroic** [hə`roɪk] adj. 英雄的，英勇的

▲ The heroic young man saved the hostages.
這位英勇的年輕人拯救了人質。

heroics [hɪ`roɪks] n. [pl.] 英雄表現，英勇事蹟

▲ Ben's heroics made the kids admire him very much.
Ben 的英雄表現讓孩子們對他仰慕萬分。

6. **incline** [ɪn`klaɪn] v. (使) 傾向；(使) 傾斜

▲ The rescue team inclined to take action as soon as possible. 救援隊傾向於盡快採取行動。

incline [`ɪn,klaɪn] n. [C] 斜坡，斜面

▲ There is a beautiful house at the top of the incline.
斜坡頂端有間漂亮的房子。

💡 gentle/slight/steep incline 緩 / 陡坡

7. **ironic** [aɪ`rɑnɪk] adj. 嘲諷的，諷刺的 (also ironical)

▲ It is ironic that such a small man is called "Big" John. 諷刺的是，這樣矮小的男人叫做「大」約翰。

💡 ironic smile/remark 嘲諷的微笑 / 言語

ironically [aɪ`rɑnɪklɪ] adv. 嘲諷地

▲ Ironically, the seats in the economy section of the concert hall were still quite expensive.
諷刺的是，音樂廳的經濟座位仍然相當貴。

8. **lethal** [ˋliθəl] adj. 致命的 [同] fatal, deadly
   ▲ The house was on fire and full of lethal fumes within minutes.
   房子起火了，幾分鐘之內就充滿了致命的毒氣。

---

9. **lure** [lʊr] n. [C] 誘惑 (力) (usu. sing.)
   ▲ Tony couldn't resist the lure of the chocolate cake.
   Tony 無法抗拒巧克力蛋糕的誘惑。
   lure [lʊr] v. 誘惑 <to, into, away from>
   ▲ We lured him away from the company by offering him a much higher salary.
   我們提供更高的薪資誘惑他離開那家公司。

---

10. **moody** [ˋmudɪ] adj. 喜 怒 無 常 的 ，情 緒 多 變 的 (moodier | moodiest)
    ▲ It's not easy to get along with moody people.
    喜怒無常的人不好相處。

---

11. **oasis** [oˋesɪs] n. [C] 綠洲；舒適宜人的地方 (pl. oases)
    ▲ The grassy oasis is a natural habitat for animals in the desert.
    這片碧草如茵的綠洲是沙漠動物的天然棲地。

---

12. **outrageous** [aʊtˋredʒəs] adj. 駭人聽聞的，令人難以接受的，離譜的
    ▲ The suspect committed an outrageous crime.
    那名嫌犯犯下駭人聽聞的罪行。
    outrageously [aʊtˋredʒəslɪ] adv. 離譜地

▲ Everything in that restaurant is outrageously expensive. 那家餐廳的每一樣東西都貴得離譜。

13. **perch** [pɜtʃ] n. [C] 高處

▲ We had a good view from our perch on the hilltop.
我們在高高的小山頂上視野很好。

perch [pɜtʃ] v. 棲息

▲ The eagle perched on the top of the tree.
老鷹停在樹梢。

14. **preach** [pritʃ] v. 傳教，講道；倡導，勸說

▲ The minister preached to the crowd on forgiveness.
牧師以寬恕為題對大眾講道。

💡 preach the gospel 傳福音 | preach at/to sb about sth
向…嘮叨勸戒…

15. **puff** [pʌf] n. [C] 一口氣；蓬鬆的東西

▲ Bob blew out the candle in a puff.
Bob 一口氣吹熄了蠟燭。

💡 powder/cream puff 粉撲 / 奶油泡芙

puff [pʌf] v. 抽菸 <on, at>；噴出 (蒸汽等)

▲ The old man puffed on his pipe. 那位老伯抽著菸斗。

💡 puff out sb's cheeks 鼓起兩頰

16. **refute** [rɪˋfjut] v. 反駁，駁斥

▲ The speaker spoke with such certainty that it seemed impossible to refute his argument. 那位演講者說得如此肯定，令人似乎無法反駁他的論點。

17. **rigorous** [ˋrɪgərəs] adj. 嚴謹的，嚴格的
   ▲ The recruits received rigorous military training.
   那些新兵接受了嚴格的軍事訓練。

18. **sermon** [ˋsɝmən] n. [C] 布道，講道；(令人厭煩的) 說教
   ▲ The priest is preaching a sermon in the church.
   牧師正在教堂裡講道。

19. **sneaky** [ˋsnikɪ] adj. 偷 偷 摸 摸 的 ，鬼 鬼 祟 祟 的
   (sneakier | sneakiest)
   ▲ Don't play any sneaky trick on me!
   別對我玩什麼偷偷摸摸的花樣！

20. **stationery** [ˋsteʃənˏɛrɪ] n. [U] 文具
   ▲ The store at the corner also sells stationery, such as
   pens, paper, and envelopes.
   轉角那家店也有賣筆、紙、信封等文具。

21. **superficial** [ˏsupɚˋfɪʃəl] adj. 表面的，表皮的；膚淺的
   ▲ It's lucky for you to escape with only superficial
   wounds in such a serious accident.
   你很幸運，在這麼嚴重的意外事故中只受到皮肉傷。

22. **tilt** [tɪlt] n. [C][U] 傾斜，歪斜 (usu. sing.)
   ▲ The painting seemed to be at a slight tilt.
   那幅畫好像有點傾斜了。
   💡 (at) full tilt 全速地
   tilt [tɪlt] v. (使) 傾斜，(使) 歪斜 [同] tip；(使) 傾向，
   (使) 偏向 <toward>

▲ Allen tilted his chair back against the wall.

Allen 把椅背斜靠在牆上。

---

23. **underpass** [ˋʌndəˏpæs] n. [C] 地下道

▲ The underpass is closed because of flooding.

地下道因為淹水而關閉了。

---

24. **vine** [vaɪn] n. [C] 藤本植物或攀緣植物 (的藤蔓)

▲ The vines have been trained around the window frames. 藤蔓被修整成圍繞著窗框生長。

---

25. **wrinkle** [ˋrɪŋkl̩] n. [C] (皮膚的) 皺紋；(布料等的) 皺褶 (usu. pl.) [同] crease

▲ The model tried the cream to reduce the fine wrinkles around her eyes.

那名模特兒試用乳霜來消除眼睛周圍的細紋。

wrinkle [ˋrɪŋkl̩] v. (使) 起皺紋 <up>；(使) 起皺褶 [同] crease

▲ The boy wrinkled up his nose at the smell in disgust.

男孩聞到味道，厭惡地皺起了鼻子。

💡 wrinkle sb's brow 皺眉

Unit 40

1. **expiration** [ˏɛkspəˋreʃən] n. [U] 到期，期滿

▲ Can I renew the lease before its expiration?

我可以在租約到期前就先續約嗎？

💡 expiration date 到期日，有效使用期限

2. **foe** [fo] n. [C] 敵人

▲ These two nations joined together to fight their common foe. 這兩國聯合起來對抗共同的敵人。

3. **gloom** [glum] n. [U][sing.] 陰暗；憂鬱 [同] depression

▲ Leona saw an animal emerging from the gloom of the hallway.

Leona 看見陰暗的走廊中出現了一隻動物。

gloom [glum] v. (使) 憂鬱，(使) 消沉

▲ Emma gloomed for several months after her lover passed away. Emma 在愛人過世後消沉了數月之久。

4. **heterosexual** [ˌhɛtərə`sɛkʃʊəl] adj. 異性戀的

▲ Whether in heterosexual or homosexual relationships, people should respect each other. 不管是在異性戀的或是同性戀的關係中，人都要互相尊重。

heterosexual [ˌhɛtərə`sɛkʃʊəl] n. [C] 異性戀者

▲ All people, whether heterosexuals or homosexuals, should show respect for each other. 所有的人，不管是異性戀者還是同性戀者，都應該要互相尊重。

5. **incur** [ɪn`kɝ] v. 招致，引起，遭受 (incurred | incurred | incurring)

▲ This controversial movie incurred the wrath of the public when it was released ten years ago.

這部有爭議的電影十年前上映時，引起了大眾的憤怒。

6. **irritable** [ˈɪrətəbl̩] adj. 易怒的，煩躁的 [同] bad-tempered；
(器官等) 敏感的
▲ The hot weather made me irritable.
炎熱的天氣使我煩躁。

7. **liable** [ˈlaɪəbl̩] adj. 要負法律責任的 <for>；可能…的，
容易 (遭受)…的 <to>
▲ The careless driver was liable for the damage he
caused.
那位粗心的駕駛必須對他造成的損失負起法律責任。
💡 be liable for a debt 有義務償付債務

8. **madam** [ˈmædəm] n. [C] 太太，小姐，女士 [同] ma'am
▲ May I help you, madam? 小姐，我能為您效勞嗎？

9. **motherhood** [ˈmʌðəˌhʊd] n. [U] 母親身分
▲ Mary tries to strike a balance between her career and
motherhood.
Mary 試著在事業和母親身分之間找到平衡。

10. **oatmeal** [ˈotˌmil] n. [U] 燕麥片，燕麥粉，燕麥粥
▲ Christopher usually eats oatmeal for breakfast.
Christopher 通常吃燕麥片當早餐。
💡 oatmeal bread/cookie 燕麥麵包 / 餅乾

11. **peril** [ˈpɛrəl] n. [C][U] (重大的) 危險
▲ Firefighters put their own lives in peril to rescue
people from dangerous situations.
消防員為了救人脫離險境，置自己的生命於危險之中。

peril [ˋpɛrəl] v. 將 (性命等) 置於危險之中 (periled, perilled | periled, perilled | periling, perilling)

perilous [ˋpɛrələs] adj. 非常危險的

▲ Icy roads are very perilous to drivers.
結冰的道路對駕駛人來說很危險。

12. **precede** [prɪˋsid] v. 在⋯之前

▲ Sam preceded the report with a brief introduction.
Sam 在報告之前先做了一個簡短的介紹。

precedence [ˋprɛsədəns] n. [U] 優先 <over> [同] priority

▲ I believe quality always takes precedence over quantity. 我認為質永遠比量重要。

13. **punctual** [ˋpʌŋktʃʊəl] adj. 準時的

▲ Kevin is always punctual for appointments.
Kevin 約會一向準時。

punctually [ˋpʌŋktʃʊəlɪ] adv. 準時地

▲ The employees are required to arrive at work punctually every day. 員工被要求必須每天準時上班。

14. **rehabilitate** [ˏriəˋbɪləˏtet] v. 使康復或恢復正常生活；修復

▲ We need plans and places to help rehabilitate drug addicts. 我們需要協助藥物成癮者恢復正常生活的計畫和地方。

15. **ripple** [ˋrɪpl] n. [C] 漣漪

▲ A gentle wind made ripples on the surface of the pond. 微風使池面泛起漣漪。

💡 a ripple of laughter/applause/excitement 一陣笑聲 / 掌聲 / 騷動

ripple [ˋrɪpl] v. (使) 起漣漪

▲ A soft breeze rippled the lake.
輕柔的微風在湖面吹起漣漪。

---

16. **setback** [ˋsɛt͵bæk] n. [C] 阻礙，挫折 <to, for, in>

▲ The CEO's resignation was a serious setback to the company. 執行長辭職對公司而言是個重大的打擊。

💡 suffer/receive/experience a setback 遭遇挫折

---

17. **snore** [snor] v. 打鼾

▲ My father snores horribly every night.
我爸每天晚上打鼾的聲音都大得嚇人。

snore [snor] n. [C] 鼾聲

▲ My father's loud snores woke me up.
我爸響亮的鼾聲吵醒了我。

---

18. **stature** [ˋstætʃɚ] n. [U] 身高 [同] height ；名望，聲譽 [同] reputation

▲ The boy's short stature prevented him from joining the basketball team.
那男孩因為身材矮小而無法加入籃球隊。

💡 gain/grow/rise in stature 聲望提高

19. **superintendent** [ˌsupɚɪn`tɛndənt] n. [C] 主管，負責人
   ▲ The superintendent of our department asks us to report to him once a week. 我們部門的主管要求我們每週一次向他報告工作情況。

20. **tiptoe** [`tɪp͵to] n. [C][U] 腳尖
   ▲ I walked up the stairs on tiptoe.
   我躡手躡腳地走上樓。
   💡 stand/walk on tiptoe(s) 踮起腳尖站立 / 走路
   tiptoe [`tɪp͵to] v. 踮著腳尖走
   ▲ We tiptoed so we would not make a sound and wake up the baby.
   我們踮腳走路以免發出任何聲響吵醒嬰兒。

21. **vineyard** [`vɪnjɚd] n. [C] 葡萄園
   ▲ Eric owns a vineyard that can produce 500 gallons of wine every year.
   Eric 擁有一座能年產五百加侖葡萄酒的葡萄園。

22. **yearn** [jɝn] v. 渴望 <for, to> [同] long
   ▲ The prisoner yearned for his freedom.
   這囚犯渴望自由。

23. **yogurt** [`jogɚt] n. [C][U] 優酪乳，優格
   ▲ A bowl of yogurt with fruit makes a delicious and nutritious breakfast.
   一碗優格加水果是美味又營養的早餐。

24. **zoom** [zum] v. 激增 [同] escalate；快速移動，疾駛而過
   ▲ Interest rates have zoomed from 5% to 15% in the
      past few days. 利率在過去幾天內已由 5% 漲到 15%。
   💡 zoom in/out (鏡頭) 拉近 / 遠
   zoom [zum] n. [C] 變焦鏡頭 (also zoom lens)
   ▲ Take a close-up with a zoom.
      用變焦鏡頭拍一張特寫。

NOTE 🖉

單字索引

單字索引

340

單字索引

單字索引

單字索引

單字索引

單字索引

單字索引

我的進度檢核表，
學習完成就打勾☑！

PLUS	①②③④⑤⑥⑦⑧⑨⑩

Congratulations!

Unit 1

1. **ace** [es] n. [C] 一流的發球
   ▲ Peter hit an ace on his first serve.
   Peter 一開始就擊出了一個漂亮的發球。
   ace [es] adj. 一流的
   ▲ David's an ace football player.
   David 是一流的美式足球選手。

2. **artifact** [ˈɑrtɪ͵fækt] n. [C] 人工製品 (also artefact)
   ▲ Artifacts such as bowls were created in prehistoric times.
   像碗之類的人工製品在史前時代就被製作出來了。

3. **barefoot** [ˈbɛr͵fʊt] adv. 赤腳地
   ▲ I love to walk barefoot in the sand at the beach.
   我喜歡光著腳走在海邊沙灘上。

4. **chatter** [ˈtʃætɚ] v. 喋喋不休 [同] jabber；(機器、牙齒等) 咯咯作響，顫動
   ▲ Stop chattering and finish your work.
   不要再喋喋不休，做完你的工作吧！
   chatter [ˈtʃætɚ] n. [U] 閒聊
   ▲ My roommates' endless chatter is annoying.
   室友們聊天聊個沒完，真令人受不了。

5. **clench** [klɛntʃ] v. 咬緊；握緊 [同] grasp
   ▲ The girl clenched her teeth to hold back the tears.

女孩咬緊牙關忍住淚水。

---

6. **crook** [krʊk] n. [C] 彎曲處 [同] bend
   ▲ The vet held the puppy in the crook of her arm.
   獸醫將小狗抱在她的臂彎裡。
   crook [krʊk] v. 使彎曲 [同] bend [反] straighten
   ▲ My supervisor crooked his finger, gesturing for me to
   go to him. 主管彎曲手指，示意我過去他那邊。
   crooked [`krʊkɪd] adj. 彎曲的 [同] bent [反] straight；欺
   詐的 [同] dishonest [反] honest
   ▲ Many collisions happened along the crooked road.
   這彎曲的路段發生過許多撞車事件。

---

7. **dissuade** [dɪ`swed] v. 勸阻 <from> [同] deter [反]
   persuade
   ▲ The father dissuaded his daughter from marrying her
   boyfriend. 這位父親勸阻女兒不要和男朋友結婚。

---

8. **doorstep** [`dɔr,stɛp] n. [C] 門口的臺階
   ▲ A cat is sleeping on the doorstep.
   一隻貓在門口的臺階上睡覺。
   💡 on one's doorstep 在某人住家附近

---

9. **ebb** [ɛb] n. [C] 退潮 (usu. sing.)
   ▲ The tide is on the ebb now. 現在正在退潮。
   💡 the ebb and flow 潮起潮落；(人生、事業等的) 盛衰
   ebb [ɛb] v. 衰退 <away> [同] decline [反] grow
   ▲ The injured soldier felt his life ebbing away.

受傷的士兵感到生命力正在流失。

---

10. **expel** [ɪk`spɛl] v. 驅逐 <from> [同] dismiss [反] accept
(expelled | expelled | expelling)

▲ The student was expelled from school for hitting a
teacher. 這名學生因毆打老師而被學校退學了。

---

11. **fret** [frɛt] v. 苦惱 <about, over> [同] worry (fretted |
fretted | fretting)

▲ Susan spent most of her time fretting about trifles.
Susan 大半時間在為小事煩惱。

---

12. **hairdo** [`hɛr͵du] n. [C] 髮型 [同] hairstyle

▲ Mrs. Wang got a new hairdo in that hairdressing
salon. 王太太在那家美容院做了一個新髮型。

---

13. **hereafter** [hɪr`æftɚ] adv. 從今以後 [同] from now on

▲ Mr. White will hereafter be in charge of our
company's computers.

從現在起由 White 先生來管理我們公司的電腦。

hereafter [hɪr`æftɚ] n. [sing.] 來世 (the ～) [同]
afterlife

▲ My mother believes that she will meet my father
again in the hereafter.

我媽媽相信死後會和爸爸再相遇。

---

14. **incidental** [͵ɪnsə`dɛntḷ] adj. 附帶的 <to>

▲ The bill includes several incidental charges.

這帳單包含了幾項雜支。

---

15. **nonviolent** [nɑn`vaɪələnt] adj. 非暴力的
    ▲ Dr. King led nonviolent protests against racial discrimination.
    金恩博士領導非暴力抗爭反對種族歧視。

    nonviolence [nɑn`vaɪələns] n. [U] 非暴力 (主義)，消極反抗
    ▲ Mahatma Gandhi is a proponent of nonviolence.
    聖雄甘地是非暴力主義的倡導者。

---

16. **preface** [`prɛfəs] v. 為⋯作序文，為⋯作開場 <with>
    ▲ I prefaced my speech with my sincere gratitude to the organizers.
    我以我對主辦單位誠摯的感謝作為演說的開場白。

---

17. **prune** [prun] v. 修剪 <back> [同] trim；刪除，刪減 <back> [同] eliminate
    ▲ John spent the weekend pruning back the hedges.
    John 整個週末都在修剪樹籬。

---

18. **retaliate** [rɪ`tælɪ‚et] v. 報復 <by, against> [同] revenge
    ▲ Tom slapped Jack, so Jack retaliated by kicking Tom's ankle. Tom 打了 Jack 一巴掌，於是 Jack 踢 Tom 的腳踝來報復。

    retaliation [rɪ‚tælɪ`eʃən] n. [U] 報復 <against, for> [同] revenge
    ▲ The citizens lived under the terrorists' threats of

retaliation. 市民們活在恐怖分子報復的威脅中。

---

19. **spire** [spaɪr] n. [C] 尖頂 [同] steeple
   ▲ The spires of the Catholic church were visible in the distance. 那座天主教堂的尖塔從遠處就可看到。

---

20. **streak** [strik] n. [C] 條紋 [同] stripe；傾向
   ▲ There were streaks of mascara on your cheek. 你臉頰上有一些睫毛膏。
   ♥ a streak of lightning 一道閃電 | a cruel/mean/jealous/ romantic streak | 性格殘暴 / 卑鄙 / 善妒 / 浪漫
   streak [strik] v. 在⋯留下條紋；疾馳
   ▲ Alan was streaked with sweat after exercising.
   運動過後，Alan 身上都是汗水的痕跡。

---

21. **tempest** [ˋtɛmpɪst] n. [C] 暴風雨 [同] storm
   ▲ A violent tempest blew the ship off its course.
   猛烈的暴風雨把船吹離了航線。

---

22. **trot** [trɑt] n. [C] 騎馬疾行；[sing.] 奔走，小跑步
   ▲ The cavalry went at a trot. 騎兵隊快馬前進。
   trot [trɑt] v. 快步走，急速前進 <along> (trotted | trotted | trotting)
   ▲ The dog trotted along after the sheep.
   狗快步地追趕著羊。

---

23. **uphold** [ʌpˋhold] v. 支持，維護 [同] support (upheld | upheld | upholding)
   ▲ The president vowed to uphold the rights of minority

groups. 總統誓言維護少數族群的權利。

24. **victorious** [vɪk`torɪəs] adj. 獲勝的 <in, over> [同] triumphant

▲ We were victorious over our opponents.
我們擊敗了對手。

25. **zinc** [zɪŋk] n. [U] 鋅

▲ The iron bar is plated with zinc to stop it from rusting. 這根鐵棒被鍍上鋅以免生鏽。

Unit 2

1. **arctic** [`ɑrktɪk] adj. 北極的 (also Arctic) ; 極寒的 [同] frigid

▲ This moss is usually found in Arctic regions.
這種苔蘚通常可以在北極地區找到。

Arctic [`ɑrktɪk] n. [U] 北極區 (the ~)

▲ Penguins live in the Antarctic, and polar bears live in the Arctic. 企鵝住在南極,北極熊住在北極。

2. **asylum** [ə`saɪləm] n. [U] (政治的) 庇護 [同] shelter

▲ A Russian athlete asked for political asylum while attending the Olympic Games.
一名俄國運動員於參加奧運時請求政治庇護。

💡 grant sb asylum 給予…庇護

3. **barometer** [bə`rɑmətɚ] n. [C] 氣壓計;變化指標 <of>

▲ Thunderstorms are likely to occur when the barometer falls suddenly in the summer.

夏天氣壓突然下降時，很有可能會出現雷雨天氣。

---

4. **carbohydrate** [ˌkɑrboˈhaɪdret] n. [C][U] 碳水化合物，醣類

▲ Soda pop contains carbohydrates.

汽水裡含有碳水化合物。

---

5. **check-in** [ˈtʃɛkˌɪn] n. [U] (機場、旅館等的) 報到 (手續)；[C] (機場、旅館的) 報到處

▲ E-tickets make check-in easier.

電子機票使報到手續更簡單。

checkout [ˈtʃɛkˌaʊt] n. [C] 收銀臺；[U] (旅館等的) 退房，結帳離開

▲ During the summer vacation, I worked part-time at the checkout in a supermarket.

暑假時我在超市兼差收銀。

---

6. **commence** [kəˈmɛns] v. 開始 [同] begin [反] end

▲ Classes will commence in February.

課程將於二月開始。

---

7. **deficiency** [dɪˈfɪʃənsɪ] n. [C][U] 不足 <in, of> [同] lack [反] sufficiency；缺陷 <in> [同] flaw

▲ Many elderly people suffer from broken bones caused by calcium deficiency.

很多老年人因為鈣質不足而骨折。

deficient [dɪˋfɪʃənt] adj. 缺乏的 <in> [同] inadequate ；有缺陷的 <in> [同] defective

▲ Junk food is deficient in nutrients.
垃圾食品缺乏營養。

💡 mentally deficient 智能不足的

---

8. **distort** [dɪsˋtɔrt] v. 扭曲 (聲音、圖像等)；曲解事實 [同] misrepresent

▲ Linda's face was distorted in the broken mirror.
從破掉的鏡子裡看，Linda 的臉變形了。

---

9. **ecstasy** [ˋɛkstəsɪ] n. [C][U] 欣喜若狂

▲ The people of Morocco went into ecstasies over the historic victory in the World Cup. 摩洛哥人民因在世界盃足球賽取得歷史性的勝利而欣喜若狂。

---

10. **expertise** [͵ɛkspɚˋtiz] n. [U] 專門的知識技術 <in>

▲ The job requires expertise in computer programming.
這項工作需要專業的電腦程式設計能力。

---

11. **exquisite** [ˋɛkskwɪzɪt] adj. (品味等) 敏銳的，有鑑賞力的 ；(工藝等) 精美的，細緻的 [同] delicate

▲ Mrs. Smith had exquisite taste in clothes.
Smith 太太穿著的品味高雅。

---

12. **generalize** [ˋdʒɛnərəl͵aɪz] v. 概括而論 <about> [同] conclude ；歸納 <from>

▲ The author generalized that people who live in a big city are indifferent and selfish.

作者概括而論地說大城市的人都冷漠且自私。

---

13. **heavenly** [ˈhɛvənlɪ] adj. 天堂的 [同] divine；極好的 [同]
wonderful [反] awful

▲ This song is like a heavenly melody.
這首歌如同天堂之樂般悅耳。

💡 heavenly Father 天父，上帝

---

14. **oar** [or] n. [C] 槳

▲ We need a pair of oars to row the boat.
我們需要一對槳來划船。

---

15. **prick** [prɪk] v. 刺，戳洞 [同] puncture；刺痛

▲ Potatoes cook faster if you prick them before baking.
烤馬鈴薯前先在上面戳洞會比較快熟。

💡 prick one's conscience 使某人良心不安

---

16. **quarrelsome** [ˈkwɔrəlsəm] adj. 好爭吵的 [同]
argumentative [反] agreeable

▲ The two brothers are quarrelsome. They are always
fighting. 這兩兄弟愛吵架。他們總是爭吵不休。

---

17. **reel** [ril] n. [C] 一卷

▲ Robert put a reel of film in the camera and started to
take pictures. Robert 把一卷底片放入相機開始拍照。

reel [ril] v. 用捲軸捲；蹣跚 [同] stagger

▲ The angler is reeling in his catch.
垂釣者正把魚拉上來。

18. **ruby** [`rubɪ] n. [C] 紅寶石

▲ A ruby ring is my favorite type of jewelry.
紅寶石戒指是我最喜歡的珠寶類型。

ruby [`rubɪ] adj. 紅寶石色的

▲ The wine is ruby in color. 這葡萄酒有紅寶石的色澤。

---

19. **smack** [smæk] v. 拍打，掌摑 [同] slap；(看到食物而) 咂嘴

▲ The mother punished her son by smacking his bottom. 那位母親用打屁股的方式處罰兒子。

smack [smæk] n. [C] 摑掌，猛擊 [同] slap；咂嘴，大聲親吻

▲ Ian got a smack in the face from his friend.
Ian 被他朋友打了臉。

---

20. **stump** [stʌmp] n. [C] 樹樁

▲ The trees were cut down to a stump.
樹被砍到只剩樹樁。

💡 the stump of a candle/tooth/tree 蠟燭頭 / 斷齒根 / 樹樁

stump [stʌmp] v. 使困惑 [同] bewilder

▲ This sudoku puzzle stumps me.
這個數獨題目難倒我了。

---

21. **thrift** [θrɪft] n. [U] 節儉

▲ Jenny's parents asked her to practice thrift.
Jenny 的父母要求她力行節儉。

thrifty [`θrɪftɪ] adj. 節儉的 [同] economical

▲ My wife is a thrifty shopper, always looking for the cheapest prices.

我老婆買東西很省，總是在找最便宜的價格。

22. **topple** [ˈtɑpl̩] v. 傾倒 [同] overturn；推翻 [同] overthrow

▲ The pile of bricks toppled over onto the ground.

那堆磚塊坍倒在地上。

23. **umpire** [ˈʌmpaɪr] n. [C] (棒球、網球、板球等的) 裁判

▲ The umpire called the batter out. 裁判判打者出局。

umpire [ˈʌmpaɪr] v. 裁判

▲ Mr. Green was asked to umpire the game.

Green 先生被要求當這場比賽的裁判。

24. **urine** [ˈjʊrɪn] n. [U] 尿液

▲ The doctor needed a sample of her urine for a further medical examination.

醫生需要她的尿液樣本來做更進一步的化驗。

25. **utmost** [ˈʌt‚most] adj. 極度的 (the ~) [同] ultimate

▲ The commander drew up a plan with the utmost care.

指揮官極度審慎地擬定計畫。

utmost [ˈʌt‚most] n. [sing.] 最大限度

▲ The car mechanic did his utmost to fix my car.

修車工人竭盡全力要把我的車修好。

💡 to the utmost of one's ability 盡某人能力的極限

Unit 3

1. **armor** [`ɑrmɚ] n. [U] 盔甲

   ▲ In the Middle Ages, knights wore suits of armor when going into battle.

   在中世紀，騎士上戰場時會穿盔甲。

2. **beckon** [`bɛkən] v. 示意 <to> [同] signal ；吸引 <to> [同] attract

   ▲ The police officer beckoned me to follow him.

   警察示意要我跟著他。

3. **besiege** [bɪ`sidʒ] v. 包圍 ；(以問題等) 煩擾 <with> [同] bombard

   ▲ The army besieged the fort until their enemies surrendered. 軍隊包圍堡壘直到敵人投降為止。

4. **brisk** [brɪsk] adj. 敏捷的 ，輕快的 [同] quick ；涼爽的 [同] refreshing

   ▲ A group of soldiers traveled across the field at a brisk pace. 一群士兵以敏捷的步伐穿過原野。

   briskly [`brɪsklɪ] adv. 敏捷地，輕快地

   ▲ Nancy walked briskly, and her cheeks turned rosy.

   Nancy 輕快地走著，臉頰潤變得紅潤起來。

5. **clan** [klæn] n. [C] 宗族，大家族；同黨，團體 [同] group

   ▲ Ivan said in jest that the whole clan was coming to stay with us for the New Year holiday.

Ivan 開玩笑說整個家族都會來與我們共度新年假期。

---

6. **clutch** [klʌtʃ] v. 緊握 <at> [同] grip [反] loosen

   ▲ The boy clutched at the rope in case he would fall.
   男孩緊抓著繩子以免掉下去。

   clutch [klʌtʃ] n. [C] 離合器 ; [pl.] 抓住 , 掌控 [同] control

   ▲ To drive a car with manual transmission, you have to push the clutch in and then put the car into gear.
   開手排車，你必須踩下離合器然後進檔。

---

7. **degrade** [dɪˋgred] v. 貶損 [同] debase ; 使惡化 [反] improve

   ▲ Don't degrade yourself by telling such a lie.
   不要撒這種謊來貶損自己。

---

8. **distrust** [dɪsˋtrʌst] n. [U] [sing.] 不信任 <of> [同] mistrust [反] trust

   ▲ The villagers have a deep distrust of outsiders.
   村民非常不信任外來者。

   distrust [dɪsˋtrʌst] v. 不信任 [同] mistrust [反] trust

   ▲ I have distrusted David ever since he lied to me.
   自從 David 對我說謊以後，我再也不信任他了。

---

9. **elite** [ɪˋlit] n. [C] 精英

   ▲ The intellectual elite have been trying to improve the government's tax system.
   這些知識精英不斷試著去改進政府的稅務制度。

---

10. **fad** [fæd] n. [C] 一時性的流行 [同] fashion
   ▲ Roller-skating was once a fad among youngsters.
   溜滑輪曾是年輕人的時下流行。

11. **famine** [ˋfæmɪn] n. [C][U] 饑荒
   ▲ That country is experiencing a terrible famine.
   那個國家正經歷嚴重的饑荒。

12. **glisten** [ˋglɪsn̩] v. (潮溼或具光澤的表面) 閃閃發光
   <with> [同] gleam
   ▲ Hermione's eyes glistened with tears as she read the
   letter. Hermione 讀信的時候，眼睛閃著淚光。

13. **heed** [hid] v. 注意，留心 [同] mind [反] neglect
   ▲ You should have heeded my words.
   你早該聽我的話。
   heed [hid] n. [U] 注意，留心 <of, to> [同] attention [反]
   disregard
   ▲ My husband took no heed of my advice.
   老公沒有把我的忠告聽進去。

14. **mellow** [ˋmɛlo] adj. 醇熟的 [同] full-flavored
   ▲ Helen enjoyed the mellow taste of wine.
   Helen 享受醇酒的滋味。
   mellow [ˋmɛlo] v. (使) 成熟 [同] mature
   ▲ Age has mellowed Shawn, and now he is a
   sympathetic person.
   歲月使 Shawn 成熟許多，現在的他很有同理心。

15. **outdo** [aʊtˋdu] v. 勝過，超越 <in> (outdid | outdone | outdoing) [同] excel

   ▲ Henry outdoes me in every subject.
   Henry 每一個科目都勝過我。

---

16. **pierce** [pɪrs] v. 穿洞 [同] puncture

   ▲ Mindy had her ears pierced. Mindy 穿了耳洞。

   piercing [ˋpɪrsɪŋ] adj. (眼光) 銳利的 [同] penetrating

   ▲ Lily's piercing eyes made James uncomfortable.
   Lily 銳利的眼神讓 James 覺得不舒服。

---

17. **query** [ˋkwɪrɪ] n. [C] 疑問，質疑 [同] question [反] answer

   ▲ The man raised a query about my motive.
   那人對我的動機提出質疑。

   query [ˋkwɪrɪ] v. 詢問 [同] inquire；懷疑 [同] doubt

   ▲ Andrew queried my reason for leaving the post.
   Andrew 詢問我離職的原因。

---

18. **rumble** [ˋrʌmbl̩] v. 咕嚕咕嚕作響；隆隆作響

   ▲ Lindsay's stomach rumbled because she didn't eat breakfast.
   Lindsay 因為沒吃早餐，肚子咕嚕咕嚕作響。

   rumble [ˋrʌmbl̩] n. [C] 隆隆聲

   ▲ I just heard a rumble of thunder. 我剛剛聽到雷聲。

---

19. **safeguard** [ˋsef͵gɑrd] n. [C] 保護物，保護裝置 <against> [同] protection

▲ That lock is a safeguard against improper operation.
那個鎖是防止不當操作的安全裝置。

safeguard [`sef͵gɑrd] v. 保護 <against, from> [同]
protect [反] endanger

▲ The copyright law serves to safeguard the rights of
authors or publishers.
版權法是用來保護作者或出版者的權利。

---

20. **smother** [`smʌðɚ] v. 使窒息 [同] suffocate；抑制 (感情
等) [同] suppress

▲ The murderer smothered the victim with a pillow.
兇手用枕頭把被害人悶死。

💡 smother anger/irritation/self-pity/giggles/jealousy 壓
抑怒氣 / 憤怒 / 自憐 / 竊笑 / 嫉妒

---

21. **stunt** [stʌnt] v. 阻礙生長，妨礙發展

▲ Lack of sufficient nutrition will stunt a child's
growth. 營養不足會阻礙一個孩子的成長。

stunt [stʌnt] n. [C] 特技 [同] trick

▲ Jackie performed a stunt in the show.
Jackie 在節目中表演特技。

💡 stunt man/woman 特技男 / 女演員；男 / 女替身 | pull
a stunt 耍噱頭，耍花招

---

22. **substitution** [͵sʌbstə`tjuʃən] n. [C][U] 代替；代換

▲ In my experience, the substitution of gum-chewing
for smoking doesn't work.

就我的經驗來說，以嚼口香糖來取代吸菸不可行。

23. **throb** [θrɑb] v. 抽動，跳動 <with> [同] beat (throbbed | throbbed | throbbing)
   ▲ My head throbbed with pain as I hadn't slept for forty-eight hours straight.
   我的頭陣陣劇痛，因為我已經連續四十八小時沒睡了。
   throb [θrɑb] n. [C] 跳動，搏動
   ▲ Carol is so nervous that she can feel the throb of her heart. Carol 緊張到可以感覺自己的心跳。

24. **understandable** [ˌʌndəˈstændəbl] adj. 可以理解的
   ▲ Your disappointment is perfectly understandable.
   你的失望是完全可以理解的。

25. **valiant** [ˈvæljənt] adj. 勇敢的 [同] brave
   ▲ Maggie made a valiant attempt to compete with the world champion. Maggie 勇敢嘗試去對抗世界冠軍。

Unit 4

1. **auxiliary** [ɔgˈzɪljərɪ] adj. 備用的 [同] supplementary [反] chief
   ▲ Since the main engine was broken, we had no choice but to use the auxiliary one.
   由於主引擎故障，我們只好使用備用引擎。

2. **bazaar** [bəˈzɑr] n. [C] 市集 [同] market

▲ The tourists were bargaining for souvenirs in the bazaar. 觀光客在市集裡針對紀念品討價還價。

3. **bleak** [blik] adj. 荒涼的 [同] barren；黯淡的 [同] depressing

▲ There is an abandoned hut on the bleak hilltop.
荒涼的山丘上有一間廢棄小屋。

4. **caress** [kə`rɛs] v. 撫摸 [同] stroke

▲ The mother gently caressed the back of her baby.
母親溫柔地撫摸寶寶的背部。

caress [kə`rɛs] n. [C] 撫摸

▲ Mike gave his lover a caress to comfort her.
Mike 輕撫他的愛人以安慰她。

5. **cocoon** [kə`kun] n. [C] 繭 <of>

▲ The caterpillar came out of its cocoon and became a beautiful butterfly. 毛毛蟲破繭而出變成美麗的蝴蝶。

cocoon [kə`kun] v. (為保護而) 把…裹起來 <from, in> [同] protect

▲ Refusing to work, Andy was still cocooned in his father's wealth.
Andy 拒絕工作，並且仍受他父親財富的庇護。

6. **commemoration** [kə,mɛmə`reʃən] v. 慶祝 [同] celebrate；紀念 [同] memorialize

▲ We commemorated our school's 60th anniversary.
我們慶祝六十週年校慶。

commemorate [kə`mɛmə͵ret] n. [C][U] 紀念，紀念儀式
▲ A series of concerts were held in commemoration of the 200th anniversary of Mozart's death. 為了紀念莫札特逝世兩百週年舉行了一連串的音樂會。

---

7. **denounce** [dɪ`naʊns] v. 譴責 <as> [同] condemn [反] praise；告發，指控 <as, to> [同] accuse
▲ Some politicians openly denounced the mayor's inability to deal with the emergency.
有些政客公開譴責市長在處理緊急事件上的無能。

---

8. **dosage** [`dosɪdʒ] n. [C] 一劑的藥量 (usu. sing.)
▲ The correct dosage is one spoonful four times a day.
正確的藥量是每天四次，每次一湯匙。

---

9. **dreary** [`drɪrɪ] adj. 沉悶的，乏味的 [同] gloomy [反] cheerful
▲ It was a dreary December night—cold, dark, and wet.
這是個沉悶的十二月夜晚——又冷、又黑、又溼。
drearily [`drɪrɪlɪ] adv. 沉悶地
▲ The old woman was dressed drearily in gray.
老婦人穿著灰沉沉的衣服。

---

10. **federation** [͵fɛdə`reʃən] n. [C] 聯盟 [同] league；聯邦
▲ Several countries formed a federation to develop international trade.
幾個國家組成聯盟以發展國際貿易。

---

11. **flare** [flɛr] v. 火光閃耀 <up> [同] blaze；突然發怒 <up>

[同] explode

▲ The bonfire flared in the wind.

營火在風中熊熊燃燒著。

flare [flɛr] n. [C] 火光閃耀 [同] blaze

▲ There was a sudden flare as Anderson struck a match. Anderson 一劃火柴，火花就迸出來了。

---

12. **grope** [grop] v. 摸索 <for> [同] feel about ；搜尋 <for> [同] search

▲ Jack groped his way across the dark basement.

Jack 摸索而行，穿過黑暗的地下室。

---

13. **herald** [ˋhɛrəld] n. [C] 預兆 [同] sign

▲ Dark clouds are the heralds of bad weather.

烏雲是壞天氣的預兆。

herald [ˋhɛrəld] v. 預告…的來臨；宣告 <as> [同] announce

▲ The invention of the steam engine heralded the beginning of a new era.

蒸汽機的發明預告了新時代的來臨。

---

14. **hysterical** [hɪsˋtɛrɪkl] adj. 歇斯底里的，異常激動的 [反] calm

▲ The little girl became hysterical when she couldn't find her parents. 小女孩找不到爸媽時變得歇斯底里。

---

15. **militant** [ˋmɪlətənt] adj. 好戰的，好鬥的 [同] aggressive

▲ Ben is unpopular among his peers for his militant

attitude. Ben 因咄咄逼人的態度在同儕間不受歡迎。

---

16. **oversleep** [ˌovəˈslip] v. 睡過頭 (overslept｜overslept｜oversleeping)

▲ I overslept this morning and missed the train.
今天早上我睡過頭而沒趕上火車。

---

17. **ransom** [ˈrænsəm] n. [C][U] 勒贖金

▲ The terrorists demanded a ransom of five million dollars for the safe return of the journalist. 恐怖分子要求五百萬美元贖金，才會讓該名記者安全回來。

ransom [ˈrænsəm] v. (支付贖金) 贖回

▲ The boy's father ransomed him for two million dollars. 男孩的父親支付兩百萬美元贖他回來。

---

18. **rustle** [ˈrʌsl] v. (使) 沙沙作響

▲ Jessica's silk dress rustled as she moved through the fair. Jessica 穿過市集的時候，她的絲綢洋裝沙沙作響。

rustle [ˈrʌsl] n. [sing.] 沙沙聲

▲ We heard a rustle in the bushes and were petrified.
我們聽到樹叢裡的沙沙聲，整個嚇壞了。

---

19. **salvation** [sælˈveʃən] n. [U] 救贖；救星

▲ The religious leader's message of salvation has changed many lives.
這個宗教領袖的救贖信息改變了很多人的生命。

---

20. **shun** [ʃʌn] v. 迴避 [同] avoid；避免 [同] avoid (shunned｜shunned｜shunning)

▲ Harvey was shunned by his friends because of the sex scandal.

因為這個性醜聞，Harvey 的朋友都避著他。

---

21. **snare** [snɛr] n. [C] 陷阱 [同] trap ；(騙人的) 圈套 [同] trick

▲ The hunter laid snares for the rabbits on the grassland. 獵人設陷阱捕捉草原上的兔子。

snare [snɛr] v. 用陷阱捕捉 [同] trap

▲ Sully snared the fox that had eaten his chickens.
Sully 用陷阱捉到了那隻吃他雞的狐狸。

---

22. **tariff** [`tærɪf] n. [C] 關稅 <on>；價目表

▲ The government should reduce tariffs on imported cars. 政府應該減少進口汽車的關稅。

💡 impose a tariff 徵收關稅 | raise/increase the tariff 增加關稅

---

23. **tranquil** [`trænkwɪl] adj. 平靜的，平穩的 [同] peaceful

▲ I enjoy the tranquil atmosphere of this coffee shop.
我享受這咖啡館的寧靜氣氛。

tranquilize [`trænkwɪ͵laɪz] v. 使鎮靜，使麻醉 [同] soothe

▲ This drug is used to tranquilize animals.
這種藥是用來麻醉動物的。

tranquilizer [`trænkwɪ͵laɪzɚ] n. [C] 鎮定劑

▲ These tranquilizers will help you to relieve anxiety.

這些鎮定劑可以幫助你緩解焦慮。

24. **validity** [və`lɪdətɪ] n. [U] 正當性；有效性
▲ The validity of the law is questionable.
這條法律的正當性令人質疑。

25. **wade** [wed] v. 涉水渡過 <across, through>
▲ The river is too deep to wade across.
河水太深無法涉水而過。

Unit 5

1. **ambush** [`æmbʊʃ] v. 埋伏襲擊 [同] entrap
▲ The security guard was ambushed by the gunmen while on duty.
這位保全人員在執勤時受到持槍暴徒的襲擊。
ambush [`æmbʊʃ] n. [C][U] 埋伏 [同] trap
▲ The soldiers fell into an ambush near the border.
士兵們在邊界附近遭到埋伏攻擊。
💡 lie/wait in ambush 埋伏

2. **blizzard** [`blɪzəd] n. [C] 暴風雪 [同] snowstorm
▲ We were stuck at the airport for two days because of the blizzard. 因為這場暴風雪，我們被困在機場兩天。

3. **blunder** [`blʌndə] n. [C] 愚蠢的大錯 [同] error
▲ I made/committed a blunder by taking him for his younger brother. 我犯了個把他誤認為他弟弟的大錯。

blunder [ˋblʌndɚ] v. 跌跌撞撞地走 [同] stumble；(因愚蠢或粗心而) 犯錯

▲ Aaron blundered about in the dim room.
Aaron 在昏暗的房裡跌跌撞撞地走著。

---

4. **charcoal** [ˋtʃɑr͵kol] n. [U] 木炭；炭筆

▲ Don't forget to buy some charcoal for tomorrow's barbecue party.
別忘了買些明天烤肉派對要用的木炭。

💡 a stick/piece of charcoal 一根 / 一塊木炭

---

5. **coil** [kɔɪl] n. [C] 捲曲之物

▲ Bring me that coil of wire on the shelf in the basement. 幫我把地下室架上那卷鐵絲拿過來。

coil [kɔɪl] v. 纏繞 [同] wind

▲ The python coiled itself around a tree trunk.
蟒蛇纏繞在樹幹上。

---

6. **companionship** [kəmˋpænjən͵ʃɪp] n. [U] 情誼

▲ Having lived alone for two years, Lily misses the companionship of her old friends.
獨居兩年之後，Lily 想念老朋友的情誼。

---

7. **disgraceful** [dɪsˋgresfəl] adj. 可恥的 [同] shameful [反] honorable

▲ The cheating student should feel ashamed of his disgraceful behavior.
這名作弊的學生該為自己可恥的行為感到羞恥。

---

8. **dissident** [ˋdɪsədənt] adj. 持異議的，反政府的
   ▲ The dissident writer was put in jail.
   那位反政府的作家被捕入獄。

9. **eloquence** [ˋɛləkwəns] n. [U] 口才 [同] rhetoric
   ▲ The politician always speaks with great eloquence.
   這位政治人物說話總是很有口才。
   eloquent [ˋɛləkwənt] adj. 口才好的 [同] rhetorical
   ▲ The lawyer made an eloquent plea to the judge.
   這個律師口才便給地向法官提出申辯。

10. **fiddle** [ˋfɪdl] n. [C] 小提琴 [同] violin
    ▲ My little sister plays the fiddle in the school band. 我
    妹妹在學校的樂團中拉小提琴。
    fiddle [ˋfɪdl] v. (無目的地) 撥弄，把玩 <with>
    ▲ Can you stop fiddling with your pencil?
    你可以不要一直玩你的鉛筆嗎？

11. **flick** [flɪk] n. [C] (快速的) 輕打，輕彈，輕擺 [同] flip
    ▲ The lady called the waiter over with a flick of her
    hand. 這名女士揮了揮手叫服務生過來。
    flick [flɪk] v. (快速地) 輕打，輕觸 [同] flip；輕彈，輕拂
    ▲ The machine started working after the engineer
    flicked the switch.
    工程師按下開關後，機器就開始運作了。

12. **hardy** [ˋhɑrdɪ] adj. 強壯的 [同] strong [反] weak
    ▲ You have to be hardy to work as a construction

worker. 你必須要夠強壯才能當建築工人。

13. **incense** [ˋɪnsɛns] n. [U] (尤指宗教儀式中的) 香，薰香

▲ The temple burns incense every day.
這間寺廟每天燒香。

💡 a stick of incense 一炷香

incense [ɪnˋsɛns] v. 激怒 [同] irritate

▲ The writer was incensed by the rude remark.
這位作家被無禮的評論激怒了。

14. **nuisance** [ˋnjusn̩s] n. [C] 令人討厭的東西 (usu. sing.)
[同] annoyance

▲ The noisy factory is a public nuisance to the neighborhood.
這嘈雜的工廠對附近居民而言是項公害。

💡 make a nuisance of oneself 惹人討厭

15. **peck** [pɛk] v. 啄 (食) <at>；輕吻 <on>

▲ The sparrows were pecking at the grains.
麻雀在啄食穀粒。

peck [pɛk] n. [C] 輕吻

▲ The foreign guest gave me a peck on the cheek as a greeting.
那位外國貴賓親了一下我的臉頰當作打招呼。

16. **ravage** [ˋrævɪdʒ] v. 毀壞 [同] ruin

▲ The village was completely ravaged by the war.
這個村莊被戰爭徹底地摧毀了。

ravages [ˋrævɪdʒɪz] n. [pl.] 損壞 (the ～) <of> [同] devastation

▲ The deserted windmill was left to the ravages of the rain and the wind. 廢棄的風車被擱置，任由風雨摧殘。

🔘 the ravages of war/time/disease 戰爭 / 歲月 / 疾病的摧殘

---

17. **rhythmic** [ˋrɪðmɪk] adj. 有節奏的 (also rhythmical)

▲ The rhythmic sound of the rain hitting the tin roof is like a song.

雨有節奏地打在鐵皮屋頂上的聲音就像一首歌。

---

18. **saloon** [səˋlun] n. [C] (尤指昔日美國西部的) 酒館 [同] bar

▲ The two cowboys promised to meet again at the saloon. 兩位牛仔約定在酒館再次見面。

---

19. **sanction** [ˋsæŋkʃən] n. [C] 制裁 (usu. pl.) <against> [同] punishment；[U] 認可，批准 [同] permission [反] disapproval

▲ Many countries have imposed economic sanctions against Russia since the Ukraine war.

烏克蘭戰爭開打後，已有多國對俄羅斯採取經濟制裁。

🔘 give sanction to sb/sth 認可⋯

sanction [ˋsæŋkʃən] v. 認可，批准 [同] approve [反] disapprove

▲ The president refused to sanction the use of nuclear weapons in the time of crisis.

總統拒絕在危機時期批准使用核子武器。

---

20. **shudder** [ˈʃʌdɚ] v. 發抖 [同] quiver；搖動 [同] shake
   ▲ I shudder to think what my mother will say when she sees my poor grades. 想到媽媽看到我糟糕的成績會說什麼，就讓我不寒而慄。

   shudder [ˈʃʌdɚ] n. [C] 發抖 [同] shiver
   ▲ The girl gave a shudder of horror when she entered the haunted house. 女孩進入鬼屋時，嚇得發起抖來。

---

21. **sneer** [snɪr] v. 譏笑 <at> [同] mock
   ▲ The naughty students sneered at the principal's warning. 頑皮的學生們對校長的警告嗤之以鼻。

   sneer [snɪr] n. [C] 譏笑
   ▲ The boy curled his lips in a sneer when the teacher scolded him. 被老師責備時，男孩不屑地撇了撇嘴。

---

22. **tart** [tɑrt] n. [C] 塔，餡餅
   ▲ Would you like to have a fruit tart?
   你要來個水果塔嗎？

   tart [tɑrt] adj. 酸的
   ▲ The apple is really tart. 這顆蘋果真的很酸。

---

23. **tread** [trɛd] v. 行走 [同] walk ；踩踏 <on> [同] step on
   (trod, treaded | trodden, trod | treading)
   ▲ The runaway girl was treading a path through the forest. 逃跑的女孩正沿著一條小徑穿過森林。
   💡 tread water 踩水；原地踏步，沒有進步

tread [trɛd] n. [sing.] 腳步聲；[C][U] (鞋底、輪胎的) 紋路

▲ My little cousins' heavy tread on the floor keeps me awake the whole night.
小表弟們重踩在地板上的腳步聲讓我整晚都睡不著。

---

24. **verge** [vɜ˞dʒ] n. [C] 邊緣 [同] brink

▲ The golf player pushed the ball from the verge of the green. 高爾夫球選手從果嶺的邊緣把球推擊出去。

💡 on the verge of sth 瀕臨⋯；將要⋯

verge [vɜ˞dʒ] v. 緊鄰 <on> [同] border；接近 (某狀態) <on>

▲ My estate verges on the lake. 我的土地緊鄰著湖邊。

---

25. **wail** [wel] v. 痛哭，嚎啕大哭，哀號

▲ The baby wailed for her mother. 寶寶哭著要找媽媽。

wail [wel] n. [C] 鳴聲；痛哭 (聲)，哀號 (聲)

▲ Did you hear the wails of police sirens?
你有聽到警笛鳴聲嗎？

Unit 6

1. **amiable** [ˈemɪəbl̩] adj. 和藹可親的 [同] friendly [反] hostile

▲ Sally's amiable personality allows her to get along with others easily.

Sally 和藹可親的個性讓她很容易和別人相處。

2. **bog** [bɑg] v. 使陷入泥沼 <down>；使落入困境
(bogged | bogged | bogging)
▲ Our truck was bogged down in the mud.
我們的卡車陷入泥沼中。

3. **bombard** [bɑm`bɑrd] v. (連續) 砲轟 [同] bomb；(以大
量問題、要求等) 困擾某人 <with> [同] assault
▲ The enemy ruthlessly bombarded our coastal cities.
敵軍無情地轟炸我方的沿海城市。

4. **chuckle** [`tʃʌkl] v. 咯咯竊笑 [同] giggle
▲ Andrew chuckled at his mother's funny dress.
Andrew 對他母親滑稽的洋裝咯咯地笑了起來。
chuckle [`tʃʌkl] n. [C] 咯咯竊笑 [同] giggle
▲ Lily gave a chuckle when she saw me fall.
Lily 看見我跌倒，發出咯咯的笑聲。

5. **conceit** [kən`sit] n. [U] 自負 [同] arrogance [反]
humility
▲ Celine's conceit prevented her from seeing her own
faults. Celine 的自負使她無法看清自己的缺點。
conceited [kən`sitɪd] adj. 自負的 [同] arrogant [反]
humble
▲ Many workers dislike the young and conceited
manager. 很多員工不喜歡這個年輕又自負的經理。

6. **confer** [kən`fɝ] v. 交換意見 <with> [同] discuss；授予

<on, upon> [同] grant [反] deprive (conferred | conferred | conferring)

▲ Before answering any questions, the company had better confer with its lawyers.
在回答任何問題前，該公司最好和它的律師商議一下。

---

7. **deteriorate** [dɪˋtɪrɪəˏret] v. 惡化 [同] worsen [反] improve

▲ The air quality in the area has been deteriorating steadily since the factory was built.
自從工廠建好以來，這個地區的空氣品質日益惡化。

---

8. **drawback** [ˋdrɔˏbæk] n. [C] 缺點 <of, to> [同] defect [反] advantage

▲ The two major drawbacks to living in a big city are the traffic jams and the air pollution.
住在大城市的兩大缺點是交通堵塞和空氣汙染。

---

9. **embark** [ɪmˋbɑrk] v. 登船，登機 [同] board [反] disembark；著手從事 <on, upon> [同] launch

▲ The passengers were waiting to embark at Keelung for Japan. 乘客們在基隆等待登船前往日本。

---

10. **flap** [flæp] v. 擺動 [同] flutter；拍打，拍動

▲ The national flag was flapping in the strong wind.
國旗在強風中飄揚。

flap [flæp] n. [C] (一面固定的) 下垂物；輕拍 [同] flutter

▲ Farmers wear caps with flaps to protect their faces

from the sunlight.

農夫戴有布罩的帽子以保護他們的臉免受陽光照射。

💡 tent flap 帳棚門罩

---

11. **flicker** [ˋflɪkɚ] v. 閃爍 [同] sparkle；(表情、想法等) 閃現 <across, on>

▲ The candlelight flickered in the wind and gradually diminished. 燭光在風中閃閃爍爍，漸漸黯淡下去。

flicker [ˋflɪkɚ] n. [C] 閃爍 [同] spark；(希望、情緒等的) 閃現 <of>

▲ I absent-mindedly stared at the flicker of the flames in the fireplace.

我心不在焉地盯著壁爐裡閃爍的火光。

---

12. **humanitarian** [hjuˌmænəˋtɛrɪən] adj. 人道主義的 [同] humane

▲ The government sent humanitarian aid to the victims of the disaster. 政府提供災難受害者人道援助。

---

13. **inward** [ˋɪnwɚd] adj. 內部的，向內的；內心的 [同] inner

▲ The speaker took an inward breath and continued her speech. 講者吸了口氣，繼續她的演說。

💡 inward satisfaction/panic/relief 發自內心的滿足 / 慌張 / 安心

---

14. **peddle** [ˋpɛdl] v. 沿街兜售 [同] hawk；傳播 (思想等)

▲ My uncle peddles souvenirs on the streets every day.

我叔叔每天都在街上兜售紀念品。

---

15. **pesticide** [ˋpɛstə͵saɪd] n. [C][U] 殺蟲劑 [同] insecticide
   ▲ The overuse of pesticides will pollute the environment. 過度使用殺蟲劑會汙染環境。

---

16. **pious** [ˋpaɪəs] adj. 虔誠的 [同] religious [反] impious
   ▲ The pious old lady never missed a single church service.
   這位虔誠的老太太從未缺席任何一次教會禮拜。
   piously [ˋpaɪəslɪ] adv. 虔誠地
   ▲ The man prayed piously to God.
   那人虔誠地向上帝禱告。

---

17. **redundant** [rɪˋdʌndənt] adj. 累贅的，冗餘的 [同] excessive [反] essential
   ▲ It is redundant to say "a sad tragedy."
   「悲哀的悲劇」是累贅的說法。

---

18. **rite** [raɪt] n. [C] 儀式 [同] ceremony
   ▲ People practice different rites of passage in different cultures. 在不同的文化中，人們遵行不同的生命禮儀。

---

19. **sanctuary** [ˋsæŋktʃʊ͵ɛrɪ] n. [C][U] 避難所，庇護 [同] refuge；[C] 禁獵區 [同] reserve
   ▲ The country is considered to be a sanctuary for political refugees. 該國被視為政治犯的避難所。
   💡 find/seek sanctuary 尋求庇護

---

20. **simmer** [ˋsɪmɚ] v. 用小火煮 [同] stew；內心充滿 (情緒等) <with>

▲ The soup is simmering. 湯正在用小火燉煮。

🍃 simmer down 平靜下來

simmer [ˋsɪmɚ] n. [sing.] 用小火煮

▲ To make a hearty soup, chop two onions and bring them to a simmer first.
要做一道豐盛的湯，切碎兩顆洋蔥並先用小火煨煮。

---

21. **sprawl** [sprɔl] v. 四肢攤開地躺；延伸 [同] extend

▲ The strong winds of typhoons can send people sprawling to the ground.
颱風的強風可以把人吹倒在地。

sprawl [sprɔl] n. [sing.] (尤指城市雜亂的) 延伸

▲ The countryside is being destroyed by urban sprawl.
都市無計畫地擴展使鄉村地區受到破壞。

---

22. **taunt** [tɔnt] n. [C] 嘲弄 [同] mockery

▲ The helpless girl could do nothing but endure those guys' taunts and insults. 這無助的女孩什麼也不能做，只能忍受那些男生的譏笑和侮辱。

taunt [tɔnt] v. 嘲弄 <about, with> [同] tease

▲ The two soccer teams taunted each other during the entire game. 這兩支足球隊整場比賽都在互相叫陣。

---

23. **tremor** [ˋtrɛmɚ] n. [C] (輕微的) 震動 [同] quake；顫抖 [同] tremble

▲ There was a small tremor this morning.

今天早上有個小地震。

24. **victimize** [`vɪktɪ,maɪz] v. 使犧牲，使受害，欺凌
   ▲ Some ethnic minorities are victimized by mainstream society. 一些少數民族受到主流社會的壓迫欺凌。

25. **whirl** [hwɝl] v. 旋轉 <around> [同] rotate
   ▲ The elegant dancers whirled around in front of the king. 優雅的舞者們在國王面前迴旋起舞。
   whirl [hwɝl] n. [C] 旋轉 (usu. sing.) [同] spin ；[sing.] 混亂，騷動
   ▲ A whirl of sand blocked the sailors' vision.
   飛旋的風沙擋住了水手們的視線。

Unit 7

1. **anecdote** [`ænɪk,dot] n. [C][U] 軼事 [同] tale
   ▲ A book on the anecdotes about the former president was published recently.
   最近出版了一本關於前任總統軼事的書。

2. **bout** [baʊt] n. [C] (拳擊、摔角的) 比賽 [同] match；(疾病的) 發作 <of, with>
   ▲ Sam beat his opponent in the wrestling bout.
   Sam 在這場摔角比賽中擊敗他的對手。

3. **braid** [bred] n. [C] 髮辮，辮子
   ▲ Lily never goes out without wearing her hair in two

braids. Lily 每次出門必定綁著兩條髮辮。

braid [bred] v. 綁辮子

▲ On the beach, some women make money by braiding tourists' hair.

在海灘上，有些女子替觀光客綁辮子來賺錢。

---

4. **clamp** [klæmp] v. (用工具) 夾緊 <together> [同] fasten [反] loosen；強行實施 <on> [同] impose

▲ Clamp the two planks together until the glue gets dry. 將兩片木板夾緊，直到膠水乾透。

💡 clamp down on sth 強力取締…

clamp [klæmp] n. [C] 夾鉗

▲ The blacksmith fastened the two pieces of plates with a clamp. 鐵匠用夾鉗固定這兩片板子。

---

5. **constituent** [kən`stɪtʃʊənt] adj. 組成的 [同] component

▲ In order to understand the sentence better, we need to consider its constituent parts.

為更理解這個句子，我們需考慮到它的組成部分。

constituent [kən`stɪtʃʊənt] n. [C] 成分 <of> [同] component

▲ What is the major constituent of the new medicine? 這種新藥物的主要成分是什麼？

---

6. **counterclockwise** [ˌkaʊntɚ`klɑkˌwaɪz] adv. 逆時針地 [反] clockwise

▲ Mike unscrewed the cap counterclockwise to open

the bottle. Mike 逆時針旋轉瓶蓋以打開瓶子。

---

7. **devalue** [dɪ`vælju] `v.` 貶低價值 [反] enhance
   ▲ Dennis tends to devalue his own achievements because of his lack of self-confidence.
   Dennis 因缺乏自信而傾向貶低自己的成就。

---

8. **displease** [dɪs`pliz] `v.` 使不悅 [同] annoy [反] please
   ▲ Leo's carelessness displeased the professor.
   Leo 的粗心使教授不悅。

   displeased [dɪs`plizd] `adj.` 不滿的 <with, at> [反] pleased
   ▲ Sandy is very displeased with you because you are always late. Sandy 對你非常不滿，因為你總是遲到。

---

9. **enact** [ɪn`ækt] `v.` 制定法規 [同] legislate
   ▲ The country's congress enacted several new laws.
   這個國家的國會制定了幾條新法律。

   enactment [ɪn`æktmənt] `n.` [U] 制定 [同] legislation
   ▲ The enactment of the abortion law is still in dispute.
   墮胎法的制定仍有爭議。

---

10. **fling** [flɪŋ] `v.` 猛扔 [同] hurl；猛然移動 (身體、手臂等)
    (flung | flung | flinging)
    ▲ The boy flung the book down on the sofa and stamped out of the living room.
    男孩把書摔在沙發上，重重踱步離開客廳。

---

11. **foil** [fɔɪl] `v.` 阻撓 [同] hinder

▲ An attempt to assassinate the governor was foiled by police. 警方阻止了一起暗殺州長的計畫。

foil [fɔɪl] n. [C] 襯托物，陪襯 <for, to> [同] complement；[U] 箔

▲ The dress is a perfect foil for Lucy's terrific figure. 這件洋裝完美地襯托出 Lucy 極好的身材。

💡 gold foil 金箔 ｜ aluminum foil 鋁箔

---

12. **installment** [ɪn`stɔlmənt] n. [C] 分期付款

▲ Jim paid for the laptop in/by six monthly installments. Jim 以六個月分期購買筆記型電腦。

💡 installment plan 分期付款計畫

---

13. **jeer** [dʒɪr] v. 嘲笑，嘲弄 <at> [同] sneer

▲ The crowd jeered at the candidate.
群眾嘲笑那位候選人。

jeer [dʒɪr] n. [C] 嘲弄，嘲笑 (usu. pl.) [同] taunt

▲ The jeers and boos made the performer feel uncomfortable. 嘲笑和噓聲讓表演者感到不自在。

---

14. **massacre** [`mæsəkɚ] v. 屠殺 [同] slaughter

▲ Japanese soldiers massacred Chinese civilians during World War II.
日軍在第二次世界大戰期間屠殺中國百姓。

---

15. **peg** [pɛg] n. [C] (衣物的) 掛勾；(固定物體的) 釘，栓，椿 [同] pin

▲ James took off his raincoat and hung it on a peg

outside the door.

James 脫下雨衣，掛在門外的掛勾上。

💡 tent/wooden peg 營釘 / 木釘

peg [pɛg] v. 用釘子固定 <down> (pegged │ pegged │ pegging)

▲ We pegged down the tent at the campsite.

我們在營地以釘子固定帳棚。

---

16. **pollutant** [pə`lutənt] n. [C] 汙染物

▲ When these wastes are burned, pollutants are released into the air.

這些廢棄物燃燒時，汙染物會被排放到空氣中。

---

17. **relish** [`rɛlɪʃ] n. [C][U] 佐料；[U] 享受 <with> [同] enjoyment

▲ I'd like some relish on my hot dog.

我要在我的熱狗上加些佐料。

relish [`rɛlɪʃ] v. 享受，喜歡 [同] enjoy [反] dislike

▲ The greedy man relished the idea of cheating others out of their money.

那名貪婪的男子滿心想著要從別人身上騙取錢財。

---

18. **ridicule** [`rɪdɪ,kjul] n. [U] 嘲笑 [同] mockery

▲ John has become an object of ridicule among his colleagues. John 已經成了同事們嘲笑的對象。

💡 hold sb/sth up to ridicule 嘲笑…

ridicule [`rɪdɪ,kjul] v. 嘲笑 [同] mock

▲ Mr. Wang is often ridiculed for his accent.

王先生常因說話的口音受到嘲笑。

---

19. **sane** [sen] adj. 神智正常的 [反] insane；合理的，明智的 [同] rational [反] irrational

   ▲ As far as I can judge, Roy is perfectly sane.
   依我的判斷，Roy 的精神狀態相當正常。

---

20. **snort** [snɔrt] v. (表示不屑而) 發出哼聲

   ▲ The workers snorted at the employer's answer.
   工人們對雇主的答覆發出不屑的哼聲。

   snort [snɔrt] n. [C] (表不認同等的) 哼聲

   ▲ Billy gave a snort of contempt after I expressed my opinion. Billy 在我表達意見後嗤之以鼻。

---

21. **stammer** [`stæmɚ] v. 結巴 [同] stutter

   ▲ The secretary often stammered when she felt uncomfortable. 那位祕書感到不自在時，常常會結巴。

   stammer [`stæmɚ] n. [C] 結巴 (usu. sing.) [同] stutter

   ▲ Otis spoke with a stammer because he was lying.
   Otis 因為說謊的緣故，說話結結巴巴的。

---

22. **terminate** [`tɝmə͵net] v. 終結 [同] stop [反] start

   ▲ The contract terminates on June 30.
   這份契約於六月三十日終止。

---

23. **trespass** [`trɛspəs] v. 侵入 (私有土地) <on> [同] invade；濫用，占用 <on>

   ▲ The sign read, "No trespassing."
   告示牌上面寫著「禁止入內」。

trespass [ˋtrɛspəs] n. [C][U] (對私有土地的) 侵入 [同] invasion

▲ The thief was charged with criminal trespass.
這個小偷被控非法入侵。

---

24. **visualize** [ˋvɪʒʊəlˏaɪz] v. 想像，在心中描繪 [同] imagine

▲ Can you visualize what you will be like in ten years?
你能想像自己十年後的樣子嗎？

---

25. **whisk** [hwɪsk] v. 攪拌；迅速帶走 <off, away>

▲ The baker is whisking together the yolks and sugar.
麵包師傅正在將蛋黃和砂糖攪拌在一起。

whisk [hwɪsk] n. [C] 攪拌器

▲ Dad used a whisk to mix the batter for the cake.
爸爸用攪拌器混合做蛋糕的麵糊。

Unit 8

1. **antenna** [ænˋtɛnə] n. [C] 天線 (pl. antennas, antennae)；(昆蟲等的) 觸角 (pl. antennae)

▲ The soldier was twirling the radio antenna, hoping to send out signals successfully.
那名士兵轉動無線電的天線，希望能成功發出信號。

---

2. **brew** [bru] v. 釀造 (啤酒)；醞釀著，即將發生

▲ Craft beer is usually brewed in small quantities.
精釀啤酒通常都是少量釀造。

brew [bru] n. [C][U] 釀造的酒
▲ This pub serves home brew. 這家酒館賣自家釀的酒。

3. **brooch** [brotʃ] n. [C] 胸針 [同] pin
▲ Anyone attending the ceremony is required to wear a diamond brooch.
任何參加這個典禮的人都必須佩戴鑽石胸針。

4. **contemplation** [ˌkɑntəmˋpleʃən] n. [U] 深思 [同] reflection
▲ Looking at the old photos, Sophie seemed lost in contemplation. Sophie 看著舊照片，似乎陷入沉思。

5. **corps** [kɔr] n. [C] 部隊，兵團 [同] crew (pl. corps)
▲ After graduating from high school, Jerry joined the Marine Corps. 高中畢業後，Jerry 加入海軍陸戰隊。

6. **crouch** [krautʃ] v. 蹲伏 <down> [同] squat
▲ The boy crouched behind the tree while playing hide-and-seek. 男孩玩捉迷藏時蹲伏在樹後。
crouch [krautʃ] n. [sing.] 蹲伏 [同] squat
▲ Ruth lowered her body in a crouch to hide from the killer. Ruth 蹲下身來以躲避殺手。

7. **designate** [ˋdɛzɪɡˌnet] v. 任命 <as, to> [同] appoint；指定 <as, for> [同] specify
▲ Sharon is the first woman designated as a cabinet member. Sharon 是第一位被任命為內閣成員的女性。
designate [ˋdɛzɪɡnɪt] adj. 已任命但尚未就職的

▲The prime minister designate is preparing to take office. 即將上任的首相正準備接任職位。

---

8. **disregard** [ˌdɪsrɪˋɡɑrd] v. 不理會，無視 [同] ignore

▲Let's disregard Johnny's criticism and go on with our work. 我們別理會 Johnny 的批評，繼續工作吧。

disregard [ˌdɪsrɪˋɡɑrd] n. [U] 漠視，無視 <for, of>

▲The violent suppression of the demonstration has shown total disregard for human rights.
對示威遊行的暴力鎮壓展現了對人權的完全漠視。

---

9. **enclosure** [ɪnˋkloʒɚ] n. [C] (以籬笆、牆等圍繞的) 圈地；(信或包裹的) 附件

▲The family grow vegetables in the enclosure.
那戶人家在圍起的空地裡種菜。

---

10. **flutter** [ˋflʌtɚ] v. (旗子等) 飄動 [同] flap；(心臟因緊張或興奮而) 快速跳動

▲The sails of the pirate ship fluttered in the wind.
海盜船的船帆在風中飄動。

flutter [ˋflʌtɚ] n. [sing.] 緊張，慌亂

▲Traveling by airplane always puts me in a flutter.
搭飛機總是讓我很緊張。

---

11. **gobble** [ˋɡɑbl] v. 狼吞虎嚥 <up, down> [同] devour；併吞 <up>

▲The hungry boy gobbled up two sausages.
飢餓的男孩狼吞虎嚥地吃下兩條香腸。

💡 gobble up sth 快速消耗…

---

12. **irritation** [ˌɪrəˋteʃən] n. [U] 惱怒 [同] annoyance；[C] 惱人的事物

▲ My neighbor yelled at my dog with irritation because it pissed on his lawn.
鄰居惱怒地對我的狗大吼，因為牠在他家草坪上撒尿。

---

13. **lame** [lem] adj. 跛的 [同] disabled；缺少說服力的

▲ The car crash had left Jim lame for the rest of his life.
那場車禍讓 Jim 終生跛腳。

💡 lame duck (因表現不佳而) 需要協助的人

---

14. **lament** [ləˋmɛnt] v. 表達悲痛，感到惋惜 [同] mourn

▲ We all lamented the death of the firemen.
我們都對那些消防員的死深感悲痛。

---

15. **mouthpiece** [ˋmaʊθˌpis] n. [C] (電話的) 話筒，(樂器的) 吹嘴；代言人，發言人 [同] spokesperson

▲ Miles blew into the mouthpiece of the trumpet, but no sound came out.
Miles 對著小喇叭的吹嘴吹氣，但吹不出聲音來。

---

16. **plight** [plaɪt] n. [C] 困境 (usu. sing.) [同] difficulty

▲ The plight of the people in the concentration camps was pitiful. 集中營裡人們的困境令人同情。

---

17. **pluck** [plʌk] v. 拔 (毛) [同] pull out；撥彈 (琴弦) <at>

▲ The farmer's wife plucked the chicken's feathers and

---

chopped it into pieces.

農夫的妻子拔去雞毛，將雞肉剁成小塊。

---

18. **repress** [rɪ`prɛs] v. 壓抑 [同] restrain [反] release ；鎮壓 [同] suppress

▲ I could not repress a smile. 我忍不住微笑。

repressed [rɪ`prɛst] adj. 被壓抑的 [同] suppressed

▲ Painting is a good way to release repressed emotions for Barbara.

對 Barbara 來說畫畫是抒解被壓抑的情感的好方法。

repressive [rɪ`prɛsɪv] adj. 壓迫性的，壓制的

▲ The regime has repressive laws on women's rights.

該政權有著壓迫女性權力的法律。

repression [rɪ`prɛʃən] n. [U] 壓迫；壓抑 [同] oppression

▲ Many people fled the political repression in that country. 許多人逃離該國的政治壓迫。

---

19. **shrewd** [ʃrud] adj. 精明的，聰明的 [同] wise

▲ The manager came up with a shrewd solution to the problem. 經理想出了解決問題的聰明辦法。

---

20. **sprint** [sprɪnt] n. [C] 短距離賽跑；[sing.] 全速衝刺 [同] dash

▲ Ben won the 100-meter sprint.

Ben 獲得一百公尺短跑勝利。

sprint [sprɪnt] v. 全力衝刺 [同] dash

▲ Kelly sprinted down the road to catch the last train.

Kelly 為了趕上最後一班車而沿路狂奔。

---

21. **stout** [staʊt] adj. 堅固的 [同] strong；肥壯的，粗壯的 [同] fat [反] skinny
  ▲ The stout ship was unharmed through the strong winds and rain.
  這艘堅固的船在強風大雨中沒有受到一點損傷。

---

22. **toil** [tɔɪl] n. [U] 辛勞 [同] hard work
  ▲ Nancy finished the project after years of toil.
  歷經多年的辛勞後，Nancy 完成了那項計畫。

  toil [tɔɪl] v. 努力，辛苦工作 [同] work hard；艱難緩慢地行進
  ▲ Sue toiled away at the task.
  Sue 為了那項差事拼命工作。

---

23. **triumphant** [traɪˋʌmfənt] adj. 勝利的 [同] victorious；得意的
  ▲ The triumphant team celebrated its victory.
  勝利的隊伍慶祝勝利。

---

24. **vogue** [vog] n. [C][U] 流行 (usu. sing.) <for> [同] fashion
  ▲ This hairstyle was in vogue in the 1960s.
  這種髮型在 1960 年代風行一時。

---

25. **wring** [rɪŋ] v. 擰，擠 <out> [同] twist；扭轉，搓揉 (wrung | wrung | wringing)
  ▲ I wrung out the wet towel and hung it on the rack.

我把濕毛巾擰乾並晾在架上。

💡 wring sb's neck (氣到想要) 扭斷…的脖子

Unit 9

1. **antibody** [ˈæntɪˌbɑdɪ] n. [C] 抗體

▲ Breast milk contains antibodies which can protect newborn babies from infection.
母乳含有保護嬰新生兒對抗感染的抗體。

2. **brood** [brud] n. [C] (小雞、小鳥等的) 一窩

▲ The hen walked back and forth to feed her brood.
母雞來回走來走去餵牠的小雞。

brood [brud] v. 沉思，憂思 <over, about> [同] worry

▲ Tyler was brooding over his parents' divorce.
那 Tyler 憂鬱地想著他父母親的離婚。

3. **buckle** [ˈbʌkl] n. [C] 扣環

▲ Hugo's wife gave him a belt with a gold buckle as a birthday present. Hugo 的太太送他一條有黃金扣環的皮帶當作生日禮物。

buckle [ˈbʌkl] v. 扣住

▲ You should always buckle your seat belt when riding in a car. 搭車時應該都要繫上安全帶。

💡 buckle up 繫上安全帶

4. **cleanse** [klɛnz] v. 清潔 [同] clean [反] dirty；使純淨，滌淨 <of, from> [同] purge

▲ James cleansed his wound thoroughly and then put a bandage on it. James 仔細清理他的傷口後纏上繃帶。

▲ Helen believes that religion can cleanse her soul of sin. Helen 相信宗教可以除去罪惡，淨化她的心靈。

---

5. **cordial** [ˋkɔrdʒəl] adj. 熱誠的，誠懇的 [同] friendly

▲ The host family gave Maria a cordial welcome when they first met.
當他們初次見面時，寄宿家庭給予 Maria 熱誠的歡迎。

---

6. **crunch** [krʌntʃ] v. (發出嘎吱聲地) 咀嚼 <on>

▲ Bella crunched on some buttery popcorn while watching the movie.
Bella 邊看電影邊咀嚼著奶油爆米花。

crunch [krʌntʃ] n. [sing.] (咀嚼、踩踏發出的) 嘎吱聲

▲ The dog barked when it heard the crunch of footsteps outside the door.
聽到門外傳來嘎吱的腳步聲，狗叫了起來。

crunchy [ˋkrʌntʃɪ] adj. (食物) 酥脆的 [同] crisp

▲ The cucumber is fresh and crunchy.
這條小黃瓜又新鮮又脆。

---

7. **dismantle** [dɪsˋmæntl] v. 拆卸 (機械等) [同] disassemble；撤除 (組織、制度等)

▲ The bomb technician tried to dismantle the explosive device found by the police.
拆彈技術員試著拆卸警方發現的爆炸裝置。

---

8. **drizzle** [ˋdrɪzl̩] n. [U] [sing.] 毛毛雨 [同] sprinkle

   ▲ There was a light drizzle last night.
   昨晚下了一場毛毛雨。

   drizzle [ˋdrɪzl̩] v. 下毛毛雨 [同] sprinkle

   ▲ Come inside the house. It's drizzling now.
   進屋來吧。現在正在下毛毛雨。

9. **erode** [ɪˋrod] v. 侵蝕，腐蝕 [同] destroy

   ▲ The waves and the wind are constantly eroding away
   the cliff. 海浪和風正不斷地侵蝕懸崖。

   erosion [ɪˋroʒən] n. [U] 侵蝕，腐蝕；逐漸削弱

   ▲ These trees are planted in order to prevent soil
   erosion. 這些樹是種來防止土壤侵蝕的。

10. **foresee** [fɔrˋsi] v. 預見，預測 (foresaw | foreseen |
    foreseeing) [同] foretell

    ▲ Economists have foreseen an economy recovery after
    the COVID-19 pandemic.
    經濟學家已預見了新冠肺炎疫情後的經濟復甦。

11. **gorge** [gɔrdʒ] n. [C] 峽谷 [同] canyon

    ▲ A narrow rocky path winds through the gorge.
    一條滿佈石塊的小徑蜿蜒在峽谷中。

    💡 Taroko Gorge 太魯閣峽谷

    gorge [gɔrdʒ] v. 狼吞虎嚥地吃 <on> [同] gobble

    ▲ The children gorged themselves on chocolate cakes
    at Christmas.

孩子們在聖誕節狼吞虎嚥地吃著巧克力蛋糕。

---

12. **ingenuity** [ˌɪndʒəˈnuətɪ] n. [U] 獨創力

▲ The architect showed great ingenuity in designing the spherical concert hall. 建築師在設計這座球體音樂廳時展現了極佳的創造力。

---

13. **lyric** [ˈlɪrɪk] n. [C] 抒情詩；[pl.] 歌詞

▲ Emily Dickinson is a poet famous for her lyrics.
艾蜜莉狄金生是一位以抒情詩聞名的詩人。

---

14. **menace** [ˈmɛnɪs] n. [C][U] 威脅 [同] threat

▲ Nuclear weapons are a great menace to world peace.
核子武器對世界和平是一大威脅。

menace [ˈmɛnɪs] v. 威脅 [同] endanger

▲ The country has been menaced by war for a long time. 這個國家長期飽受戰爭威脅。

menacing [ˈmɛnɪsɪŋ] adj. 威脅的 [同] threatening

▲ The teacher stared at the naughty children with a menacing look.
那老師用威脅的眼神盯著調皮的孩子們。

---

15. **pact** [pækt] n. [C] 協定，合約 <with> [同] treaty

▲ The government signed a peace pact with the rebels last month. 政府和叛亂分子上個月簽署了和平協定。

---

16. **picturesque** [ˌpɪktʃəˈrɛsk] adj. 美麗如畫的 [同] beautiful

▲ Lucas lives in a picturesque village near Florence.

Lucas 住在靠近佛羅倫斯一個風景如畫的村莊裡。

---

17. **pocketbook** [ˋpɑkɪtˏbʊk] n. [C] (女用) 手提包 [同] handbag

▲ Jean keeps her scarf in her pocketbook.
Jean 把圍巾放在她的手提包中。

---

18. **resolute** [ˋrɛzəˏlut] adj. 堅決的 [同] persistent [反] irresolute

▲ The explorer was resolute in carrying out his expedition to the Arctic.
這個探險家決心實現他的極地遠征之旅。

resolutely [ˋrɛzəˏlutlɪ] adv. 堅決地

▲ David resolutely refused to give up his parental rights over his daughter.
David 堅決地拒絕放棄對女兒的親權。

---

19. **sewer** [ˋsuɚ] n. [C] 下水道

▲ Don't pour the kitchen waste into the sewer.
不要把廚餘倒入下水道。

---

20. **stern** [stɝn] adj. 嚴厲的，嚴肅的 [同] strict

▲ With a stern voice, Lucy asked her son to explain why he skipped class.
Lucy 用嚴厲的語氣要求她的兒子解釋為何他會蹺課。

---

21. **tact** [tækt] n. [U] 周全，得體，圓滑 [同] diplomacy

▲ As a diplomat, Frank always handles risky situations with tact. 身為一個外交官，Frank 總是能周全地處理

危險的情勢。

tactful [ˋtæktfəl] adj. 周全的，得體的，圓滑的 [同] diplomatic [反] tactless

▲ It was not tactful of you to turn down her offer.
你拒絕她的提議可真是失了分寸。

---

22. **tramp** [træmp] n. [sing.] 沉重的腳步聲 ；[C] 流浪漢 [同] hobo

▲ As the soldiers approached, we could hear the tramp of their boots.
當士兵走近時，我們可以聽到軍靴的沉重腳步聲。

tramp [træmp] v. 以沉重的腳步走 [同] stomp

▲ Lily heard someone tramping up the stairs and guessed it was her drunken husband. Lily 聽到有人腳步沉重地上樓，猜想那應該是她喝醉的先生。

---

23. **unpack** [ʌnˋpæk] v. 打開 (行李等) [反] pack

▲ Ivan went into his bedroom and unpacked his suitcase after arriving home.
Ivan 回家後進到臥室，打開他的行李箱。

---

24. **vulgar** [ˋvʌlgɚ] adj. 低俗的 [同] crude

▲ Some people thought that great literature should not contain the vulgar language.
有些人認為偉大的文學作品不應該包含粗俗的語言。

---

25. **yarn** [jɑrn] n. [U] 紗線

▲ You need a lot of yarn if you are going to make a big

quilt. 如果要做一床大棉被，你需要很多的紗線。

Unit 10

1. **artery** [`ɑrtərɪ] n. [C] 動脈
   ▲ A heart attack is usually caused by blocked coronary arteries. 心臟病發作常是因冠狀動脈阻塞造成的。

2. **brute** [brut] n. [C] 殘忍又野蠻的人 [同] savage
   ▲ Allen beats his pets whenever he gets drunk. He is such a brute. Allen 一喝醉酒就會打他的寵物。他真是個殘忍又野蠻的人。

   brute [brut] adj. 粗野的 [同] savage
   ▲ The police used brute force to push the suspect into the patrol car. 警察使用暴力將嫌犯推入警車。

   brutish [`brutɪʃ] adj. 殘忍的 [同] brutal
   ▲ The brutish man abuses his wife and children almost every day.
   這個兇殘的男人幾乎每天虐待他的太太和小孩。

3. **cellar** [`sɛlɚ] n. [C] 地窖，地下室 [同] basement
   ▲ John is a wine collector. He has stored a lot of wine in the cellar. John 是一位葡萄酒收藏家。他在地窖裡儲藏了許多葡萄酒。

4. **cosmopolitan** [ˌkɑzmə`pɑlətṇ] adj. 世界性的，國際性的 [同] international；見多識廣的 [同] worldly

▲ Christchurch is a city with a cosmopolitan atmosphere. 基督城是一個具有國際化氛圍的城市。

---

5. **covet** [`kʌvɪt] v. 覬覦 [同] yearn for

▲ Tina coveted the manager's position, but she never made it. Tina 覬覦經理的職位，但從未成功。

---

6. **dart** [dɑrt] n. [C] 飛鏢；[sing.] 猛衝 [同] dash

▲ The brown bear is killed by a poisoned dart.
這隻棕熊被淬毒的飛鏢毒死了。

dart [dɑrt] v. 猛衝 [同] dash；投射 (視線等) <at>

▲ Students darted into the classroom on hearing the bell ring. 學生一聽到鐘聲就飛奔進教室。

darts [dɑrts] n. [U] 擲鏢遊戲

---

7. **dispatch** [dɪ`spætʃ] v. 發送 (信、文件等) [同] transmit；派遣 <to> [同] send

▲ The telegram was dispatched immediately.
電報立即被發送。

dispatch [dɪ`spætʃ] n. [U] 發送，派遣

▲ Some aid workers were in charge of the dispatch of food and clothing.
有些救援隊員負責食物和衣服的發送。

---

8. **dynamite** [`daɪnə,maɪt] n. [U] 炸藥 [同] explosive

▲ Before digging a tunnel, workers blasted the rock with dynamite.
在挖掘隧道前，工人們用炸藥爆破岩石。

dynamite [ˋdaɪnəˌmaɪt] v. 用炸藥爆破

▲ The rebellious troops dynamited the power plant in the city. 叛軍用炸藥炸掉城裡的發電廠。

---

9. **emphatic** [ɪmˋfætɪk] adj. (語氣) 強調的 <about, that> [同] assertive

▲ Our manager is emphatic about the importance of punctuality. 我們的經理強調守時的重要。

---

10. **frail** [frel] adj. 脆弱的 [同] fragile [反] firm；虛弱的 [同] feeble [反] healthy

▲ Don't touch the frail antique. It is worth more than 10 million dollars.
請勿觸碰這脆弱的古董。它價值超過一千萬美元。

---

11. **glee** [gli] n. [U] (因成功、勝利等而產生的) 喜悅，快樂 [同] joy [反] sadness

▲ The candidate announced the outcome of the election with glee. 該名候選人高興地宣布選舉的結果。

---

12. **gulp** [gʌlp] v. 大口地吞食 <down> [同] swallow [反] nibble；抑制 <back>

▲ The thirsty boy gulped down a glass of water.
這個口渴的男孩大口地灌下一杯水。

gulp [gʌlp] n. [C] 一大口 (的量)

▲ The snake swallowed a hen in one gulp.
這條蛇一口吞下一隻母雞。

---

13. **magnitude** [ˋmægnəˌtjud] n. [U] 規模 [同] size；[C] (地

震等的) 規模

▲ A project of such magnitude will take considerable time to complete.

這樣大規模的企劃將需要相當多的時間來完成。

---

14. **materialism** [məˋtɪrɪəlˌɪzəm] n. [U] 物質主義

▲ Materialism plays a major role in modern society.

物質主義在現代社會扮演重大的角色。

---

15. **migrate** [ˋmaɪgret] v. (動物依季節而) 遷移；移居 <from, to> [同] emigrate

▲ Some birds migrate south to Taiwan to overwinter in fall. 一些鳥類在秋天時南遷到臺灣過冬。

---

16. **poach** [potʃ] v. 盜獵 [同] hunt illegally；水煮 (荷包蛋、魚、肉等) [同] simmer

▲ Rhinos are often poached for their horns.

犀角經常因為牠們的角遭到非法獵捕。

poacher [ˋpotʃɚ] n. [C] 盜獵者

▲ Poachers constantly invaded the national park.

盜獵者經常侵入這座國家公園。

---

17. **prop** [prɑp] n. [C] 支撐物 [同] support；道具 (usu. pl.)

▲ We need to find something as a prop to keep the tree from falling.

我們需要找個東西撐著，讓這棵樹不要倒下來。

💡 stage props 舞臺道具

prop [prɑp] v. 支撐 <on, against> [同] support

▲ Ian propped the ladder against the wall.
Ian 撐起梯子靠在牆上。

18. **recur** [rɪˋkɝ] v. 再發生 [同] reappear <to>；重複出現
   ▲ Our team tried to make plans carefully to ensure that the accident would not recur.
   我們團隊試圖仔細制定計畫，以確保事故不會再發生。
   recurrence [rɪˋkɝəns] n. [C][U] 再發生 <of>；重複出現 <of>
   ▲ The government should take measures to stop the recurrence of drunk driving.
   政府應採取措施制止酒後駕車再次發生。
   recurrent [rɪˋkɝənt] adj. 頻頻發生的 [同] frequent
   ▲ Sheila had a recurrent nightmare of being chased by a beast. Sheila 經常做被一隻野獸追趕的惡夢。

19. **signify** [ˋsɪɡnəˌfaɪ] v. 表示 [同] convey；意指 <that> [同] mean
   ▲ Please signify your agreement by raising your hand.
   請舉手表示贊成。

20. **stoop** [stup] v. 俯身 <down>；彎腰駝背
   ▲ The little girl stooped down to put on her shoes.
   小女孩俯身穿鞋。
   stoop [stup] n. [sing.] 駝背；[C] 門前臺階
   ▲ The old lady walked with a stoop.
   這名老婦人走路駝背。

21. **temperament** [ˋtɛmprəmənt] n. [C][U] 氣質 [同] nature；性情 [同] mood

▲ Dan's artistic temperament always attracts many girls. Dan 的藝術家氣質總是吸引著許多女孩。

temperamental [ˌtɛmprəˋmɛntl̩] adj. 喜怒無常的 [同] moody

▲ A temperamental person is often unreliable. 喜怒無常的人通常不太可靠。

---

22. **trample** [ˋtræmpl̩] v. 踩壞，踐踏 <on> [同] stamp；蔑視 (權利等) <on>

▲ There was a sign to remind people not to trample on the lawn. 有一個告示提醒人們不要踩壞草坪。

---

23. **upbringing** [ˋʌpˌbrɪŋɪŋ] n. [C] 養育，教養 (usu. sing.)

▲ Having a strict upbringing, Ryan was never allowed to go out playing with his classmates. 因為受到嚴格的教養，Ryan 從不被允許和同學出去玩。

---

24. **withstand** [wɪθˋstænd] v. 抵抗 (withstood | withstood | withstanding) [同] resist

▲ The tableware cannot withstand intense heat. 這種餐具不耐高溫。

---

25. **yeast** [jist] n. [U] 酵母 (菌)

▲ Yeast is used to make bread rise. 酵母被用來使麵包膨脹。

PLUS 索引

PLUS 索引

NOTE

NOTE

20分鐘稱霸大考英文作文

王靖賢 編著

- 共16回作文練習，涵蓋大考作文3大題型：看圖寫作、主題寫作、信函寫作。根據近年大考趨勢精心出題，題型多元且擬真度高。
- 每回作文練習皆有為考生精選的英文名言佳句，增強考生備考戰力。
- 附方便攜帶的解析本，針對每回作文題目提供寫作架構圖，讓寫作脈絡一目了然，並提供範文、寫作要點、寫作撇步及好用詞彙，一本在手即可增強英文作文能力。

Intermediate Reading:
英文閱讀 High Five

掌握大考新趨勢，搶先練習新題型！

王隆興 編著

★全書分為 5 大主題：生態物種、人文歷史、科學科技、環境保育、
  醫學保健，共 50 篇由外籍作者精心編寫之文章。

★題目仿 111 學年度學測參考試卷命題方向設計，為未來大考提前
  作準備，搶先練習第二部分新題型——混合題。

★隨書附贈解析夾冊，方便練習後閱讀文章中譯及試題解析，並於
  解析補充每回文章精選的 15 個字彙。

英語 *Make Me High* 系列

進階英文字彙力 4501~6000 PLUS 隨身讀

彙　　　整	三民英語編輯小組
責任編輯	楊雅雯
美術編輯	曾昱綺

發 行 人	劉振強
出 版 者	三民書局股份有限公司
地　　　址	臺北市復興北路 386 號 (復北門市)
	臺北市重慶南路一段 61 號 (重南門市)
電　　　話	(02)25006600
網　　　址	三民網路書店 https://www.sanmin.com.tw

出版日期	初版一刷 2023 年 9 月
書籍編號	S872650
I S B N	978-957-14-7613-1

三民書局